For the Love of Carrie

Jill A Sanders

good friend of Joans

ISBN: 1484846958
ISBN-13: 9781484846957

For The Love of Carrie

Dedication

This book is dedicated to all child welfare workers. May peace be with you.

chapter 1

1995

The basement was dank and dark except for the dusty glimmer of light peeking through the mud covered window. Six-year-old Paula Thompson hung on by a thread. The floor was damp and cold. If she let herself think about it, a cold chill permeated her body. She tried not to think about it. She tried to remember the good days, when it was her and her mom. Even those memories were fading. It was hard to focus, hard to care anymore. Nobody else cared. She had no doubt she should give up any hope at all. She stopped crying long ago. It did no good. What did she do wrong? She knew, if she could figure it out, maybe things would get better. Maybe she should have been quieter. Maybe she asked for too much food. Maybe she yelled at her younger brothers too much. Or maybe she shouldn't have wanted Mommy to hug her so much. Maybe she should have tried to love Ed, her stepdad, more, but he scared her. She was tired, too tired to feel anything anymore. But she couldn't remove the incredulous want she had for her mother to come hold her, and tell her everything would be okay. It was the one thought that wouldn't abandon her, for her mother to come and love her once again.

She heard the bolt on the basement door unlock. Each time the lock clicked, Paula was filled with the tiniest sliver of hope she'd be rescued. Only for it to evaporate when she would hear Ed's bellowing voice. "Now don't you waste any time getting straight back up here. You hear me Darlene? I mean it!"

Darlene hurried down the creaky basement steps carrying a bowl of cold oatmeal in her cigarette stained hands. As she approached her daughter, she admonished her. "Now don't start any of your whining or begging, Paula. You know I can't take it. And I can't do nothin' about it." She set the cereal on the cardboard box, then, reached up to loosen the ropes. Paula's hands fell to her sides. "Now hurry up and eat it. I gotta get back upstairs." Darlene lit a cigarette as she stood over her daughter watching her eat. She blew puffs of smoke all around her, and then started her hacking cough.

Paula devoured the five spoonfuls of oatmeal, not caring or noticing it was cold and hard. Her upper lip was still sore from where the duct tape was ripped off of her mouth earlier. She was so hungry she barely noticed. She learned her lesson, though, not to scream even if spiders were crawling up her leg. She counted five spider webs hanging from the basement's ceiling. Some webs had other bugs entwined within them. She tried hard not to think about sharing her space with the creepy crawlers. "I have to pee, Mommy."

"Well, I don't have time right now. Ed is really mad. You'll have to hold it. I'll come down later. Now gimme the bowl." Paula cried silently, without tears. There were none left. This time Darlene let her sit on the cardboard box while she tightened the ropes which led to the water pipes strung across the basement ceiling. Her raw skinned wrists sported marks that were rooted deeply into her from where the rope dug into her skin. At least this time, she wouldn't have to stand. Her legs ached badly from the previous hours of standing all night long. Paula was grateful for the small kindness.

Darlene turned her back. Without saying another word, she left her six-year-old daughter. Paula heard her younger brothers' feet running across the floor above. They were laughing and chasing each other about, having fun. She couldn't remember when she last saw three and four-year-old Barry and Davy. How many days was it? It seemed like an eternity. Paula couldn't begin to count how many days the sun came up and peeked through the small window. She wished she could play with her brothers. Maybe she could after her punishment was over. She tried again and again to think about what she did wrong, so she could be sure not to do it again. But her mind wouldn't work anymore. She longed to leave the basement and be with her brothers and her mother. She knew she was bad because she often wished Ed would die. Maybe that was why she was being punished.

Paula fell back into her semi-conscious state. Her body was extremely thin and frail. The circles under her eyes were growing darker with each day. She realized she peed on herself when the cardboard box caved in. She didn't care anymore. She didn't notice the musty stink of the urine. She didn't notice anything, even the tormenting ache in her arms. Although her physical body continued to endure, Paula was barely alive.

chapter 2

May 29, 2014

She heard the cardinals in the window box feeder beckoning her to arise. She didn't want to awaken. She wanted to linger and bask in the dream she had making love to her soul mate. It felt incredibly real. She relished the thought of never leaving, but he was not hers to have.

The birds loudly chattered their morning reveille, forcing Carrie back into the waking world. In all of these past dreary, dreadful months, Carrie found comfort with the birds. Her favorite bird, the pileated woodpecker never came to the feeder. He was often a ground feeder, feasting on grubs, and bugs found in old dead logs and fallen trees. Their distinctive call always delighted her. But to see one was a rare, but heartwarming sight. She imagined they came from an ancient line due to their dinosaur like characteristics. Perhaps they descended from the mythical phoenix, she imagined.

Carrie reveled in myths and fairy tales. In those stories, she found purpose, meaning and a happy ending. This wasn't her experience in real life, especially as a child welfare social worker. Real life was tough, hard, and painful with only bits of joy spread here and there. Joy that needed to be captured and held tight or it would crumble and vanish quickly, leaving only sweet and tender memories. These memories prompted Carrie to believe hope was alive, and there was good in the world.

Having not slept well for the last year, this morning Carrie felt strangely well rested and energized. Her mind traveled back to last night. She remembered she made a critical decision after torturous deliberation. Yes, she had a long talk with the good Lord last night. She poured out her heart and soul, trying to rid herself of the pain possessing her constantly. Clarity was the gift given to her in return. She knew how to end the pain. She understood what was required of her to move on, even if it was to go to a different realm. Once again, she reviewed her decision to assure this was the right course of action as there would be no turning back once it was implemented. It was how Carrie worked: make a decision and never look back. She was tired of the dilemma. She was tired of being tired. She wanted to move on. Yes, she thought, I feel steadfast in my decision to end it all. Carrie felt a new energy surging through her veins.

She stretched in the comfort of her bed. She pointed her toes towards her head to lengthen her muscles. She let out a hefty loud yawn. A new day was about to begin, along with a new chapter in her life. It was an opportune time to get started. Her birthday was tomorrow and births were a time for a new beginning. This was in line with Carrie's plan, a new beginning for herself. Enough of feeling dead inside, she might as well be dead with that constant feeling.

She gazed around her bedroom. The morning sun streamed through her bedroom window. The pattern of her eyelet lace curtains lay on her bed and arms with the morning sun casting its shadows. Carrie rolled her head and noted the few cracking noises it made. She gazed on the pastel blue walls and smiled when she saw the glass blown angel wings hanging from a ceiling hook, swaying slightly in the gentle spring breeze. The artisan remarkably captured exquisite detail in the feathering of the wings. The sun caused the wings to sparkle so brilliantly, Carrie could feel the angelic energy emanating from within. It was the perfect gift Jeff gave her on their wedding day.

Finally, her eyes rested upon the precious photograph of her twin sons and Katy, the three most important people in her life. Scott and Todd were four years younger than their sister. They were identical twins with light brown hair. Scott had dark blue eyes. Todd had soft brown eyes. If not for their different eye color, it was impossible to discern which was which. She threw the photo a kiss and forced herself to get up and get going. She had much to do. The phone rang, and caller ID announced it was her daughter Katy. She smiled and answered.

***

Katy put her phone back on its charger. Strange, she thought. Mom sure seemed to be chipper. Perhaps she caught wind about what she and her uncle Carson were up to. No way, no way possible, she mused to herself. Whatever the reason, she was happy Mom was seemingly less depressed. It was a painfully difficult year for all of them. Perhaps the toughest times were behind them. She was glad her mother was finally going to emerge from her home. It would be the first time she ventured out alone in nearly a year.

The phone rang. "Hello," answered Katy.

"Hi, Katydid." It was her Uncle Carson. He gave her the nickname when one spring a katydid landed on her nose, which sent the then four-year-old into a screaming panic. She's since made up with insects and all creatures of nature, having adopted her mother's loving attitude toward all living beings. But the nickname stuck. "I'm checking in to see if everything is set for the momentous day tomorrow. Anything you need me to do?"

"Nope, I think everything is covered. I talked to Mom this morning and she seemed, well, happy. You didn't do anything to cue her in about tomorrow, did you?"

"Really? Well, I'm glad to hear that. It's about time. But no, I haven't talked to her in over a week. Maybe it's because this spring has finally turned a corner, and it's warming up, and the rain stopped. You know how your mom loves springtime with the flowers blooming and the fresh smell of the outdoors. Hey, by the way, do you have any suggestions for me about what to buy her for her birthday? I certainly don't want to show up without a gift tomorrow."

"I don't know. Mom is hard to buy for. She has everything. In fact, she told me she might buy a dress today to wear tomorrow. She actually has believed our story - hook, line and sinker. Perhaps you could purchase a corsage for her to wear. Calla lilies are her favorite flower. She'd love it."

"Thanks for the tip," Carson replied.

"Uncle Carson, you don't think she'll be mad at us, do you? After all, you know how she hates to have people fuss over her. With all she's been through, this might be quite overwhelming for her. She seemed to be better today. I don't want to create a setback for her. Maybe we went a little too far. Maybe we went over the top. I will understand if she gets quite irritated with us. Well, you *know* what I mean," Katy said anxiously.

"Katydid, take some of the advice your mother always gave you, don't worry. Besides it's too late now to change anything. Tomorrow will be the perfect cup of tea for her. I can't wait to see the look on her face. She'll laugh, yell, cry or hit us, but whatever it is, it'll be better than the sorrow she's been swimming in. Besides, it's her birthday. She's always worked and planned diligently for our birthdays. It's only fitting she finally experiences being on the receiving end. And Katy, you know how much your mother loves you. She wouldn't want to disappoint you. She'll be fine. Remember she's a trooper. "

"Yeah, Uncle Carson, you're right. She's one tough old bird. Maybe that's why she likes birds. She's one of them." Katy giggled. "Well, I guess I'll see you tomorrow. Thanks for all of your support and help. Love you."

"Love you too. Bye."

Katy believed she and Uncle Carson came up with an ingenious story. Carrie thought she would be attending a luncheon where her brother was going to be honored for all of his community service. Carson was a pillar of the community, so it made their story credible. He was quite the philanthropist for their Midwestern city. As an architect, he designed a community center which was a shining pearl in a ravaged neighborhood. It was built in a circular pattern with glistening white enamel bricks and a bright red tiled cone-shaped roof. He succeeded in emulating a shaker style round barn. The outer walls were laced with large beveled glass square windows, providing a perfect fish bowl effect. It was the pride of the community and was featured in "*Architectural Digest*." He dedicated his services for free. But he didn't stop there. He headed a fund-raising drive which garnered a sizeable endowment for on-going support and maintenance. He was truly remarkable and generous as this was only one of his many endeavors. He and Carrie both have a giving spirit.

***

Meanwhile, Carrie readied herself for a day out alone, the first in a long time. She hopped out of bed, and then noticed her white cotton night gown was covered with grass stains. Her memory of the evening before flooded back. She fell to her knees on the dew covered ground while engrossed in a deep conversation with God. It was no wonder there were deep green stains on her night gown where her knees buried into the wet grass. All of her pain was exposed last night. Nothing was left to hide in her shadows within. Ask and you shall receive. She asked for an answer, and she received one. Soon, she thought. Soon all of the earthly pain will be gone. It was time to get on with it.

Shopping was first on this day's agenda. This time she would venture out alone. Freedom. It felt good. She needed a few items for what she planned to do and started to create a list. Her garden hose did not overwinter well and sported a crack. She thought she might repair it with some duct tape, maybe even pick up a new hose. It couldn't hurt to have two. She needed a new shower curtain. She needed to refill her prescription, and look for a new dress. Her brother was chosen to receive the coveted

Ben Franklin award for community service. The YWCA was sponsoring a luncheon reception to honor him at the prestigious Hyatt Hotel. Besides, she thought, a new outfit can double as a birthday present I give to myself. Carrie was never one to splurge on herself. She needed a compelling reason to give herself permission to buy an ensemble.

chapter 3

Rena Cameron lifted herself out of her overstuffed gray leather computer chair. She was glad she finally completed the program formatting to be distributed at the Ben Franklin honorary luncheon tomorrow. Her teapot started vibrating its screaming note announcing the water was ready. She stood up begging her muscles to relax and stretch as she walked towards the kitchen. She was in need of hydration and tea would be thirst quenching. The sun was a welcoming force and beckoned her to drink her tea on the veranda, which wrapped itself around the old wooden home. She dumped all of her teabags into an old large round antique fish bowl, cleaning out the various sixteen boxes taking up too much space in her cupboard. She typically labored over which tea to drink, but now the dilemma was easily resolved. She blindly put her hand in the large bowl, and whatever bag of tea she captured would be the flavor of the moment. Today, her fingers selected Chai tea, one of her favorites. She thought a bite to eat might round out a perfect moment. She removed a biscotti from the large rose-laden ceramic cookie jar. As she walked out to the veranda, she breathed in the cinnamon vapors of the tea.

Sipping her tea, she watched the first spring hummingbirds come to the hanging feeder. She couldn't help but think of Carrie Cathers. What an incredibly remarkable woman she must be. There were sixty-one entries this year for the coveted Ben Franklin award, an honor bestowed upon a citizen who gave exemplary service to the community. In years past, the selection was always difficult, but this year the most compelling essay was written by Carrie's daughter, and captured the hearts and minds of all of the YWCA panel members. Additionally another entry also nominated Carrie, a quite touching entry by a man named Martin Barnett.

Each year the panel of women would read the nominations, and then rate the top three on their ballot. Without fail there wouldn't be a majority agreement at the start, so the mediating process would begin. It was emotionally draining, and some women would leave feeling personally wounded when their choice was dismissed. It took several ballots to find a winner. Rena likened it to selecting a Pope. But this year was unlike any other. Carrie Cathers was the number one choice for eighteen of the ballots and ranked second or third on the other six ballots. It was phenomenal. She won it hands down. Rena was excited to meet this extraordinary woman.

***

Paula Cameron steered her bicycle into the driveway, stopping at the side of the porch where her mother was sitting with her tea. "What's up, Mom?" She inquired. "I thought you would be inside working on the computer."

"Oh, I finished early," Rena replied. "How was your psychology class today?"

Paula was attending the local community college three miles from their home. She enjoyed bicycling back and forth to class now spring was here. She has slender, long legs, a trim body and beautiful, thick, jet-black hair, which she pulled back into a ponytail. She was exotically beautiful. She loved her old-fashioned Victorian home, and all of the detailed scrolled woodwork lining the inside, not to mention the leaded stained glass windows momentarily leaving rainbows dancing on the walls. The house had character, unlike the cardboard cutout houses of the suburbs.

"Class, it was okay. Do you know the psychology professor has worn the same outfit every day since the beginning of the semester, green pants and a white shirt? I think he's trying some experiment on us to see how long it is before we react to it. Well, I have to check on some stuff. Is it okay if I use the computer?" Paula asked.

"Sure, close my page, it's already saved. I ran to catch the teapot, so I didn't close it down," Rena said. As Paula bounded up the steps into the house, Rena gazed upon her daughter thinking how blessed she was to have been given the privilege to adopt her. She's such a beautiful, loving spirit. God surely blessed me when she came into my life, she reminisced.

Rena sipped her tea. She bit into the biscotti, savoring the dark chocolate wrapped around the cookie's base. The almond flavor was distinctive, delighting her taste buds. Suddenly she heard a compelling scream from her daughter. "Mommm, Mommm, oh my God, Mommm!" Rena's heart thumped hard in her chest. Something was desperately wrong. She flew into the study where her daughter was sobbing at the computer. Her shoulders were heaving. Her voice was unclear through the torrential tears as she tried to speak.

Her daughter stood and tried to talk, but her emotions impeded her. Rena clutched her into a bear hug and in a whispered voice gently coaxed her. "What is it Paula? What happened?" Paula clung to her mother and simply let her tears flood out of her eyes. She soaked her mother's blouse with her teardrops. Slowly she regained control as her sobbing and breathing quieted.

"Mom, who's that woman," Paula asked as she pointed to the picture of the woman who was highlighted on the program for the Ben Franklin award.

"Why do you ask?" Rena responded.

Paula continued. "Do you remember when I was younger and would dream of a woman's face at night? Remember, I repeatedly dreamed of some woman. I never knew who she was, or why I would dream of her, but she was there every night. It never scared me, but it was always curious. I used to think maybe she was an angel. Do you remember?"

Rena silently sucked in a long breath. How could she forget? Paula had this same image nightly for five years or longer. Neither she nor Paula understood why. She wasn't plagued with this memory, or at least spoken of it for years. "Yes, darling, I do remember."

"Mom, the picture on your computer is her! Who is she? "

"How can you be so sure?" Rena asked tentatively.

"Well, I know this face. It's an older face than the one in my dreams, but I know it's her. Not many people possess one brown eye and one blue eye, and this woman does. As she gazed once again at the photo, recognition began to set in. Paula gasped. It was long ago when she allowed her mind to travel back to that time. Mom, I remember who she is now. She's the one! She's the one! She's the one who saved me from the basement!"

chapter 4

Carrie felt free as the hot cascade of water flowed over her slender body. The heaviness left her. She had a plan now to end her pain, and she was anxious to get going. No soaking in the bathtub crying and feeling sorry for herself. She was determined to have no more. She was moving forward into a brand new realm. No, a shower was the ticket for this day. It would keep her moving, standing not sitting. She realized she hadn't washed her hair in two weeks. Now was time to take charge of her life again. She oozed the shampoo from its container and worked it into her scalp vigorously. As she scrubbed, she imagined she was ridding herself of all of her pain, watching it disappear down the drain. Well, not all of the pain, but a considerable portion of it. The rest would be gone soon.

She pulled on a pair of jeans she hadn't worn in months. They used to fit her perfectly, shy of being snug. Now they hung loosely on her, but not overly so. She looked in the mirror and was stunned by her appearance. She didn't realize she lost so much weight. Her gaunt look surprised her. No wonder Katy was worried about her. No need now, she would soon leave this life behind. She smiled at the thought. She riffled through her closet, found a lightweight cranberry sweater with a square neck, adorned with a few tiny sequins along the edge. It was perfect for the beautiful bountiful spring day. Her salt and pepper hair had grown to shoulder length, and easily wrapped into a neat bun at the base of her neck. It made her look tidy.

She grabbed her purse and headed toward the garage. It was, then, she realized she hadn't driven in a long time. As she placed her hand on the garage door knob, she took an anxious breath. Can I handle this, she wondered. Of course you can, she said to herself. You've handled far worse things. Don't back down now. You're no longer the pathetic Carrie, you're strong. You're on a mission. Go for it. She opened the door and peered into the garage. There it was - Jeff's candy red Porsche coupe. It was waxed to a brilliant shine as Jeff left it. Tears began to slide down Carrie's cheeks. She wiped them away with the back of her hand. Enough, she said to herself. Go forward. Remember the good parts. Don't let yourself ruminate on the last day. You've done that enough.

She forced a weak smile onto her face. There were happy times, weren't there? Jeff was a steadfast, loving husband. Better than she deserved, she often thought. He was attentive, a good provider, a great father. He loved this car. It was his dream car, the most precious possession he owned. Carrie thought of the days she watched him washing and waxing Zippy, the name he fondly gave to this car, his second love as he referred to her. Of course, he always reminded Carrie she was his first and only real love, but Zippy was close behind her. And that was Jeff.

Carrie thought about how Jeff treated her. She never worried he would be unfaithful to her. That wasn't his character. Through the years, she kept hidden her knowledge she knew he loved her more than she loved him. She loved him, but it was in a quieter, less intense fashion. And this was part of her grief, feeling guilty she couldn't return his love with equal due measure. It wasn't in her.

Jeff wasn't a social creature, he was more down-home. He was happy to be with his family. He was a steady-eddy. He was an accountant, a CPA with a manageable and financially successful client load. Jeff wasn't prone to becoming overly excited about anything. She often wished he would be more animated and thrilled with life. After all, he was an accountant. He was content puzzling around with numbers all day. But Zippy awakened Jeff from sleepwalking through his life as Carrie characterized it, although she knew it probably was an unfair portrayal. He loved his children with fierce passion, as well as he loved her. She needed him to be more actively engaged with the rest of the world. But they had many wonderful, tender moments. Carrie whispered a silent prayer up to Jeff, "Please forgive me for not loving you as you were. Now you're gone, I miss you badly."

Carrie hit the garage door opener and let the pine scented spring air in. She slid into the driver's seat and gripped the leather bound steering wheel. She bent down and sniffed it to see if there were any traces left of Jeff's cologne, Old Spice. She thought she detected the slightest whiff, but it probably was her imagination. Thank goodness Jeff opted for an automatic, even though it was uncool for a sports car. Jeff wasn't into being cool. He was a creature of comfort and ease.

Backing Zippy out slowly, Carrie thought her best bet would be to run over to Sears. They likely would have all she needed: hose, duct tape, shower curtain and maybe even a new dress. One-stop shopping sounded good to her today. She didn't want to overdo it. As she stopped the car at the end of the driveway to check for on-coming traffic, she gazed at her house. She and Jeff moved into this smaller home after the children left. It was a quaint house, made with redwood siding. It had an etched-glass red rimmed door. She loved the bay window which she adorned with a variety of green plants. Sadly, she neglected them terribly, and it showed.

Carrie loved the lot of land they secured. It had a generous back yard, butted up to a woodland area, which contained a small neighborhood park. Thankfully the park's shelter house and playground equipment weren't visible to them. It was perfect for watching the joy of nature contained in the treed land. Meditation came easily for her, when she would ease into one of their Adirondack chairs and listen. Yes, she had good years in this home.

The way was clear. Carrie backed Zippy out into the street. She was on her way. It felt good to open the windows and let the wind glide past her face. She reached to turn on the radio, but then, instead, pushed the CD button. She was curious what Jeff might have last played. Eric Clapton sang melodiously, moving Carrie to tears. Oh, this wasn't a good idea. "Let it grow, let it grow, let it blossom, let it flow. In the sun, the rain, the snow, love is lovely, let it grow," came forth. This was their song. It secretly held a different meaning for Carrie than Jeff. She planted her love *hopes* with Jeff, and hoped her love would grow stronger with time. Jeff planted his love, and he let it grow freely. If only she could have a rewind with Jeff. She would be a better wife.

Carrie met Jeff when she was flustered with preparing her annual tax return. She stumbled into the first CPA business she could find. She received a small inheritance from her parents' estate, but sizeable enough she was afraid to fill out the tax forms by herself. She wasn't proficient with math or numbers. And there he was sitting at his neatly organized desk displaying his name plate: Jeff Cathers. He stood quickly while extending his large hand out to her for the required business handshake. He was average looking, six feet tall, brown hair, brown eyes and slightly overweight, probably from sitting behind his desk all day. When he smiled, he was all teeth, large and pearly white. He deftly prepared her tax return. It was all prim and proper. As she rose to take the tax return to the post office, she tripped over her own feet, lost her balance and fell into the wastebasket sitting next to his desk-butt first! She was extremely embarrassed. Jeff, the gentleman, offered her his hand again to help free her from the confines of the wastebasket. This time his hand felt warm and welcoming. She laughed nervously. He timidly asked her to dinner. How could she not accept given the circumstances? And that's how it began.

chapter 5

1980

As he sat in his yellow Grand Prix outside of Carrie's place, he searched for the hand towel he threw in his car as a last minute thought. His hands were oozing with sweat, and not because it was a hot sizzling day. Jeff looked in the rear view mirror and checked his hair once again, having already combed it twice during his drive to Carrie's apartment. He rehearsed in his mind how best to greet her. Jeff felt unusually discombobulated. "Get it together," he said to himself. "Geez, what's wrong with me?" He was twenty minutes early, the last thing he wanted to be especially on a first date. He decided to take a short drive and come back.

Carrie was rushing to get ready. She came in from a three mile run to clear her head. Forget about it, she mused to herself. So what if I was a klutz and fell into his wastebasket? He still asked me out. She stepped into the shower. Her thoughts continued. He's tall and has a decent OP quotient. Yes, he's quite optically pleasing. She remembered his hands, how strong but gentle they were. When he touched her, she felt safe.

She reached for her towel and wrapped it around her. She scampered toward her walk-in closet. As she passed her bedroom window, she noticed a strange yellow car out front. She quickly towel dried her hair, looked back up and the car was gone. Strange, she thought. Carrie fingered through her clothes, gathered up a khaki skirt, and an aqua V-neck long sleeved top. She slipped on tan earth sandals, preened in the mirror for two seconds, and then added a shelled necklace with matching sand-dollar earrings. She was satisfied.

Jeff returned, now angry with himself. He was seven minutes late. He hated people who weren't punctual. He quickly leapt up to her door, was about to ring the doorbell, when the front door opened. There she was, smiling. He waited for the expected admonishment about his tardiness, but none came.

"Hey," Carrie began. "Welcome. Come in and have a glass of iced tea. It's awfully hot out there." She surreptitiously noticed his sun-colored car, and took note it was him earlier.

"Sure, I'd love to," Jeff responded. Carrie's easy going manner was a welcomed relief. "Do you like seafood? I thought we might go to the Windjammer tonight if you're not allergic to fish."

"The Windjammer, I love that place. I grew up on the shores of Lake Erie. Seafood comprises probably eighty percent of my body's make up. I'm surprised I haven't grown gills in my neck," Carrie laughed. "When I was seven-years-old, my father wouldn't let us swim in the lake due to all of the pollution. He said they traced hepatitis cases to it, or something similar. We were allowed to play in the sand, but couldn't go near the water. It was kind of a bummer, know what I mean?"

She's easy to be around and so unpretentious, Jeff thought. Her allure was immediately intoxicating to him. He felt almost dizzy, and his heart began to race. Calm down. Pull yourself together, he told himself.

"Here you go," Carrie said as she handed him his iced tea. "Do you want lemon or sugar? Well, I mean sugar as I'm out of lemons."

"No, I'm good to go as it is," he retorted, then took a long slow thirst quenching drink. "What kind of tea is this? It has a delightful flavor."

"Oh, I made it myself, sun tea. I threw some Irish Breakfast and Earl Grey in the decanter, then added some lemongrass and basil leaves. The herbs kind of give it a lift. Glad you like it." Carrie pondered Jeff's face. She noticed even with the evidence of whiskers, he had a baby face quality about him. He exuded a gentle energy, a bit nervous though, she thought. He wasn't in his confident professional CPA mode. She liked that.

Jeff was a consummate gentleman. He opened her car door for her, and she slid into his immaculate interior. When they reached the restaurant, Carrie automatically reached to open her own car door, but Jeff suggested she should wait for him to play the role of gentleman. "Allow me," he requested. She thought he was a bit assertive, but in a kind way. Carrie thought this whole protocol of men opening doors for women a bit archaic, and implied women were in need of help even with the easiest of tasks. But she assented. She felt silly sitting there until he graciously opened the door, and held out his hand to assist her upward. Door opening was another of his jobs, she noted. He did well opening every door they encountered. She had to admit it made her feel a bit special.

The hostess led them to a quaint booth made of dark wood. Fish nets hung above filled with glass artifacts, starfish and fake lobsters. The table had a fisherman's lantern adorning it, exuding a soft yellow light. There was a piece of rope sitting on top of each placemat. The challenge was to tie the rope into one of many possible knots as demonstrated on the placemats. Carrie sat opposite Jeff, not quite ready to sit next to him.

"Would you like a glass of wine," Jeff inquired, "or maybe a beer, or a root beer?"

"Not a root beer," Carrie giggled. "A glass of Riesling might please my palate. How about you?"

"Sounds good. A bottle of Pies Porter Riesling please," he advised the waitress. After a quick study of the menu Carrie decided on the lobster pot special. She didn't want to cause Jeff to have an exorbitant bill, and specials were usually a decent bet. Jeff agreed. After pouring the wine and securing the bottle in the ice bucket, the waitress whisked herself back to the kitchen.

"To a great evening," Jeff toasted as they clinked their glasses together. "To a good beginning," replied Carrie. The wine quickly impacted Carrie as she began to feel light and breezy. I should have eaten some carbs after my run, she thought. Wine on an empty stomach might not have been the best choice, but she was happy and having fun. It was a long time since she sincerely enjoyed herself.

"Let's see who can whip this knot up first," Carried giggled, "as she pointed to the most complicated looking one on the placemat. She was tipsy after the first glass of wine, which wasn't surprising with her waif-like appearance. Jeff was up for the challenge, relaxing a bit as the time rolled by. He was still in control of his faculties, or so he thought. He was intoxicated, not by the wine, but by this curious, confident, apparently slightly competitive woman. He sat back and pretended to manipulate the rope. To him the knot was simple, logical and consequently easy, but he was going to let her win. He basked in her facial features. He knew if he let her, she could mesmerize him. Hell, who was he kidding? She already had.

The dinner arrived, and the waitress placed the lobster pots in front of each of them, along with a tall butter tureen heated with a candle in its base. Carrie delighted in the sweet succulent taste of the lobster as it melted on her tongue. She let the buttered bite slither down her throat.

"Hmm," she purred. "This is so good." Jeff grinned. This was going far better than he expected. He loved to see a woman who was not shy about enjoying her food. There was no pretense here. Jeff poured both of them a second glass of wine. By now, Jeff was also feeling the magic of the alcohol.

Carrie and Jeff chatted the night away with easy abandon. Jeff, who was typically reserved, seemed to be more animated than usual. He began to talk expressing himself with his hands instead of resting them quietly on the table top, as was his usual style. He didn't know what overcame him, but he was happy. And then it happened. As he was flailing his hands about describing something, he tipped over the hot butter. It tilted toward Carrie, then, dribbled off the table onto her lap. He was mortified! She moved quickly bunching her napkin on her lap into a heap. It caught the butter without any damage being done. "I'm glad you did that," she smiled. "Now I'm not the only klutz sitting at the table!"

Jeff slid another foot deeper into loving Carrie. She was kind. She quickly changed what he considered to be a horrific situation into something light and non-consequential. He gazed fully into her eyes for the first time but became confused.

"Don't know where to look?" piped up Carrie. "Most people settle looking at the bridge of my nose." She was accustomed to people being stymied with her eyes, one was blue and one was brown. It was an infrequent condition. People were intrigued. She knew they felt like their eyes were bouncing back and forth from blue eye to brown eye, but she never noticed it. They both heartily laughed. Jeff knew he was a goner. She had him, if only she wanted him.

At night's end, Jeff dared to wrap his arm around her waist as he escorted her to her apartment door. She turned to face him and thank him for the fun evening. Forcing himself to remember he was a complete gentleman, he took each of her hands in his own, lifted them to his lips and kissed each one softly. He knew, if he dared kiss her on those beautiful full lips, he would never want to let her go. It pained him to leave her, but leave he did.

Carrie contentedly stepped inside. She couldn't stop smiling. It seemed to be a perfect date.

chapter 6

May 29, 2014

Carrie pulled into the parking lot and found a remote space to park Zippy. She wanted to be cautious and avoid the car from accidentally being nicked by another car. She knew better than to park it in a zigzag fashion taking up two spaces as many people did. She did not want to give anyone any reason to leave an indelible scratch on her car with a key.

Besides, she thought, a longer walk in the fresh air would feel good.

Where to start, she pondered? She hadn't been inside a Sears store for years. She found the tool section, looking for some duct tape first. Buy the smallest item first, so not to lug around the larger ones while still shopping was her motto. When she found the duct tape shelf, she was surprised to discover duct tape came in not only the color silver, but there were red, green, yellow, blue and black tape, too. When did that happen, she wondered?

A sales clerk in his fifties approached her and asked, "Anything I can help you with ma'am?"

She turned her head toward him and said, "No, not really, just picking up some tape."

"Why Ms. Singer, is that you?" the sales clerk said excitedly. Ms. Singer. Carrie hadn't been addressed by her maiden name in ages. She looked at him curiously, trying to recognize who he was. "You're probably wondering who I am. I wouldn't expect you to remember me. I'm Robert. Robert Winfield. My mother was Myrtle Winfield. I sure do remember you. I'm so glad to see you, again. What's it been, maybe almost thirty or forty years?"

Robert Winfield. Yes, she remembered him, quite vividly. Carrie always had trouble recognizing people's faces, especially after years may have passed. But she had a steel trap memory for all of the other details. She clearly remembered Robert, his mother and his four siblings, Carl, Vicky, Michelle and Jerry. His family was one of her first cases as a child welfare caseworker. She received a concern Robert was failing in school and sleeping through his classes. His grades fell dramatically from the beginning of the school year. His physical appearance deteriorated, and he came to school with disheveled dirty clothes.

Her first encounter with him was in a small office at his school in 1972. He walked in with his shoulders slouched, his pants sinking way below his waist, long before it became the trendy style, and he wore a tattered zipped up stained gray sweatshirt, which was too short for his long girth. He appeared sullen, with sad, mournful eyes. It was clear to Carrie he was carrying a heavy weight of some kind for his tender age of sixteen.

It took her time to coax him to talk to her as he didn't trust people. She tried to reassure him she was there to help in any way, if only she could understand what was happening in his life. At least, she hoped she could help. She wasn't as sure as she sounded. She was a novice in this role. Carrie thought she came across as confident to Robert, but he probably saw through her and noticed her own apprehension.

Perhaps that was what allowed Robert to begin to share with her. She, also, was vulnerable. He told her he stayed up all night long to keep an eye on his family as his dad was in prison for receiving stolen goods. His mom moved them to a smaller apartment. She had little money since his father was no longer contributing. The neighborhood was scary. You could hear clamor all evening long in the streets and in the apartment building. His brothers and sisters were scared. As the oldest, and now the man of the family, he felt it was his job to watch out for the family. Night was the worst time. Consequently he slept with 'one eye open' all of the time. Yes, Carrie remembered the Winfields. They were indelibly etched into her mind.

"Yes, Robert, yes, I do remember you and your family. How are you and your parents and brothers and sisters?" Carrie responded. "It's good to see you again. You're right. It has been a few years, probably decades I guess. You look terrific."

"Well mom and dad have passed on. Carl, unfortunately, is in jail, drug stuff, you know. But Vicky, Michelle and Jerry are all married and doing well. I became a grandfather. Can you believe it?"

"Well you beat me. I'm still waiting for grandchildren to appear." Carrie was struck by the fact she was six years older than Robert. "You look like you're doing well. I'm happy for you."

"Ms. Singer, I can't thank you enough for how you helped my family. I always said if I ever run into Ms. Singer again, I'm going to let her know she made all of the difference. You changed my life. I wouldn't be here today if it wasn't for you. I'm serious Ms. Singer. Now don't look at me like that. It's true. If you hadn't come along when you did, I don't know what would've happened. I'd probably be in jail alongside Carl, or be a druggie, maybe would've even killed somebody. You showed me a different path. You were about the only one who really gave a damn about me, excuse my language, but it's true. I always remember you in my prayers," Robert went on. "Vicky feels the same way. Now you know you saved her. It's good to see you, Ms. Singer, I can't tell you. The good Lord has blessed me today!"

"Well, thank you, Robert. I appreciate the sentiment, but you give me too much credit. You pulled yourself up. It's good to see you again. I'm glad life is good for you. Please give my regards to all of your family. Well, I have to get going. Take care." Giving Robert a quick hug, Carrie left to gather her other items.

As she walked toward the domestic section in search of a shower curtain, her thoughts turned back to the Winfields. It was an eye-opening, no an eye-popping experience for her. She remembered the small apartment Myrtle moved her family into after Don was sent to prison. It was meant to be an efficiency apartment for one person, one large room and a small kitchen and a bathroom with a tub and no shower, no bedrooms. The entire family slept on the cracked and dirty linoleum floor, amid what little possessions they owned. Clothes were strewn about and piled in heaps here and there. A couple of broken toys were present. Cockroaches were crawling everywhere. They had no heat. It was winter, and it was cold. Without heat, they had no hot water. The ceiling was stained with watermarks from the toilet leaking from the apartment above them. They didn't have a landlord, they had a slumlord. He didn't give two hoots about the conditions. He didn't care he packed a family of six in the rat hole. He was happy to take what little welfare money they had for the rent.

Myrtle Winfield had vacant eyes. She looked as though the world battered her about because it did. She was short and not quite obese. Dark circles under her eyes were her constant companion. She had little vocal expression in her voice. Carrie, although not a psychologist or diagnostician, was confident Myrtle was in the throes of depression. How could she not be? She wondered how Myrtle came to this place in life. Her childhood likely wasn't a happy story. Carrie felt sorry for them. She was determined to do whatever she could to help them. She would often have trouble sleeping at night knowing families like this, especially the children, suffered for all the other ills of the world. It was always the children who paid somehow. And the adults, they usually were those same children in their earlier life. It was all such a vicious unending cycle.

Her first visit to the family home was a true culture shock for Carrie. Myrtle had a pot of something cooking on the stove. Carrie wasn't sure what it was, but she thought she saw some type of animal feet sticking out of it. When she inquired what was cooking, Myrtle said, "Raccoon. Robert and Carl caught one last night. They make real good eating, not as good as groundhogs, but good enough to get some meat in your belly." Carrie checked herself from expressing her horror as her stomach rumbled and suggested it wanted to erupt. She never imagined city dwellers would resort to eating wild animals. She realized she genuinely didn't understand the reality of surviving poverty. They didn't teach this in college.

She remembered when Myrtle called her from a payphone and said the slumlord was going to let her family move to another apartment with two bedrooms, one block away. It was larger, with hardwood floors, and appeared to be in better condition, but the cockroaches lived there also. Carrie helped her get the gas turned on, so they would have heat and hot water. She took her down to the welfare office and advocated for her to get the full range of benefits her family needed. Myrtle didn't do this before. She was illiterate and overwhelmed with the government bureaucracy. Don always took care of the finances. Carrie contacted a local church group and arranged to get the children their own beds, a luxury they never before knew.

It wasn't long after they moved, when their home burned down, along with the other three apartments in this row type housing. Luckily, no one was injured. The Winfields started to put their lives back together, once again. It was devastating. The Red Cross and other charitable groups helped, but they couldn't fix the mental anguish everyone felt.

Yes, the Winfields taught Carrie about the meaning of poverty. Oh, they talked about it in her college classes. They put numbers and tables on the chalkboard to show what little could be purchased with the state's assistance. They never spoke of the actual outcomes poverty caused. University professors were isolated in their theoretical worlds. That's what they taught her, theories. She didn't learn about real life until she became a caseworker.

Robert fell behind in school. Although a junior, his performance, and reading level was at a fourth grade level. Schools passed him over and passed him on. It was easy to look the other way. There were so many Roberts. He was a good kid, though. He had a good soul. He cared about his family. The burden on him was too great for him to handle. Of course, he was sleeping in class. It was the only safe time to sleep. Classes held no real life relevance for him. Learning about the Civil War wasn't going to help him survive the next day.

Carrie found a program, the Job Corps, which was tailored to try to help kids like Robert. The requirements included: the applicant was between 16-21 years of age, behind in school and came from poverty. The youths could have no serious mental health problems and no serious juvenile court record. Robert fit perfectly. It required him to leave his family and move to one of their facilities. Carrie thought Robert went to Indianapolis. Their focus was vocational training, providing them a skill matching their abilities. They also had on-site counselors for personal problems. Robert thrived in that program. Myrtle was reluctant to let Robert go. She came to depend on him since Don was gone. It took serious persuasion on Carrie's part to get her to agree.

Carrie remembered one summer day when she had an appointment with the Winfields. As she approached their apartment, Michelle stood in front of the screen door wearing a dress two sizes larger than what her thin frame required. She looked quite forlorn as she stared out of the door. This eight year old child pierced Carrie's heart with an overwhelming sadness she hadn't experienced before. Typically considering herself an extremely strong individual, Carrie couldn't bring herself to stop the car and keep her appointment, and thus drove onward. The image of Michelle in her mind was the perfect snapshot of how children paid the price for poverty, forlorn, fragile and vulnerable. It literally hurt Carrie's heart. She stopped the car near a community park and tears flooded her eyes. Then she started to bawl. She knew people walking by might see her, but she didn't care. It was too much to endure.

She returned the next day. She felt guilty all night for not stopping. She couldn't reach the Winfields to alert them she was unable to come as they had no phone. Michelle asked Carrie, "Why didn't you come see me yesterday? I thought I saw your car drive by. I was waiting for you."

Carrie took one silent gulp and told Michelle she had an emergency and came today instead. Carrie, then, made up her mind she had no right to put her own needs first. Sure it was hard to see children suffer. They lived the horror of what she felt for them. She could never feel the true essence of their pain. She felt she was selfish by attending to her own needs rather than Michelle's need. Carrie gave her a giant hug and promised her she wouldn't break an appointment again if she had any say in the matter.

Michelle hugged her back and said, "That's okay Ms. Singer. I forgive you," whereupon Carrie used all of her energy to stifle back her own tears as she marveled at the ease with which children could forgive. Adults could learn a thing or two if they paid attention to the children, she thought.

When Carrie thought things couldn't get any worse for the Winfields, she received notice Carl, age thirteen, was picked up and placed in the detention home. He would have a court hearing this afternoon at 1:30. She needed to be there.

Carrie scanned the crowded waiting room in the courthouse to find Myrtle. She sat on one of the back benches that once were church pews, now carved with numerous graffiti slogans. Her head hung low, and she barely reacted when Carrie sat next to her. "What happened," Carrie quietly asked.

In words broken and almost imperceptible Myrtle replied, "Carl stabbed my brother with a butcher knife." Carrie tried to keep her mouth from falling to her knees. She couldn't believe what she heard. Carl was a shy kid, sensitive and kind. "He went off," Myrtle continued. "He found out my brother, Larry, was doing sex stuff to Vickie. When Larry fell asleep on our couch, he went to the kitchen, pulled out a butcher knife and stabbed him."

Carrie never saw this coming. How could she not know Vickie was being sexually abused? It made sense, though, the fact Carl would try to defend his sister. After all, Robert was gone in the Job Corps, and Don was still in jail.

Carl was placed on probation and sent to counseling. Vickie joined a therapeutic group for girls, who were victims of sexual abuse. Her uncle Larry went to jail, but only after Vickie found the courage to tell her tale of sexual abuse in the public courtroom for all to see and hear. It was required. Carrie remembered the legal system didn't give a damn about how such public testimonies revictimized the children, requiring them to relive their most horrific moments publically.

Hell, she thought, most adults wouldn't have the courage to come forth with their secrets, let alone sit there and let some stranger cross examine them, suggesting they were liars. And that act, the final act of a child sitting in a courtroom's witness chair, after taking a vow to tell the truth, only the truth and nothing but the truth; that act also required a child, without adult coping skills, to be cross examined, questioned and harassed about the most revolting, soul searing wound and depraved action taken against her by a sexual perpetrator, who was supposed to be a safe and trusted relative; that act required her to disclose publicly the details of the hands touching her body, forcing her to open her legs so the pervert could ram his penis time and time again into her; that act required her to put his penis into her mouth as he held an iron grip on her head; that act required her to tell how he bent her over the side arm of the couch and anally penetrate her over and over; that act of the courtroom drama was only the last of the many acts previously played out leading to this last act. Telling her story time and again, first to her mother, then to the police, to the hospital doctor, to the hospital social worker, to the child welfare worker, to the victim's assistant worker in the prosecutors department, to the prosecutor, to the guardian ad-Litem, to the sexual abuse therapist all preceded the final act. Each time repeating her story, she was required to relive the horror, to be victimized over and over and over again by the system designed to protect her. She learned children were chattel, nothing more, unimportant living beings with no voice, no need for gentle handling, and no concern for their emotional well being. It sickened Carrie. She shuddered as the memories poured forth.

Yes, Carrie remembered the Winfield family. She cut her teeth on them. They were a vehicle for her learning. She kept them in her prayers as part of a constant daily vigil. Carrie tried to forget, but she never could. She couldn't forget any of the kids, not just the Winfields.

chapter 7

Carrie meandered through the aisles at Sears until she found the domestic department. She found the shower curtain section and quickly picked up a new shower curtain liner, deciding that's all she actually needed. Now it was time to trudge to the women's section for an outfit to wear to her brother's honorary reception. This was the part of shopping Carrie disliked. She never understood women who reveled in this activity. It all seemed quite vain. Carrie's taste went to the practical, in concert with the way she lived her life - no fluff, no muss.

What little free time she did have certainly wasn't going to be spent inside a store acquiring stuff she didn't need. She preferred spending time with her children and being outdoors. She always felt a tinge of guilt she wasn't a stay at home mom. She secretly knew such an existence would drive her crazy. She rationalized she was a better mother with the stimulation of work to carry her through the day. As a result, she appreciated every moment with her children. And the children never knew any other way. They seemed fine with it.

Carrie squarely faced why buying a new outfit was needed. She simply lost enough weight her clothes were baggy on her. She did have some pride. She didn't want to embarrass her brother tomorrow; therefore she relented to the process.

She scanned the clothing racks for some possibilities. She picked out a brown linen dress with a rope belt, a navy blue polyester suit with some epaulets and gold braiding, a red and black print A-line dress, and a couple of pants suits, one purplish set with a light weight lavender sweater top and darker purple pants, and a green silky set with a mandarin collar tunic top with gold square buttons. She didn't look forward to the dressing rooms. "Ugh," she said under her breath, "let the process begin."

Off came her sweater and jeans and on went the brown dress. "It looks like a baggy sack," she groaned talking to herself. "With this rope belt I might as well join a monastery. I look like a monk. Maybe God is trying to tell me something," she snickered. Next she adorned the navy blue suit. "Aye, aye sir," she saluted in the mirror. "I don't think so," Carrie continued. The A-line black and red was next in line. "This one looks like it came from the devil," she laughed. It jogged a memory of hers.

She owned a flannel black and red, large-checked shirtwaist dress with a wide circle skirt falling to her mid-calf. The skirt portion had enough material to make it into a tablecloth, she often thought. She was remembering one particular day at work when she was in the restroom. After peeing, she pulled up her underpants and her pantyhose, another torturous fashion design she believed. This particular time, the hem of the back of her skirt got caught in the elastic waistband of her pantyhose. She, unknowingly, left the restroom with her skirt hiked up, allowing anyone and everyone to take a glance at her backside. Because the skirt had ample volume, she didn't notice. Her co-workers let her walk around for about ten minutes before she heard the raucous uproar of laughter. The minute she realized her situation, her face turned as red as the material. Carrie thought quickly. She figured she had two choices: get mad at them for having a healthy laugh at her expense, or laugh with them. She chose the latter.

"Quit daydreaming and get back to business," Carrie reminded herself. Next was the purple pants suit. Her ass swam in the pants, likely because she had no rear end. "Please," Carrie pleaded to the thin air, "let this last one be the one." As Carrie removed the green tunic top from the hanger, she enjoyed the feel of the smooth silk-like material. Her fingers easily glided over the fabric with the muted sheen. She put on the pants, and they also were a bit roomy in the back but not quite as baggy as the purple pants. She slipped on the top, and it easily covered up her slimness in the pants. It was comfy. She loved it, and green was her favorite color. "Perfecto," she announced. "Next, the garden department," she directed herself.

She grabbed a twenty-five foot green and white striped hose. This will do, she thought. BIRDSEED ON SALE begged the flyer next to the stacked bags of birdseed near the checkout counter. Carrie stopped short and pondered and pondered again. Why not, she decided. She grabbed a fifteen pound bag and threw it on the checkout counter.

chapter 8

Paula Cameron trembled. Her body involuntarily shook, as if she went into shock. Her mind raced with thoughts tumbling over one another. They were coming fast and furiously. Even though it was a warm spring day, she became chilled. Rena became scared when her bi-racial daughter turned ghost white. She didn't know what was happening to her, but knew she needed to get her off of her feet. As Rena guided her to the love seat in the corner, she grabbed the orange afghan Paula brought with her the first day she came to her home. She wrapped it around Paula and snuggled her as she folded her arms around her. Paula let out a loud, long wail as if she was expelling all of the evil events embedded in her. Rena sat silent, rocking her. She was speechless, dumbfounded and knew with all of her being she shouldn't let go of Paula. Rena tried to hold back her own tears, but it was impossible. She hurt from the depths of her soul for her child, as she knew Paula must be reliving a past real life nightmare. However, she couldn't begin to imagine what horror her daughter knew. They sat together as the crescendo of emotions diminished into an unsettling quiet. Forty minutes passed since either of them spoke a word.

"Mom, you'll never know how much I love you," Paula began and then, once again, her raw emotions usurped her body. She shed tears she didn't know she had left in her. Paula intellectually comprehended what was happening to her. She knew she needed to succumb to the process. She had many years of therapy following her removal from her home, but she was only six-years-old. She didn't have the vocabulary to put it into words, or the ability to recall many of her past life experiences. She hid them from herself to survive. Shadows and fleeting glimpses of darkness and pain were all she remembered then. The therapist explained to her she may never remember the events at all, let alone many of the details, or they might come flooding back to her at some future point. No one could predict. What saved Paula from total insanity was her gifted brilliant mind. She compartmentalized those events and stowed them away somewhere deep in her psyche. So deep, she couldn't access them until today. The picture of Carrie Cathers was the trigger allowing her to find the key and open the door. Carrie Cathers *was* her angel.

1995

As she hung tied to the water pipes above, Paula could hear all of the sounds above her. The floor boards were old and creaky, and sound traveled easily between the upstairs and the basement. Her mother and Ed fought frequently, typically ending in her mother screaming, followed by a loud thud on the floor above. She could hear glasses or plates breaking, imagining Ed was throwing things at her mother. She could hear Barry and Davy scurrying into the corner next to the couch. "Go get me another beer, woman," he'd say in a loud authoritative voice. "Get me my cigs." "Come suck my dick." "Don't you sass me, bitch." Whack, whack, whack. Bitch, whore, cunt, asshole, nigger lover were words frequently falling out of Ed's mouth with wild abandon. Paula didn't know what they meant, but his tone suggested they were bad words. "I'm going to take my sons and leave you and your bastard daughter to the wolves." Paula literally thought she might be eaten by wild animals, which took her fear to levels of unimaginable heights. She learned to stop listening. She imagined she and her mother would live in a castle, and she was a princess. Or she would be at her grandmother's house helping her with her garden. She dreamed of being back in school with her friends, playing and having fun. But she always returned to the intolerable excruciating existence no person should have endured.

When Ed would leave the house, her mother would come down and be with her. She cherished those moments. Mom would untie her and hold her. She would bring her some few scraps of food, but Paula didn't notice or taste the food. She quickly gobbled up the offering. She would bring her a bucket to use to pee and poop. As time wore on, Mom came down less often. She had multiple bruises on her arms and face. Once she looked as if she was missing a patch of hair. Paula would beg her mother to let her come upstairs, whereupon Darlene would look away and tell her to hush.

Once, Darlene was in the basement when Ed came home. She couldn't get up the stairs fast enough before he discovered she was with Paula. "I told you never to go into the basement when I'm gone, didn't I bitch! Answer me. I said answer me! I guess I'm going to have to teach you a lesson. You think she has it bad now? Well I'm about to show you how bad it can really get. This is your fault. I told you damn woman, you better listen to me." Ed came stomping down the basement steps. Paula was terrified. He was big and mean. He reeked of alcohol and stale cigarettes. "Get your fat ass down here. You're going to watch this cunt. I said GET YOUR FAT ASS DOWN HERE NOW!"

Darlene wanted to die, but she was afraid if she didn't listen to Ed, that's exactly what would happen. He would kill her. She came down. "Now sit your mother-fuckin' fat ass on the steps, shut your mouth and watch. Remember, you made me do this. It's because you won't fuckin' listen. I'm going to get me a piece of nigger, like you did six years ago."

Paula's eyes couldn't get any bigger. She could hardly breathe. She knew she was in the bowels of the devil. Ed yanked her arms free of the ropes causing serious rug-like burns along her forearms. He forced her to the basement floor, took a jackknife out of his pocket, brandished its shining steel blade about her face and then roughly cut off her pants. He spread her legs and forced himself inside of her. Paula screamed. She became unconscious. It made no difference to Ed. He decided he was going to have his way with her until he was satisfied. He continued to ravage her unconscious body. When she came to, she was lying on the floor with her hands and feet tied up. Blood stains were splattered on the floor where she lay. She lay still as if she was dead. She didn't want to alert Ed she was awake. She wished she died. She was alone. Her body began to convulse into violent shaking. Once again, she lost consciousness.

May 29, 2014

Paula knew there was no way she could tell her adopted mother the full details of her memory. There were some things not meant to be shared and brought to the light of day. It would serve no purpose, and she didn't want Rena to have to bear the burden of the horror. She didn't want pity. Curiously Paula was calm and resolved. That was in her past, a past no child should have lived through, but she survived. She remembered she prayed to God while on the floor. She prayed He would save her and send her one of His angels. And He did in the form of Carrie Cathers. Not only did God save her, but He delivered her to the most incredible mother in the universe, Rena Cameron.

"Mom," Paula began again, "some awful things happened when I was a little girl. My step-dad and mom kept me locked in the basement. It was for a long time. I don't even know how long. I was real lonely, and some pretty nasty things happened. I hope you'll understand I can't talk about it right now. But I'm alright. It was a long time ago, and they can't hurt me anymore."

Rena knew when she adopted Paula she was a traumatized child. The agency shared with her what they could, but even they didn't have the full picture. Paula was in a severely compromised physical condition, from which they said she would recover fully. Rena also knew Paula was placed in a great therapeutic foster home, Rena's own sister's home. Paula was emotionally and sexually abused, but due to her inability to express what happened to her, no one actually knew.

"Mom, I can tell you this. The woman you're honoring tomorrow, Carrie Cathers, she was the one who got me out of the basement. She was the one who carried me up those basement stairs and made all of the bad stuff go away. She was the angel I prayed for God to send to me and come save me. Mom, I want to skip my classes tomorrow. I need to be at the luncheon and see her again. I owe her my life. Do you think I might say a few words?"

"Of course, darling, are you sure?"

"I've never been surer of this than anything else in my life. I'm positive," said Paula with a tone in her voice making the angels sing.

***

Rena placed a phone call to Barbara Douglas, president of the YWCA board. "Barb," she began, "I wanted to check tomorrow's program's speakers list with you before I publish the bulletin. I have it completed on my computer and want to get it printed for tomorrow."

"Great!" Barbara said excitedly. "I think tomorrow is going to knock the socks off of a lot of people. How do you have the speakers lined up?"

"Well first we'll have Chaplain Kennedy give the invocation, followed by lunch. Then, you and the mayor will start with some opening remarks. Then, I thought we decided Katy Cathers-York would read her essay, followed by Martin Barnett and his entry. Next, I have state representative Cindy Prehm, then the Public Children Services Policy Initiative's director Elliot Marquette, who will present her with the award. Did I get it right?"

"That's what we agreed upon; however, there may be another addition even at this late date, but it isn't set in stone. Cindy suggested that the Undersecretary to the Office of Health and Human Services from Washington D.C. might attend, and if he can make it, he'd like to say a few words! I can't believe it, but apparently Cindy knows him personally, knew he might be in town, and asked if he might be a guest. Can you believe it? Someone from the President's staff might be here!"

Once again, Rena was awestruck with the day's unfolding. "No, I can't, but it's beyond anything we expected if he can come. Do you want me to add him to the program?"

"I think it's best if we don't. He may not show. Cindy said because it was a last minute request, we shouldn't go to any trouble. Besides, if he can't make it, then there'll be no explaining to do. And if he can, he'll be a welcomed surprise. What do you think?"

"I'm inclined to agree with you," Rena responded. "But I've yet another pretty amazing surprise for you."

"Oh, really?" Barbara inquired as her left eyebrow rose as it did when she was caught off guard.

"You won't believe this," Rena started, "but Carrie Cathers was apparently the social worker who first rescued our Paula from her birth parents! Paula had a startling flashback when she saw Carrie's picture on the bulletin. It was the most intense emotional scenario I've been part of or witnessed. I wasn't sure if she was going to come through the experience as it took her down an intensely rough set of memories. But her resilience is remarkable. She actually wanted to know if she might say a few words tomorrow. I told her she could without even thinking to check with you first. Anyone who would've seen the emotion bursting from her, wouldn't have the heart to deny her request, especially after all she's been through. I hope you don't mind. I thought I could give her a few minutes after Cindy Prehm."

"Wow, what a mindblower! Are you sure Paula is up for this?"

"Absolutely, I think to deny her would be devastating to Paula. Carrie's impact on Paula, let alone our community as a whole, has been overwhelmingly unbelievable. I didn't know people like Carrie could keep on going, carrying such a heavy load. I've never felt better about our choice this year," Rena said reflectively, "and to think she did this for forty years. It's unfathomable!"

"I can't imagine having the energy reserves she must have possessed," Barbara remarked. "If you sense Paula genuinely wants to do this, I'm sure a few moments would be fine. She's such a bright and sensitive young woman. Whatever she has to say would likely enhance the afternoon. Feel free to add her.'

"Thanks, Barb. Can't wait for tomorrow. See you then."

chapter 9

Carrie walked slowly back to Zippy. "Should I or shouldn't I," she debated to herself. "Well, it's now or never." She lifted the birdseed and hose into the small trunk, hung her outfit in the car, wiggled herself into the driver's seat and was on her way. It was a beautiful day, and she wasn't ready to go back home. She had enough of being home. She drove along the road towards the cemetery. It was strangely beckoning her back. It was four days shy of one year since the funeral, and she hadn't been back. It was time. She was resolute.

As she passed through the iron arch announcing Dane Forest Cemetery, memories came flooding back in torrents. Until one year ago, the cemetery was a place of joy and beauty for her and Jeff and the kids. It was three hundred and fifty acres of forest lined rolling land, with a large stone and marble mausoleum from circa 1850 overlooking a pond with mallard ducks, Canadian geese and their babies, and a pair of swans. The many paths winding through the beautiful land were lined with state champion trees including a Black Maple, a Douglas Fir and a Chinese Juniper. They were among the dozens of a variety of trees creating a breathtaking arboretum. Dawn Redwoods lined the main drive through the memorial park leading to the century old stained-glassed chapel with ivy clinging to its walls. Two hundred species of different birds made this area their home, and bird watchers from all over the Midwest came to catch a sighting to add to their repertoire.

Springtime was magical here with all of the wildflowers blooming, the fledging birds learning to fly and other curious wildlife. An albino squirrel who took up residence was often a key find. With a quick eye, one might spy one of the red foxes or coyotes running along the woodland's edge nearest the river tributary meandering lazily along one side. Headstones of every size and shape adorned the ground. You could see the progression of the ornate hand-carved stones of yore to the machine laser-cut stones of modern day. One hundred and fifty thousand interments were the last count. There currently were fourteen different sections overall. Four of them were military areas: Civil War, World War I, World War II and the Korean and Viet Nam war. They recently designated a newer fifth area for our more recently fallen. The oldest sections had sunken and erupted headstones, leaning every which way as the land shifted throughout the years. The saddest, heart tugging area for Carrie was the section designated "Lullaby Land" for infants and children. Most of these headstones had carved angels. There were so many, it was as if they created a large standing precious silent choir.

Carrie drove Zippy slowly to her favorite area, the butterfly garden and bird feeding station. She languidly eased out of the car, as she searched for the smooth marble bench positioned on the perimeter of the bird garden as Scott would call it. She smiled at the memory of Scott and Todd chasing each other around the bench in a game of tag when they were four years old. She hoisted the bag of birdseed from the trunk and climbed up the small grassy incline toward the feeders. They were neglected, utterly empty, Carrie noted sadly. She ripped open the bag of seed and filled them until there was none left to give.

Wearily, her earlier vibrant energy gone, Carrie sat her sixty-four-year-old bones down on the marble bench. The sun highlighted the feeders and the birds began to swarm in to fill up their bellies with the peanuts, sunflower, safflower and thistle seeds. The chickadees arrived first, followed by the nuthatches and titmice. Carrie delighted in the fluttering of their wings. The finches began to change their winter grayed yellow into bright canary yellow, the purple finches deepened their red markings. Her mind couldn't help but wander to earlier times.

This is where she and Jeff spent many of their happiest moments. They volunteered their time and energy here for the past twenty-five years. She could see Jeff helping to cut the sod to create the butterfly garden. She remembered the smell of the soil as she moved the cool dirt to plant the verbena, liatris, royal catch-fly, butterfly bushes and butterfly weed plants. Her back remembered the slight ache it would create after hours of weekly weeding. But it was all worth it. The butterflies exploded onto the scene without fail each summer, dancing their coats of color as they flitted from flower to flower thirsting for the precious nectar in each flower's offering.

Hide and seek was an oft played family activity. The children delighted in hiding but couldn't stop their giggling long enough to stay hidden. Before coming to the cemetery, the family would stop at the library, and each child would choose a book to be read to all. The family gathered on a large, old, bedspread printed with a fern design and laid carefully on a grassy spot they designated as theirs. Carrie would pack a picnic lunch they'd feast upon as they watched the birds and butterflies. As the children grew older and became involved in sports, music and other activities their schedule became quite hectic. Yet still, the tradition at Dane Forest continued. It was their time of loving one another. It was a magical place. A quiet, serene, peaceful time filled with happiness and devoted affection. As Carrie remembered, she fought through the painful longing for times past.

On the other side of the small narrow road leading to the birding area, Carrie saw the gravestone of her parents. Carl and Helen Singer started this tradition after they purchased some plots during a bonanza sale. In fact, they thought ahead and purchased six plots, one for each of them, and two for each of their children hoping they'd grow up, marry and lay themselves nearby when their time came, but, not for many years to come. Well, thought Carrie, the time came sooner than expected now, didn't it?

***

It was the evening of her birthday, one year ago. She was born on Memorial Day, May 30, when Memorial Day was the same date each year before they made it into a three day weekend. Even as a child Carrie felt an unsettling sensation when she understood her birth was on the day of honoring dead people. It was morbid, not joyous. When she was a young child, her mother tried to make her feel better about her birth date by telling her the park service personnel hung the swings at the neighborhood park just for her as they did this on the Friday of the Memorial Day weekend. She didn't know this date would personally affect her with a visit from death.

It was a rainy spring season. Jeff slipped out of the house to pick up a birthday gift for her he purchased earlier and stored at the twins' apartment. The wind picked up fiercely, and the rain became torrential. Carrie thought about worrying for a split second, but decided that'd be bad karma. She busied herself chatting with Katy, who came to spend the night and celebrate her mother's birthday. Katy's husband, Luke, was out of town on business.

The storm swelled to a fierce pitch. The rain came down in blankets. All of the windows flashed an enormous blinding light through them, followed by an immediate, monstrous, crackling thunder. The earth released a small tremble. The two large white oak trees, standing guard at the edge of the woodland in their back yard, were speared by a tremendous forked bolt of lightning, as if the god Thor, himself, pitched it. Carrie and Kate both immediately screamed and jumped uncontrollably at its inception.

The women ran to the back windows overlooking the yard. Two large thuds shook the ground and floor of the house as they watched the mighty trees fall to their death. "Oh, my God, oh, my God!" they both said in unison, "oh, my God!" The trees lay silently. Carrie ran to phone the twins. She hoped Jeff hadn't started to come home in this storm. She was going to warn him to stay put until it passed over, not to hurry home because it was her birthday. The phone was dead. Jeff took the cell phone with him. Katy's cell phone's battery was dead. Carrie took some small comfort knowing Jeff drove her car, instead of Zippy. Her silver Toyota Camry was more stable on the road in this type of weather.

"Don't worry, mom. Dad will be fine," Katy said trying to soothe her. "You know Dad is anything but a risk taker. Hey, let's play a game of Scrabble in the meantime," she said hoping to take her mother's mind off her concern.

Scrabble was a family favorite. Carrie and Jeff both delighted in words and their sounds. They made up many word games to play during their courtship, rhyming games, spelling challenges, Boggle, Hangman, trying to best one another with each and every opportunity. They'd buy identical crossword puzzle books and see who could finish each puzzle first. Jeff wasn't a risk taker. He wasn't searching for excitement in the company of many. He didn't enjoy parties and social events. He was content to be home with her alone. Jeff would read poetry to her as they lingered in each other's arms. They passed down their love of words and reading to all of their children. Theirs was a quiet life.

⁂

As Carrie became lost in her memories, a Rose-breasted Grosbeak bird flew to the nearest feeder and hungrily fed. She loved their plumage as they reminded her of a bird wearing a tuxedo with a red ascot. To see this bird was an infrequent sighting as they were only passing through on their migratory pilgrimage to places farther north. Where's your mate, Carrie wondered? The next thing she knew, the dowdier multi-brown colored female settled next to her partner. He placed a large peanut into her beak. How sweet, Carrie thought.

⁂

She looked across the road and reverted back to her memories. Jeff was a gentle, thoughtful, quiet man. He would do anything Carrie wanted as his goal in life was to make her happy. After their first date at the Windjammer, Jeff sent a dozen roses to her work the following Monday. The note simply said: Thank you for taking a chance on me. After their second date, their third date, their fourth date, and every date thereafter for the first six months, he sent her a dozen roses to her office. It became an office inside joke, but each and every woman who worked there secretly wished they had a man who demonstrated such care for them. The roses came with such regularity every Monday the receptionist quit looking at the card to see whom they were for, for they all knew, they were for Carrie. One Monday Carrie received two deliveries of a dozen roses. It wasn't until Wednesday she realized one set wasn't for her but for another co-worker, who came to her office when her boyfriend was concerned she didn't receive the roses he sent her.

Carrie thought about their first kiss. It was after their third date. Jeff took her to the art museum, where they strolled through the halls hand-in-hand. Their tastes were different. Carrie enjoyed the brighter bolder colors, the abstract paintings begging you to make sense of them. She employed her imagination and offered grand interpretations to Jeff about their hidden meaning. "This one means," as she studied a Pollock painting, "the world is full of chaos, with little pockets of happiness here and there," as she pointed to spots of yellow and green circled in black with purple and red paint drips surging toward the dark circle. All Jeff saw was paint splatters. Jeff's taste leaned toward the obvious: a man plowing his field as the sun set, a group of people frolicking at a bar, a vase of flowers on a table accompanied with apples and oranges. These made sense to him. Jeff liked his world to be predictable.

Carrie wondered as Jeff drove her home if he was ever going to kiss her. He certainly wasn't too forward by any means. She made up her mind, if she had to, she would initiate the lip lock. Once again, the total gentleman, he took each of her hands in his and began to lift them for the gentle kiss goodbye, whereupon Carrie flung her arms around Jeff's neck and planted a big fat smooch on him. What Jeff feared most happened. He couldn't let her go and kissed her again and again and again. His force of will alone kept his hands from touching her breasts, her butt, and everywhere else his body was screaming for him to touch. He was breathless. He started to sweat profusely and knew he better leave now or else he didn't know what would happen. He didn't want to ruin it. He didn't want Carrie to find a reason to find him distasteful. He pulled her arms down, kissed her hands and left. The next Monday, she received two dozen baby pink roses.

It wasn't until the fourth month Jeff relented, and felt safe enough to speak of his love for Carrie to her. He never before told a woman he loved her. Tonight was huge. He made a grand plan. He arranged for them to take a cooking class at Maya's house. She was a burgeoning new local chef, who offered classes to small groups of interested people in her downtown loft. Tonight, the class would consist of only Carrie and Jeff. Jeff planned the menu. First a cheese fondue, so he could feed her gently the bits of bread and sliced green apples. Like the Grosbeaks, Carrie thought. Next they would whip up a chicken linguini Alfredo as he imagined the spaghetti scene in the movie "Lady and the Tramp." And lastly, chocolate covered strawberries to match the color of her succulent lips. Jeff was quite proud of his plan but extremely nervous. The evening moved along better than he could imagine. They started with a bottle of Kendall Jackson chardonnay, something to loosen up the evening. Of course, the cheese fondue dribbled all over the place, being the klutzes they were. The linguini was overcooked and stuck together, causing uproarious laughter as they tried to move their lips smoothly around a linguini to meet in the middle, for it only to break and splatter. The strawberries squirted their juices and ran down their shirts. With the wine playing its part, Jeff and Carrie amused themselves and laughed until it hurt. They profusely thanked Maya for the evening fun, jumped into his Grand Prix and headed over to Jeff's place.

Jeff had a single flat apartment, meticulously decorated and shiny clean. His dwelling reflected he liked order. Perhaps that's why he was an accountant. Everything was always in proper order. He had a plan. Jeff always had a plan, a plan to please Carrie. But Carrie screwed it up. "Jeff," she said in a sultry voice, "you've made a mess of me with all of the fondue and linguini and strawberries. Do you mind if I take a shower?" Taken aback, Jeff replied, "of course not. Feel free. The towels are in the linen closet in the hallway."

"I know silly man," she giggled.

Jeff could hear the shower running and tried not to imagine her nakedness in his shower. This isn't how he planned it. Next Carrie called out to him, "Jeff, do you have a shirt I could throw on. Mine is sticky." Jeff grabbed a button down cotton shirt and opened the bathroom door widely enough to let his arm enter with the shirt. "Don't be shy. I've got a towel wrapped around me." She opened the door wide. Jeff could see her long slender legs from top to bottom. Her breasts were pinched together by the towel wrapped around her chest, leaving inviting cleavage and gluing Jeff's eyes to her sweetness.

"I love you, Carrie, I love you, I love you," he blurted out uncontrollably. "I love you so much." This wasn't how he planned it. He imagined Carrie would think he only said those words because she was in such a compromising position, and his hormones, not his heart, were speaking.

But Carrie knew better. She drew him towards her and said, "Carry me to your bedroom, sweetheart. I love you, too."

***

Now sun gleamed into Carrie's eyes breaking up her reverie of days long past.

It would be sunset in about eight hours, Carrie guessed as the sun shot a gleaming ray straight into her eye. She shielded her eyes for a moment. She, once again, gazed longingly at the family plot of headstones from the marble bench. She didn't have the courage, yet, to draw herself closer to the site. Perhaps there was no need to get closer, no need to get down on her knees and once again bask in more sorrow. She needed the grief to go away. A Tiger butterfly flitted about her head and then she spotted a Red Admiral, one of the first butterflies to welcome in the spring. It was as if they came to cheer her, but her memory of the last fateful day was still begging to be played in her head.

***

Carrie was interrupted in her momentary daydreaming as she heard Katy calling to her.

"Mom," Katy said, "where did you put the Scrabble game? It's not here in the chest.

"Oh, I think I put it in the basement, honey. It's back in one of the plastic bins in the far corner." Katy went to retrieve the board.

Carrie worried for a quick moment about Jeff and the weather. Stop, she said to herself. Her memories, then, drew her to the night Jeff asked her to marry him. Once again, he methodically planned the evening. She came over as she did many other evenings. They took turns going to her place and then his. This night, a full moon night, they were at his place. Jeff purchased a bottle of Chianti, Roca del Mace, a delicate tummy warming smooth red wine. He placed the Scrabble game on the coffee table and carefully planned where specific letter tiles could be collected and then placed on his rack. When it came time to play, he pulled the tile with the letter A, allowing him to create the first word. He was giddy. They picked up seven tiles each and the game began. First they toasted with their wine glasses, "to a great night." Jeff anxiously placed his tiles on the center of the Scrabble board. M-A-R-R-Y-M-E.

Carrie gasped. She didn't see this coming. She smiled at him, held up her finger as if to say "Wait." She studied her tiles with the letters B, K, E, I, A, Y, and S. She carefully picked up four of the tiles, attached them to the letter M which was on the board, and spelled out the word M-A-Y-B-E. Jeff looked at her forlornly, and her heart started to break for him. She immediately snuffed out the laughter about to emerge from her own supposed cleverness. She quickly grabbed the letters back and used his Y and added the letters E and S, Y-E-S. She melted into his chest and gave him a long lingering kiss, dancing her tongue around his.

"Mom," Katy said waking her mom from her daydream. "I set the game up, are you ready to play."

"I'm sorry, dear, I was. . . "

"I know, mom, you were worrying about Dad. Now stop and let's play."

As Kate and Carrie delved into their Scrabble game, the winds outside started to quiet down, the storm was dissipating. O-N-Y-X was formed on the board by Carrie, heartened she finally got rid of the letter X. She briefly reflected on the black onyx ring Jeff gave her, mounted in a delicate silver laced setting. This night has been as black as onyx, she thought.

Kate remarked, "Mom, you didn't leave me any decent options on this board. This game hasn't been an easy one." An unexpected uneasiness and chill passed through Carrie. It gave her the shudders. She wished Jeff would get home. Then the doorbell rang. "I'll get it," Kate announced as she jumped up from her chair. Strange, Carrie pondered, Jeff must have forgotten his key, feeling relieved he was finally home. I wonder why he didn't enter in through the garage. Maybe the bolt of lightning tripped up the electrical circuit so the garage door couldn't open.

Kate answered the door and immediately recognized Ellen. "Why Ellen, what a surprise! Do come in. I supposed you stopped by to wish Mom a happy birthday. It's good of you to remember, and in this weather!"

Ellen Lewis long worked alongside Carrie throughout her years as a child welfare caseworker. They'd been through many rough times, trials and tribulations together. Ellen was one of the few people who understood the emotional toll this work exacted from the Children Services staff. Ellen, as a police officer, often was with Carrie and saw the ravages child maltreatment caused. She saw the vacant staring eyes of children and understood the hurt and pain on a far deeper level than the superficial. Ellen also knew Carrie's heart. She was the most giving, unselfish and spiritual woman she knew. In fact, Carrie was the reason Ellen continued in the work she did. They became fast and loving friends, despite their fifteen year age difference.

"Katy," she gulped, her eyes watering. Stay strong, stay strong this one time for Carrie, she thought. It's the very least you can do. Every fiber in Ellen's body wanted to relent to her emotions. She wished within the deepest part of her soul she wasn't standing here at this moment. She couldn't imagine the pain which would rip through her dear friend when she delivered the unimaginable news. "Kate, dear, I'm here on semi-official business," she said quietly as tears began to stain the side of her face as they left the corners of her eyes.

Carrie slid her chair back from the table, stretched and ambled toward the front door to greet Jeff. "Why it's about time you got here, I was worried with the storm and . . ." Her words trailed off as she realized it was Ellen at the door, in uniform. She couldn't help but notice Ellen was highly emotionally charged and not in a good way. She looked at Katy, who'd turned as white as a ghost. Her thoughts raced and without anyone having to say a word Carrie knew. Carrie knew something terrible happened to Jeff. The cold shudder she felt earlier wasn't random. "No, no, no," her half cry came spewing from her depths. A brief moment of hope mounted an assault. "Where is he, which hospital?"

Ellen grabbed Carrie, held her tightly and whispered in her ear, "He's gone, Carrie, he died in a car crash." The three women huddled together and heaved flooding tears. They'd momentarily quiet until one of them began again. The tide of emotion kept rising, ebbing and swelling again and again like the waters in the oceans until all three were utterly spent. Carrie called upon her reserves of strength to pull it together, quite like she did many times before with all of the children. She was pragmatic. She, long ago, learned to accept reality, accept the world had pain to give. Today she was its target and not a helpless child. Then she thought of her own children, poor Katy and Scott, and Todd. She'd need to be strong for them now. The Kleenex box was ravaged by the women. "Katy, dear, do you think you could get us something to drink? Let's go into the family room," Carrie paused with the reminder of the word family and theirs' would never be the same again, "and sit down."

Katy, sniffing the whole way, brought in three tall ice filled glasses of mint sun tea Carrie prepared earlier in the day. All three took a small sip. "Ellen," Carrie began, "I appreciate you brought me this news, rather than a stranger. I can't imagine what you've been through this night. Please tell me what happened."

That was like Carrie, Ellen reflected, worrying about everybody but herself. "I'm not sorry it was me," Ellen began, "I couldn't bear the thought of someone else telling you. Carrie, he died quickly. By all accounts, he didn't have time to suffer at all." Katy began to weep again, tried to stop but couldn't. Carrie cradled her in her arms gently, assuring her it'd be alright.

"Please, Ellen, go on," Carrie pleaded.

"Well, as you know, it's been a terrible stormy night. The rain's been thick." Carrie became aware the night transformed into a hauntingly deathly quiet now, not a sound could be heard. It was eerily peaceful. "Jeff was on his way home. The light turned green for him to pass through the intersection at Teaberry Lane and Star Rd. The on-coming car failed to stop and broadsided Jeff at a racecar like speed. He never knew what hit him. The car rolled three times and crashed into the gasoline pumps at the Shell station. It burst into flames. By the time any help could get to him, he was gone. The car was entirely burned along with the majority of the gas station." Ellen wished she didn't have to relate this to them. It was serious enough Jeff was gone, but the details made it even more horrific. But she knew Carrie wouldn't want to be coddled.

Katy's sobs turned to asthmatic-like whimpers. Carrie stared into the beyond as she rocked Katy gently. "We'll be alright, we'll be alright," Carrie kept affirming to herself. "We'll get through this, we're strong, we will, you'll see."

Ellen watched the two women supporting each other. Her police officer training taught her she was watching the beginning of the grief cycle; she saw it many times before. Shock, total shock set in first. The body and the mind would let you get through. Shock would let you slowly process at a speed you could handle and not go berserk. Even though Carrie appeared to be the Rock of Gibraltar, Ellen wasn't sure how long she could manifest this state. This was the part she dreaded, there was more. She wanted to vomit. She didn't want to tell her the whole story. Maybe she should give her more time before hearing the rest. What would Carrie want, she considered? Carrie was the strongest person Ellen knew, but even this might be too overwhelming for even her. Hell, it was too much for me, Ellen thought, let alone what it was going to do to Carrie and Katy. I should have brought some more people with me. Ellen knew deep down Carrie would want the whole truth of the matter. There simply was no easy way to stop the crushing blow about to be delivered. She prayed to God to give her the strength to continue and be strong for her good friend. She prayed to God to give Carrie and Katy even more strength.

"Carrie, Katy," Ellen began, "there's more." She sucked in her breath and sent up yet another prayer enabling her to continue. "Jeff wasn't the only person in the car, the twins. . ."

Carrie went deaf after the word twins. She could hear no more.

chapter 10

The sun was about six inches from the horizon. It was turning into an orange hue rather than a brilliant yellow. Carrie rose from the bench and began to saunter over to the gravesites. She felt compelled to draw closer. She did it. She faced it fully square in the face. Surprisingly there were no more tears. There was only peaceful resignation.

Carrie didn't attend church, even though in younger years she gave some thought about becoming a minister. She held a deep belief in God and often held conversations with Him, but she found church anything but inspiring. For her, it was another method to control people, often making them feel guilty for their humanness. She felt she didn't need someone to intercede on her behalf to reach God. She preferred to talk to Him directly, and she did often. It was what got her through all of those years with the many, many, many hurt children with broken spirits she encountered. Carrie liked to think of herself as a spiritual being. Perhaps that's why she enjoyed nature. She could see how the Lord painted the world with an artist's eye. It was in the solitude of nature she felt connected with Him.

Carrie remembered many conversations she and Jeff had regarding how to handle their deaths, well, their funerals. They both wanted something remarkably different from the other. Jeff was traditional. He imagined there should be a wake and a funeral, perhaps two days of a wake. Of course, the body should be embalmed and placed in an open woodened casket. Everyone should gather at the cemetery and pay their last respects as the casket was lowered into the ground for burial. Afterwards, there should be a reception where all could indulge in food and share memories while comforting one another. Carrie cringed at the thought of this scene, but they agreed to respect the other's wishes.

Carrie wanted nothing similarly. She didn't want people to last remember her lying dead in a casket. The dead body wouldn't be her. It would be the remnants of a body she once inhabited. She would no longer be there. Her energy would have moved on. Carrie knew what she wanted, the State wouldn't allow. She wanted to be buried in the sky as the Native-American Indians practiced. She wanted to allow her body to go back to nature from whence it came. She imagined her body being laid upon a platform, looking up toward the sky. She took from nature her entire life to feed and sustain her body. She took from plants and animals. Her death could be a time to give back. But Carrie, still the pragmatist, knew the government wouldn't allow it. She couldn't see herself being embalmed, staving off inevitable decomposition as long as possible. She didn't want her body to turn into an eventual gel-like substance before only bones remained, with decomposition taking decades. She had her mind set on cremation. Besides, she figured, if she needed another body in the future, the all powerful God could find her one. She trusted Him.

How ironic, she thought. The nature of Jeff's and her children's death precluded any possible way Carrie could follow through with his last wishes. She did what she could do. They held a wake and a funeral and a reception. They gathered at the cemetery, although she held vague memories of any of it. She was strangely comforted her children and husband was cremated by God himself as she defined it. She knew they were in a better realm. Their earthly trials and tribulations were taken from them, and they now walked in a new life, perhaps with God, perhaps in a place unknown. But she knew their spirit energy continued to live on. Carrie kissed her hand three times and placed a kiss upon each of their engraved names. "I love you Jeff, I love you Scott, I love you Todd." Carrie hung her head in a silent prayer as an almost imperceptible smile crept on her face. She knew the day was near when she would join them. It was time to leave.

chapter 11

Back in Zippy, back on the road, Carrie had one more stop before she went home. She needed to refill her prescription. Following their deaths, her doctor ordered Xanax to curb anxiety she may experience, "to be on the cautious side," he said. Carrie never took any kind of pharmaceutical. It was against nature's way in her mind. This time, though, she figured it couldn't hurt to have it on hand, kind of like the doctor said. Although she never tapped into her original bottle, she knew it was beyond the 'use by date'. She wanted a fresh bottle on hand for what she planned. The pharmacy was located inside her grocery store. She thought she might pick up one of her favorite foods for dinner: a filet mignon, baked potato and a salad filled with greens and vegetables with a tad of strawberry vinaigrette dressing.

She approached the pharmacy window and requested her refill. "The wait is about thirty minutes today. We're kind of backed up," the pharmacy assistant noted. Carrie went to collect her dinner items. When she finished gathering her groceries, the prescription still wasn't ready. She sat on one of the nearby benches to wait. Every time she was near a pharmacy, she couldn't help but think of Ramona.

***

Ramona was the mother to three budding teenage girls. They were referred to the agency for services as the girls were out of control, running the show. It was their father who called in the concern. He was divorced from Ramona, and wanted custody of his children as Ramona was awarded full custody at the divorce. Jim, the father, cheated on Ramona and wasn't home often. His role as father was fulfilled like a phantom ghost, sometimes there, sometimes not. The court gave Ramona full custody.

Carrie disliked these cases. The children would be fine if the parents had their act together. Often child welfare wasn't about the children's behavior but about the immaturity of their adult parents with their inability to put their children's needs above their own. Jim despised Ramona as she continued to contact the court to press charges against him for non-payment of child support. He remarried and had another family he was supporting. He didn't have enough money to go around for two separate households, which was his rationale for non-payment. He wanted custody of his children so his child support payments would terminate.

As she worked with Ramona, Carrie became aware that Ramona was depressed with her life as it didn't turn out according to her dreams. She was filled with hate for Jim. Her energy levels were seriously depleted. The girls did have the run of the household. Ramona spent much of her time in bed. She doctor shopped. This practice gave her many prescriptions from each doctor, all sedatives and anti-depressants. Carrie was alarmed at how easily doctors handed out these prescriptions. As a result, Carrie never got in the habit of taking any prescription drug. You need to learn to deal with life was her motto. She often saw medication as a cop out.

She formed a viable professional relationship with Ramona, and Ramona leaned on Carrie. Carrie cut her availability back as she tried to decrease Ramona's dependence on her for emotional nurturance. She linked Ramona with a professional mental health counselor, enrolled the girls in some group work, and tried to help Ramona establish rules and boundaries in the home for her children. Yet Ramona was psychologically stuck in her anger, and eventually turned it inward.

One day as she was sitting at her desk completing paperwork, Ramona called. She told Carrie she ingested seventy-seven assorted pills from her bag of collected prescriptions. She was calling to say one final goodbye. "I guess Jim wins in the end, he'll get the children," she remarked. "Thank you for all you've tried to do. I can't deal with it anymore." Ramona hung up. Carrie noticed an inflection in Ramona's voice alerting her this was no joke, no outward cry for attention. Ramona really completed an action would end her life.

Carrie acted quickly. 9-1-1 service wasn't available yet. She called the Emergency Medical Squad responsible for Ramona's neighborhood. She wasn't sure which department covered her residence as they lived out on the fringe of town. There were a couple of different townships she may be in. She called Jefferson Township. They took the information and said they'd respond. "Whew," Carrie muttered, "I'm glad I chose the right one on the first try."

About forty-five minutes later, Carrie called Jefferson Township to see what the situation was they encountered at Ramona's home. It was at this time they responded, "Oh that wasn't in our jurisdiction. It's in Grover Township."

"Did you alert Grover Township?" Carrie replied.

"No, we didn't. We had to take another run."

Carrie couldn't believe her ears. A woman ingested a potential lethal amount of prescription drugs, enough to kill a horse, and they let the call drop. She quickly picked up the telephone and dialed Grover Township EMS. They responded. They found Ramona unconscious and on the verge of death. Luckily, Ramona hadn't locked her front door. She was immediately transported to Schroeder Memorial Hospital where her stomach was pumped. She was hospitalized overnight and then transferred to the psychiatric ward for further assessment.

Carrie arranged to meet the children when they arrived home from school. She didn't want them to come home to an empty house and wonder where their mother was. Her current work project would wait. Yes, she would be late, once again, with her paperwork. But this was more important, though she knew the state's bureaucrats wouldn't understand.

Accompanied with the police, as only they had the ability to remove children from their homes without a court order, Carrie arrived to Ramona's home before the children got off the school bus. She was glad to see it was officer Ellen Lewis who came to the scene. Women police officers were less scary to children than male officers. The children were given to their father for care until Ramona was stabilized. This was one of a few rare instances Carrie knew she saved a life. Without her follow up, Ramona would never have received help in time. Carrie was the only person she called.

***

"Mrs. Cathers, Mrs. Carrie Cathers," the clerk called out. Carrie stepped up to the pharmacist's window and picked up her pills. She grabbed her grocery cart and headed for the check out aisles. As she searched for one that could quickly process her purchases, she passed by a display for Bailey's Irish Crème, one of her favorite liqueurs. She grabbed a bottle. Gathering up her checked out bags, Carrie returned to Zippy and headed homeward.

chapter 12

Carrie was glad to get home. She had an emotionally draining day. It provided her with some of the emotional release she needed to move forward. She had plans. The telephone light indicated she had messages. There were five, one from Carson and four from Katy. She imagined Katy was worried about her, but she needn't be. She was fine, finer than she was in a long while. She gave Katy a quick call back to assure her she had a good day, and she was now home safely. Carrie understood how much energy Katy spent trying to take care of her during this past year. It wasn't easy. She was proud of how strong Katy was for her. Carrie understood she wasn't the only one who suffered the loss of Jeff, Scott and Todd. After all Katy lost her father and brothers, but remained steadfast in her strength finding the reserves to care for her mother also. Carrie sent up a silent prayer of gratitude for her daughter and her son-in-law, Luke. If not for Luke, perhaps neither of them would've made it through. He had a heart of gold. It was quite clear Katy was nestled in the center of it, wrapped in the protection of his love.

Luke, in many ways, loved Katy with the same passion Jeff loved Carrie. The corner of her mouth curled upward as she thought Katy, indeed, found a husband mirroring many of her father's traits. He adored her, as did her father. He was predictable, perhaps a bit more spontaneous, but steadfast in his commitment and love to Kate. Carrie was sure it was Luke who grounded Katy throughout the past year. He never gave her a moment's grief about all of the nights she spent with Mom instead of being curled up next to him. Well, Carrie thought, Katy deserves to be released from her self-imposed bondage to me. Soon she'll be set free.

As the phone began to ring, Carrie imagined it might be Carson calling her back. "Hello," Carrie spoke into the phone. "Hi, Ellen! It's good to hear from you. No, actually I arrived home a few moments ago. I'm feeling great. I was going to throw a steak on the grill. Why don't you come over and join me? I'd love to visit a bit. Okay. Good. See you in a few." A surge of happy energy filled Carrie. She imagined she would eat in quiet solitude, but was pleased her good friend called.

It had been rough for Ellen this past year, too. After all, Ellen was at the scene of the accident. She endured the remaining image of the calamity. Carrie thanked the good Lord many times over her last memory of her family was a happy picture, not the ensuing remnants of death and destruction. Ellen wasn't spared. Many lives were impacted, thought Carrie. How we are all intertwined is unbelievable, and most of the time we aren't even aware of it. If only all people in the world could live and love one another as if we were all family, and take care and time to give more than we receive. Ah, it'd be such a better place. "That's never going to happen," muttered Carrie. The stark reality of life bore the opposite view in her life experiences. She thought about how she was challenged to live the creed she wished for the rest of the world. Taking the high road was never easy. Sticking to your principles was never easy. Carrie realized she did a lot of talking to herself. She became accustomed to it.

"Hi Carrie," greeted Ellen, letting herself in and wrapping Carrie in a big bear hug squeezing her tightly. "How are you?"

"I'm feeling quite well," Carrie responded as she began to prepare for dinner.

"Here's my steak," Ellen announced. "I ran into Kate in the wine aisle as I was picking up this bottle of Pinot Noir. Kate said you were particularly up today. What's up, pun intended," Ellen chuckled with her cleverness.

Carrie put her hands on her hips, nodded her head in agreement and said, "I decided to get on with what I need to do. I had a long talk with myself again, but this time I was serious. It feels good."

"Katy told me the YWCA is honoring Carson tomorrow. She invited me to attend and sit with you guys. I'd love to come. Are you okay if I do? You know I feel like a family member."

"Of course, I'd love to have you come. I should have thought of inviting you myself," Carrie said as she hugged Ellen. "Please, do come."

"I will, and don't feel you guilty about not thinking of it yourself. I'm sure this time of year is difficult for you because it is for me, as well. I can't imagine what's been going through your mind. It will have been a year ago tomorrow."

With a huge lingering sigh, Carrie said, "It's been pretty rough. I went to the cemetery today. I was determined to stay until, well until I could walk through it without falling to pieces. It was therapeutic. I think I needed some time alone with all three of them. Jeff, Scott and Todd would be upset if I continued to linger in a sea of nothingness, holding a self-indulgent pity party. You know, I think I was grieving not only for them all this time. I think I was grieving for all the hurt, harm and horribleness I've seen all my work life as well. I didn't realize how it impacted me. Having retired shortly before the accident, I realized I haven't really processed all I've seen and experienced the last forty years. It all kind of hit me at once. Be careful. Take care of yourself out there Ellen. You may not see all I have, but you've seen your share of it. Really, take care of yourself, sweetheart. I wouldn't want you to fall into the dark abyss I did. It's a long climb out. I don't know if I've reached the top of it yet, but I'm closer."

Trying to lighten the mood Ellen began to sing "Happy Birthday to you, happy birthday to you, happy birthday dear Carrie, my forever friend, happy birthday to you, and many more. I hope you didn't mind I sang. Last year wasn't much of a birthday for you."

"Oh, I've given up celebrating my birthday. Remember it's also the old Memorial Day, a time to honor those who've passed on. You all can celebrate it if you want, even after I've passed on. In the meantime, it doesn't mean much to me. As a kid, I was upset I was born on that day. I thought of it as morbid before I understood it was a day of honor. Tomorrow, I'll celebrate for," her voice began to crack. She paused and then gained strength again, "for all of them. They made my life happy. We had many unforgettable good times together."

"It's time to honor them and their lives, and to celebrate you, too!" Ellen chirped in.

Carrie meekly smiled thinking how wonderful Ellen was for trying to cheer her up. She decided to go along with it, for Ellen's sake. "Okay. It's a deal."

"How about a glass of wine?" Ellen suggested as she popped out the cork. Carrie pulled out two decorative wine glasses with pictures of Sequoia trees etched into them and tinted green glass stems. She and Jeff picked them out during their honeymoon at Sequoia National Park. As Ellen poured the wine, Carrie took in the aroma. She loved noticing smells, it made life more exhilarating. Clink. "To you," Ellen toasted. The smooth 'A to Z' wine left a clean finish, warming their tummies. Ellen discovered this wine at a small French Bistro in Evanston, Illinois when she attended a law enforcement conference there. The wine was one of her favorites. Nothing but the best for my dear friend, she thought.

"Hey, I've some good news! You know I've always been with the Juvenile Bureau Division of the department my whole career. Most of the officers begin there and then move on to what they consider more prestigious areas such as homicide or vice or internal affairs. Well, it finally paid off for me. I was promoted to Captain!"

"Awesome," retorted Carrie, "I'm happy for you, you deserve it. I know many of the officers think working with children, and their families are small potatoes, but I believe it makes a difference in the long run, a critical difference to their future well-being. We can't save them all, but we do save some. You'll be good, too. No one can replace the experience and knowledge you have about family strife. Let's toast again, this time to you!"

"I wish you better luck than I had with a management position. You know there was a time when I was a supervisor instead of a worker, for about three months. Administration kept prodding me to become a supervisor. I always resisted. I didn't think it would be right for me. I wanted to be on the front lines. I wanted to work with the children and their parents directly. I saw how supervisors would become disconnected from the children. It was not because their hearts wanted to, but it was because of all of the demands the system placed upon them. I didn't think it'd be right for me."

"What happened?" Ellen questioned as she leaned forward placing her elbows on her knees.

"Well, it was when Connie Preston went on maternity leave. They wanted someone to fill in for her. The other supervisors were overwhelmed. They didn't need the responsibility of additional staff. Usually they'd farm out a supervisor's unit members assigning each to another supervisor. They asked me to assume her place. I guess they figured with all my years of experience, I could easily guide the other workers. Besides they were encouraging me for a long time to move up. I'd say no, and they'd shake their heads in bewilderment. They didn't understand why anyone would want to stay on the streets instead of being inside where it was safer. On the other hand, I didn't understand why anyone would want to be cooped up all day inside. It was like committing oneself voluntarily to prison for eight hours each day. I enjoyed getting out, being able to move around in the community and meeting with my families. I loved my kids. I didn't love the paperwork. There was too much for the caseworker, let alone for the supervisor who had five times as much! No, it wasn't for me."

"What happened? You never told me about this," Ellen said.

"Well, there truly isn't a lot to tell. I thought for a quick moment, maybe they're right. Maybe I should give it a shot. You can't know for real what it's like, unless you give it a try. I said I'd do it. It seemed to be a perfect opportunity for a trial run. It was a good experience as well as a bad experience."

"How so," Ellen said intriguingly..

"It was good because it solidified for me I wanted to stay a caseworker. My heart, mind and soul wanted to be with the families the entire time I was filling in for Connie. I didn't care about the fact it paid less to be a caseworker, although I've maintained anyone who stays on the street should get paid more than those who stay inside. But that's not the point. I hated supervising other workers. It did give me a new appreciation for the role of the supervisor, but it wasn't for me. I realized it's easier to be responsible for your own work, and not answer for someone else's work. Maybe I copped out. When the workers came to me and told me how they responded to their case situations, sometimes I wanted to die. I couldn't believe how many different responses individual caseworkers had to similar situations. Some were helpful, others punitive, and still others, in fact, most of them, were outright clueless about what to do. I'm sure it was because they were beginners, but they were dependent on me for every little direction. It wore me out. It also made me realize seasoned caseworkers were a desperately needed resource. It provided me with a clearer understanding why I always seemed to get the difficult cases. Who else could they trust with them? I guess me and two other workers. I was glad to hand the reins of supervising back to Connie. But you guys at the police department, you're probably set up differently. I'm sure you'll do a fantastic job. Hey, I think the steaks are done. Let's eat."

"The meal was sumptuous," Ellen pronounced. As they cleaned up, Ellen said, "I loved the way you cut up those potatoes into small pieces and added all those herbs to them before baking them. They were delicious. Did you make the salad dressing? It was so light. What's your secret?"

"Grape seed oil, instead of olive oil. It's lighter and has more anti-oxidants, too. It costs a little more, but I find it's worth it. I also used champagne vinegar. Why don't we sit in the screened-in porch? It's such a pleasant evening still," Carrie suggested. "You can stay a bit longer, I hope."

"Of course I can. In fact, there's something I want to talk to you about," Ellen said a bit nervously.

"Really?" Carrie raised her eyebrows as she handed a light-weight quilt to Ellen, "in case you get a little chilly. What do you want to talk about?"

"I want to talk about Darren Oglesby," Ellen said hesitantly.

"Oh, really? What about him?"

"Carrie, I never understood how you were able to forgive him. After all, he was absolutely responsible for the tragic night you lost Jeff and the boys. He was way past the intoxication limit to drive. He was speeding and was reckless. Yet, you asked the judge to give him leniency. How on earth did you bring yourself to make such a request, after all he took from you? I never understood, and I really want to."

Carrie leaned back in her chair and closed her eyes. "It was required," she said sighing heavily. She knew this would be difficult for many people to understand, but she really didn't care. Perhaps, she thought, it was time to try and explain. Even her family didn't understand.

"It was required? What in heaven's name do you mean it was required?"

"Ellen, dear, I don't expect you or anyone else to understand, but I did it for myself as well as for Darren. If I didn't forgive him, I'd have swirled around in even more negativity than I have. I did it for me. I did it to release me. I had to take the high road. Besides, I kind of owed it to him," Carrie said, grabbing Ellen's hand with a light squeeze.

"You owed him! What do you mean you owed him? Were you nuts? I don't see how you owed him anything," Ellen cried out, half angry, half bewildered.

"Let me tell you the story," Carrie said with a heavy heart. "It's time."

chapter 13

Carrie began telling her story. "It started when my supervisor called me into her office". "Carrie, can you come in here for a moment? I have a new case I want to give you. This one has a bit of a different twist." My curiosity was piqued. "This case involves a ten year old boy named Darren Oglesby. He was born with a birth defect in which one leg is five inches shorter than his other leg. The hospital clinic called us to say they were concerned about his mother's lack of follow through with his needed orthotics and physical therapy. In fact, she's broken many appointments over the years resulting in his spinal alignment to be grossly compromised. If he doesn't get the needed interventions, he'll suffer some permanent long term damage and collateral organ impairments if he hasn't already. I think this case has your name written all over it. Mother apparently isn't the easiest person to work with."

"Thanks, Lysbeth, I'll get right on it," Carrie said slightly smiling.

"That's what I like about you, Carrie; you're the only caseworker who thanks me for more work. I do wish we could clone you. Good luck and keep me posted."

Carrie's heart was already captured by Darren. Kids with physical disabilities from the start of their life always had it tougher. This case was going to be challenging. She wondered what was up with Darren's mom, Geneva. She dove immediately into action and scheduled an appointment to meet with Geneva and Darren.

The family lived in the area of the city referred to as 'the hole'. It was a poverty laden neighborhood with all the earmarks of urban decay, crime, homelessness and overcrowding, with many lost, wandering souls starving for a breath of life. Hope long ago vacated this area. Chances of residents getting out of this neighborhood were slim to none, mostly none. Most caseworkers feared entering this area, but not Carrie. She discovered if you treated people with dignity and care, gave them human respect, they would respond in kind. In fact, she served many families in this neighborhood. After she established a relationship with her families, they would watch out for her. There were times when they would walk her to her car, or advise her to wait a few minutes before she left, knowing a drug deal was happening on the street then, and she wouldn't want to interrupt it for her own safety. Working in 'the hole' filled Carrie with gratitude for what she didn't endure in her own personal life, especially as a child. She had a tender place for all of the children of 'the hole'.

Darren was a quiet, bright-eyed child, but every now and then Carrie could sense a seething river of raw anger running through him. His skin tone was extremely dark, unlike his siblings. His mother, Geneva Oglesby, was in her mid-thirties, was clearly quite beautiful before the ravages of her life began to be evident on her face. Darren was the fourth child born to her. All of Geneva's children were fathered by the same man, a local pimp named Joe. In fact, he fathered a total of seventeen children to several different women, all who were forced to work as a prostitute for him. Geneva was his first victim. Joe didn't involve himself with his children. He occasionally would appear on the scene offering up his criticisms and unhappiness with whatever irritated him in any particular moment. The walls in the home displayed the evidence of his anger, with several holes punched through the dry wall. It saddened Carrie to see the children try hard to gain his affection, when he had none to give. Carrie could only imagine he, too, probably suffered some unconscionable maltreatment as a child, but she wasn't here to help Joe. She was here for Darren.

The culture inside 'the hole' was survival of the fittest, and Darren was losing the race. His physical disability wasn't his only handicap. He was also failing in school, could barely read, often was the target of bullying, came from a fractured family, and had a soft heart that was compromised daily. He wasn't a fighter. He quietly accepted the cruel actions of other children. He tried to escape within the confines of his home, which was chaotic. Fortunately Geneva didn't turn tricks in her home. She took her business to the local flea bag motel a few blocks away. Carrie wanted to swoop up this child, take him home, and away from all of this negativity, but, of course, she couldn't. Her heart broke for him instead.

Geneva didn't take kindly to the county's or the hospital's interventions. "What do they 'spect of me?" she ranted. "Take him here; take him there, as if Darren was the only kid I had to do for. And besides, how do they 'spect me to do all of this shit. They know I ain't got no car, no license, no way to get him to the clinics. Besides he's doin' fine, he can get around. So he limps, big deal. We all got troubles to deal with. I know it was Ms. Snippety social worker from the clinic who called you all. She don't have a clue about livin' here in 'the hole.' All she does is go home to her nice comfy house in the burbs and passes judgment. Well, she can kiss my ass! We're fine. We don't need no help. So you can go on back to your office, missy whoever you are. We don't need you here. We're doin' just fine."

Carrie knew she was going to have to offer something to Geneva she could grab onto which made sense for her to develop any kind of relationship with her. "Ms. Oglesby," Carrie began, "now you know I can't leave. I wouldn't be here except Darren's condition is far more serious than what anyone thought. I came to help if you'll only let me. Look, how much could it hurt if we helped get Darren some of the physical interventions he needs. I know it's rough for you. I get that. That's why I want to help. I'm not saying you're a bad mother, I know better. I know you love your children. You need some assistance. Everybody needs a helping hand once in a while. Now please, don't let your pride get in the way of helping Darren. He's a good kid," Carrie pleaded while praying at the same time. Ms. Oglesby stood there with her hand on her hip, staring a burning hole into Carrie. "I promise. I'll do everything within my power to help you. I can give you bus tickets so you can get him to the clinic. I'll be glad to come by and take you and him there myself. Now I know you don't want Darren to suffer. Please Ms. Oglesby." It wasn't beneath Carrie to beg for her children if it'd help.

"You'd do that? You'd do that for me and Darren?" Geneva said tilting her head and calming her tone.

"Yes, I would if you'll only allow me. Please. For Darren."

"Okay, okay, I'll give you a try. But if you're lyin' to me, you better never come back around here ag'in. Can't say what might happen to you. Know what I mean?" Geneva suggested trying to maintain some power in the relationship. "You git it?"

"Yes, I get it," Carrie replied gratefully.

Carrie worked with Mrs. Oglesby and her family through many trials and tribulations for the next two years. She slowly watched the family dynamics deteriorate even though they had moments of triumph along the way. She often thought 'the hole' was aptly named. Did anyone get out in good condition or even fair condition? The odds were astronomical. Geneva's two older daughters both became pregnant by the time they were sixteen. Brandy was put on the street to work as a prostitute by her so-called father. Tawana was the target of a rape for a local boy's gang initiation. Life was rough. You were lucky if you survived at all without going crazy. Geneva tried. She tried with what few resources and skills she had. She was able to provide her children with their basic needs, food, clothing and shelter. Carrie knew she loved her children, even though Geneva felt coddling them would only make them soft and put them at greater risk in their neighborhood. Perhaps she was right.

During her involvement, Darren did get more physical therapy. Carrie referred them to the Easter Seal Society. They provided him with the special shoes he needed to even out the length of his legs. Darren, however, felt embarrassed by the clunky looking shoes and would get teased mercilessly because of them. His feet also grew at an alarmingly fast rate, and his entitlement to new shoes didn't come quickly enough at times. Resources for the poor, even for the children on Medicaid weren't nearly generous enough. As a result, Darren would discard his shoes as they pinched his feet too tightly. Once, Carrie used her own money for the shoes, even though the agency forbade such practices. She didn't care. It broke her heart to see him suffer.

Geneva would have a black eye and bruises on occasions when Carrie met with them. "Part of the job," she'd say. "'sides I didn't get killed. Brings in what little money I git." She would never press charges. If she did, was a sure way for her to sign her own death warrant, if not by one of her clientele, then by Joe. Besides, she would likely end up in jail for her prostitution as she would have to declare how she received her injuries. She wasn't about to snitch out her johns.

Their lifestyle would never be portrayed on the television screen. The masses wouldn't tolerate it. They wouldn't believe it, and if they did, they might have to feel uneasy about it for a minute. The networks tried a series about it once. It was called "Eastside, Westside", but it went off the air shortly after it began. It was far too gritty and uncomfortable for the audience as the show captured the challenges of poverty all too well. People didn't want to watch it.

School was torturous for Darren. His gentle nature allowed him to be crushed by the meanness the other kids dished out to him daily. The thought of going to school was anything but pleasant for him. Not only was his physical condition the frequent target of jeers, his inability to read, coupled with his tenderness put him in double jeopardy. School was a lose-lose proposition for him. He began to cut school with regularity by the time he was twelve. The local drug dealers quickly usurped his street time. They used him as a drug mule. He actually was given no choice.

Carrie was never a caseworker who quickly wanted to separate children from their parents. Especially when the parents were doing the best they could do and were able to provide for their basic needs, which Geneva did with regularity. Children weren't placed in care for quality of life issues alone. If that was the case, every child living in 'the hole' would be removed from their parents. Certainly the community had no ability or stomach for such action. But Carrie could see Darren slipping away. She knew if a dramatic intervention wasn't provided for him, he would either end up in jail or be dead. He didn't use drugs, but he started to drink alcohol. It gave him a false sense of bravado, which would eventually lead him into greater trouble. It also deadened his daily pain and misery. Carrie pleaded with Lysbeth to allow her to approach Juvenile Court for a temporary order of custody and place Darren in a therapeutic group home. She knew he wouldn't blend well into a foster home, due to loyalty and bonding issues with his mother. Residential care would be another arena where he would be taken advantage of by the other residents. A group home wouldn't require him to bond intimately with a family, but it could offer him some structure and opportunity in a safer, smaller environment.

"Lysbeth, you know I rarely come and ask for this. I know if we don't give Darren a chance, he's going to end up being another statistic. We're supposed to protect these children. It's our job, isn't it?" Carrie implored.

Lysbeth knew Carrie was right, but she enforced the agency's rules. She hated this. "Carrie, you know we're supposed to protect these children from harm from their parents," she responded in an exasperated voice. "You know we can't take in every child because of the dynamics of their community. Besides, these kids need to learn to live within the norms of their culture. And you know they'll return right back home when they turn eighteen."

Carrie argued with Lysbeth more strongly than she did before. She realized she raised her voice in protest, and was seen as unreasonable.

"I think, perhaps, you've allowed yourself to get too personally involved with this case. Maybe I should transfer it to a different worker," Lysbeth suggested.

Carrie put on a stiff upper lip, even though every fiber of her body wanted to scream. "No, there's no need to transfer this case. Ms. Oglesby probably wouldn't tolerate a new worker. I'll be okay. Maybe I can find Darren a male volunteer to act as a big brother. Let me give it a try. It can't hurt." Carrie kept the case. She could never find a volunteer willing to take on Darren due to the neighborhood he lived in. Volunteers were too afraid. Carrie understood. Once again, he didn't count or matter. Carrie thought of Darren nightly as she tried to sleep. His situation haunted her.

One day, as Carrie was sitting at her desk, she received a call from Ms. Oglesby, which was highly unusual because she didn't have a telephone. "Ms. Carrie," a weak and raspy voice filled the phone, "I thought I should let you know I'm in the hospital. I got beat up by Joe, and he hurt me bad. I'm really worried about Darren. I know he's going to do something that's going to get him into a mess of trouble. Can you go talk to him? You're the only person he half listens to," she said in obvious pain.

"I'm on my way," Carrie replied as she gathered her car keys and bolted toward the exit.

Joe beat Geneva with a baseball bat. He was angry because she brought in less and less money. In a rage, he fractured her hip. Darren was out on the street looking for him. Before Carrie could find Darren, it was too late. He found his father standing on a street corner among a group of men. In a blind rage, seeking revenge against his father's wrong doing, Darren stabbed Joe in the back near his upper left shoulder with a kitchen butcher knife. He was only fourteen years old, but seemed to have the strength of a full grown man. The police were called. Joe was treated and released from the emergency room. Darren was carted off to the Juvenile Detention Center, charged with aggravated assault. Joe, once again, was free as Geneva wouldn't press charges against him. She knew he would maim her further or kill her if she did. There were no witnesses to Geneva's beating. Joe knew not to batter her with any witnesses present. Darren was found guilty, then sent to the State Department of Youth Corrections to be held until he reached the age of twenty-one, the next seven years of his life. He was marked as a throw away child.

Carrie knew she failed him. She should have tried harder to get him the help she clearly understood he needed. She should have insisted Lysbeth plead her case for Darren to the agency's executive director to get him admitted to a therapeutic center before the underlying anger manifested as it did. She should have searched harder for a volunteer. She should have done something more than sit around and see this gentle soul become destroyed.

"You see, Ellen," Carrie continued, "I was given my opportunity to help save Darren one more time. Yes, it wasn't right he was driving a car with no license. And yes, it wasn't right he got behind the wheel of a car being as drunk as he was. But I know in my heart of hearts he never meant to hurt anyone. Putting Darren away in jail for a lengthy sentence would only continue to contribute to this cycle of pain and punishment. I couldn't do it."

"Unbelievable!" Ellen replied.

"Besides I went and saw him unbeknownst to you all. I went up to jail and met with him. I had to see him. I had to look him in the eyes to see if that gentle Darren still existed. When he saw me, he burst into tears. He didn't know it was my family he killed. He knew me as Ms. Singer, my maiden name, not as Ms. Cathers. He said over and over he was sorry. He kept saying, "I didn't mean to, I didn't mean to." He looked pathetic. He limped badly. He was in terrible pain both emotionally and physically. It was no surprise to me he turned to alcohol to deaden the pain of his life. At least he avoided heroin. His spine was terribly misshapen. At age thirty-six, he cried like a baby. It wasn't forced tears, he didn't cry for effect or for my pity. I saw the little twelve-year-old boy, once again, life thoughtlessly kicked to the side. The deepest part of my spirit forgave him. I forgave him for him, as well as for myself."

"I wrote a letter to the judge and shared with him my reasons for wanting leniency. The judge met with me upon receiving the letter. I shared with him my understanding of Darren's life. He agreed he would allow leniency on the condition Darren was placed in a substance abuse treatment halfway house prior to his full release. He said, "If you can forgive him, who am I to give him a severe punishment? You, my dear, are the true victim in this situation."

Of course, I disagreed with him. Darren was the victim his entire life. I was content, for in some small way, I was finally able to get him the treatment he desperately needed. And there you have it. I've never regretted my decision."

"Carrie," Ellen paused, "you've the grace of God with you unlike anyone else I've known." After a quiet interlude Ellen added, "The reason I asked you about Darren to begin with is our department received notice he is being released from prison. He is being transferred to the Agape halfway house to complete his last six months, where he'll be required to enter into alcohol and substance abuse treatment. I wasn't sure how you would react. I didn't want you to find out accidentally. I thought you had a right to know."

Carrie smiled contentedly. "That's the best piece of news I've received in a long time."

chapter 14

After Ellen went home, Carrie sat a bit longer on one of the porch's lounge chairs. She placed some sandalwood incense in the ceramic lotus flower incense burner. Another gift Jeff gave her. They loved this aroma. She wrapped herself in a quilt and put her feet up. She watched the moon begin to rise as it peeked from behind the large sycamore tree branches. She let her mind drift back to the beginning of her life as a social worker. A curious thought struck her. She was an active social worker for more hours in her life than she was in any other role, longer than a mother, wife, daughter, sister or friend. She was a thoroughbred of sorts. She amused herself with the thought - a thoroughbred child welfare worker. Most workers didn't make it past their second year, especially in child welfare. Yes, she was one of a rare breed, even rarer for having stayed on the streets for forty years. She didn't feel special. She felt it was her calling. Somebody had to do it. This is where she felt alive and needed, where she belonged. She didn't actively choose this field. It chose her.

Carrie intended to be a nurse. She was accepted into the university's nursing program and began their rigorous college curriculum of biology, calculus and organic chemistry, which nearly killed her entire college career. These certainly weren't the courses a social worker would choose. Following a year of tough general sciences, she forged into anatomy, physiology, and pharmacy. And she thought organic chemistry was tough! However the straw that broke her back wasn't the course work at all. It was the actual hospital field internship. She discovered she had a weak stomach, not for blood, but for cancer sores, puss, burns, infections and any number of diseases capable of physically ravaging the body. The decaying smells, the lingering look of the patients' hopelessness, the curt manner of doctors too busy to take time to see the patients as a person, plus their condescending manner toward nurses and other staff, and the pleading eyes of the patients were all too overwhelming for Carrie. She knew this wasn't her place in the world. She could do it. She knew she was tough. It didn't resonate with her. It wasn't her calling.

What should she do? She briefly thought about becoming a minister her senior year in high school, but she knew it was for all of the wrong reasons. It was vanity driving the idea. She, as only a teenager could imagine, thought if she could become the first female minister in her church's denomination it would be cool. It wasn't a thought promulgated by a desire to serve God. She wasn't sure she possessed a strong enough faith to be worthy of such a title. The thought quickly subsided. She knew she had to find another path. She, then, stumbled upon the college of social work. It was a close match without a spiritual or religious requirement, but still would serve the needy. She could even graduate on time as the courses she already took would be accepted by the college if she designated them as her electives, even though she didn't plan to take any hard sciences for electives. She was planning on ceramics or equestrian options, not microbiology and like courses she already had. Oh well was her thought. You didn't always get what you wanted in life, but she was grateful for the opportunity to attend college. She didn't have time to whine about what might have been.

Upon graduation, there was the next key decision. Where to work? Social work had many options: mental health, medical, gerontology, child welfare, developmental disabilities, vocational rehabilitation, nursing homes, child development, schools, community centers. As she explored these options, it became quite evident the desirable areas required a master's degree. She only had a bachelor's degree, which limited her choices. She took a civil service test for child welfare. A test the state dismissed as unnecessary three years later, but required at this time to enter the field. Children held a special place in Carrie's heart. She banked on this path, which panned out. Never did she imagine it would usurp her entire life! Yes, taking this job was unbeknownst to her, a critical life changing decision. Her plan was to give it a couple of years, get some experience every other place required, then move on. But, she told herself, everyone has to start somewhere. This was as good a place as any.

Her first supervisor was a jovial, African-American man. He had a wide grin, large bright eyes and was a bit chubby, but he clearly was no man's fool. His quick wit and ability to assess a situation compared to no other. Thomas W. White, Jr. was terrific for Carrie. He guided her past the pitfalls new, naïve, idealistic workers fell into. He provided an arena of utter freedom for Carrie to express herself without passing judgment while teaching her, not only about social work practice, but about life. Carrie laughed to herself as she thought of the many times Thomas clasped his hands together on his rounded belly as he let out a loud bellowing laugh while she delivered her singularly narrow assessment of family situations.

She was naïve about life's realities. She felt she was brought up in a cloistered life, probably because she was in her suburban middle class neighborhood. She didn't see the ravages of poverty, the pain of abuse or agony of neglect hundreds of children bore daily. She didn't understand what hunger in the belly did to people. What a life without hope brought forth. How frustration along with lack of opportunity manifested in outward demonstrations of anger both towards others and self.

Yes, any naivety she brought with her, this job took from her. She could never get it back, no matter how badly she wanted to rewind the clock. When she signed her name on the dotted line accepting the position, no one in the personnel office even whispered what they would take from her while paying her wages barely above the minimum wage, (so much for the value of her college education, or more importantly, for the value of saving children.) It was anything but lucrative or held in high esteem. Carrie soon learned children were still society's discardable chattel.

The first time Carrie heard Thomas's low resonating laughter was when she recounted for him her first client visit. He later admitted her experience was quite unusual, but nonetheless it underscored everything about her lack of experience, her youth, her cultural ignorance and her dogged determination to never get caught off guard again.

Thomas assigned her what was believed to be a relatively easy case, as he attempted to introduce her gently to this new world. The mother's name was Nancy Robinson. She had five children, the oldest twelve. The intake worker opened the case for services to help Ms. Robinson control her burgeoning adolescent oldest child, Samuel. Mrs. Robinson was a single mother and had no sustaining adult male role model in the home for Samuel. He was reported to be creating some minor mischief in the federal housing community in which they lived. The intake worker suggested the caseworker assigned might help Sam enroll in some community outreach programs which would provide some structured social interaction for him during non-school hours, leaving him with less time for meandering about his neighborhood. Mother was overwhelmed watching out for him while tending to her four younger children. Sam wasn't a delinquent. He was unruly. A misguided youth was the euphemism used.

Carrie remembered how excited and nervous she was to begin her career in earnest. She hadn't been to a federal housing area or even saw one from a distance. As this mother had no telephone, Carrie sent a letter to Mrs. Robinson informing her of her intended home visit at ten in the morning. An appointment time the seasoned caseworkers suggested to her because the outside activity in the depressed area wouldn't have yet ramped up for the day, whatever that meant. As she approached the area, she took a long lingering gaze at the environment, gently inhaling a long slow breath. The clustered brick apartments appeared to be in desperate need of maintenance. Garbage was piled up in overflowing bins. The parking lot was full of rusted and dented vehicles with peeling paint. Various cars were missing wheels, up on blocks. The picture of poverty greeted her this morning.

"Okay, you can do this," she said to herself, and then promptly drove around the block three more times before she actually manufactured enough gumption to get out of the car and knock on the door. After all, she thought, who am I to tell a woman in her thirties how to manage a twelve year old child? What do I know about parenting? Absolutely nothing. Carrie felt all of her confidence and her book learning drain from her body as if it was a giant sieve. But Carrie wasn't one to be easily crushed into defeat. Mustering her courage, she knocked on the door. In all of her college education, she was not prepared for what greeted her at the door.

"Why hello," said Mrs. Robinson. "Do come in." And there she was. Mrs. Nancy Robinson dressed in a flimsy negligee, leaving absolutely nothing to the imagination. Her hair was impeccably coifed. It was later Carrie realized she wore a wig. Her pendulous breasts swayed underneath her gown revealing her large protruding nipples. Carrie didn't dare look below the belly button. She was lost for words. She was sure her facial expression wasn't as controlled as she wished.

Mrs. Robinson continued. "Won't you come into the kitchen where we can sit down and talk? The children are at school. You must be Carrie Singer. I received your letter."

Then, Carrie realized she was utterly speechless. She even forgot to introduce herself. "Yes, yes I am. And you're Mrs. Robinson, correct?"

"Yes, that's right." Mrs. Robinson led Carrie to the kitchen, now providing Carrie with a full view of her entire backside. Four of the six chairs around the kitchen table were occupied by men!

"Please, please do sit down, Ms. Singer," Mrs. Robinson suggested with a knowing grin on her face. "Let me get you a cup of coffee." The smell of coffee and earlier cooked eggs permeated the air

"Yes, yes, sit down miss, please, make yourself at home," came the chorus of bass voices from the group of men, all widely grinning.

Carrie reluctantly declined both the chair and the coffee. She actually disliked coffee and rarely drank it. "Mrs. Robinson is there somewhere where we could talk privately? I don't think these gentlemen," Carrie gulped while her stomach was easing into a slow flip flop, "would really be interested in what we need to talk about. You know, it's kind of personal stuff." Carrie was thoroughly taken aback by the presenting situation. For one of the first times in her life, she was at a loss for words or a viable thought. Here was this woman prancing about, nearly nude in front of four men and a county governmental official. Yet, it didn't seem to bother Mrs. Robinson in the least. School didn't prepare her for this at all. Neither did her supervisor or her new co-workers.

"Oh, child, pay no mind to them. I ain't got nothin' to hide," she giggled, "as you can plainly see for yourself. Go on ahead with what you got to say."

Think, think, get it together, Carrie desperately instructed herself. "Ah, Mrs. Robinson, I can't really begin with your company present. Before I can discuss your situation and county business, I would need you to sign a release of information form, because of confidentiality rules. And I'm sorry to say I didn't bring any with me. I didn't know I would need them. Perhaps I can come back at a more convenient time for you, when you would be alone. How about tomorrow? Is there a time when it could be me and you?"

"Aw, sure honey," replied Mrs. Robinson, "how about eleven?"

"Eleven would be perfect. I'll come back tomorrow. I'll let myself out the door. See you then." Carrie scurried toward the front door, but it failed to open.

Mrs. Robinson followed behind as she heard Carrie fumbling with the lock which was tricky. She smiled kindly at Carrie, and opened the door so she could exit. "See you tomorrow, Ms. Singer. Have a good day," Mrs. Robinson said in a cheery voice.

As she walked toward her car, she heard the loudest and longest uproar of male laughter suggesting they were rolling around on the floor. Once Carrie secured herself into her car, settled her mind down, and grabbed a few breaths of fresh air, she, too, began laughing. She realized the absurdity of the entire situation. Yes, they had a genuine laugh at her expense. It was a valuable first lesson. At least, she thought, Mrs. Robinson has a strong sense of humor. I think we'll get along well.

It was, then, the irony hit her. Her name was Mrs. Robinson! Carrie reminded herself of the movie "The Graduate", and the tantalizing Mrs. Robinson seducing Dustin Hoffman. Carrie realized she must have presented as outrageously nervous and flustered as Dustin Hoffman did in the movie. Of course, they had a good laugh at her expense. Carrie appreciated the scenario. She began to think she quite liked Mrs. Robinson. Mrs. Robinson could teach her a great deal more about life than what she probably was going to provide back to her. This was her first introduction into the culture of poverty. These people felt more alive and real, less stifled than the persons she mingled with in her life. This was going to be interesting.

This was Carrie's beginning. She forged forward learning at every step and turn along the way. There were many families and cases. She couldn't even begin to remember them all. But there were those few who stood out, having touched her some significant way. She couldn't forget them, even if she wanted to.

Carrie's non-social worker friends couldn't understand what drew her to her profession. How could she expose herself day in and day out to work with these lazy, no good, government parasites? All they did was have children so they could live off of the tax-payer's money. As far as they knew, these people were worthless, throw away trash. Forget them, they reproached her. Carrie learned early on there was no use in trying to explain to her 'educated friends' how their moral judgments and understanding of the nature of poverty and child maltreatment was misguided. They had no ears to hear. They didn't want to hear. They wanted to stay in their shallow, lavish life, and not think about the vagaries of those who have less opportunity. They needed to feel superior because they were emptier on the inside than those with less. Carrie wanted to scream at them about their superficialness, but she knew time would teach them, maybe. She learned to distance herself from them as she perceived their lack of interior depth and compassion. Carrie thought maybe she was becoming a reverse snob.

But not all of her clients were poor. She had interventions with some of their community's finest, pillars of society as they were esteemed. However, professionalism ruled the day, and her lips were sealed. What some people did for status astounded her. Carrie's memory took her back to the afternoon she pulled her 1973 silver Capri with a brown fender into one of the wealthier neighborhoods to meet a well respected attorney's family. They were referred for possible physical abuse of their daughter. Everyone, who was outside, scanned her car for it clearly wasn't of a make, model, or condition belonging in this neighborhood. As she arrived at the listed address, Carrie realized she was pulling up to the largest mansion on the street. She was never before this close to wealth. The mother, who obviously didn't have to work outside of the home, was puttering among the plants in the landscaping wrapping around the brick home with gables and leaded glass windows.

Carrie introduced herself. The mother invited Carrie into the house through the large mahogany double doors. Here, Carrie observed her first sunken living room with a plush rounded couch pit, an indoor pool off the family room with a flowing waterfall, gold embossed ceiling inlays with Renaissance like paintings, the stone fireplace opening to both the living room and dining area, the long teak wood hand-carved dining table, and all of the other luxurious amenities, including an elevator. The smell of bleach drifted through the air. It all seemed sterile. Carrie thought about how many children suffered because of their poverty while others basked in such a lavish, and Carrie thought, gaudy lifestyle. It seemed unfair.

Getting down to business, Carrie shared a concern was called in their fifteen year old daughter had bruises on her arms, and a large swollen bump on the back of her head. The report indicated she was forcibly grabbed by her father and shoved up against a wall during an episode of his anger. Once again, Carrie was in for an unwelcomed surprise.

This mother became quite agitated and indignant about the alleged concern. "Abuse," she said through seething teeth, "you think my daughter was abused, do you? Well, I can tell you there is nothing to that. If you want to see abuse, look at this!" The mother turned her back to Carrie and pulled her shorts and underpants down fully exposing her oversized buttocks, which were black and blue from where her husband kicked her frequently. Carrie was amazed women would tolerate this type of behavior so they could stay in the circles of the rich. Clearly there were problems in this home. Mother was caught up in her own dilemma, and not her daughter's. This family was clearly in need of an intervention. However, because the father was a well-known lawyer, it was likely they wouldn't enter the county child welfare system. Through his connections, he could make it go away, and his daughter would be a continued victim. The justice system often seemed to hand out "justice" only to the less monetarily endowed.

Carrie thought her friends wouldn't want to have considered people of such affluence would behave in such fashion. Hurting children was the business of the wretched poor only. She had no need to burst their bubble. She only needed to remove herself from such small mindedness.

chapter 15

As the moon rose above the boles and the branches of the trees, it began to cast its bright light down upon the backyard lawn. Carrie gathered her quilt and thought a cup of chamomile tea would be the perfect complimentary ticket to round out the evening. She pulled out her favorite tea mug. She and Jeff purchased this mug during their one and only lavish vacation to Hawaii. They decided to spare no expense and spoil themselves rotten. Carrie felt guilty the entire time, thinking this money could have been used for needier causes. Jeff insisted. He had a good heart, but he didn't feel compelled to exhaust it beyond his family realm.

The teapot steamed and whistled announcing the water's readiness. Carrie steeped the tea bag for a few minutes watching the tea turn the water into a crisp light brown. The heat swirled toward her nose and tempted her sense of smell to bathe in the sweet scent. She opened a jar of honey and added a small dollop of sweetness. With tea in hand, she left the covered porch and walked outdoors. She sat in one of the Adirondack chairs which allowed a full view of the night sky. She nestled herself into the chair with her quilt as a chill was creeping into the air. Venus hung brightly in the sky with its gentle blue aura dancing about it. To her left was the sparkling red Mars winking at her. The constellation Orion, defender of all in Carrie's perception, shone brightly above as if to guard her against all harm. Sipping the tea, the inviting taste warmed her.

She thought about how blessed she was. She was grateful, not only for the earthly comforts surrounding her, but for the gifts of knowledge and understanding of the human experience. She felt she wasn't denied anything, and her life's path suited her perfectly. She experienced great love and great sorrow. To have experienced life on both ends of the continuum, only magnified each experience with greater clarity. Carrie trusted God knew what he was doing as he carved out individual paths for each of his creatures to travel, learn and grow, but sometimes it was difficult. Even the most joyous times were overwhelming and difficult to accept with grace. But it always came to an end. The key was not to let the ending scar you, leaving you wanting for more and feeling forever cheated. The key was to hold tightly onto the wonderful memories. Let them live on in your spirit, never dying, always there to taste of them once again, if only metaphorically. "Aaahhhh, life can be sweet," Carrie spoke softly. "And it can be painfully harsh." It was all mixed up together like a tossed salad of experiences.

Carrie closed her eyes as she laid her head against the pillowed portion of the chair's covering. Her mind wanted to wander back in time, yet again. This time she revisited the family which finally drew her to the conclusion she needed to get her Master's degree.

1976

Bill and Claire Anderson were opened for on-going services. They had three children, Angela, 15, Crystal, 13 and Bill, Jr., 9. Bill, Sr. requested help for his daughter Angela stating she was out of control, not minding the rules, arguing with her mother constantly and setting a terrible example for Crystal, who was beginning to follow in her footsteps. Angela's school performance was deteriorating, and he caught her smoking his cigarettes. He characterized her as easy, likely having unprotected sex, although he wouldn't consider giving her birth control. He felt it sent a message saying: go ahead, have sex. No, he wanted the department to stop the activity. He described her acting like a trollop and wearing gobs of makeup, which made her appear clown-like. He wanted help in nipping her disturbing behaviors in the bud.

Although he presented himself as the unchallenged dominant man of the house, he failed to exercise any kind of reasonable control of his family situation. He came to the agency for help. He frequently suggested to his daughter he'd have Children Services come and take her, as a viable threat for her to 'straighten up her act'. She called him out on his threat, told him to go ahead. Thus, he had no choice except to ask for help or lose face, and he couldn't stand to lose face. Carrie was to be this family's savior.

Carrie's first appointment with the Andersons was arranged for them to come into her office at their request. Bill wanted to make sure he had ample opportunity to express himself without his children overhearing the conversation. Carrie realized from the inception of this relationship, Bill wanted to direct it, and establish the foundation upon which the intervention would occur. He traditionally stepped into the role "king of the hill" within his family. The fact his daughter, Angela, called him out for a true battle was quite disconcerting to him. He didn't much care a female worker was assigned to the family. He requested a male worker. But given this was a primarily female dominated profession, except for the administrative roles which were male intense, there were few men available. And there was none to give to Bill and his family. He would discover Carrie was as tough as any man they may have provided him. She was the better choice for Claire, Angela and Crystal.

Carrie's first impression of Bill, Sr. suggested he was insecure in his manhood because he needed to have his way of doing things accepted without challenge. He was about five foot seven inches tall and sported a military style haircut, even though he was never in the military. Carrie later discovered the military rejected his request to serve. He had a blue collar job, working as a machinist in a local factory with sixty employees. He was physically strong, but was far from having honed his body into a classic masculine pleasing shape. He was built like an apple, with skinny legs. Carrie noticed his fingernails were long and embedded with dirt or oil. Long fingernails on a man creeped her out. He wore a plaid cotton short-sleeved button down shirt and a pair of blue work pants covered with grease stains. As they entered the interviewing room containing a conference table, Bill immediately began to direct where everyone should sit, including Carrie.

On the other hand, Claire had a different energy about her. She was taller than Bill, Sr. Strange, thought Carrie, he would marry a taller woman. Claire was thin, with a deep olive- colored skin tone. Her hair was black with streaks of gray, long and tangled, falling to the middle of her back. Her eyes were outlined with dark circles. She walked solemnly, with her shoulders hunched over as if she had the beginnings of osteoporosis, although she didn't. Her eyes stayed in a downcast course throughout the interview, only glancing up for a brief moment when Carrie touched her arm and asked her a question. Typically Bill would insert an answer for her until Carrie asked him to desist and allow Claire to speak for herself. She could tell Bill was agitated with the request, as he offered up a harrumph and snorting sound. When Claire spoke, it was barely audible, reaching a level above a whisper. She clearly seemed to be beaten down. By what, Carrie wasn't sure.

By the end of their first meeting Carrie collected a plethora of information. Bill and Claire married at a young age, both nineteen. Claire came from a more affluent family than Bill, and her parents objected to the relationship. As a result, they went to Monroe, Michigan and eloped. Claire's mother was crushed by Claire's actions. Her family disowned her. She and Bill weren't welcomed into their home. She was cut from any family contact or communication. She was dead to them. How dare she defy them? They never met their grandchildren. They showed no interest in their welfare. Instead, they gave their lives over to indulging their two sons, who also carried the family torch of no contact with Claire.

This situation, however, suited Bill fine. He had no desire to ingratiate himself to these arrogant snobs, secretly understanding he would never measure up. He didn't need or want their constant indignation and rejection. He felt a sense of pride he took their only daughter from them. She was trapped, and that was to his liking. It gave him the control he desired. He seemed to care less how this impacted his wife, boasting how she belonged to him now and not them.

Even though money was tight, Bill forbade Claire to work outside of the home. He provided them with necessary food, clothing and shelter, a small three bedroom ranch-style home in a working class neighborhood. They learned how to do without extras. He wasn't going to have his wife parading around outside of the home working. The world didn't need to know he couldn't give them everything they wanted. They had what they needed according to him.

Claire slightly nodded in silent agreement with Bill as he proclaimed he and his wife had a good, thriving, loving relationship. Why, there couldn't be a better husband out there, than he was. Yes, it was all good.

Carrie pondered. She asked Bill, "If everything is all good and wonderful, then how is it you're here? I don't understand."

That was all the prompting Bill needed before he launched into his diatribe about the vagaries of his daughter. He cast her in such a light Carrie believed she may have her first visit with the child of Satan shortly. Angela was anything but an angel according to him. In fact, he suggested it was the trick of the devil which made them name her Angela. As Bill ticked off Angela's behavioral inventory one by one, Carrie noted Claire's head slowly hung lower and lower. It was as if she was showing tacitly her disagreement with Bill's assessment, but she never dared to speak up with even one word. Carrie knew she was looking at an emotionally beaten down woman. Bill ended his monologue with, "I'm not even sure she came from my loins. I can't believe any daughter of mine would ever act like that!" Carrie knew this wasn't the time to question him about his stance regarding having fathered Angela. Already too much emotionality was expressed in this meeting. Carrie was concerned for Claire and her ability to not emotionally decompose right in front of her. Bill, however, made it quite clear his actions played absolutely no part in his child's misguided behavior. In fact, he should have won the father of the year award to put up with her obnoxious and toxic behavior.

Carrie had arranged to meet Angela after she came home from school, and before her father was home from work. She wanted to have time alone with this child to further her assessment. She, then, ended the meeting.

Carrie had only a brief moment to speak with Claire before Angela arrived home. Once again, Claire appeared to be uncomfortable in opening up about how she perceived what was happening within her family. She repeated Bill was a good provider and Angela, although far from perfect, has a good heart underneath it all. Primarily Claire kept busy preparing for her children's momentous return from school. Carrie wondered if it wasn't a ploy to keep from engaging in a heart-to-heart conversation with her. There were secrets in this family, and she suspected Claire knew of them. She had yet to develop a trusting enough relationship with Carrie for her to share. Besides, Carrie assumed Bill, Sr. gave her strict instructions about what she could and couldn't say. Maybe talking with Angela would help broaden her understanding.

The home was neatly organized and spotlessly cleaned. Their furniture wasn't plush or even comfy looking, but it was durable and appeared to survive years of use. The colors in the home were flat and dull, nothing bright and cheery. They had a large picture window overlooking their yard and the street. Their driveway was formed of gravel, leading to a single unattached garage. It was full of tools and other stored items, leaving no room for a car. The garage door had a large dent and the window panes were broken. The backyard was fenced and housed their mixed breed sad-eyed dog, a cross between a terrier and golden retriever. He badly limped as if his hip hurt. They called him Buster, who appeared to be busted both physically and emotionally. He seemed to be a fitting mascot for the family.

Carrie imagined Angela would present with a punk look. Most likely she used make-up heavily, lots of eye shadow, heavy mascara, fingernails painted in blue or black, and short skirts all embodied by a girl with a bad attitude. But when Angela entered the room, Carrie questioned if she came to the right residence. Angela was a beautiful fifteen year old child. Her hair was clean and bouncy, light brown in color. Her cheeks were flushed with a healthy glow of natural pink. A tad of light pink lipstick was tastefully applied. She was dressed modestly wearing long loose fitting pants, and a tunic length top with a thin gold-chained belt hanging tastefully down. Her smile brightened the room.

"Hello, I'm Angela," she spoke as she reached out to shake Carrie's hand. Her touch was gentle and warm. "My dad said you needed to speak with me." Carrie noticed Claire took Bill, Jr. outside, leaving them to have some privacy, as Crystal had yet to arrive home. Angela presented herself as a thoughtful, well spoken young lady. She shared school was harder for her this year and her grades dropped to mostly C's, but she was working hard to bring them up. Boys did call home to talk to her, but this was no surprise. She seemed to be quite delightful. Angela knew her father was quite upset with the attention the boys gave her. She swore up and down she didn't have sex with any. In fact, her father wouldn't even let her date. The only times she was allowed to be in mixed company was when she involved herself in some youth group activities sponsored by a local church. Her parents didn't attend church, but her father was hard pressed not to trust the kindly older minister, who made assurances nothing improper would happen under his watchful eye. Yet, when she would come home, he persisted she was with boys in a sexual manner, when she wasn't. Angela was quite perplexed by this, and she was aware she was building a slow bubbling resentment toward her father because of these accusations.

"Mom can't really help me. Dad tells her to be quiet, and she shuts down. Sometimes I get angry at Mom because I feel as no one believes me. If mom does, she doesn't come to my aid with Dad. It's like he has some kind of magic spell over her. I guess I'm never supposed to talk to boys at all. But it's hard because I can't help it when they call me. I don't give them my phone number or anything, but I know my friends passed it out. But again, Dad doesn't believe me. Sometimes I wish I could run away from home. That's why I told Dad to go ahead and call you guys. I think maybe I would be happier living somewhere else. But then I know I'd worry about my brother and sister and Mom. I don't know what to do," Angela said while tears began to form in her eyes. Carrie's heart began to hurt for Angela. She wasn't sure what would help this family. She knew she needed to engage Claire more. Claire knew more than she was telling.

Carrie worked with this family for three months, and still no new information came to light. Claire, having few female friends, was happy to see Carrie. She began to talk more readily, but it was never anything of substance enabling Carrie to understand the family dynamics. Since the agency's involvement, Bill, Sr. calmed down his rhetoric about Angela. Carrie's presence, alone, seemed to have helped this family to find a more balanced even keel. Yet, Carrie was hard pressed to define why she remained involved. Bill, Sr. called them to save face, she remembered. He wasn't going to have backed down from the threats he made to Angela about having the government come and get her. Perhaps it was time to bow out of this case. She called the Andersons and advised them of her decision to close the case.

As Carrie sat at her desk completing the dreaded paperwork to close the Anderson case, she received an urgent call from Claire. This was the first time Claire initiated a call to her. "Carrie," she began, "please don't close our case. We've run into some additional troubles. We didn't tell you sooner, perhaps we should have, but Bill didn't want me to. He's been laid off of his job. It's been about three weeks, and we're running out of money and food. I'm worried about what to do. Can you help?" Of course, Carrie knew she could help them get some assistance with their basic needs. She reassured Claire she would help and put away the paperwork that she began to complete for the case closing.

Bill wasn't happy Claire called Carrie. His male pride really did get in his way. Carrie tried to be as gentle and cautious as she could be as she explained how welfare assistance was meant for situations such as theirs. In fact, Bill paid taxes over the years to help support these programs. It was only right he should be able to access them when his family was in need. Bill viewed welfare recipients as moochers and lazy ne'r do wells, and he didn't want to be seen among them. Carrie helped him to shift his view, at least temporarily, about the facts of people who received welfare benefits. The vast majority of welfare recipients only received benefits for an average of eighteen months, and were as motivated as he was to become self sufficient. She did acknowledge there were some families who seemed to depend on welfare payments from generation to generation, but typically these families were fraught with any number of disabilities, laden with suffering of a different kind. Bill should be thankful his family didn't have to contend with such issues. Bill reluctantly followed through with what he believed to be a humiliating process and filed an application for food stamps and a medical card. His income level qualified him and his family. It provided them with a stop gap measure until he could pick up work again.

Carrie kept the case open for another two months. Bill was called back to work. There were some family squabbles and fights, not unlike any other family. Bill would occasionally resort back to his degrading name calling toward Angela. She seemed to take it in stride. This typically happened when Bill would get drunk or over stressed. Angela began going to her bedroom closing the door. She quit arguing with him. It did no good. She was actually quite mature for her age. Carrie felt sorry for her, but there was nothing more she could do. Once again, she informed the family she would close the case.

The following Monday morning shortly after the agency opened, Carrie received a call from the front desk receptionist. "Carrie, a Mrs. Anderson is here in the office and hopes you can come and talk with her." Strange, thought Carrie, this is highly unusual behavior.

Carrie put her current work project aside and went down to the first floor to greet Claire. She escorted her into one of the interviewing rooms. Something was up. Carrie saw Claire was visibly trembling and began to shake harder when she sat down. "Claire, what's wrong?" Carrie asked.

"Carrie, you can't close our case," Claire began. Then, her body heaved, and she began to sob uncontrollably. Carrie immediately got up and put her arm around Claire in a comforting way. She pulled a tissue from the Kleenex box on the table and handed it to Claire.

"Claire, please, tell me what's happened," Carrie pleaded.

Claire lifted her head, blew her nose and blurted out, "I wouldn't be surprised if Bill wasn't having sexual relations with Angela!" She began to sob again.

Carrie closed her eyes. She felt the clarity of the pain Claire was carrying with her all of these months. It made perfect sense. Why didn't she put it together? Carrie was harder on herself than she should have been. She carried the guilt of not understanding these dynamics with her for a long time. It wasn't until she was trained thoroughly in the sexual abuse cycle; she was able to forgive herself. She simply didn't know.

Typical indicators of sexual abuse by a male figure in the household included calling the victim degrading sexual names. Bill called her every name in the book: tramp, floozy, whore, cunt and bitch. They would accuse their victims of seeking out sexual activity. They would characterize them in the most unflattering manner, even if reality suggested something different. They would seek to isolate their victims and limit their contact with other males and outsiders. That explained why Bill would get angry when boys would call Angela. Bill possessed all of the classic symptoms. Carrie simply didn't know the indicators. If she knew them, it would've been obvious. She let Angela down. Angela was actively assaulted by her father all of this time, too fearful to speak out.

Sexual perpetrators found ways to keep their victims silent, either through bribery with money or gifts, or through threats of violence toward their victims or their loved ones. In this case, Bill threatened not only to hurt Angela's mother, but also to bring Crystal into the bedroom with them, as well. Angela felt compelled to stay silent to save her mother and her sister. She was an extraordinarily brave young woman.

Perpetrators have self-image problems. Carrie knew Bill was sensitive about his maleness, asserting himself in positions of authority where possible. Being laid off of his job only exacerbated his own insecurities. And Claire, how long did she know? What courage she must have summoned up to reveal the family secret. Carrie wondered what threats Bill used with her. Carrie wanted to throw up every time she thought about how she failed this family for many months. How many more times was Angela victimized because of her stupidity? Carrie would have trouble sleeping at night knowing she failed to keep Angela safe.

This family, along with many others such as Vickie Winfield, haunted her nightly when she would lay her head on her pillow desiring needed sleep. Often it came slowly, leaving her to think endlessly. This was another one of the job's gifts they didn't tell her about at human resources. Sleep, which typically came easily for Carrie, became elusive. The nightly ritual was there to greet her. The voice always talked to her before she was allowed to drift off. "Did you keep a child safe? Do you leave a child in an unsafe place? Will they be abused or neglected again? Did you act too quickly? Were your actions an appropriate measure to the circumstance? Should you've taken the child away from their parent? Would removing the child cause more harm than leaving him at home or vice versa? Did you do everything you could? Did you think of all of the possible solutions before you acted or failed to act? Were you good enough? Did you do the best possible action?"

It wasn't a comforting nurturing voice. It was the critical, challenging, voice. The questions it asked were provoking, scary and left Carrie with a sense of potential dread. The voice was her constant companion nightly for forty years. She remembered when the voice died. It was a sudden and quick death, timed with the evening of her retirement. It tried to revisit her a few times, but there were no more situations for which the voice would have questions. One last lingering question persisted, which slowly abated, "Could you've done better?" Her answer was the same. I did the best I could do.

chapter 16

"Aaahhhh," Carrie murmured in contemplative resignation. She inhaled another whiff of the scented night air, smelling the peony bush nearby. Yes, the Anderson family was the straw which broke the proverbial camel's back. Carrie made mistakes before in her assessments, but none carried the everlasting devastating effects of this blunder. "Social workers need a crystal ball in their tool kit," Carrie noted. "Those were the days. Those were the days." She sipped her chamomile tea, closed her eyes and drifted backward in time. Thinking is the fastest way to travel, and travel she did, back to her graduate school days.

1976

The graduate school application came in a bulky manila envelope with seemingly endless pages to fill out, upon which she began the begging process for admission. Paperwork was the mascot of social work. It was endless, and the admission process was no different. Carrie was grateful her undergraduate grade point average was high enough she wasn't required to take the dreaded GRE's. She did poorly on standardized tests. Her brain seemed to click off when she knew the end score was vital for her next endeavor. She received her highest grades from essays or oral exams, never from a multiple choice questionnaire a computer could score. The last page of the admission packet, according to those who went before her, was the most critical, and it was an essay question: Why do you want to get your master's degree in social work? "Why did I?" she mused to herself. It was funny to Carrie this question felt different at the end of her career rather than at the beginning. She understood. She understood she didn't know what she didn't know then, and if she knew then what she knew now, would her answer have been different? Carrie quickly tucked the thought away as it was no longer relevant. It didn't matter.

> But Carrie remembered her original answer. *I want to receive my graduate degree in social work because I need a stronger foundation upon which to grasp human behavior. I have worked as a child welfare worker for five years, and I know I have only scratched the surface of understanding human functioning. I don't want to make mistakes, even though as a human I know I will. I want to minimize wrongful judgments which cause undue harm to others. I need more education, perhaps more distance from day to day field work so I can gain a new perspective armed with greater discernment of why people hurt, why people hurt others, and especially why people hurt children. I currently have many leaves of knowledge with no tree upon which to place them and find order in them. I have seen appalling human behaviors as well as loving behaviors. I need a more thorough comprehension of the different cycles of human interaction from domestic violence to sexual abuse to emotional abuse to drug addiction to mental health issues to poverty issues to cultural issues to policy issues to ethical issues to why the hell do we do what we do to each other as human beings.*
>
> *I have often considered leaving this career track for many reasons: more money, fewer work hours, less danger, greater benefits, better working conditions, and finding a job which doesn't haunt you night and day and night and day, etc. But I know deep down in my heart of hearts this is my true calling. It would be quite difficult for me to walk through this life and not have a responsive care for the plight of others who are less fortunate. I can't do it. Please allow me entry into this greater world of knowledge. Your time and energy won't be wasted on me.*

Carrie wasn't one to belabor her answer. It was painfully honest and true to her heart. This is the only way she knew to respond. Carrie wasn't a game player when it came to real life. She was about being upfront and real, not about bullshit. And this answer was a real reflection of what motivated her. She sent the admission packet along its way and hoped she would be found worthy. Others who already walked down this path informed her, a small envelope reply was a rejection. You wanted to see the larger envelope. And she did. Two months later, the reply came: You're in!

A genuine smile swept Carrie's face as she allowed her memory to come flooding back. The packet announced she was required to come to a two hour orientation meeting before the official start of school. One hundred applicants were accepted from the three hundred and six applications. The college scheduled ten orientation sessions each allowing ten students to attend. At the time she attended, Carrie had no inkling how her life was going to change.

It was August of 1977. Carrie and eight others crowded into a small conference room at the College of Social Work. She was surprised the room accommodation was exceptionally small. There was barely enough room for them to sit around the large table in the room, but they wriggled in, feeling tightly packed like sardines. There was one empty chair next to the professor leading the session. Carrie couldn't help but check out the other students, it was in her nature.

The first person to talk to her was a male student Matt, who wore white socks with his laced dress shoes. He appeared to be strong despite his slight chubbiness. She figured he was countrified, especially when he talked about leaving the farm. There was Sylvia, an African-American woman in her mid-thirties with round cheeks who dressed in a colorful dashiki. She sported glasses slipping down her nose, which turned into a waterslide due to the heat of the day. When she talked she peered above the upper rim of her glasses with her head slightly bent downward. Carrie almost missed seeing Eloise. She was diminutive, apparently shy and clearly the oldest member of the group. Carrie guessed she was in her mid-fifties. She appeared to be a reticent but hip type of grandmother. Vanessa was a gabber, talking non-stop from the minute she entered the room and continued on even during the professor's introductory statements. Carrie pegged her as rude and self-absorbed. Michael looked like he consulted GQ magazine before getting dressed. He was impeccably clothed. Carrie thought him to be a bit obsessive-compulsive. Richard was a tall slender man with a pock marked face, a quiet voice, and a gentle spirit. Lydia was dressed in a business suit and seemed to be impressed with her own self-importance. And, of course, the group contained the vibrant, effervescent Susan, who drew you into her energy field unyieldingly. Yes, it was going to be an intriguing adventure, this graduate school.

Carrie wondered what first impression she might be making. She knew she was wrong to be judgmental so quickly of her soon to be peers, but she couldn't help it. It was her nature. She was required to assess people daily for the past five years in her job, and it became part of her. Carrie also knew she might be wrong about each and every one of them.

Fifteen minutes into the meeting, the door swung open with impressive speed banging loudly into the wall. The last of the group of ten joined them. "So sorry I'm late," Ben remarked as he gave the professor an irresistible impish grin. Carrie could tell the professor wasn't impressed.

"And may I ask what was so important you couldn't be timely?" the professor inquired.

As he struggled to pull his chair towards the table, barely fitting between the chairs already occupied on either side, Ben answered, "I'm sorry, but I got stuck in the bathroom, been there for about twenty minutes. Totally unexpected, you know. I didn't plan for it to happen, but it's what it was. Oh, by the way, I'm Ben." The rest of the group nervously giggled, and Ben answered them with an adorable wink of his eye. Ben began to scan the group one by one and nodded silently as he caught the eye of a few of them as the professor droned on. When his eyes locked in on Carrie, she felt a surge of energy emanating from him entirely discombobulating her. Every molecule in her body vibrated, as if at a rave. She didn't know how quite to characterize him or understand her body's reaction to him. She caught herself taking in a deep breath. Handsome, cute, good looking all fit him. Mischievous also came to her mind. Reality oriented as proffered by his reason for being late. The quality striking her most vividly was electric, he was downright electrifying. He was one of those guys who could charm you instantly no matter whom you were. She thought to herself to keep her distance.

"As I was saying," Professor Tamara Forsberg continued on, "this two year journey towards your master's degree has a standardized curriculum the first year. There are no electives until year two. You'll all be required to take a year of social work policy, social work practice, research, human functioning and ethnic studies. This will accompany your requirement to perform sixteen hours of field instruction at an agency or institution that will be assigned to you. Your schedule will be delivered to you one week before the beginning of the college quarter. Are there any questions?" This was the part Carrie hated about school, someone always had questions. Ms. Forsberg adeptly explained everything but, inevitably, someone had questions.

It started with Lydia. "Ms. Forsberg, are you saying there won't be an opportunity for us to select an elective course of study the first year?"

Carrie thought what part of what she said was unclear to you? She made it perfectly clear in her introduction.

"Yes," replied Professor Forsberg.

"I see. Does this mean I'll have to wait until next year to take a course addressing abnormal human behavior?" Lydia continued. Carrie sighed deeply to herself. She had little patience for those who needed to be heard for the sake of recognition alone. Carrie reminded herself to keep her mouth shut and carefully choose when to reveal herself. She had little need to draw attention to herself unnecessarily. She knew there would be many future opportunities to make herself known. Now wasn't one of them, especially when she could feel Ben slyly checking her out. Unease filtered through her bones, a condition which was foreign to her. One she didn't appreciate.

Richard spoke next. "I don't have a driver's license or a car. Will that be a problem?"

Professor Forsberg replied, "We can work around your situation, but you'll need to be assigned to an agency accessible through our public transportation, and one not requiring you to transport clients."

"You mean I might have to drive clients around in my car?" jumped in Mr. GQ. "I wasn't prepared for that possibility. I've nothing against them, but I don't want them in my car stinking it up. And I don't want to be responsible for them in traffic."

Carrie wondered how he was able to get past the admission process. She couldn't detect any compassion here. She laughed to herself as she imagined his car to be as immaculate as himself. She found it humorous if an obese client with body odor crushed his seat springs as she smoked a cigarette and gulped down some soda, accidentally spilling it onto his carpet. He, on the other hand, likely opened his window trying to hang his head outside to breathe some fresh air while suggesting she should not smoke in his car, for it to fall on deaf ears. Stop, she thought. You're not being any more compassionate toward Mr. GQ, than he may be towards a future client. Besides he's young, likely came to graduate school directly from undergrad and doesn't have a clue about real life social work experiences. But the more she tried to stop the scene in her head, the funnier it became as her brain added a noisy farting session to the situation. She began to let out a slight giggle, which caused all to turn their heads and stare at her. Oh, this was not what she wanted to happen. Please, she offered up to the good Lord, do not let anyone ask me to share what I find to be funny.

"Ms. Singer would you mind sharing with us what's so funny," asked the Professor. "We could all benefit from a bit of humor right now."

Carrie knew what she was about to say would be critical to their beginning understanding of whom she was. This wasn't the propitious moment she imagined. Why Lord, why did you let her ask? What should I say? The truth? Think. Think fast. "I was thinking about how as a social worker you must be prepared for the unexpected, while maintaining a professional response, when every fiber of your being may not want to. Michael's reaction to driving clients around reminded me of my first encounter with a family I was asked to help, and how it taught me we must maintain a healthy sense of humor if we are going to get through without going crazy." Thankfully Mrs. Robinson came to her mind.

"You make an excellent point," countered Professor Forsberg.

Oh, please don't have said that, thought Carrie. All eyes were on her as if she won some coveted prize from the professor. This isn't what Carrie wanted to project as her first impression. She wanted to be nearly invisible. Ben didn't fail to notice as he placed his palms together and gave her a slight bow. Carrie squirmed.

Professor Forsberg continued. "In closing I want to say I'm honored I'll be your college advisor during your graduate years. As a result, the ten of us will have some group sessions together throughout your time here. Please, call me Tamara. I look forward to getting to know you all. Take care and I'll be seeing you soon."

Everyone began to shuffle about to leave. Their hard backed oak chairs screeched on the linoleum floor as each struggled to release themselves from the crowded table. Carrie held back, purposely moving more slowly than the others. She wanted to exit surreptitiously to avoid an encounter with that Ben guy. She peered through the doorway and observed Ben was talking to Susan in the hallway. A good time to make a speedy exit, she thought. She gathered her belongings and headed toward the doorway. As she stepped into the hallway, Susan turned away from Ben leaving him free to catch Carrie.

"What a save," Ben beckoned to Carrie. "Even got kudos for it. I wonder, what were you honestly thinking? It was obviously not what you spouted off to the professor, so much for her observation skills." Ben continued to speak as he approached Carrie. "How about sharing with me. What was going on in your mind?"

Carrie could feel her heart beginning to race. She didn't want this encounter. This Ben guy was too sure of himself, and of her. She wanted to scream: GO AWAY! As he came closer, she noticed he had the greenest of green eyes that begged her to swim deliriously in them. What was happening to her? She felt as if a spell was cast upon her causing her to be mesmerized by this man. Get a grip, she thought. Come back to reality. She forced her mind to find the words to stop this interaction.

"Perhaps," she began, "you've assessed the situation incorrectly. I was actually thinking about how humor is needed to get through the day, thank you kindly."

"Okay, my apologies. I'm sorry I missed the introductions at the beginning of the meeting. My name is Ben Randall. And you're?"

"I'm Carrie Singer." Ben held his hand out to shake hers, and she reluctantly offered her hand. His mere touch of her hand sent a quick warming sensation through her body. She was caught off guard. "It's nice to meet you. I'm sorry, but I need to run. I'm sure we will meet again, when classes begin. Gotta go. Bye."

"We will," Ben proclaimed, "that we will. See you then. Nice meeting you too."

Carrie hurried back to her office. She had three weeks left to prepare her caseload for her departure. She needed to update all of her written records and make sure she informed all of her clients she would be leaving. This was the part she dreaded. Carrie became attached to her families. She felt as if she was abandoning them. It was actually more than a feeling. It was the reality of the situation. She was leaving them, handing them off to yet another caseworker. This made her feel sick to her stomach. It was no wonder clients hated the system. How many times were clients required to reinvest their life story with yet another stranger? Carrie thought about this process and likened it to her own life.

How often would she be willing to give up her family's secrets to a new stranger? How willing would she be to enter into a system requiring such blind faith, so you would trust the next caseworker? Hell, she wasn't willing to trust her life history with persons she chose as friends, let alone endeavor to share with strangers. And newly assigned caseworkers were strangers to their families. Strangers coming with some foreknowledge of their life circumstances, something they read in their case record. Yes, clients were right to feel like system fodder because they were. Clients were clearly on the short end of this equation. Strange caseworkers would approach their door with knowledge of all of their foibles and problems, and they, on the other hand, had no knowledge of the caseworker at all. It was definitely one sided, requiring immense trust by the client.

Carrie had high hopes of introducing the new caseworker personally to her families. However, she was informed her replacement wouldn't arrive until the Monday following her departure. The agency didn't want to pay for two caseworkers to serve the same families even for one week. It was viewed as a waste of taxpayer money. The system didn't care it would've been money well spent to ease the transition for the clients and the new caseworker. They didn't matter. Even though the clients' mere existence provided jobs for all of the agency staff, their nominal additional needs for a smooth transition between workers were secondary and unimportant. The system, not the individual caseworkers, didn't actually care.

Carrie struggled with this concept. It kept her awake at nights during this time. She felt she should abandon her need for education and stay with her clients. Both needs, hers and the clients, couldn't be served simultaneously. She felt selfish. She vowed she would never abandon her clients again after she got her master's degree. It didn't help her to sleep any better. She kept her vow until the day of her retirement.

Carrie was fortunate enough to receive some state stipend money to help pay for her school expenses. It came with a contract requiring her to return to the field of child welfare for two years. If she failed to serve her time, she would be required to return the funds. This wasn't an issue for her. Her commitment was already made in her heart. But this alone wouldn't cover all of her costs. She was able to secure an evening shift positions as a screener with her agency. It was going to be a rough two years with little personal time. She looked forward to the new challenges, the new possibilities, and the new friendships which would come. Ben crossed her mind. "Go away," she admonished him.

chapter 17

Professor Forsberg invited all of her assigned students to a welcoming gathering at her home. Carrie felt compelled to attend. She arrived wearing a mid-calf, gauze, green and blue print skirt with a green, peasant blouse. It was a hot and humid early evening, and she wanted to wear something which wasn't clingy, not too casual, but not formal. Her skin was already glistening with a thin layer of sweat. She opted to place a small drop of rosemary oil behind each ear. Carrie rarely used perfumes, finding them to be nauseating and discovered essential oils did the trick as well, but with a lightness of scent.

Sylvia arrived simultaneously with Carrie. "Hi, Carrie," Sylvia called out with a grinning smile showing her large white teeth.

"Hello, Sylvia, it's good to see you again."

"We're in the big show now," she exclaimed with a full grin. "I never thought I would be getting a master's degree. It's a dream come true for me. How about you," Sylvia inquired.

"I'm right with you Sylvia. It should be an adventure. I hope I'm up to the task," she added.

"Up to the task, darling, are you even kidding me? You've already scored big with the professor. I've heard she's one of the hardest professors to please. And you did it with ease at our orientation. I almost went back to the college office to see if I could request a different advisor, but thought better of it. And did I catch Ben eyeing you? He was quite a trip wasn't he?"

Her comment caused Carrie to want to turn and run away. She forgot about Ben for a quick minute, but the sheer mention of him caused her nerve endings to stand at attention again.

"Susan was enamored with him," Sylvia continued. "I think she hopes to link up with him beyond schoolwork."

"Really," Carrie smiled, "I wish her well. I saw the two of them talking briefly after the orientation in the hallway."

"Susan ran into me outside of the building after orientation. We went and had some coffee together. All she could talk about was Ben. He made a big first impression with her, especially with those gorgeous green eyes and his thick sandy brown hair. And what a voice! Those deep resonating notes in his voice almost could convince me I'm not married. I pity the woman who marries him. Women will be chasing him eternally. In fact, I think Susan was hoping to get some kind of additional moment with him, but he said he had to catch up with someone else then. Oh, listen to me drone on," Sylvia said as she flipped her hand downward. "I need to learn to keep my mouth shut. At least that's what Howard says. Howard's my husband. Well, are you ready to go in to the festivities?" The two women joined the group in the professor's backyard. It was pungent with smells from the gas grill cooking some burgers.

"Welcome, I'm glad you came," said Professor Forsberg. "Make yourself comfortable. I was hoping we'd all get to know each other a little better tonight. Quite informal. No agendas. Remember, call me Tamara. Now you're Sylvia, and you're, of course, Carrie, right?"

"Yes," Carrie and Sylvia replied in unison. "Thank you for having us," Carrie continued. "You have a lovely setting here."

"Thank you. Well enjoy while you're here. I need to go check on some food in the kitchen." Tamara left Carrie and Sylvia to their own amusements. Carrie noticed Matt was engaged in a conversation with Eloise near a small stone crafted waterfall fountain. Lydia, Vanessa and Richard were laughing as they stood near the potted herb plants. Susan corralled Ben and Mike at one of the glass topped tables with a bold red umbrella. Sylvia made her way to join the laughing group. Carrie opted for Eloise and Matt. As she passed by Ben, Susan and Mike, Ben reached out and grabbed her elbow.

"Hey, there," he chimed. "Good to see you again!"

"Oh, hello. Yes, it's good to see you again too, as well as Susan and Mike. Hello everyone," Carrie said as she was feeling her insides twittering unexpectedly.

"Sit with us," Ben insisted. "Come on, we have an empty chair here begging for you to join us." Susan cast Carrie a furtive glance suggesting she should move on. Meanwhile, Mike moved the empty chair out from under the table so Carrie could sit next to him and across from Ben.

"I'll come back in a minute," Carrie said as she raised her index finger in the air suggesting one minute. "I want to get something to drink first," as her throat caused her to swallow when nothing was present to swallow. Carrie headed for the outdoor bar.

"What can I get for you?" asked Tamara's husband Steve.

She fully intended on asking for some iced tea, but when her mouth opened to speak she heard herself say, "I'll have a gin, lemon and 7, please." Gin, lemon and 7!!! Whatever am I thinking? It will be good for you, you know. Calm your nerves, her inner voice whispered from somewhere deep within. You have to admit it. You say you want to live in reality, don't you? Well the r-e-a-l-i-t-y is, and you might as well face it head on, the reality is you're extremely attracted to Ben. No, no, it can't be. But it is what is. No, no, no. Why are you fighting it? You're human. You can have human feelings and emotions for love, and the comfort found in the arms of another, can't you? No, say it isn't so. Not with him. He'll only cause me trouble. I can feel it. Cause you trouble? Maybe, but not the kind you're thinking of. You'll figure it out kiddo. Now go on back over there and enjoy yourself. I caused you to order the drink, it'll help you out. Trust me. Now go on over there. Her inner voice subsided.

As Carrie wended her way back to the table over the patterned brick patio, she couldn't believe the conversation she just held with herself. Mike and Ben greeted her back with smiles while Susan pretended she was happy to share her company with Carrie. Carrie rather liked Susan's energy. It felt fresh and bouncy. She knew she and Susan could become friends. It would take only a while before Susan would realize Carrie posed no threat to any plans Susan might have for Ben. Carrie maneuvered to sit down and pull her chair toward the table. She took a quick sip of her drink, looked up and decided to take the offensive and ask a question, rather than have to respond. Yes, respond to anything Ben might want to explore. Oh my gosh, did I think *explore* she mused to herself as her thoughts betrayed her with scenes of Ben exploring her lips, her breasts, her thighs, OH, STOP! "What have you all been up to these last three weeks?" Carrie asked the group.

The group began to chat away about what they did. Susan finished moving into her new apartment. Mike was working out in the gym regularly, and it showed. Ben remained intensely silent throughout. Carrie threw in a word or two but mostly for acknowledgement and support of the other's stories. Carrie couldn't dismiss the underlying energy passing between her and Ben. She refused to look into his eyes and forced herself to keep her focus on Susan and Mike as they spoke. Susan leaned to her left toward Ben and turned her perfectly featured face toward his and coaxed him to explain his sudden silence. Carrie took a large gulp of her drink. What Susan didn't realize was, Ben wasn't quiet at all. His entire body was resonating, and Carrie could feel it as you feel music swathe you as the notes dance in the air. Before Ben could respond, Eloise and Matt approached the table bringing two chairs with them and joined the group. Susan's question was forgotten.

The evening's gathering turned out to be quite pleasant. Carrie enjoyed the other students. They were all different from one another. Professor Forsberg ran her own agenda during this event as well, though she earlier announced there were no agendas. Carrie's appreciation grew for this "tough" woman, when she created a challenge for the group to get to know one another better. Tamara tossed all of their names into a baseball cap and pulled two names out at a time so they would be randomly paired up: Matt and Sylvia, Eloise and Vanessa, Michael and Susan, Richard and Ben, and Lydia and Carrie. Carrie was relieved she wasn't paired up with Ben. She wasn't too sure of Lydia. She seemed to have an underflow of angry energy. Carrie hoped she was wrong. Their assignment was to discuss with their partner one life changing event which helped shape their current lives. After which, their partner would share with the larger group each of their moments.

Whew, Carrie thought, Professor Forsberg pulls no punches. It was down to brass tacks right away. Which moment to choose? This could get interesting. It was also a peek into the lives of all of them. What one would choose to share could also be particularly telling. As expected, some students were immediately open with the details of their life; others chose to be more reserved. Carrie wondered what Tamara would think of each of their choices.

Lydia and Carrie sat down on the bar stools to chat. Lydia insisted Carrie reveal her moment first. Controlling, that's what Lydia is, controlling, thought Carrie. Carrie decided not to fight it. "I almost drowned once," Carrie began. "A friend and I started out canoeing on a perfect summer day. We were both inexperienced and found ourselves in some currents stronger than our skills were. Our canoe overturned and threw both of us out of it. I was scooped up and placed in the middle of a nasty whirlpool, one which I couldn't get out of. I noticed my friend was able to make it to the river's edge and up onto the shore. The next thing I knew I was dragged down under the water. I fought my way back to the surface only to be pulled down over and over again. I swallowed a fantastic amount of water. I struggled, bobbing up and down until my strength was fast diminishing. My thoughts turned to, you're going to die here. You're going to drown. I had no strength left. My friend couldn't reach me. Dread began to set in. I started thinking about all of the people I would never see again.. Then, I know you're going to think this is crazy, but then I heard a voice as clear as day, a voice sounding as it was talking to me as clearly as you're talking to me now. The voice simply said, "Don't panic." It wasn't a voice coming from inside of my head. It came from outside of me. "Don't panic." I let myself fall to the bottom of the river, maybe about twelve feet, and then I was able to push up with my feet and bob up once again to the surface where a large tree branch was floating by. I grabbed it with all of my might and flowed further down the river until I could paddle kick myself to the river's shore. I knew, then, guardian angels were real. Nothing else could explain why I'm alive. I should have drowned."

"It absolutely deepened my belief in a higher power watching over us. Before I wasn't sure, but now I never question the possibility of God. Well, I figured I better do something good with my life as God believed it was worth saving. Now I try to help others who need a hand up, and hope my life was worth saving."

Lydia's mouth slowly dropped open suggesting astonishment. "You mean, you actually thought for real you were going to die?"

"I didn't think it, I knew it with every last breath I was trying to gulp for air and then realized I was gulping water! I was a goner. It could have only been a divine intervention which saved me. At least that's what I believe with my whole being. It really did change my entire perspective on life. The preciousness of it was lost on me before. I now realize the entire event was actually a gift. Before the incident, I never gave life much thought, figured I would live to be old. I think it goes with being young and feeling indestructible. But now I take greater care for how I spend my moments here on Earth. I try not to waste my time frivolously, although I'm okay for having fun. I think it's vital to bring joy to situations where possible. Don't you?"

"You bring up an interesting point," Lydia said contemplatively. "I never have spent time thinking about how I live my life. I have thought, rather, about how to survive on a day to day basis. Now I'm not saying I had any true brushes with death, I haven't. But there are other kinds of deaths if you know what I mean. Death of spirit, perhaps, lost in a quicksand pool stealing your self-esteem and suffocating you until you genuinely lose who you are. I feel like I fought that fight all of my life. People were quick to tell me I would never amount to anything. Forget your dreams, they would say. You need to understand your place in this life."

"People would really say that to you?"

"Not people, but my family, my mom, my dad, aunts, uncles. It was the culture of the neighborhood. Hardly anyone got out. In fact, one of my defining moments was the day I won the city's spelling bee contest when I was in the eighth grade. I grew up in Washington D.C. I lived in a rough neighborhood filled with drugs, gangs, and guns. It wasn't safe to go out on the streets unless you had protection. Protection in the form of some big burly guy, who would watch your back for you. Young girls were often targeted to be raped as part of gang initiations. I rarely went outside, and if I did I never went outside alone. As a result, I read voluminously at home. I think I checked out every library book the school had to offer. It was a safe way to escape the chaos we lived in."

"I'm sorry. No child should live like that," Carrie said understanding and thinking back to the lives of many of her former clients. Carrie began to feel differently about Lydia since their first meeting. She began to understand how her first impression of Lydia came to pass. She had to be tough and hard to survive. Carrie was stymied Lydia was willing to share as much as she did with her. Carrie imagined Lydia wasn't always this forthcoming.

"Don't be sorry for me, Carrie. It made me strong. I don't want anyone's pity."

"I really wasn't feeling pity. The world can be harsh, and children shouldn't need to deal with all of those travesties. One of the reasons I became a child welfare worker was to help children avoid those experiences. I guess I see myself as an eternal rescuer. I was once rescued, so I'm trying to pay back. Please tell me more about how winning the spelling bee changed your life."

"Well my father," Lydia continued, "was a gang member and ended up in jail when I was about eight years old. My mother became a drug addict and found ways to survive on the street if you know what I mean. Both of my parents chastised me for having dreams of going to college, let alone a dream of graduating from high school. They said I needed to understand how life was for us in the ghetto. You don't get out, they would say, and the sooner you understand, the better off you'll be. Neither one of them graduated from high school. I don't think they were trying to hold me down. They wanted me to accept the reality of their life, and they couldn't see any further. But I kept reading and reading and reading. Words fascinated me. If I started talking like the language of my books, I would get yelled at and told to stop being uppity and come back to the real Earth. I actually watched what dialect I would use. When in the ghetto, talk like the ghetto. When anywhere else talk like the books did."

"I can't imagine what life was like for you. How did you get through it all?"

"I owe a lot to my grandmother. She was the one there for me. My mother had her own problems. My dad, well he was gone. My grandmother was the only one who encouraged me. Our school had a big event for the spelling bee, and I won. No one was as surprised as I was. Grandma said she knew I could do it. My mom didn't even show up. It was the first time in my life I won anything. I remember I couldn't stop smiling. Some kids told me they would wipe the smile off my face if I didn't stop."

"And then what happened?" Carrie said intrigued.

"Well I had no idea the winner of the spelling bee would be sent on to compete with the other schools' winners for the city championship. I was extremely nervous. There were about twenty four of us competing. I was glad grandma came. She kept telling me not to mind the others, keep my head on straight, and I would win. And I did! Pneumonia was the word which won it for me. I couldn't believe it. Everyone I knew told me I was going to fall off the high horse I was riding. They said I was begging for a big fall. I won and proved them all wrong. It was the first time I felt quite happy with myself. After winning I changed. I knew I could do anything I wanted to do if I didn't pay any mind to the naysayers. It was then I knew I could get out of the ghetto, as long as I was able to dodge the stray bullets which would cut down some innocent bystander. Even if you were inside your own home, didn't mean you were safe from the street violence. I guess I must have some guardian angels around me, too," Lydia said with a gentle smile. "Your story helped me see that."

Carrie and Lydia became so engrossed in sharing their stories; they failed to realize they were called upon to join the larger group for the greater sharing. Ben came over and put an arm around each of their shoulders to usher them to the waiting group. Once again, Carrie needed to calm herself down with his touch. She hoped he didn't notice his mere touch quickened her breath. "Ladies," he said, "while you were chatting, we all decided the last to join the group should be the first to share their defining moments."

"If you're willing," added Tamara, "but someone does need to start."

"I'll start," said Lydia. "Carrie was touched by a guardian angel. Once you've been touched by an angel, there is no going back to the way you were before you were touched. This girl, I mean woman, nearly drowned in a canoeing accident. I say nearly because obviously she didn't. However it was the encouraging voice she heard while drowning guiding her to not panic. As a result, she floated to the bottom of the river and then pushed herself back to the surface only to discover a large tree branch waiting for her to grab. She swears there was no branch available the other dozen times she surfaced to get air. Why it became a defining moment for her was it caused a shift in her own consciousness about God. It strengthened her belief. It didn't make her religious, only more spiritual. And it's with that same spirit she's been able to do all of the child welfare work she has without the overlay of burnout, at least, not yet. And there you have it."

"Thank you Lydia. Carrie do you've anything you want to add?" asked Tamara.

"Lydia captured the essence of the experience. I wake each morning knowing I will never be able to predict what gifts each day will bring me. It makes life more interesting. Don't you think? The experience did strengthen my belief in hope, and I don't think you can be an effective social worker without hope. If we don't have hope, how can we expect our clients to have dreams?"

Once again, Carrie obviously impressed Professor Forsberg. "You seem to possess wisdom others never quite seem to capture. Thank you for sharing with us. Okay, who wants to share next?" continued Tamara.

The evening rapidly passed as each of their defining moments was shared. The group began to open up with dialogue and coalesce. Many ooohs and aaahs were exchanged along with hearty and cheerful laughter. The last one to have their defining moment shared was Ben. Richard spoke gently and softly. "Ben shared with me the birth of his daughter, Alexis, was by far the greatest defining moment of his life. In his own words, not only did he strut around like a peacock in full plumage, but her entry into the world caused him to have to put aside childish endeavors sooner than he would have. He did the 'right thing' and married his high school sweetheart, Jane, after learning of her pregnancy at the age of eighteen. Alexis is now ten years old. Ben and Jane worked hard to complete college, raise their child and stay sane as he put it. He said he learned the value of commitment to hard work in school, marriage and fatherhood. Not all things come easy, and we should appreciate what we've been given. Even though we might not be given what we think we want, we'll be given what we need, if we only look. Did I get it right Ben?"

All eyes turned to Ben as he raised thumbs up to Richard followed by a magnanimous grin. Carrie was flabbergasted as were a few others. She had no idea he was married. He didn't wear a wedding band. Then she felt foolish. The fact he was married was a good thing, she convinced herself. Wasn't she actively trying to avoid him? She knew he would be trouble. She didn't think of this scenario. Besides she didn't enter graduate school to find a man. She didn't have the time. All things considered, this was very good news. Ben is married. No problem. Now if she could get her body to be as logical in responding to the news, maybe it would calm down when it was in his energy field. Of course, it will. Carrie glanced over at Susan and noticed her effervescence faded. She felt sorry for her in a way. Carrie decided to approach her and commiserate a bit. "I don't think any one of us saw that coming," she quietly said in Susan's ear. Susan nodded with eyebrows raised followed by a heavy sigh.

As Carrie drove home, she couldn't help but review her past encounters with Ben, all two of them including this evening. Upon retrospection, she admitted he never did anything to her suggesting he was interested in her in a romantic way at all. He tried to be friendly, and she read too much into it. Oh, but his impish smile and those eyes invited you in. Thinking about him now caused her body to start a warming glow within. Stop, she told her body. Stop now. He's married. He isn't available. Besides you didn't want to get involved anyway. She vowed to focus on real possibilities in her life, not Ben.

And it began - this uneasy interaction between Ben and Carrie filled with curiosity, vibrant energy and potential sexual synergy. It wasn't what Carrie planned. She didn't have time to dabble in a relationship at this point. Especially with school beginning, as well as her evening position at the agency, answering the hotline for abuse and neglect. Neither Ben nor anyone else was figured in her plans. Although she couldn't deny, even to herself, Ben intrigued her on many planes. All in all, Carrie attempted to put Ben out of her mind.

chapter 18

The first quarter of school was nearing. Carrie settled into her small desk space for her evening position on the Abuse Hotline. She barely knew her coworkers in this department, having only seen them for a few moments when they would arrive to work, and she would leave for the day. This second shift was going to be a challenge. Carrie traditionally flopped into her bed about ten o'clock each night, but with this position she wouldn't get home until midnight. Classes started at nine each morning and continued through the day until four. She had to be at work by five, giving her little time for a relaxing dinner or any type of personal sustenance. It's only for two years, Carrie reminded herself. I can get through this. Besides, this is the only way I can afford to pay for school without going into greater debt. You've handled rougher situations than this one. Carrie often gave herself little pep talks.

She liked her new supervisor, Tanner Hill. He was a tall, jovial bearded man. If you asked him a question, he gave you an answer. Perhaps not the one you wanted to hear, but at least he would give you an answer. Some supervisors always put her on hold, unsure of themselves when Carrie would ask a question. They wanted to take her concern or question up the line to the director. This used to make Carrie crazy waiting for an answer. Well there were supervisors, and then there were supervisors. She could never figure out how some people were promoted into the position, especially if they were fearful to make a decision without consulting others. She didn't believe those types were competent supervisors, only competent conduits to transfer information for someone else to decide. Luckily Tanner wasn't of this type. He would listen intently and then decide. This worked for Carrie. However, Carrie didn't consistently consult with Tanner in the same steady fashion she did with prior supervisors. Perhaps it was because the nature of the job changed. She no longer was on the street, no longer providing the primary intervention and services to clients. Instead, she was answering the telephone and talking to the caller regarding their concerns for children who were allegedly maltreated. Her job, now, was to discern who had information rising to the level requiring a thorough investigation, and which information wasn't appropriate for their agency to act upon.

At first Carrie thought this job would be a breeze compared to actually working person to person with clients in the street. This was dispelled for her on her first evening, when she informed the caller their concern wouldn't be addressed by the agency as it didn't meet the standard for further investigation.

"What good is your God damn agency anyway? What has to happen to a kid before you do anything? Die. You're all a bunch of useless good for nothing leeches, living off of the tax payer dollars. You all ought to be taken out and shot. Why even have this stupid hotline number anyway? "

"Sir, we can't investigate your concern unless you give us additional information suggesting a child is at risk for maltreatment. Simply reporting a ten year old child is screaming next door isn't enough information for us to act upon. Checking on every child who simply screamed would be next to impossible. Do you have any other information or indicators something is seriously wrong?" Carrie asked patiently.

"Forget it. Forget it. Wait until your tax levy comes up again. You can sure bet I'll vote against it." The caller slammed down the phone and Carrie imagined him walking away in a huff.

Later, Carrie received a call from someone who was unmistakably intoxicated. Words were so slurred she had a hard time understanding what they were saying. "Yeah, I wanna report about, Jesus Christ quit trying to take the phone away from me, about these kids out here, I said leave me alone. I'm making an 'portant call here. So sorry about that. Now what was I saying? Oh yeah, these kids out here are runnin' around crazy. Somebody's gotta do somethin'. Oops, now I spilled that all over the floor. They have trampled my flowers and scream the awflest names at me. Damn it, Zee, git your hands off this phone. Damn it. Now leave me alone, go. Give me the damn phone back." Carrie heard a click and the caller was gone. This would be the first of many such calls. Drunks and druggies seemed to rule the evening.

The calls never stopped. As soon as she would hang up the phone, there would be another call waiting. Neighbors would call on neighbors because of a spat having nothing to do with the children. They would blatantly lie to cause unneeded disturbance to their neighbors' family with a child welfare investigation. Carrie couldn't believe people would use a child abuse hotline service as retribution to settle some frivolous neighborhood or family squabble. But it seemed to happen all of the time.

Anonymous callers were also plentiful. Regardless of the source, the agency was required to assess the information given and act on it accordingly. Anonymous callers bothered Carrie. If they were concerned about the children they were reporting, why wouldn't they provide their name? Why would they not stand up and be counted? All referral sources were required to be kept confidential by the agency. People run scared most of their lives she thought, even when they tried to do the right thing. Or they were merely vindictive and wanted to cause undue stress to others out of revenge, hurt, or anger. It left her with a sad and empty feeling. When she discovered seventy percent of all of the calls taken, assessed, and investigated were found to have no discoverable valid information, her sense of hope for humankind as a good and loving species further evaporated, taking an emotional toll from her. Yet deep inside, folded into the fabric of her being, she refused to be conquered by the despair always trying to creep in.

Her first night home she was exhausted. She dreamed her ear transformed into a telephone receiver. She did battle with many unknown faces ending in her trying to choke the living daylights out of them. She woke up feeling spent. "This isn't good, this is not good," Carrie whispered to herself during a yawn and a large stretch of her arms and legs. "Get your butt out of bed. You have to get to school."

As she drove to school she was experiencing a basketful of emotions: excitement, fear of failure, nervousness, doubt, joy, freedom, anticipation. Many thoughts were swirling around in her head. She wondered what recipe all those emotions might be whipping up for her to experience this day. What she liked about social work was she never knew what the day would bring. No day was predictable. You may go home exhilarated or anguished. It was the surprise element, the adrenaline rush to which she was addicted. Graduate school would likely be an addiction all over again wrapped in a different package. Today curiosity was killing the cat. Today she would find out what assignment she would be given for her field experience occurring two days per week. She only knew child welfare up to this point, with faint brushes with other social work avenues. Oh, where will I land, she wondered?

As she walked across the university's grounds, the colors and smells of autumn sang to her. The sun was rising, beginning to highlight the red and gold tones in the leaves as they gave one last gift of color before they floated to the ground, shriveled, crumbled and returned to the soil from which they came. Autumn aromas tickled her nose, as the crunching sound of shuffling through leaf piles tickled her ears. This was her favorite time of the year.

As she walked she passed by many others students, most with their heads down, walking swiftly. Oh, look up, look around, engage yourself with this beauty called fall, she wanted to tell them. Instead she began to say "hi" or "hello" to the passerbyers, jolting them from their oblivious passage to wherever. They would look up at her with a question in their eyes: Are you talking to me? Typically they would slightly lift their already weary looking heads and offer a smile or let out a meek reply back. Some wouldn't notice or respond at all. Others were too engrossed in each other, unaware there were other people trying to engage them. Some of them were obviously lovers by the way their energies resonated together even as they walked. She envied the lovers. Sometimes she wished she had more hours in the day for loving herself. Later, she mused. I'm too busy now. Thinking of lovers, Carrie's mind jetted to thoughts of Ben. He's married, she admonished herself. Besides, remember you weren't interested.

The social work college was encased in one of the historical buildings on campus, adorned with a large carved stone arch announcing its entryway. Climbing up its steps, Carrie felt a mixture of excitement and anxiety. She was headed for the same conference room her orientation meeting was in with Professor Forsberg. "Remember she wants to be addressed as Tamara," she reminded herself. It seemed awkward to address a professor by her first name. Slowly the ten began filling in around the conference table. Carrie purposely sat next to Susan wanting to get to know her better.

"Hello Carrie," Susan said brightly. "It's good to see you again!"

"Hi, yeah it's good to see you too. How're you doing?"

"I'm feeling really nervous. I could hardly sleep last night. How 'bout you?"

"Oh, I slept like a rock," Carrie replied, "but then again I always have slept without any difficulty, after I actually fall asleep. Once I slept all night on a rock pier in a lake in the Upper Peninsula in Michigan. I was out moon watching and fell asleep right there on my back until the sunrise. Sometimes being able to sleep soundly isn't good. I woke up literally covered with hundreds of bug bites. If it was Halloween I wouldn't have needed a costume. I looked a fright, and itched incessantly. I put mittens on my hands to keep from scratching my very skin off!"

"No way!" Susan exclaimed.

"Oh, yes, I have pictures to prove it."

"Well, I couldn't get my mind off of where my field assignment might be. I hope I'm up to the task. I'm a bit afraid. I think some places could be pretty scary," Susan said and feigned shivering.

"You'll be fine," Carrie said comfortingly.

Susan noticed Ben approaching down the hallway. "Now there's a snake," she said nodding her head in Ben's direction. "You know he knows he's attractive and has sex appeal times one thousand. Yet, he let me think he was available. I certainly didn't appreciate that at all."

Carrie's curiosity was piqued. "Really, he did? What did he say to you?"

"It's not what he said to me. It was what he didn't say to me. I mean I'm sure he could read I was interested in him, yet he let me babble on about everything. I felt like such an idiot when Richard announced he was married. I'm sure Ben had a good laugh at my expense. Ben is a snake in the grass who intentionally sets up women with his charm only to crush them later. That's what I think. His character cancels out his physical attributes."

"I see," Carrie responded as Ben walked through the doorway. He still took her breath away. Tamara followed on his heels. She was carrying a small folder containing the secrets of their field placements.

"Everyone is here and accounted for," Tamara announced. "Let's get started. I'm sure you're all anxious to find out where you'll be placed. A few words first. I want to thank all of you for coming to my home. I enjoyed getting to know each of you a tad bit better." She smiled which seemed to lighten the atmosphere a bit. "Next, each of you'll be required to put in sixteen hours at your placement site. We tried to take into consideration any special requests you might have. These assignments are not interchangeable. Are there any questions before we get started?"

Lydia, of course, raised her hand. "Do you mean if we find someone to trade assignments with, it won't be honored?"

"Yes. That's correct. We considered several different variables in the matching process. Your assignment is non-negotiable. Listen, everyone," as Tamara glanced around at all of the eager eyes, "I know it may seem harsh, but we've our reasons. Part of being a professional social worker includes your ability to adapt to any number of scenarios. You all were given the opportunity to inform us prior to your assignment of any special circumstances, and we took those into consideration. If you simply think you won't like your placement, isn't reason enough to exchange to another place. We've limited space in the community for field placements for all of our students, both graduate and undergraduate. Short of something rising toward a near catastrophe, we won't be making any changes. Any other questions?"

Fidgeting was evident around the table. Fingers tapping, feet shuffling, heavy sighing, notebooks opening, purses being zipped, bodies wriggling in their seats, nervous energy abounded everywhere. "Okay, let's get started," Tamara said as she drew out a pack of papers. "Ellie, you've been assigned to the Easter Seal Society. Vanessa, you've been assigned to the American Lung Association, Susan, you've been given the Early Childhood Development Center. Carrie is going to the Mid-State Psychiatric Center." The last announcement caused the group to giggle when the Professor said going rather than assigned.

"Yeah" Vanessa erupted, "you're going to the crazy joint."

"Shall we continue," Tamara inquired. "Lydia, you've been placed at the free clinic here on campus. Sylvia, you also are going to the Mid-State Psychiatric Center."

Sylvia gave Carrie a wink. "I guess we will have to be crazy together," Sylvia piped up as she made circles with her finger around her ear and grinned.

"Uh huh," Tamara continued showing slight irritation, "Matt, you've been assigned to the County Welfare Department. Michael, the department of Juvenile Corrections has your number, you won't have to drive any clients around in your car," more snickering ensued. "Richard was given the Federal Housing Authority and that leaves Ben. Ben, due to your request for second shift hours, you've been assigned to one of the few agencies with a second shift field placement opportunity, Children Services."

Carrie dared to glance at Ben and saw, once again, his beaming smile. Of course he didn't know she would be working there. Again she started to get all jumpy inside. He has a wife and child, he has a wife and child, he has a wife and child, she kept repeating to herself.

"Now you'll all need to sign these contracts pertaining to your placement before you leave. Additionally your copy will provide you with your agency's address and field instructor's name and contact information. You should all be good to go. Any last questions?"

The familiar hand of Lydia was raised. "I have a weak immune system. Do you think it's wise I be placed in the free clinic? You know, with all of those germs. I never thought to indicate it on my initial information inquiry page."

"As I clearly stated earlier, these placements are non-negotiable. I'm sure you'll be fine. Anyone else? Okay. Good luck out there. See you next month." As Professor Forsberg rose from her chair, the screeching of all of the chair legs on the linoleum floor began again and reached a fever pitch. The room was eerily quiet as each member considered their future plight.

Carrie considered approaching Ben to let him know she would be working alongside him, but thought better of it. He'll find out soon enough. Besides, what does he care? She scampered on to her first class, human functioning.

chapter 19

As she slid into her chair for her evening shift of telephone calls, Carrie felt exhausted. She could close her eyes and easily take a catnap. "I'll get used to this," she told herself. After all what did I expect would happen, she thought? First day of school and meeting so many new people, attending classes again after five years, and working full time, what did I expect of myself? I guess I'm learning the lesson I'm not invincible. Okay enough. Concentrate on what you're getting paid to do. Answer the phone. Carrie obeyed her own instructions and took the next call.

"Hello, this is Children Services. My name is Carrie Singer. How may I help you?"

"Yes, this is Sandy Jones of Children's Hospital. I'm calling about a four year old girl who has sustained a third degree burn on her buttocks having been forced to sit on the hot grid of a heater." Carrie felt a huge impulse to break into tears, imagining the condition of the child and her pain. Instead she wore her professional voice and stoic composure and gathered the necessary information. At the end of her shift, Carrie robotically moved with a singular goal in mind, get to bed and sleep. As she began to exit the area, she heard Tanner call out to her.

"Carrie, can I see you for a quick minute before you leave?"

"Yes, of course," she replied as she entered his office wondering what was up. She quickly did a scan of her night's activities and couldn't imagine there was any problem.

"Carrie, I know you're only into your second week of working this shift, but I've a favor to ask of you?"

"Oh, okay. What can I do for you?"

"Carrie you have the strongest foundation in child welfare of all of my evening staff. Even though you're new to screening calls, it's clear to see you execute your responsibilities with professionalism, dignity and composure."

"Why, thank you Tanner. I'm glad to get good feedback," she said with a smile.

"It's for this reason I would like to impose and ask if you would be willing to share your skills and knowledge in coaching others. You handle all of the calls well, even the callers who don't deserve it. Well, you know what I mean. Carrie, I think you've a true talent, or gift if you will, to engage with even the most difficult of people and maintain such calm composure. It really is awesome to watch you interact with our clients."

"Thank you. I don't quite know what to say."

"Then say yes, Carrie. Say yes you'll be the primary coach for our new graduate student, a man named Ben Randall. He'll be here two nights a week and I need to assign him to one of the screeners, and you're my best bet."

Carrie didn't see this coming. She let out a gasp.

"Did I say something to upset you," Tanner inquired.

"No, no. Are you sure? I mean maybe there would be somebody else who would be better suited for this," Carrie stammered. Her mouth became dry. Why am I acting like this, she pondered. Quit it. You're not a petulant adolescent, gather your wits, be professional.

"I've thought this over carefully, and I'm convinced you're the right person," Tanner continued. "Now you're not going to let me down, are you?"

"Of course not," she found her grip. "Send him my way when he comes in."

"He'll be here tomorrow night. I've arranged for you to take the larger office with the second smaller desk in it. Ben can claim the smaller desk. Thanks Carrie. I appreciate it. Let me know if there's anything you need. I think it's best if he shadows you for the first two weeks."

"Thanks, Tanner. See you tomorrow night." Carrie was too tired to let her brain play around with this new scenario. She drove straight home, zombie like, whipped off her clothes, brushed her teeth and flopped into bed. Sleep came swiftly, but her brain conjured up disturbing dreams of Ben Randall.

She dreamed she was entering her office and went to place her coat on the coat rack when the coat rack hooks became Ben Randall's arms slowly entwining around her, holding her close. Then her dream jumped to a scene on a public street. She was standing in front of a store, nude, as Ben emerged from its front door. Not wanting to be caught naked by him, she jumped into an uncovered sewer hole and hid. However, inside the sewer hole she was in someone's bedroom. She landed on the bed, still naked. Ben's reflection was cast in a mirror. She could see he was unclothed. Next she was sitting in a classroom with a book opened to read an assignment for her human functioning class only to find Ben's face plastered on each page. She slammed the book shut. She ran out of the classroom and searched for a bathroom. She had to pee, bad.

Carrie abruptly woke up and stumbled into the bathroom. As she placed her hands on her head, sitting on the toilet, she was astonished by her dreams. "What the hell is wrong with me? Listen brain, leave me alone about Ben," she pleaded out loud. Her brain produced a question: Surely you must admit you feel his compelling energy? Denying your attraction to him doesn't make it go away, does it? "Aaaarrrrrrghh!" came flowing out of her mouth as a sad wailful longing. As she eased back into her bed, she prayed for sleep, no dreams.

The alarm clock jolted her out of a dead sleep. It was six a.m. and time to get up, get in the shower and move forward. As the cool water streamed down her face she began to recollect having an uneasy feeling about her dreams last night. Try as she might, though, she couldn't remember any of the details. However, the feeling something wasn't right stayed with her. Oh, well, she thought, forget about it. Consciously she would forget.

***

Today marked the first day of her field placement at the Mid-State Psychiatric Center. She found herself filled with curiosity layered with some apprehension. Carrie worked with a few clients with mental health challenges, but none so severe they required hospitalization. She knew at times patients could erupt into unpredictable behavior and perhaps become violent. She was glad Sylvia was given the same assignment. At least she would have one person to commiserate with, if commiseration was called for. Carrie hoped not.

As she entered the reception area, she saw Sylvia. When she saw Carrie, she broke into her wide grin and became quite animated. "I'm glad to see you," Sylvia blurted out. She stood and started to move her body in excitement with her hands jiggling and her feet pumping up and down on her toes. "I didn't realize how nervous I was to come here. It wasn't until I saw you enter the door; I was able to calm myself down some. Look at me. I'm still hyper. I'm so happy we were assigned together!"

"Me too," replied Carrie. "It may be quite an adventure, don't you think?"

"I hope it's a good one. I'm glad you're on this ride with me. Crazy people kind of spook me out." Then the door to the waiting room opened and a tall large woman approached them. She looked like an old Olympian, very strong with long golden braids swirled about pinned to her head. Carrie thought she looked like a Valkyrie woman from days of yore.

"Hello, my name is Willa Kearns. You two must be Carrie and Sylvia, right?"

"Yes, I'm Carrie"

"And I'm Sylvia."

"Welcome to our facility. Won't you come this way to my office?"

The starkly adorned office reeked of government thriftiness. An old wooden desk was scarred with wear and stacked high with piles of papers begging to be organized. In the corner were some dented gray filing cabinets topped with a picture of what appeared to be Willa's family. Willa's college degree was framed and hung crookedly on the wall. The sunlight shone in through the tall framed window panels pouring light onto Willa's desk. She pulled her squeaky wheeled wooden desk chair forward and began.

"First, I want to welcome you to our facility. It's old, you might say ancient, having been built in the mid 1800's. We've approximately 2,000 patients in residence here from all over the state. Some have been permanently committed to us. Others are here for a short interim stay until they can be stabilized. We've three resident psychiatrists on staff, not nearly enough for the population size, but we do what we can. We also have a host of nurses, and nurses' aides. In addition to the two of you, we welcome students from many different disciplines including medical, physical therapy, occupational therapy, art therapy, nursing, music therapy, and dietary nutritionists as well as teachers. I think you'll find your experience here quite diverse and enlightening. In a moment I'll give you a tour of the building but I want to prepare you for what you'll see."

"I want you to know all of the staff here wish this facility was able to provide a higher standard of care for the patients than what our budget allows. What you'll see can be quite disturbing. We do have policies in place requiring a certain standard of care for our residents; however, they do not meet a quality standard, only a minimal subsistence standard, which is far short of anyone's comfort level. As a result, we try to manage the patients' care in a way promoting dignity, but sometimes circumstances make this impossible. Many of our patients have nowhere else to go and thus they stay, as they do not have the life skills required to be on the outside. Local communities don't have the resources or facilities to care for these individuals; therefore it has become the state's responsibility. I know I gave you a real short summation about our program, but I'm sure you'll learn more as you work with us. Any questions?"

It was a lot to take in. What did she really mean? Carrie ruminated. Her curiosity was piqued. She thought about the many themes Ms. Kearns brought up: budget problems, staffing problems, dignity issues, subsistence level of care, ethical issues, and community resources. Did she also provide an apology of sorts about what they were going to soon witness? Willa even acknowledged full time staff wasn't comfortable with the conditions. Yes, it was a lot to take in at once. Carrie wasn't one compelled to keep a conversation going, and she was glad to hear Sylvia pose a few questions. She was only half listening, lost in her own thoughts and emotions of the moment. Carrie never heard any person put succinctly together so many burgeoning issues in such a short paragraph and with such ease. She imagined this wasn't the first time she delivered such a message.

Willa turned and looked at Carrie, "Any other questions?"

"No," Carrie replied, "I'm anxious to get started, thank you."

"Well, then, let's begin. I'll show you where the two of you'll be sharing an office. Then we will walk through our facility so you can become familiar with the surroundings."

"This building was built in the mid 1800's," Willa began as their tour started. "It has the distinction of having the longest hallway yet built at the time of its construction. Actually in America, only the pentagon has a longer hallway today. The hallway has been divided by a series of doors leading from one residential section to the next. The residents' rooms are located along the hallway corridor, similar to a medical hospital. The second and third floors each have sixteen individual units. The first floor houses the administrative offices, the cafeteria, maintenance offices, laundry room, and admitting offices. The smaller residential section on the first floor houses in-coming patients for observation to determine if they need to be admitted full time, or if they can be released after treatment requiring only a shorter stay of up to thirty days. We also have a room dedicated for judicial probate hearings. Lastly the first floor also houses our adolescent population."

"We shall start with touring the second floor. This is where the women are housed. Ready?" Willa asked as she searched for a key, one out of many on the largest key ring Carrie saw. There must have been at least fifty keys dangling from the silver ring including some skeleton keys. It felt eerie. "Ah, here it is," declared Willa, as she slid the key inside the door's keyhole. Gripping the door handle with both hands, she pulled the heavy steel door, as it loudly squeaked open. Carrie and Sylvia scurried inside. Ms. Kearns followed behind, again tackling the door to close it as it screeched into place. When the lock clicked shut, Carrie felt a surge of anxiety she quickly put in check. It was a bad strange feeling to be locked inside this facility. As she peered down the longer than expected wide hallway, she observed the many doors leading to the individual rooms. The floor was covered with cracked and broken tiles resembling a black and white checkerboard pattern. Clanking brown steam pipes snaked their way along the top of the walls leading to a twelve foot ceiling. Windows were placed well above viewing site, smudged and dirty allowing small streams of sunlight to filter through. The plastered ceiling also sported meandering cracks and an occasional water spot. The walls were in need of new paint as the institutional green was faded and peeled in some areas baring concrete. Carrie felt as if she stepped back in time to the 1800's.

"These residents are among our most functional. Their behavior responds positively to the drugs they are given. It does control their impulses to act out in random nonsensical behaviors. For the most part, they are harmless to you or themselves. However, without their medication their behavior deteriorates and they lose any consistent structured functionality they have. It really is sad, but the upside is many of them are able to leave our grounds and maintain themselves for short periods of time in the community. Some of them have part-time jobs in Sheltered Workshops."

"Additionally these residents have no need for help with self-care such as hygiene and dressing themselves appropriately. Many of them are quite fun to be around. Some have a great sense of humor. You know psychological problems are not the same as mental retardation. There is no cure for the mentally retarded, but there is help for the mentally disturbed, at least for many of them, unfortunately not for all of them."

"Come along, we are going to pass through the next door," Willa encouraged. As Carrie walked down the hallway, many of the residents acknowledged her with a pleasant 'hello' or wave of the hand. Some were knitting, some playing cards with each other, one was playing the small and quite out of tune spinet piano in the far corner. Each note resounded loudly as it bounced off the wall creating a slight echoing. A few were lying in their beds apparently sleeping. Carrie tried to imagine what it must be like to live in such an environment. It seemed overwhelming to her more than it appeared to be to the women residents. Or were they resigned to their fate, Carrie wondered.

"Now understand as we continue to walk from door to door the condition of the patients will worsen. You'll begin to notice a change in their ability to function as we continue."

"Ms. Kearns," Sylvia began, "did you say there are sixteen areas such as this one, all connected like this from door to door?"

"Yes, that's correct."

"If my calculations are correct," Sylvia continued, "each section includes about sixty patients?"

"Yes. Each cell or living area is composed of ten rooms on either side of the hallway. Each room holds three patients. We've four nursing aides per each area, two RN's, and security guards where needed."

"This would be way too crowded for me!" Sylvia shuddered. "A girl couldn't find any privacy here!"

Carrie agreed. It felt a bit claustrophobic as well, especially with all of the locking and unlocking of each door, and the clanking of the keys as they moved on the ring.

Two thirds of their way through the facility, they entered the geriatric sections. Nothing could have prepared Carrie and Sylvia for what they were about to see. It was horrific. The smell greeted them first, an intense musky dank smell of urine. Many of the women were strapped into wheelchairs, naked. The aides explained the patients wouldn't keep their clothes on. They were sitting there with their heads hung low. Their eyes appeared vacant, staring off into apparent nothingness. Carrie wondered what was going on inside their brains. What kind of mental life might they be having? All of a sudden one of the women pointed her finger straight at Carrie and started screaming. There was a look in her eye for a brief moment, when her eyes directly connected with Carrie's eyes, a look of powerlessness coupled with a plea for help. This image, this connection was branded into Carrie's memory bank. It would frequently haunt her. An aide quickly came to the woman's side and helped to quiet her.

Carrie was glad to move on to the next area. It, too, housed senior residents. Most of these women were ambulatory. A small frail looking lady came shuffling toward the threesome. In her blue flowered duster and terry cloth slippers, her thin white hair gently flying around her head, as if bees were buzzing about, the octogenarian outstretched her arms reaching toward Sylvia. "There you are, your Aunt Millie has been waiting for you so long," she said gleefully as she wrapped Sylvia into a hug laying her head on Sylvia's shoulder.

"You'll have to excuse Millie," Willa explained. "She's easily confused. She never has visitors and thinks anyone who isn't a staff member here is a family member of hers. She really is harmless and quite loveable. She's lost herself along the way."

As they approached the last area, Willa suggested they all go outside and get a breath of fresh air. It wasn't until they actually were outside Carrie realized how tense she was. She inhaled air deeply, and was reminded of how good it felt to breathe fresh air once again; similar to when she nearly drowned. It felt good to be free outside. Her heart ached for the residents. She wished conditions such as she saw, both the human condition and the physical conditions of the facility, didn't exist. She wanted the world to be better than this.

"Carrie, Sylvia, how are you?" Willa inquired. "I know that was a lot to experience and can be overwhelming. Are you okay?"

Carrie began, "Yes, I'm good. I never imagined the conditions were so, so …."

"Dismal?" offered Willa. "Unacceptable, shameful. You can choose whatever adjective suits you and I wouldn't disagree for one moment. These are our lost adults. Lost to themselves as well as lost in the system. Each year the state cuts our budget, but asks us to take on more patients. It's appalling. We've a few state legislators who are trying to pass a bill to change the conditions; however the condition of the disempowered person isn't high on the state's priority list. If these conditions don't anger you, they should. These patients have no strong voice fighting for them. Anywhere. They only have a dedicated few who have invested themselves in attempting to bring about some sorely needed changes. And thank the good Lord for them!"

"I'm sorry, I didn't mean to get on my soap box," Ms. Kearns said, "but it isn't right, it isn't right! I'm sure you gals have seen enough for the day. I know it was a lot to take in. Generally people need some time to decompress after they have their tour. Why don't you both leave early and take care of yourselves? "

"But we haven't finished the tour yet," Sylvia suggested. "We haven't gone through Cell 16."

Willa gave Sylvia and Carrie a knowing smile. "Yes, you're right, but I think it's best if we postpone the rest of the tour for another day. We will have ample time this year to complete it. I promise. Go ahead girls and enjoy the rest of your day!"

"Thank you," they yelled in unison. "See you Friday."

Carrie and Sylvia discussed what they saw as they walked toward the parking lot. "I'm glad we didn't finish the tour today," Carrie remarked.

"Really," Sylvia said somewhat surprised. "I wanted to get it all over with. I wonder why she stopped when she did."

"Well I imagine what was behind Cell 16 was the worst of the worst. Remember how she said as we progressed through each corridor the patient's conditions would become increasingly more difficult? Well Cell 16 is at the end of the line and I don't think I'm ready to absorb the secrets behind its door yet. I've seen enough for one day. I'm exhausted."

"Oh, you're right, I forgot. Carrie, how did you get to be so damn logical?" Sylvia said as she let out a loud ripple of laughter. "Oh, it feels good to laugh, especially after today!"

Carrie caught the sparkle in Sylvia's laugh and eyes and joined in. It was a wonderful release. Then their laughter evolved into a vicious cycle of contagion between them and they laughed until their ribs began to hurt their sides. They heaved their lungs trying to capture some of the crisp autumn air. Slowly they calmed themselves down, only to start again into uproarious laughter. After a while they didn't even know why they were laughing, but they were glad to have one another in the moment.

***

As the moon rose higher into the night sky and the stars began to twinkle brightly, Carrie shifted in her Adirondack chair. She rearranged her blanket, realizing her brain was in high gear. She couldn't stop thinking about the past. Then it dawned upon her, she was reviewing her life. She decided not to fight the compulsion as it would do no good. She sipped on her nearly finished tea savoring the sweetness. She knew what was coming next, yet she was compelled to review it in detail. Carrie allowed herself to settle comfortably back into her chair, close her eyes and remember. This time she would remember guilt free, a gift she decided to give herself.

chapter 20

Driving home from the psychiatric hospital, Carrie felt spent. She wondered why some people were afflicted with such mental suffering and was reminded to count her own blessings. She had five free glorious hours before she needed to report in to work. She grabbed a quick bite to eat, peanut butter and jelly and some carrot sticks. She thought about reading some of her classroom assignments and pulled out a thick tome entitled "The History of Child Welfare Policy and Social Change." She opened the book and began reading. The material was dry. It was hard for her to keep her eyes open. She inadvertently fell asleep in her recliner. She woke up when the pain in her neck reached the sensory center in her brain and sent out an alert to her system. As she lifted her head upward from the bent down sideways position gravity took it to, her book slid off her lap and onto the floor. The thud of the book fully awakened her and she glanced at the clock. She was out cold for three hours! She massaged her neck to try to restore its full range of motion. Her mind wandered back to the psych hospital and she hurt for all of the vacant eyes she met there. "Oh, my goodness, I've got to get ready for work!" Carrie remarked as she ran up her stairs to splash some water on her face, brush her teeth and get ready for an evening of unrelenting phone calls.

As she pulled into the agency's parking lot, Carrie remembered her last conversation with Tanner. Ben was coming this evening. She felt a mixture of dread coupled with unwanted excitement. She told herself to be professional. She was good at professionalism. She could maintain even under this circumstance. Besides, he's married, she reminded herself. You need to keep that in the forefront of your mind. Try to get to know him as a friend. Hormones, I'm ordering you to stand down, hear me: stand down.

She pushed opened the door and walked to her desk only to remember Tanner advised her he was changing her office to accommodate Ben as well. Tanner left a cardboard box on her desk to help her move her gear.

She was relieved to see her newly designated office was empty. It was larger than her previous one, but there were no windows in the long rectangular space. She felt like she would be working inside a manila folder. The office was tucked away into the back corner of the screening area. She plopped her cardboard box onto her desk and started to arrange her belongings. As she finished placing her last item, a picture of her parents, on her desk, she could hear Tanner's familiar voice approaching. "And back here we've arranged for you to be seated with one of our best employees, who will coach you along the way." Carrie sucked in a long slow breath. Tanner's head popped in, "Okay if we come in?" he inquired.

"Sure," Carrie replied.

"Ben, this is Carrie Singer, Carrie, Ben Randall," Tanner said as he made introductions. Carrie looked up and saw his beautiful smiling face. She knew she was blushing internally everywhere in her body, and hoped her face wasn't flushed.

"Carrie!" Ben exclaimed. "I had no idea you would be here! It's great to see you again."

"You know each other?" Tanner said with surprise.

"Hi Ben, it's good to see you again," Carrie managed to say matter-of-factly. "Actually, Tanner, Ben and I are in school together. We happen to be assigned to the same faculty advisor."

"Of course, I should have known, I mean I should have known you were both in the same program. Well, this shouldn't be a problem, should it? I mean, there won't be any conflict of interest, will there?"

Ben jumped in, "Absolutely not, at least not from my vantage point. How about you Carrie? Any problems with this?" he said as his deep emerald green eyes twinkled and winked at her.

"No, none at all," she stammered.

"Well, then all is good," Tanner continued. "Carrie, Ben, I'll leave the two of you alone and you can get started. Perhaps you can start with a tour of the building and take him to the supply area to get him set up at his desk. Ben, if you need anything, give me a hoot."

"Will do," Ben replied. "Thanks for everything."

"No problem," Tanner said as he moseyed back to his office.

As Tanner walked away, Carrie was feeling unsettled, a feeling uncommon to her. She reminded herself any fancy she felt toward Ben was one sided. He was a perfect gentleman towards her. Any outreach he initiated was only in the venue of friendship from one student to another. She knew she had the ability to put her feelings on hold. She did it repeatedly to get through some days at work. If she allowed, she could have been overwhelmed by all of the dreadful situations of children she encountered, yet she was able to persevere and even talk to those she believed were some of the most heinous individuals. She couldn't deny, though, the invisible current of magnetism she felt whenever Ben was in her presence. He, on the other hand, appeared to be cool, calm and collected. Well, she wasn't to be outdone by Ben, and she, too, would ramp up her own version of cool, calm and collected.

"What do you say? Shall we go capture some supplies for you?" Carrie began.

"Whatever you say, boss," Ben retorted.

Carrie hesitated, "Ben, I don't want this experience to be awkward for either of us. I'm not your boss. I happen to have some experience in child welfare, and I'm a team player. When Tanner asked me to guide you, I agreed and I'm happy to do it. But please, call me Carrie, okay?"

"Okay, boss," Ben said with a quirky smile on his face. When he saw Carrie's unimpressed response he felt compelled to continue, "Okay, Carrie. I don't feel awkward, and sure don't want you to feel awkward either. I'll be good. Promise, Boy Scouts honor," he said as he lifted his hand to make the Boy Scout promise sign.

Carrie realized she was likely overreacting to the situation at hand. She let out a little laugh. "Okay, well let's go get some supplies. They are down the hall in the black supply cabinet." As Carrie led the way, she imagined she could feel Ben's eyes watching her from behind. She remanded herself to stop being foolish. "You'll need some intake forms, pens, paperclips, and a stapler. That should do it."

"Down this hallway are the employees' bathrooms, each one contains a shower. Sometimes the children come in here so disheveled and dirty we need to give them a shower. There is a large sink in the women's bathroom for cleaning babies. Outside of the bathroom area is another large supply closet which holds plenty of clothing for all sizes and ages."

"On the north side of the building, we have visitation rooms, clerical offices and a large meeting room. The nurse's office is located beyond the screening area. All children who come to us and need to be placed elsewhere are required to get a physical examination to assure they do not carry any communicable diseases, and to document any injuries they may have received. The Public Health Department has contracted with us to provide this nursing service."

"Opposite the nurse's station is a small office for our law enforcement officer. He or she rarely sits in here. Mostly they stay in the reception area to assure all remains as quiet as possible. You know removal of children, when it happens, can cause people to become quite volatile. We are grateful for their presence. Remind me to tell you the story of when we were given police security on a full time basis. It was an interesting event."

"Let's see, supply cabinets, restrooms, nurse, police, visitation and meeting rooms, clerical area, oh yes, we also have a small kitchen. It's around this corner. Sink and stove, a water cooler and some vending machines. The child welfare caseworkers who go into the field have their offices down the other hallway. Well, there you have it, the grand tour! Oh yeah, the second floor holds all of the offices for the people who work during the day shift, except for screening. They are alongside us on the first floor."

Ben took in the environment. These were certainly anything but lavish accommodations. Actually they provided the bare minimum. He noticed some water stains on the ceiling and pointed them out to Carrie.

"The water stains," Carrie responded, "are a result of the roof leaking when it rains. Actually the water drips out of the overhead lights. We've reported it to our administration, and they swear there is nothing unsafe about it, however, it's frightening when you actually see it happen. I guess if we had better conditions the taxpayers would be upset about the money being spent on that rather than the children."

After they settled back into their office, Carrie explained the telephone system. "What you should probably do first is listen in on the conversations so you can begin to get a feel for what we do in screening. Any questions?"

"Can't think of any, but I'm sure they'll come with time."

"Alright, time to get started." Carrie sat in her chair and punched the button in on the telephone to take the next call. Ben followed suit as he was instructed.

"Hello, Children Services, this is Carrie Singer. How may I help you?"

The caller responded. "I'm not sure if I should be calling you or not," came an elderly voice.

"Okay, why don't you tell me what's concerning you?"

"My grandson has been diagnosed as having hyperactivity. He has been prescribed Ritalin; however my daughter and son-in-law refuse to give it to him. They say they don't like the effects of it for him."

"Alright, what would you like to see happen?" Carrie inquired.

"Well, I believe if a doctor says you should take a medicine, then you should. After all, they are the doctors. They should know best, shouldn't they?"

"Can you tell me why the doctor prescribed the medicine for your grandson?" Carrie pursued.

"Well, my daughter said she was receiving calls from his teacher requesting they get him the medicine, because he is easily distracted in the classroom. And they did. But they stopped giving it to him. They said it made him zombie like."

"I see," said Carrie. "In a situation such as yours, child welfare can do very little, I'm afraid. Unless we receive a doctor's statement or concern stating this medicine is critically vital to his overall health and well being, there is very little we can do."

"But his teacher said it really helps him at school," the caller persisted.

"I understand. ADHD conditions often contribute to classroom distractions for the teacher as well as the children. However, there is nothing in our legal code requiring a parent to give a child this medicine for behavior management issues. I'm afraid, absent any other concern; this isn't a situation in which Children Services can effectively intervene. Your best option is to discuss your overall concerns with his parents."

"Oh, believe me, I've tried. But they don't seem to care. They keep telling me to mind my own business. And I keep telling them my grandson is my business, isn't he? I don't know what else to do. I don't want to see him do poorly in school. He's only seven years old. I was hoping you would be able to talk some sense into them."

Carrie sighed. These calls were tough. She understood both sides of this argument. But she had no choice. "Unfortunately, at this time we won't be able to approach your family, unless we hear from a physician. I'm sorry," Carrie said with a clear note of compassion.

"Well," the grandmother continued, "at least I tried. Thank you for your time."

"You're welcome." Carrie place the phone back down on the receiver and turned to Ben. "There you have it! That's what we do all shift long. You never know what person or concern is going to be presented each time you pick up this phone. It's like the lottery. Some calls go well, others don't. This caller for example, was polite and disappointed but not challenging of us. Another person may have heard we couldn't respond, and then would've proceeded to release a spew of venomous words about how ineffective the agency is. What most people don't understand is we are guided by our state laws, policies and procedures. We can't be everything to all people. That's what it seems like many of them want, but it isn't possible. Listen to me prattle on," Carrie ended as she shifted uncomfortably in her chair.

"I love listening to you," Ben inserted. "You've such a melodic voice. Its tone has the ability to put people at ease immediately."

Carrie laughed. "You say that now, but wait. My voice certainly doesn't have that effect on everyone. There are plenty of callers who would challenge the validity of your statement." And please don't say you love anything about me, Carrie silently wished.

"Well, I love your voice. You have me mesmerized," Ben smiled.

Carrie decided to take the bull by the horns right then and there. She had to because, otherwise, she could see Ben might suck her right into him and it wasn't going to happen. "Ben, if I didn't know better, I would think you're flirting with me."

"Guilty!" Ben unabashedly retorted and then continued. "Carrie I'm sorry, I don't mean to make you uncomfortable. Trust me, I've sensed from the first moment we met you clearly do not want anything to do with me. It feels like you've avoided me as much as you can. Really, I want to be your friend. Do you think we could start over?"

Carrie couldn't believe what she was hearing. Yes, I was flirting with you! Oh, why did he have to be married? She, also, didn't realize how she must have projected a stronger energy than she calculated in avoiding him. He was aware. She avoided him because she had to, not because she wanted to. Could she manage to be his friend? It would be tough given the enormity of magnetism between them, but given the circumstances the situation called for her to accept him into her world. Reluctantly she acknowledged to herself there are some things she could not control. This was one of them. True to herself, she made the best of each moment. "It's a deal," she said, and clapped her hands together. Their friendship began.

As the evening progressed, there was a lull with in-coming calls. Carrie would use these moments to complete writing up her referrals. She would get backed up if the phones rang constantly, not leaving enough time to finish the paperwork. Ben offered to help her with one of them. She gladly relinquished writing one. It gave Ben a chance to practice capturing all of the details on paper. "This isn't as easy as I anticipated it would be," Ben announced. "I can see how this job could wear one down after a while. Especially if calls continue to come in at the fast pace they have been coming in this evening."

"It's important for you to remember one of your roles in this position," Carrie offered, "is you're a critical public relations person for this agency. You're likely the first person our callers interface with, and the first impression we give them will likely determine how they characterize us in the future. It gets really tough to stay professional all of the time, especially with all of the different kinds of callers we have: disgruntled callers, callers with a specific agenda other than child safety, drunk or drugged out callers, callers with anger issues and you become the convenient person to dump it on, callers with mental health concerns, who really don't have a foot squarely in reality, callers who use this agency and call in false referrals to cause trouble for someone they have an issue with, callers who want to share vital information but are afraid to and you have to pry it out of them. Patience, I find, is critical. I try to remember each and every one of these callers is hurting in some way, either for a child or for themselves. I find some of the toughest calls come from other professionals who have no problem letting us know they do not appreciate our response to situations."

"Really," Ben said as he arched his eyebrows. "How so? Can you give me an example?"

Carrie began, "Without naming names, many teachers feel unless we remove a child from their parents, we've done nothing. They'll often remark they don't know why they are mandated to call us about situations, when we will do nothing to change the child's living situation. What they don't understand is removal of children from their home should be our last action, only after all of the other interventions we offer can't or won't work. They really don't understand the trauma children experience due to a removal. They think placing a child into a "nice" home is all they need. One teacher in particular always gives us her take on our ineffective services each and every time she calls. On the other hand, if you ask this same person if she's contacted the parent with her concerns, she acts aghast we would suggest she should try to interface with them. It really is sad. And it isn't only teachers who feel this way. We get it from medical professionals as well. You learn it's impossible to be all things to all people. Sometimes it's hard for me to stay professionally nice to them."

"I can't imagine any of this gives you difficulty. You seem to do it with such ease," Ben said, "really! I'm being sincere."

"Thanks," Carrie replied as she let a small smile creep out.

"On a different note," Ben continued, "you said I should remind you to tell me about how police security was established in this building."

Carrie let out a small laugh. "Well, it's a funny story. I mean the situation was anything but humorous, but you'll come to learn child welfare workers have a different kind of humor. If we can't laugh about some of our atrocities, we would go insane. The "normal" person may find some of our humor is anything but funny. And they are right. Except when we laugh, we understand the context. The situations are horrendous, but that's what sometimes makes them funnier. We never make light of the people, only their choices. Police officers understand this humor. It's kind of like a fraternal understanding of ludicrous insane circumstances."

"Okay, what happened?"

"Well, we've a supervisor here who's in her mid-fifties, never has been married, and has led a rather sheltered life. She actually never was a child welfare worker on the street. She was hired in from another state, Kentucky or Tennessee I think, and I'm not sure what all of her background is. I know she's quite religious, Baptist I think. Anyways it's important for you to imagine her demeanor to understand why this is funny."

"It doesn't help her first name is Prudence. She has good intentions. She's a good person, but I feel she's quite fearful of many things. I can't imagine why she came to child welfare, except her heart probably wanted to save children. It takes a certain kind of toughness to be a child welfare worker. She doesn't have toughness when she actually has to interface with our clients. I don't mean to diminish her. She's good at assessing from a distance with second hand information given to her by her workers. She's not good at handling the clients herself."

Ben's interest was piqued, "Okay."

"The father of this eleven year old girl was asked to come in to discuss a referral we had suggesting he was sexually inappropriate with his daughter. His ex-wife, with whom he had a strained relationship, called in the concern. The assigned worker wasn't in the office when he arrived. Prudence, as the supervisor, had to conduct the interview. He was angry about the entire situation, completely maintaining his innocence. He arrived here about 4:45. We lock our agency doors at 6:00. Once they are locked you need a key to unlock them as they are double key locked doors, no flip lock on the inside."

"Gotchya," Ben said.

"Well, Prudence wasn't done talking to this man, but this man was done talking to Prudence. He wanted to leave. Prudence refused to unlock the door for him so he could exit. She felt if she talked to him a little longer, she would get him to admit to his actions or something. She was blindly unaware or ignored all of the signs of his increasing agitation. He asked three times for her to unlock the door. She refused. He said something to the effect he refused to be her hostage in this building. That's when he went ballistic."

"I don't know if you noticed or not, but our reception area is very inexpensively built. The reception desk wall and counter are made out of plywood and cheap paneling. We used to have glass windows along the one side hallway leading to the reception area. This man, after his third denied demand to be let out of the building, grabbed the receptionist counter and literally tore it down. Needless to say he spewed a slew of profanities during this tirade. The receptionist quickly left the area, as did Prudence. He proceeded to take the two typewriters at the desk and throw them through the hallway windows, shattering glass which flew everywhere. He screamed at the top of his lungs he would be no one's prisoner. Then his eye caught sight of a large fire extinguisher. He took the extinguisher and let its contents loose all over the reception area. Then he heaved the fire extinguisher through the front picture window and it landed on the sidewalk outside. It happened a police cruiser was passing by when they noticed the extinguisher taking a flying leap through the window and their curiosity was raised. The officers couldn't believe what they saw. What were the chances a cruiser would've passed by at that precise moment? It all felt unreal, kind of like you were watching a movie, a dark comedy. The man was arrested."

"That's quite a story," Ben said as he shook his head. "Essentially this man was arrested because Prudence refused to let him out?"

"Well sort of. He did destroy the place. But you're right. Prudence had no right to deny him exit from the building. If she opened the door none of it would've happened. But that isn't the end of the story. After the police left with the client, the executive director, who was called over to the building, went to see how Prudence was doing. She was surprised to see him and asked him to what could she attribute the honor of his presence. He was perplexed. How could she not know why he was there? The bottom line is she had no memory of what happened. When she went to the reception area to view the damage, she was amazed and asked in her slightly southern tone, whatever happened here? She embarked upon a total case of temporary amnesia. She really had no conscious idea about what her role was in the event. Administration took her to the local mental health center for an assessment. She was told to take a week off, and eventually her mind might remember. If she did remember, she never acknowledged it!"

"That's kind of how it goes around here. Never a dull moment. Each day brings new surprises and situations. If you tried to make them up you couldn't. Real life is far more creative than what we can imagine. I could go on and on with stories about unbelievable human behavior, and I wouldn't be offended if you didn't believe me. In fact, I would be surprised if you did. Most people don't believe some things I've personally seen really happen. They say I'm spoofing them. I wish I were. It truly is sad, but often there is enough twist to situations it makes you laugh. Otherwise you would cry." Carrie's eyes became distant as if she were remotely lost in memories. "Well, enough of that, got to get back to those phones. I hear them ringing again."

As the evening wore on, Carrie and Ben were engrossed in responding to the endless calls. At shift's end, Ben checked back in with Tanner, and Carrie headed straight for her car. She moved slowly her energy slipping away quickly. Her body wasn't tired but her brain was. It was a draining night. She was grateful she was too tired to think. Her mind was focused on her bed and getting into it.

***

As Carrie reflected back upon her life several special memories came to her mind. It was as if she was fast forwarding through her life. In a strange way, she was thoroughly enjoying the reverie.

She thought of Ben again, and was saddened her life circumstances didn't allow her to maintain an active friendship with him throughout the years. They became best of friends their first year in graduate school. Neither of them spoke of or acknowledged their growing attraction for one another. Carrie decidedly shelved all such thoughts in some secured and locked corner of her brain, and then threw the key away. She handled many of life's cruel ironies by forgetting about them. She knew she never could really forget, but she was damned good at pretending she could. Although her conscious mind was an expert in this exercise, her unconscious mind wasn't. But there was one time, one time even her conscious mind would never forget.

It was near the end of their first year of graduate school. Carrie came to enjoy Ben's presence at work those two days. She knew other staff members talked about them behind her back, mostly untrue gossip. They could see what she denied. The electrical bond between them was extremely evident. They easily could finish each other's sentences and laughed freely and often. In Carrie's world, there was no place for her and Ben to be anything but friends.

Ben explained to Carrie he and his wife were high school sweethearts. As fate would have it, Jane became pregnant the night of their senior prom. He did the honorable action and married her. Their marriage wasn't a bed of roses, but they managed. Their love for their daughter, Alexis, was unquestioned. When Ben spoke of Alexis his eyes beamed with pride and joy. She was his light and his heart. He and Jane, on the other hand, respected one another but as they matured their youthful exuberant love for one another faded. Their goals in life took a fork in the road as well. Jane was about achieving professional success as measured by the amount in a paycheck. She graduated with a PhD. in genetic engineering, the year before Ben started graduate school. She was making a rather decent income, decadent by social work standards. Ben, on the other hand, cared less about money and cared more about the well being of his spirit and the well being of others. Jane didn't understand. They stayed together not to disrupt Alexis's life. Ben and Jane never argued. They simply led uniquely different lives.

On this one particular evening, the universe dealt Carrie and Ben a small taste of a delicious moment. A large delivery truck hit the electrical pole nearest their office and caused the electricity as well as the phones to go out. Their office had no windows or any windows close by to shed any ambient light into their office, which caused the small space to be pitch black. It was similar to being deep inside Mammoth Cave. They couldn't see their hands two inches from their face. The agency had no back-up generators, it was too costly. The only option, other than sitting in total darkness, was to find your way toward the front of the building and hope to gain some small stream of light from the night lamp posts outside, if they were working.

"What happens now?" Ben inquired.

"We've not any choice. We need to find our way to the front of the building," Carrie instructed.

They each stood up relying upon their memory to successfully walk through their office doorway. Carrie walked directly into Ben's chest. Then it happened. "Sorry," Carrie stuttered and took a step to back away leaving enough lapse time, perhaps a half of a second, for Ben to calmly, serenely, and lovingly wrap his arms around Carrie. Then it all flooded in and usurped her entire body, all of those repressed emotions. Except this time, these weren't the same emotions she originally felt for Ben upon their initial acquaintance. No, these feelings had time to grow quietly and deepen immeasurably. Carrie became lightheaded instantly.

"I'm not sorry," Ben whispered in a low hypnotizing voice. His breath in her ear warmed her more. Her body instinctively pressed closer into his chest. Her mind was racing, tumbling through the vast number of reasons why she should push herself away. She was like a deer frozen with impending disaster. Ben placed his left hand under her chin and tilted her face up towards him, never letting his right hand leave her back.

"Ben, we shouldn't," was all she could muster. As his lips met hers, her entire body went into sexual overdrive. Her hormones cued every one of her nerve endings to resonate and vibrate and dance for joy. Denial was conquered. It was let out of Pandora's Box, if only for this moment. It was the sweetest, most delicious kiss she knew, wrapped in a fragile tenderness. She abandoned everything she knew to be appropriate in the moment. Carrie became lost in the kiss and yearned for it to never end. Time suspended, at least for them.

"Carrie, Ben, are you still in here?" They heard Tanner's voice as he neared their office. Then they saw the circular light of the approaching flashlight. "You need to come to the front area until the electricity comes back on. I dragged out an old camping lantern I brought into the office after the last time we lost electricity. At least it gives out plenty of light. Come on and follow me."

And that was the end of it, one fleeting, glorious and unabashed moment never to be repeated again, but to be allowed to dwell in their memories as a remembrance of a perfect moment, a perfect satisfaction, a perfect kiss. They never spoke of it, but they both knew it was a bonding memory they would never forget.

chapter 21

1978

Spring was in full bloom with cherry blossoms, dogwood blossoms, apple blossoms, and every other kind of blossom scenting the air with fragrant perfumes to tickle the nose. As their petals dropped, the school year was closing. Carrie and Sylvia met at the student union to consult with one another regarding the last assignment of their field placement. Each was to write a composition detailing one aspect of their internship with the Psychiatric Hospital. Carrie's paper reflected ethical issues in the care of the mentally ill. Sylvia's paper outlined the continuum of care required for the population of the mentally challenged.

"As I was piecing together this composition, I was compelled to reflect back to something you said to me our first day at the hospital," Sylvia began. "Do you remember saying you were fine not to see Cell 16 during our first tour of the facility and I was disappointed not to see it? Well, I suspect you had a good idea what Cell 16 was all about, didn't you?"

"Not really," Carrie answered. "But I imagined it was to be the worst of the worst. As the cell numbers progressed higher, it seemed the patients' conditions were more challenging. I only guesstimated Cell 16 housed beleaguered souls."

"Well you were absolutely right. But why am I not surprised?" giggled Sylvia. "I haven't been able to stop thinking about the condition of those poor people. Do you have any suggestions how I might capture their predicament accurately in my paper? You've always been good at capsulizing situations."

"It's a tough one. I'm still struggling incorporating that area in my paper regarding the ethical issues around their daily care. There has got to be a better way. I mean building enclosed wooden six by six foot cells with only one tiny window to peer out of from within Cell 16 itself was a shock. They looked like something from the thirteenth century; something you would see in an old horror movie, except it wasn't a movie."

"Yeah," Sylvia mournfully replied. "I still can't get Melina out of my mind. She's only twenty-three and she's been cooped up since the age of sixteen in that hospital cell! There has to be a way to get through to her."

"I'm not sure," Carrie said thoughtfully. Melina was tagged as a feral child. She was found locked in the attic of her grandmother's house at the time of her grandmother's death. It was amazing anyone found her at all. The well worn trail in the upstairs hallway stopped midway between rooms and under the attic opening suggesting someone went to the attic frequently, especially with a step ladder leaning against the hallway wall. When a police officer entered the attic, Melina bit his hand before he could even pop his head through the opening. She had no language, was filthy, and desperately frightened. The attic was covered with fecal droppings. There were two dog dishes, one filled with dog food and the other contained water. This appeared to be the daily diet her grandmother gave to her. How she came to be was anyone's guess. Perhaps she was a product of incest as she had some of the physical markers to indicate such. She undoubtedly was stowed away from public view all of her life. Melina was fully unsocialized. She had a wild cast in her eyes which frightened people. She had no need for clothes and wouldn't keep them on. She made guttural sounds. Staff would hose her down through the tiny window to keep some semblance of cleanliness about her. She was never taken outside. Staff said they heavily tranquilized her anytime someone entered her cell, or they would be immediately attacked. Staff actually wore heavy protective coveralls when they entered her personal space to keep themselves safe from her biting and clawing. She was a tormented soul. Thankfully she was in a category of her own. No other patient in Cell 16 could match her aggressiveness or challenges. That was a good thing.

"I've tried to write the truth about her," Sylvia continued, "but it sounds like science fiction. I don't think anyone would believe this truth. I wouldn't have unless I saw it with my own eyes."

"I know what you mean," Carrie added as she pushed back from the table and stretched a bit. She hung her head low. "I haven't been able to stop thinking about her myself. She's awakened me from my dreams when

I try to sleep. I agree with you, there has got to be a better way to care for her. She seems lost to reality, or perhaps her reality has been such any one of us may have reacted as she has in the same circumstances. I can't imagine how horrible a life she had. It does make me thankful for my life. When I find myself complaining about anything, she comes to mind and I shut my mouth and my heart hurts for her."

"You, too," Sylvia nodded in commiseration. "Like me. Sometimes I can't sleep at all when she comes to mind. It's hard to walk away from her. But I don't know if I have the kind of strength one needs to stand and fight for her. Know what I mean?"

"Yes, I do. It doesn't seem like anyone does. She's truly one of society's throw away children. If only she was discovered sooner, when she was younger, perhaps there could have been some hope for her."

"Carrie, I didn't mean to get you down. It's such an upsetting situation. At least you're on the front lines trying to save children from such circumstances. I now know it takes a special kind of spirit to do the kind of child welfare work you do. Melina has opened my eyes to that."

"You give me too much credit, Sylvia, but thanks."

"I mean it Carrie! How you've handled all you've seen amazes me. I know I'm not cut out for any of this. I've been thinking about trying to get a teaching position in a college social work program. At least it feels safer. And I love the collegiate environment."

Carrie smiled at Sylvia. "You would make a great teacher. I know because you have heart, you do care for all of the right reasons. We can't all be on the front lines. Some of us need to be involved in teaching others. If it resonates with you, then that's what you should do, really!"

"Tell me what field placement type did you select for next year?" Carrie inquired.

"I was glad we were allowed to have a greater say in our placement the second year," Sylvia began. I signed up to be with the senior citizens, a nursing home. It involves some public relations. How about you?"

"I chose school social work. Thought I might see what it was like to work with children from a different perspective. Besides, working at Children Services doesn't give one the opportunity to really work closely with children as you might expect. Rather, you work mostly with their parents. I'd like to spend some more time with children, but I'm likely to discover that may be a misconception as well," Carrie laughed. "Oh well, one more year! Can you believe it?"

"No, this year went fast. I'm going to miss you Carrie. I really have enjoyed our time together," Sylvia said as she reached out and squeezed Carrie's hand.

"Trust me, Sylvia, the feeling is mutual. Besides this won't be the end of our friendship. Because the year is over doesn't mean we have to be done. At least, I hope not."

chapter 22

Carrie thought about taking a vacation day away from work this evening. She had to finish her paper on ethics and wrap up for the school year's end. She had a lot to do. She hardly believed her first year of graduate school would soon be over. But the thought of skipping out on Ben's last night at the agency seemed unbearable. She came to treasure his friendship. He actively challenged her thoughts throughout the year. He raised her awareness of the macro- environment of child welfare. His interest lay in creating foundational policies advancing worker's abilities to intervene more efficiently and adeptly in order to achieve better outcomes for the children they served. He didn't have the patience or the stamina to work day after day with the clients and their overwhelming neediness. Carrie remembered the pivotal evening leaving no doubt in Ben's mind about his chosen path. It was a curiously busy night with three different situations, all emanating a higher intensity than usual.

The agency received a request to provide training to a private Christian school regarding the mandated reporter law. Many different professionals are required to report what they perceive to be child maltreatment. It was part of the state's legal code. This law was often misinterpreted by different systems and consequently the state also required them to receive training yearly regarding how to implement it. On May 11, Tanner asked Carrie and Ben to provide the training in a school asking for an early evening class. Carrie often presented these throughout the years and was happy to get out from behind the desk. This time, though, it was Ben who would lead the training. She was the back up. It was part of his educational contract with the agency – to do some public relations, and this would fit the bill.

Ben drove his green Volkswagen Bug as Carrie navigated for him. Carrie rarely needed a map. She learned every side street and alley in the city. It was a job side benefit they didn't mention when they hired her. They pulled into the church's brick complex flashing a bright neon digital sign noting the sermon's title for the day: *Cast your sin out and be healed!* They found the visitors parking section. As they walked toward the school's entrance, they noted another smaller parking lot nearer the facility. It was filled with Mercedes, Porsche and BMW cars guarded by a twelve foot high iron fence with pointed ribs. A large cross tilted diagonally between the remote controlled sliding gates. It sent a shiver through Carrie as she noted the gothic feel. This church and school had a following of approximately five thousand people. Money was apparently no problem.

Once inside the school area, it felt more like a prison. Cameras were evident along each hallway. Uniformed guards appearing mafia like, with guns in their holsters, escorted you in and out, even to the bathroom. Carrie remembered experiencing a creepy feeling and was glad Ben accompanied her. It was different from the feeling she would have when working in the community, even in the dangerous areas. It was quite unsettling, perhaps because this atmosphere was unexpected.

Fifty staff members were seated in the large classroom and a podium was placed in front of the audience. Carrie busied herself setting up the slide projector, while Ben began the program. Ben's melodious voice kept their rapt attention. It was low and exuded professional confidence. Carrie was happy to allow Ben to take the reins. She sat back and admired his easiness with people. She realized the school year would quickly come to a close and she was saddened her time with Ben would soon be over. She came to look forward to their evenings together, more than she was willing to admit to herself at the time. They became good friends, complementing one another in perfect synchronicity. Not only did their respect for one another grow, but also their feelings of genuine care and love for one another. Carrie, however, vowed never to let the boundaries required in this relationship to be breeched again after the fleeting caress and kiss they had in the darkness. It made being only friends challenging at times for Carrie. She could admit to herself if he wasn't married, he would be her perfect soul mate. But married men didn't equal soul mate possibilities in her world. She would miss him terribly. But life didn't always give you what you wanted.

"Carrie, can you please clarify the mandated reporter law for the group?" Ben requested jarring her out of her reverie. "How sure does the reporter need to be about potential maltreatment before they call it in?"

With polished perfection Carrie stood and responded. "The law doesn't require a reporter to have specific knowledge maltreatment is actually happening. The mandated reporter needs only their own personal suspicion based upon what they have seen or heard."

One of the teachers raised her hand. "It was my understanding we needed proof of maltreatment when we call. Are you stating that isn't the case?"

"Yes, it isn't the case. You only need to have a reasonable relevant suspicion. In fact, the agency would prefer mandated reporters not begin their own investigation into the validity of their concerns. That's the role of the caseworker, to determine if maltreatment exist or not."

Another hand shot up for another question. "Could you define for me a relevant suspicion?"

"As soon as you begin to think or wonder if a child is being maltreated, you have a suspicion. That's enough reason to make a call to our agency."

"Are you saying you do not want us to do any follow up before we call to assure a child has been maltreated?"

"If you have a suspicion that's all you need. Sometimes mandated reporters interpret their role to be an investigator and unwittingly they can botch an investigation. It's up to the caseworker to assess if a child is at risk or has been injured by the maltreatment. Then it's their role to prevent the child from enduring it again. It's up to the police to investigate for criminality in child abuse or neglect. They, and they alone, arrest perpetrators and refer them for prosecution. When teachers and other professionals attempt to conduct their own investigation to determine if their suspicions are correct before calling Children Services or the police, it can create difficulties in an investigation."

"Many times it will alert the family members to the concern and a potential perpetrator may take steps to hide evidence or concoct a lie to cover up. Often he or she may involve the child in the cover up as well. If it goes badly, I've known children to be further hurt because they were unable to lie well enough and the cover is blown. We would like to avoid that possibility as we want to stop the abuse if it's happening. We don't want to give any advantage to alleged perpetrators. I think you can all understand why. Having said all of that, the law states all you need is a suspicion to report, not proof."

A man in the back raised his hand. "Our school's policy is to clear all referrals through our principal before we call. If the principal believes the call is unnecessary, we are told to not proceed."

"The law also doesn't require you to have the permission of your school's principal or superintendant to make the call. I know many educational systems have this as a policy. Some policies state only the principal will call Children Services. This isn't in keeping with the essence of the law or its mandate. When a call is made to the agency, the screener will want to talk to the person who has the most direct first hand information about the concern. It's usually not the principal. When principals place the call, the screener will inevitably still need to talk to the professional with the original concern. The law is clear it wants the person with the suspicion to call. Remember, only suspicion, no proof is needed."

Another hand quickly rose up. "I want to clarify your last point. Are you clearly stating mandated reporters have a personal responsibility to make the call? What if our principal says not to call?"

"The law doesn't require a mandated reporter to get a prior clearance from their management level to make the call. The law doesn't want non-child welfare professionals to screen out any potential calls. The law clearly states the mandated reporter, who has the concern, directly call the agency."

"What you're saying is we should call, even if our principal doesn't agree with us?"

"Yes. The law doesn't require your principal's agreement."

"Okay," Ben continued, "thank you Carrie. Any other questions?"

"Yes, I have one," a meek voice began. "Can we be sued by a family member if we call in a referral and no maltreatment is found, even though we suspected the children were being abused?"

Ben glanced over at Carrie as he began to answer. "As long as you make a good faith referral, you won't be liable. It's only if you willingly and wantonly make a referral you know is false, can you be liable. Of course when it comes to being sued, as you know in our society anyone can sue anybody for anything. However, the chances of their law suit being sustained are unlikely unless they have proof you made the referral for pure harassment purposes."

Carrie slid her chair back and stood up once again. "For your information, there have never been any successful law suits against a mandated reporter in this state."

"Okay, thank you Carrie," Ben offered. "Are there any other questions?" No one raised their hand. Ben thanked the group for the opportunity to address them. He and Carrie began to pack up their belongings. One of the teachers approached them.

"I didn't want to bring this up in front of the entire group," she began, "but we have a female student here who has been telling us for the past two years her step-father has been sexually abusing her. We've discussed her situation in staff meetings and the principal has advised us to, well, stand down. He said she's a known liar and she's probably lying about this as well. He even took it to the reverend for his advice, and well, it doesn't seem right. Now hearing what you've said, I don't think I can go home at night and sleep in peace again, unless I report it."

"Oh my goodness," Carrie responded. "I'm glad you came forward. What has she said that has you concerned?"

"Well, I'm not the one she approached, but I've been part of the discussion group when the teacher brought it up. I think she said Kelly, that's the girl's name, said her step-father started showering with her when she was twelve. She's fourteen now. Her mother works nights and isn't home when it happens. I'm not exactly sure what has happened, but I think he may be having sex with her by now. He is a deacon in this church and he is quite wealthy. He gives a lot of money to the church, so no one wants to rock the boat. Kelly does lie a lot, but I'm not sure this is a lie."

Carrie's stomach started to churn. It upset her when allegedly good people did nothing to keep children safe. After gathering all the information she needed, Carrie reassured the teacher an investigation would begin within the next twenty-four hours.

Driving back to the agency Ben said to Carrie, "How can you do this?"

"Do what?"

"Do this, all of this. Stay calm. Stay composed. See this stuff every day, day in and day out. All I wanted to do was go find the principal and the reverend and beat the living crap out of them. What right did they have, not to look into the poor girl's situation? Such arrogance. It smacked of collusion to me!"

"Whatever do you mean by collusion?" Carrie inquired. "The teacher didn't suggest the principal and reverend were in on the abuse."

"No, she didn't. But their lack of actions was no better than if they were part of it. Didn't she say he was a big contributor to the church? It wouldn't surprise me if the reverend and the principal might have been more concerned about an income source than about the child. Given the elaborateness of the facilities here, you know it has taken large sums of money to build this empire. Well, it was quite apparent to me they weren't concerned about Kelly. I'll tell you Carrie. I couldn't do this job and keep any professionalism about me. I don't know how you can see this stuff over and over and over and not go literally crazy."

"I don't know," Carrie squirmed a bit, "I'm probably a bit crazy. But someone has to do it."

"Well better you, than me, is all I can say."

***

Ben and Carrie stopped by Tanner's office to update him on their presentation as well as give them the referral regarding Kelly to process it to an investigator. "It has been busier than usual this evening. I'm glad you guys are back. We are going to need your help. The waiting room is full of kids the police have brought to us. The police conducted several drug raids this evening, many arrests, leaving us with many children to figure out what to do with. Staff has collected what information they could find regarding relatives and other placement possibilities. Would you mind following up with some of the relatives to assess if they can care for them? I think we've about eleven kids in all, from babies to adolescents. It's a madhouse in the holding area," Tanner noted.

"Sure, no problem," Carrie and Ben said in unison. Tanner gave them the folders with the contact information for the relatives and the two proceeded back to their office. The hallway rang with boisterous chatter from the holding area and interview rooms. The case aide had four children in the kitchen, feeding them some sandwiches and juice. Another worker was cleaning a baby in the restroom. As the teens languidly gazed at the television's droning, the adolescent area sported arms and legs sprawled all over the institutional heavy duty plastic furniture.

Ben and Carrie settled back into their office to begin to sort out relative possibilities. Suddenly Ben and Carrie overheard, "Now you don't want to do that. Calm down and hand me the gun." Ben and Carrie looked at each other and mouthed silently to each other, hand me the gun! Ben sprang up and peered into the hallway. He couldn't believe what he was seeing. A young girl, about eleven years old, was holding a gun and pointing it at the middle-aged overweight woman who was the assigned sheriff on security duty for the agency this evening. The regularly assigned officer called off ill, and this officer was his replacement. It was her first night at the agency. The child was among the bunch of children eating in the kitchen. Having finished her sandwich, the case aide asked her to return to the waiting area. The police officer was standing in the hallway with her back to the young girl as she approached. The officer didn't realize the child was behind her. The girl pulled the gun from the officer's holster and cocked it, and was now threatening to shoot the police woman! Officer Culpepper was visibly shaken and lost all color in her face.

"I always wanted to shoot me a police officer," announced Sonya, the young girl, "like you shot and killed my daddy. And he didn't do nothin' wrong."

Officer Culpepper lost all of her composure. She was lost for words. "You don't want to do that, you don't want to do that, you don't want to do that," was all she could muster.

"Copper lady, you've no idea what I want to do. I think I'll give you the same chance you gave my daddy. And that ain't much of one." Sonya's hand began to shake, but she remained steadfastly focused upon her target. "Yep, that's what I'm going to do, get me a cop. It's only fair, don't you think?"

Carrie popped her head under Ben's arm and took in what was happening. She and Ben were behind Sonya observing the standoff. Carrie whispered, "I'll call the police."

Ben retorted, "There isn't enough time for that!" Ben disappeared out of the office in a flash, quickly and quietly approached Sonya and leapt upon her back with a short flying leap, knocking her down to the floor with Ben on top of her. The gun fell out of Sonya's hand and Ben grabbed it. By then, Tanner arrived and quickly escorted Sonya out of the area, putting her into one of the visitation rooms where she could be restrained.

Carrie rushed to Officer Culpepper, who was in an apparent crisis. She noted the officer peed in her pants and took her to the restroom so she could regain her composure and clean up.

Tanner called the Sheriff's office to report the critical incident. Another officer replaced Officer Culpepper as she was taken to the local mental health clinic for an assessment of her well being. Carrie remembered they never saw Officer Culpepper again.

Ben was the night's hero, although there was consternation about his impulsive actions. Carrie realized Ben always made her feel safer.

***

It was ten o'clock and the office pandemonium calmed. Many of the children were placed with relatives or foster homes. All were taking deep sighs of relief. Tanner called Carrie over the telephone's intercom. "Carrie, we have a man who has come in who says he wants to report a sexual abuse. Would you mind interviewing him?"

"No problem, what's his name?"

"Mr. Burkey."

"Okay. I'll be out in a minute."

"You may want to have Ben sit in on this one, too."

"Gotcha."

"You ready for another one, Superman?" Carrie giggled as she raised an eyebrow Ben's way.

"Why not, the third time is a charm they say."

"We can hope," Carrie said as she placed her hands in a prayerful position.

Carrie and Ben entered the small fake wood paneled interviewing room the receptionist asked Mr. Burkey to wait in. Carrie first noticed how diminutive he appeared to be, quite short in stature and extremely thin. His face was littered with beard stubble, his skin appeared sallow, and he had many broken veins in his enlarged nose. Carrie would've guessed him to be an alcoholic from his looks.

Following brief introductions, Carrie began, "Mr. Burkey, I've been advised you came here this evening to report a sexual abuse. Is that correct?"

"Yes," he replied. He lifted his left hand to his face and began to stroke his cheeks down toward his chin. Carrie noticed his hand slightly shook. She wondered if her original thought about alcoholism was accurate, or if he was nervous.

"Well, why don't you tell me in your own words about your concern," Carrie prompted.

"I'm not sure where to begin," Mr. Burkey noted.

Carrie realized he would need more structure to tell his story. "Why don't you start by telling me the name of the child you're concerned about?"

"It's my daughter, Suzanne," he mumbled.

"I see," said Carrie. "I know this can be difficult to talk about, especially if something of a sexual nature has happened to your own daughter. Why don't you try to tell me what you know using your own words."

Mr. Burkey remained silent, moving his mouth as if he was going to speak, but no sound emitted. Carrie noticed he was swallowing often as his prominently pointed Adam's apple was pointedly moving up and down along his throat. Carrie realized his long skinny neck reminded her of a turkey. Mr. Burkey, the turkey, ran through her mind.

Carrie tried again. "I know how hard this must be for you. It's difficult for us to accept our loved ones may have been sexually violated. If this has happened to Suzanne, she's going to need some help to deal with the situation. Additionally, we would like to see whoever did this to Suzanne will no longer have any opportunity for this to happen again. Take your time and tell us what you know, please."

"I . . . . I. . . . . I," was all Mr. Burkey said when he threw his head into his hands which were supported by his elbows resting on his knees. He began to let out a long slow wail, a woebegone cry.

"You what, Mr. Burkey?" Carrie reached out and gently gave him a tissue.

He took a deep breath, lifted his head, and stared directly into Carrie's eyes. "I did it. I did it to Suzanne. And not only to Suzanne, but I did it to my daughter Margaret as well. I fucked them. I fucked them both!"

Carrie noted Ben's breathing became quicker and louder. She turned and looked at him and saw his face was quickly turning a beet red. Oh no, she thought. The last thing I need right now is for Ben to lose it. She reached over and stroked his arm and said, "I've got this one, Ben. It'll be okay."

"Be okay? Are you f-ing serious? Did you not hear what this scum told you! What's okay, Carrie? Tell me what the hell is okay here? Even this Mr. whatever-his-name is knows it's not okay."

Carrie used her steady, but strong and leading voice. "Ben, listen to me. I need you to go to Tanner and alert him to this situation. I'll be fine. Please go, now!" Ben reluctantly stood up and walked toward the door as he gave Mr. Burkey a look unabashedly showing his disgust with him.

With Ben gone, Carrie urged Mr. Burkey to continue. She knew if she didn't get the information right now, their opportunity for clarity may be lost forever. It was rare sexual perpetrators ever admitted their wrong doing and she didn't want to lose this chance. She learned how to put on a non-judgmental face. She knew the sheriff would arrest him before he left the building. He would be dealt with according to the justice system. Inwardly Carrie imagined her hands around his scraggly skinny neck, choking him while beating his head up against the wall. She wasn't impervious to the emotionality of these situations, but she understood the reality of what needed to be done to put this guy away. She stayed focused on understanding the events that happened. It was necessary if she was going to be able to help the victims.

As Carrie interviewed Mr. Burkey, Ben found Tanner in his office to alert him to the situation. Tanner took one look at Ben and was immediately alarmed. Ben's entire body was rigid, his face was steaming. He was gritting his teeth, while pounding his fists on Tanner's desk. "How the hell do you all stay so calm in this stew of degenerates? Do you've any idea what Mr. Burkey wanted to report? He is telling us he has been having sexual relations with his own daughters. He is fucking his own daughters! I can't stand this. I can't take it anymore. First church personnel cover up a child's plea for help because her step-father has been screwing her for over two years and now this man, this pathetic sick man, is having his way with his own daughters! I want to kill him!"

Tanner realized he had two crises unfolding before him, first Mr. Burkey and second, Ben. Tanner assessed quickly. Carrie was safe, and she knew what to do. He would alert the sheriff, who would step in after Carrie finished her interview, taking care of the Burkey situation.

Then there was Ben, who was obviously fragmenting right in front of him. Tanner saw this reaction before. In fact, he was surprised Ben hadn't come to this point earlier in the year. Secondary trauma is what they called it, when continued exposure to maltreatment caused a worker to lose his professionalism and be profoundly and personally impacted by the many traumatic events he would hear of or witness. He understood what Ben was going through. He had been there himself. He also knew Ben would come through it as well. He was strong, and his time left in the field placement was minimal.

Carrie, meanwhile, persisted with Mr. Burkey. She learned Mr. Burkey's wife died when his daughters were sixteen and eight years old. She was ill with cancer for a prolonged period of time before her death. As a result he turned toward his oldest, Margaret, and began to have sexual relations with her when she was fourteen. Although she's now twenty-four years old, they had sex two weeks ago. When Margaret moved out of the house two years ago, he turned to Suzanne when she was fourteen. The cycle was repeating.

Carrie wasn't shocked by these revelations. The dynamics of sexual abuse were convoluted and often difficult to understand. She knew Margaret, as an adult currently, wouldn't be able to be served by the child welfare system. However, Suzanne could and would receive all the help they could provide for her. Hopefully Mr. Burkey would find himself incarcerated. It was never a guarantee that would happen. It would depend upon the victim's ability and willingness to testify against him and to have the stamina to stand up to cross examination. If Mr. Burkey would plead guilty, there would be no need for a trial and he would be incarcerated. This rarely happened, especially when lawyers got involved.

After she finished her interview with Mr. Burkey, the police took over. Carrie quickly went to Tanner's office to check on Ben. "I sent him home," Tanner advised Carrie. "He was pretty shook up. You guys had a pretty rough evening. Are you doing okay?"

"I'm good," Carrie replied, "maybe a little tired. I'm going to finish writing up this interview and then I'll head home. Is Ben alright?"

"Yeah, he'll be okay. You know how it is Carrie. The reality of child maltreatment really hit home with him tonight. He'll come through it. He was more frazzled than usual. I think he has done as well as he has this year because of you. You're a rock. He really admires you, you know. Now get on out of here kiddo," Tanner said appreciatively.

chapter 23

As the daylight hours grew longer, the school year ended. Retrospectively the year was a mixture of different flavors and experiences for Carrie. She was physically tired and glad for the break from school. She grew close to Sylvia and would miss her abounding exuberance and continued ability to be awestruck. Carrie wished she hadn't lost her ability as she had, and marveled in happiness for those who still possessed the trait.

Mr. GQ, Michael, successfully made it through the year without having to drive a client in his car. Lydia's immune system must have improved for she was never sick, even though she was exposed to germs at the Free Clinic. Yes, all ten of their small group survived, and were wiser for their experiences. The ten of them met up at the Mascot Pub, a campus bar and grill, to celebrate the year's end and wish each other well until next September.

Beer abounded, the chatter heightened, giggling and laughter ensued. Carrie was reveling in the moment with the rest of them. She grew fonder of this diverse group than she realized. It felt good. Sylvia brought Howard along, and Richard invited his partner to attend.

"Hey, where's Ben?" Susan yelled out. "He should be here too!"

"He went to pick up his wife. They should be here any minute," Michael announced.

Suddenly Carrie felt like she was catapulted into a fog. Ben was coming with Jane, his wife. She never met Jane and she wasn't sure she wanted to. She was immediately conflicted and angry with herself, and a tad angry with Ben. She knew this was a completely irrational feeling. A surging anger grew within Carrie by the minute. It was rare for her to feel this way, discombobulated and fragmented. Her mind began to race to regain some semblance of emotional control. Carrie would never let anyone see her lose control. It wasn't in her persona. It wasn't how she defined herself.

Why are you bent out of shape, she wondered? It's not like he really means anything to you. He's a friend. Nothing more. He belongs to her. Keep it real, girl. I'm keeping it real. She fought with herself. Yeah, right. Why don't you admit your true feelings? Carrie decided she needed another beer and poured herself another glass from the pitcher sitting on the table.

Susan turned toward Carrie and said, "Carrie, you've met Jane haven't you?"

"No I haven't, not yet," Carrie offered.

"Really! That's quite surprising to me. You're going to love her. She and Ben appear to be perfect for one another," Susan continued.

I bet, thought Carrie. She was aware of her sarcasm but didn't want to acknowledge what it meant. "Then today is my lucky day, isn't it," Carrie retorted.

Susan gave Carrie a strange look of befuddlement. "Well, I guess it is," she responded.

"Oh, look, here they come now!" Susan noted.

Carrie forced herself to glance up at the front door. Immediately she was struck by Jane's beauty, long full thick blond hair, a trim svelte waist, and a dazzling smile. She seemed to be at ease with herself as she allowed Ben to guide her to the table. Carrie had to admit they made a handsome couple. She picked up her beer glass and chugged the remaining two-thirds of its contents.

Eloise, who was sitting next to Carrie, announced she was leaving. Tonight was the Easter Seal Society's fund raising gala and she had to attend. Ben introduced Jane to Eloise as they passed one another. "You're not leaving already, are you?" Ben inquired.

"Sorry, but I have to go. Besides I spared you from having to find another chair. Enjoy your evening. It's nice to meet you Jane," Eloise said as she moved through the front door.

"It's about time you got here," Michael announced. "Late as usual."

"Ah, but better late than never," Ben volleyed. "Jane, this is the group. I think you know Michael, Matt, Richard and Susan. This is Sylvia," Ben continued as he pointed a finger towards her, "and this is Lydia, Vanessa and Carrie."

Carrie pulled another swig of beer into her mouth. She noticed Jane giving her a lingering look or was it her imagination? Jane extended her hand to each of Ben's friends and greeted each one warmly. Carrie reluctantly extended her hand to Jane and noticed Jane had a firm handshake, not a soft limp one. Carrie read a lot into a handshake. She assessed Jane to be self-assured, socially adept, and her own person. She didn't likely kowtow to anyone. Jane reminded her of herself in a small measured way. She wondered what Ben told Jane about her. Suddenly Carrie began to feel uncomfortable, a rare feeling for her. But why? Why was she feeling this way? She didn't do anything wrong. She tried to ignore the feeling and tended once again to her beer.

As Ben and Jane settled in around the table, Jane seated herself next to Carrie in the chair Eloise vacated. Ben sat a few chairs further down on the opposite side of the table.

Jane began, "I'm happy to meet you, Carrie. Ben talks about you all of the time. He said he couldn't have gotten through his field placement as well as he did, if it wasn't for you."

"Ben has given me far too much credit. Ben is brilliant in his own right. But of course, you already know that," Carrie smiled and drank some more beer. "Tell me about yourself? What do you do?"

"Me, there isn't much to tell. I have my PhD. in genetic engineering. Currently I'm working on a research grant to try to improve soybeans' resistance to pest infestation. I'm tackling it from a pheromone perspective so the beans emit odors which would naturally repel the insects. It does involve some gene manipulation, but I think the end result will benefit mankind. I spend many hours in the lab with microscopes and slides. It's pretty boring stuff to people, but I like it."

"I see," said Carrie. "It doesn't concern you at all people consume genetically modified food?"

"No, not really. I can't see a downside," Jane replied as she looked Carrie straight into her eyes.

"I don't know," Carrie continued. "Has there been enough research into the area for us to be utterly sure? How long has the general public been your industry's guinea pigs? I mean you're not even required to inform us we are eating genetically modified foods. Your industry giants have lobbied against such labeling for years now, while they continue to put such foods on the market. It doesn't seem to be right, you know. It feels wrong morally. People should have the right to be fully informed so they can choose what they put into their bodies, don't you think?"

"Ben was right. He described you as an outspoken firecracker. Hey, I like your chutzpah. Not many people are willing to challenge me. Glad to meet you Ms. Carrie Singer." Jane beamed a broad smile at Carrie.

Carrie didn't like the way this conversation was going. She wanted to not have any feelings for Jane, but the truth was she liked this woman. She was a strong, independent bright woman. She wasn't afraid to speak her mind. She easily would take a bull by the horns and not back down. Carrie acknowledged she was impressed by Jane. Here was a woman who had a child at a young age, and still achieved personal goals for herself and her family. It was remarkable. Carrie could see how Ben stepped up as a man and supported his family, even though his circumstances were driven by a lustful moment during his high school senior prom. Carrie didn't want to like Jane, but she did. She could even imagine under different circumstances they may have been good friends. "Nice to meet you too, Jane Randall," Carrie saluted with her beer glass and then drank some more.

Carrie stood up to go to the restroom. Her bladder was urgently calling for some relief. She knew she drank more than her usual, which was one beer, but they were celebrating. Sylvia and Lydia noticed Carrie seemed to wobble a bit as she made her way through the aisle. "Something is up with her," Sylvia whispered to Lydia. "She's acting out of her character."

Carrie seated herself upon the toilet and held her head in her hands, closing her eyes. When she reopened them, the stall door started to spin in front of her. I must be really drunk, she thought. How did I let myself get out of control? It's surely time for me to stop and go home.

When Carrie returned to the table, she didn't bother to sit down. Instead she grabbed her purse and found her car keys. "Hey everyone, I have to leave. It was great seeing all of you. Have a great summer. See you in the fall."

Jane leaned over the table and suggested to Ben perhaps Carrie shouldn't be driving in her current condition. Ben agreed and stood up to stop her.

"Hey Carrie," he called out. "Wait a minute."

"What?" She responded.

"You had a bit to drink. I think it would be best if you waited a while before you drove home. Don't you think?"

"I don't know. I'll be alright. I'm slightly dizzy. That's why I need to get out of here and go home. I want to go to sleep."

"Carrie, please. You're in no condition to drive home," Ben implored.

Carrie stood there and stared at him. She was conflicted. She wanted to melt into his arms, but knew that was impossible. Even drunk, she knew she had to hide her innermost desires. She wanted to get out and go home. Leave all of this behind her. "I want to go home, alright?"

Jane jumped up and joined Ben. "Ben, why don't you drive Carrie home in her car? I'll follow behind and pick you up so we can go home as well. Okay?"

"Sounds like a good plan. What do you think Carrie? Do you trust me to chauffeur you home?"

"Do you really think all of this is necessary?" Carrie questioned.

The entire group, now engaged in this process, all shouted out "yes."

"Okey-dokey," Carrie slurred as she handed her keys to Ben. "I trust you." What I don't trust is myself, she thought.

As Ben headed down the highway, Carrie began to burp. "I'm sorry. Ben, you and Jane just got to the Mascot Pub. You shouldn't have to leave because of me." She burped again. "Sorry."

"It's alright Carrie. It's a short distance and Jane and I can always return to the bar. The important thing is to get you home safe right now." Ben reached out and touched Carrie's thigh in a gesture of caring and concern, giving it a light squeeze before returning his hand to the steering wheel. He apparently had no idea what his mere touch did to stimulate Carrie. She sighed and closed her eyes. She tried not to feel.

She burped again. "Ben, I think I'm going to be sick. Stop the car please."

Ben pulled over to the curb in the nick of time. Carrie swung the door open, leaned over and vomited clear yellow beer. Ben was afraid she might fall out of the car and grabbed her upper arm to help pull her up. Sitting upright in her seat, Carrie was overcome with emotion. She made such a fool of herself. She didn't want to, but she began to cry uncontrollably. She hadn't allowed herself to feel such raw emotion in ages. She didn't even try to stop herself from crying. After a while she didn't even know why she was crying. She couldn't stop. Her mind was racing with sadness. She was sad about getting drunk and letting everyone see her out of control. She was sad about all the misery she saw in the world. She was sad she was pathetic. She was sad Ben was married to Jane. She was sad she didn't have anyone in her life to hold her and comfort her. The more she wept, the more she hated herself. Finally she had no more tears. She heard Ben saying things to try to comfort her, but she wanted no part of his comfort. He belonged to

Jane. She finally managed to eke out, "Well, I guess I've made a royal mess of things. I'm okay now. Please take me home."

Ben pulled Carrie's car into her apartment complex, and walked her to her door. "Are you sure you'll be alright?"

"I'll be fine. Really. I need to go to bed. Thanks for looking after me. I see Jane is waiting for you. You better go. I'll see you next fall." Ben gave Carrie a quick hug and joined Jane in their car.

Carrie closed the apartment door and leaned back against it. She could feel some more tears begin to well up in her eyes. She rubbed them away. You've done enough crying she told herself. Get to bed and go to sleep. She got undressed, threw on an old T-shirt and slipped into bed. She pulled her blanket up to her neck and lay on her side. Then the next torrent of tears came and wouldn't be stopped. She cried hard, she was gasping for breaths. She gasped enough she sent herself into the dry heaves before falling into a deep sleep.

Carrie opened her eyes and thought the morning sun was brighter than usual, until she realized it was 11:00 am! Her full bladder was the day's alarm clock. As she peed she took note of the dullness of her thinking and was thankful it was the last of the night's remnants left with her. In an attempt to clear the cobwebs from her brain, she took a lukewarm shower. A hot shower was what her body begged for, but Carrie refused this want as a partial punishment for her bad behavior. She needed to make amends to herself. This small token of denial would serve as atonement for the event in her mind.

This was her first day of real freedom from work and school. She thought she would indulge herself and spend it lackadaisically, free from any heavy duty responsibilities or endeavors. Perhaps she would curl up with a good book. She has a wall full of them waiting to be discovered. Something light and easy would fit the bill. She put on a pot of coffee, tea would be too gentle. She needed a harsh dose of caffeine. As the coffee brewed she delighted in its aroma, remembering how she would wake to this smell each morning as a young child. She missed her mother. She missed having mom to talk to when life sent you sideways instead of forward. She became misty eyed. Now don't start crying again, she told herself. You've done enough for an eternity.

As she poured herself a cup of coffee, she heard a knock on the door. "Strange, now who could it be?" She glanced at the clock on her microwave and noticed it was noon. Her curiosity stirred as she wasn't expecting anyone. She looked through the door's peephole and saw a finger dangling a set of keys. It was Ben. Her first reaction was one of true happiness, quickly to be doused by the memory of last night and Jane. Ugh, she thought. She put on her happy face and opened the door.

"Ben! Whatever brings you here?" she greeted him.

"I know I should have called first, but I was in the neighborhood. I wanted to check in with you and see if you were okay. Also I accidentally pocketed your keys last night and thought you might need them." He held her keys out to her and placed them gently in her hand. "I see you've an angel watching over you," he said as he noted the sterling silver angel dangling from the key ring.

"Yes, I like to think so. It belonged to my mother, a gift my father gave her. Now I think of them both when I see her. It's a small comforting remembrance of them. Apparently, though, you were my angel last night. Thank you for seeing me safely home."

"No problem. I was glad to do it. There was no way I was going to let you drive home. Hey, do I smell coffee?"

"Oh, I'm sorry. Yes. Do you want some? Come on in." Carrie was perturbed with herself she allowed him to stand on the porch as long as he did. She really didn't want him to come in, but the universe was suggesting her needs would need to be dismissed.

As Ben held his coffee cup in his hands, he blew on it to cool it. He looked up at Carrie and was delighted being in her presence. "Carrie, can we talk about last night?"

"No, absolutely not!" she proclaimed adamantly.

"Oh, come on," he pleaded.

"Nope, there is nothing to say. It happened and it's over with."

"Is it? Is it over with?" he questioned.

"Ben, what do you want me to say? I simply got drunk. I know it wasn't pretty. And I do appreciate you drove me home. I'm embarrassed enough as it is. I'm glad I have the whole summer to put it behind me before I see everyone again."

"But what I keep wondering is," Ben continued, "what got you riled up to begin with? You seemed quite out of character. You know. The cool, calm and collected Carrie was missing last night. Are you sure there isn't more going on than what you're expressing?" Ben lifted his coffee cup and stared directly into her eyes.

"Yes, Ben, I'm sure." She stared back at him. "What? Can't I ever let my hair down and act a fool every once in a while without my having to have a good reason?" Carrie implored.

"No, Carrie, you can't. Not the Carrie Singer I know. You forget I've spent many hours with you this year, and I think I know you pretty well. I'm not buying your story. What's going on?" Ben wasn't going to let Carrie off the hook. He needed this conversation as much as Carrie did.

"You're wrong, Ben, nothing is going on."

"Yes, there is."

"No, there isn't!"

"Is too, and I'm not leaving until you tell me."

"Don't do this. There's no point. Please go home." Carrie felt tears trying to push through. Ben continued to gaze at her unflinchingly. Carrie realized he wasn't going to go anywhere.

"Come here," he said softly as he set his coffee cup down. He motioned for her to come. "Please."

"No. No, Ben. No."

"Okay, I'll come to you." Ben stood up and wrapped his arms around Carrie and held her to his chest. "If you won't say it, I will. Carrie, I've fallen in love with you. From the first moment I saw you at Professor Forsberg's meeting with us, I was inexplicably drawn to you, your energy, your smile, your vibrancy. I've never known a woman like you. You've more compassion in your big toe than most people do in their hearts. Courage unbeknown lies within you. Whenever I'm around you, I feel deliriously happy. Thoughts of you fill all my spare moments. Carrie, I didn't want this to happen, but I can no longer deny my feelings for you. I'm pretty sure you feel the same way towards me. And I suspect that's why you got drunk last night. Michael told me he noticed you drinking more heavily after you learned Jane was joining us last night. I don't blame you. I might have done the same if the roles were reversed."

"Ben, don't do this to me." Carrie tried to release herself from Ben's grip. "What's the point? You're married. You have a wife. You have a daughter. You've no right to love me, anymore than I've a right to love you. I didn't want to meet Jane, let alone like her. If I love you or not isn't important."

"It's important to me," Ben pleaded.

"Why, Ben, why? So we can both go our separate ways knowing we have a love which can't exist? So we can make ourselves more miserable? I don't think so. That's not the road I want to travel down." Carrie was teetering, trying to stay strong. "For whatever reason, you and I are not meant to be."

Ben's green eyes began to glisten with quiet tears, silently imploring her to respond. Carrie gave in. "Okay, do I love you? Yes. Yes, I do. There I said it. Are you happy now? I love you Ben. I love the way you think. I love the way you know exactly what to do and say to me to pick me up. I love the way you can finish my sentences. I love the look of you, the smell of you. When you touch me my whole being becomes electrified. Frankly, there isn't anything I don't love about you, except for this."

"Except for what, Carrie?" Ben beseeched.

"This, this scene. Ben I can't do this. Go home where you belong. Tend to your family. You'll thank me for this in the future. Trust me. Go home. If you honestly love me, go home. Please, go home. " Carrie prayed he would respond to her request. She didn't know how much longer she could tolerate his presence and not cave into her complete desire to allow Ben to possess her. She knew if he didn't leave soon. . . . She couldn't allow herself to even complete the thought. "Go home now, please."

Ben assented. He walked towards the door, stopped and gave Carrie one last hug. "I'll always love you, Carrie. Always." He opened the door and slowly sauntered toward his car, his head hung low. Carrie watched through her window as a tear quietly slid down her face from the corner of her eye. Ben moved slowly. He lost his unique jaunt in his step and all semblance of confidence Carrie always noticed. It was difficult to describe, but Carrie often thought it was one of his identifying traits and now it was gone. He placed his hand on the car door handle, paused and wiped his eyes. He slid into his car, started it and left.

Carrie could feel a torrent of tears welling in her eyes. She tried mightily to ignore the complete sadness consuming her. She didn't want to relent to it. To relent would be proof she didn't have a passing love fancy for Ben, but she'd fallen hopelessly, truly in love with him. The tears wouldn't be stopped. She caved in to her emotions and bawled with great sobbing heaves.

chapter 24

The summer months provided Carrie with welcomed relief from school and Ben. She realized how the last year of work and school drained her of her energy, both physically and mentally. It felt good to be back in a routine of a regular work week only. The agency had requested she spend the summer months as a floater, one who would fill in for caseworkers and their caseloads when they would take vacations. Carrie was grateful for this opportunity. It relieved her of night work as well as being tied to the telephone for her entire shift. She could actually go outside and see clients in their homes again. This is where she felt she did her best work, face to face with parents and children.

Additionally she was assigned to a special investigation. There were several reports a school bus driver was making inappropriate sexual advances to some of the children. He was responsible for thirty-eight children daily and four reports came in from different students. The reports ranged from giving unwanted hugs and kisses to fondling the children in their groin area. As a result Carrie was required to interview each and every student. This, too, was exhausting.

One of the summer's highlights was meeting Sylvia for dinner. Sylvia always made her smile. They went to a place called Jackalope's, located on a small lake outside of town. Jackalope's has a whimsical feel to it with an outside patio area as well as a dance floor on its second level. Sylvia arrived first, wearing an African print dress with a big bright green beaded necklace. When she saw Carrie enter the restaurant, her smile burst forth and her hands waved wildly in the air with excitement.

Sylvia stood up to greet Carrie. "Oh, Carrie, Carrie, Carrie. It's good to see you! I've missed you." The two embraced and settled at their table.

"What's up with you? Have you found the man of your dreams yet?" Sylvia inquired.

"No, no I haven't," Carrie kind of lied. "At least no one I can say has a place in my long term future. I went out with one of the court-appointed attorneys for a brief while, until I realized he was too kinky for me."

"Sounds interesting," Sylvia pondered. "What do you mean by kinky?"

"Well on the surface he appears to be the perfect catch. You know, bright, charming, handsome, full of promise, but he has a dark side. He asked me if I would be comfortable in the role of a, you won't believe this, of a dominatrix!"

"No, no way!" Sylvia exclaimed. "You, as a dominatrix! What was he thinking?"

"Apparently he was thinking he wanted to be sexually subservient or something. I don't know. I know I wasn't his cup of tea." Carrie laughed heartily. "It was too bad, because he really has it going on in every other way. You never really know people sometimes. Enough about me. What's up with you?"

"Well I've had the luxury of having the entire summer off. Howard said I might as well enjoy it, because it's likely the last summer I'll be free. It's been wonderful! I've been able to do whatever I want, so I reorganized my house. It was such a mess and now it feels great! I joined a Yoga class and it has really helped me to calm down. You know how hyper I can get! I love it. Hey, you ought to come with me some time!"

"Sylvia, you look great! You have a wonderful glow about you. If I didn't know better I would think it was the glow of pregnancy."

"Carrie, can I ask you something?"

"Go ahead, shoot."

Sylvia gave Carrie a surreptitious glance. She rubbed her hand on her belly and said, "Would you be upset if we named her Carrie?"

Carrie almost choked on her drink. "No way. No way. Are you telling me you're having a baby?"

Sylvia started shaking her head up and down with a growing smile from ear to ear. "Howard and I never thought it was going to happen, especially with me being this old. We gave up on the possibility. But voila!"

"Oh Sylvia, that's the best news I've heard all summer. When are you due?"

"Hopefully she'll come right around spring break. It's going to be a challenging year for me, but lots of women work through their pregnancy with no problem. Fortunately I have the summer to deal with the morning sickness. It should be gone by the beginning of the school year according to my doctor."

"How's Howard dealing with approaching fatherhood?"

"Oh, he's so cute and excited. He has discovered a second hand baby store and has become their most ardent customer. You know you can get some really good used baby things which look like they are in perfect condition and for less money. But Carrie, I was serious. I love you so much. You're such a good friend. Howard and I have discussed this and we both want to name her Carrie. I hope you don't mind."

"Mind? I'm flabbergasted and honored and speechless of course. But are you sure? Isn't there a family name you would like to have carried on, no pun intended." They both laughed.

"I love the name Carrie and I love you. I think our daughter would be honored to be named after you."

"I don't know what to say, but yes, I mean no, no I wouldn't be upset. Yes, if you're positive. I'm happy for you."

"Did you have any interesting cases this summer?" Sylvia asked.

"Not really. The usual stuff. I've spent about fifty percent of my time investigating a school bus driver. It's not been fun. I'm tired of asking children about any involvement they had. I interviewed thirty-eight kids. It became mind numbing. All of them are in elementary school, and their ages ranged from six to eleven."

"I think I read about it in the newspaper. So, you're the brains behind the investigation, eh?"

"I don't know if I would put it that way. The hardest part has been figuring out what terms the children use for their sexual parts. I can't believe so many children are clueless about their body parts and the proper names for them. What's it with people and sex parts? I've talked about boobies, and bumps, and cookies, and wee-wees, and pee pees, and peckers, and snakes, and winkers, and yum-yums, and even a one-eyed monster! Those are a few of the names kids have for their body parts. Some kids have no names at all and no sexual knowledge at all. It has been a struggle. The parents' haven't been helpful in many of the cases. Part of it I can understand. They don't think young children need to know about sex yet. Even the adults find it hard to use the correct terms. It's no surprise the children are clueless. It has been harder than I imagined. Promise me you'll teach young Carrie all of the proper body part names."

"Well you're way ahead of me Carrie. I haven't given a thought about how Howard and I might approach that subject."

Laughingly Carrie responded. "I'm sorry, of course you haven't. But Sylvia, seriously, teach your daughter the proper words for all of her body parts. After all we call a nose a nose, and an arm an arm, and an eye an eye. By changing up the proper names to something like, like a kitty, we do a disservice to the kids. If we are ashamed of the right names, what kind of message would we be sending? If I have children, they are going to know the right names for all of their body parts from the beginning – breasts, vagina, testicles and penis."

"Okay, will do. Better yet, Howard and I'll call you, the expert, over and you can help us out with the conversation." Both women giggled.

"We start school in two weeks. Are you ready for the last year, Carrie?"

"Pretty much. I'll be glad when it's over."

"Me, too. I think it's going to be a challenging year with the pregnancy and all. I'm glad my next internship is at Sunrise Horizons, the senior convalescent center and home. At least I imagine everyone will be moving at a slower pace, I hope, I hope, I hope."

"You'll be fine. And all of the little old ladies will love that you're pregnant," Carrie said encouragingly. "Most everyone loves babies, especially when all they see are other older people."

Sylvia beamed, "Yes, I sure hope so. Where is your internship?"

"I've been assigned to Oswego Middle School."

"Ugh, that age group is awfully difficult."

"Actually, I wanted to be placed in a middle school. I think that population is extremely vulnerable, especially to outside influences. I think of middle schools as sitting at the fork in the road. Kids often find themselves on the wrong path for many reasons. I don't know. I hope to help out at least one child from going down the wrong road. By the time they hit high school, it becomes more hopeless, I think. I want a chance to catch them earlier."

"Of course, I should have known."

"Known what?" Carrie said puzzled with her brow furrowed.

"I should have known you had an altruistic plan. Only you would ask for a setting due to a higher calling of sorts. Me, I want something easy, to get by this year. You, you want to change the world one child at a time. You give thought to everything you do, don't you? Do you ever jump into anything without thinking first?"

"I try not to. Usually the outcomes of those adventures are less than optimal."

"You know what I wish for you Carrie?"

"No, what?"

"I wish one day you'll be free, be free to be you without heavy pondering. Be free to be you in the spur of the moment. Be free to be you without thinking first. That's what I wish. Total spontaneity for you! You should try it."

Carrie smiled at Sylvia and reached over and took her hand. "I love you Sylvia, you're such a bright spot in my life."

chapter 25

The second year of graduate school came and went in a flash. Nothing remarkable occurred to allow this year to particularly stand out as memorable. Carrie returned to her evening screening job, again pushing her limits to work and attend school full time. She remembered how overly tired she felt by the year's end. She had little time for a personal life.

Graduation day would be in two weeks. She was still awed by the notion she would soon possess a Master's Degree. No one in her family received such a high degree. She didn't feel special. She felt worn out. Her illusions about the level of higher thinking with which a degree endowed their owner were vanquished. Real life experience was the greater teacher, not the regurgitation of lecture material tests required. Many who were graduating excelled at regurgitation, but not at actual learning, in Carrie's mind.

She learned a lot about learning this past year at Oswego Middle School. Mainly she became disgruntled with the educational system. It didn't allow for the consideration of many different variables impacting a student's ability to learn. The institution merely focused on tests scores. She remembered vividly a conversation in the teacher's lounge one afternoon. She knew she should have ignored the discussion. But she held her tongue all year. She couldn't stay quiet any longer. It began with two teachers consulting one another regarding a child named Alec, whom Carrie worked with during the past year.

"Well how do you expect a child like Alec to give you any respect?" his English teacher, Alice Greene began. "He doesn't give two hoots about school. Some kids aren't worth our time," she said in animated exasperation.

"I know exactly what you mean," responded Heather Looney, his science teacher. "Why, even his own mother couldn't care less about him. Do you know she's not responded one time to requests to come into the school for a conference about him?"

"Well, now that says it all, doesn't it," Alice continued. "If his mother doesn't care, why should we? I'm tired of wasting my time on kids like him."

"Me, too. You know last week he cut my class twice and slept through the class on the days he did attend," Heather recounted.

"Well at least when he's sleeping you don't have to put up with his smart aleck attitude. Do you know he says the rudest things? The other day he called me a bitch. Then when I questioned him about what he said and he denied it. Yep, he out and out denied it and said he called me a peach. We don't get paid enough to put up with crap," Alice pronounced. "They should put kids like him in an institution to keep them from interfering with the kids who really want to learn. I bet it would teach him a modicum of respect."

As Carrie heard this conversation continue she began to seethe. Before she thought twice, she was compelled to interject herself into the conversation uninvited and surely unwelcomed.

"Excuse me for interrupting," she began, "but are you talking about Alec Morales?"

"Yea! Why, do you know him?" Alice inquired.

"Yes, I do. But I don't quite see him in the same light as the two of you. Quite frankly, I'm appalled about your attitudes, not his."

"Why whatever do you mean, our attitudes?" Heather questioned. "What's wrong with our attitudes? We're facing reality. You know sometimes, Carrie, you have to get not all kids are meant to be, well I mean, all kids are not able to be taught. And Alec is one of them."

"You know, you're right," Carrie reflected. "Understanding Alec like I do, I can see he sees nothing of value the two of you might teach him."

There was no way Alice was going to allow Carrie's last remark to pass without further comment. "Well it's apparent whatever interaction you had with Alec didn't yield a single positive result either."

"What's it with you teachers? Are all of you so quick with assumptive leaps of judgments? Have you bothered to sit down and talk with Alec to discover what's really going on with him? Or is it a one way street? You say jump and he is suppose to blindly follow and never question you? I thought we were supposed to be teaching children how to think things through, how to challenge what's put before them, to help their minds grow and critically assess. But as soon as a child does, he suddenly becomes tagged as a problem child. That's what I see here!"

"Tell me Carrie, what do you suggest we should do differently?"

"Well have you reached out to Alec's mother beyond sending her requests she come and see you?" Carrie asked.

"Like what?" Alice said cocking her head to one side.

"Like calling her on the telephone or stopping by her house?"

"Well, no, but it's not our job," Alice responded.

"Oh, I'm sorry," Carrie continued, "but I thought it was your job to connect with your students and teach them. It seems apparent to me neither of you has spent any energy trying to connect with Alec. You've been too busy discarding him. Sometimes that path is the easier path. Heather, what period is your science class with Alec?"

"First period," Heather retorted.

"Well I'm not surprised he sleeps through your class or cuts it as you describe it. Do you know he has a paraplegic younger brother? His mother has to take public transportation by 6:00am to get to her job by 7:00am, leaving Alec with the responsibility to care for him in the morning. Getting him up and dressed and taking care of his hygiene needs isn't an easy task, especially for a thirteen year old boy. The special needs bus picks his brother up at 7:40 leaving him only twenty minutes to make it to your class on time. The fact he arrives at all is amazing!"

Now feeling a bit sheepish Heather responds, "I didn't know."

"Have you offered her a time in the evening to meet with her regarding your concerns?"

"Well, no. We don't get paid to do that."

"Did you know English is Mrs. Morales's second language? She can't read or write English. This embarrasses her tremendously. She's tried to attend night school for this, but the demands of motherhood and lack of transportation make this impossible for her."

"No," Heather and Alice responded in unison.

"Also, did you know Alec's uncle lives with them, often gets drunk and becomes violent. Alec has become hyper vigilant at night in order to be ready to protect his brother and mother if needed?"

"Well, no, I didn't know," Alice admitted.

"How do you expect a thirteen year old boy to be invested in school when he rarely sleeps well, and has taken on family burdens generally reserved for adults? What do you think he sees when teachers, such as yourself, pass judgments without understanding?"

"Listen," Carrie continued, "I'll admit I know I sound harsh and judgmental about you. But I get tired of adults making excuses for not reaching out, and then turn around and blame the kids for inappropriate behaviors, when their behaviors make total logical sense to them. Maybe over extending yourself isn't part of your paid job. What about your hearts? What about the kids? If teachers really don't care, and see students as merely widgets of a job, then what does that say about us as a society?"

Alice and Heather stood there with dumbfounded looks on their face. It was the first time Carrie saw them speechless. Carrie continued, "Hey, I like teachers, don't get me wrong. I know you have a tough job. And I know it often feels thankless, because it likely is at times. But sometimes we all need something to jolt our perspectives. It's all part of the grand learning scheme from birth to death, isn't it?"

***

Professor Forsberg invited the group to her home for a pre-graduation celebration the day before the actual ceremony. It was a warm late spring evening filled with rain. All came with a jovial spirit, happy to be done with school. Sylvia was all smiles as she presented her three month old daughter Carrie Grace to the group.

"I see our Carrie has woven her magic into you and you named your daughter after her!" exclaimed Michael. "How charming."

"What's your problem Mike," retorted Susan. "I think it's sweet. Remember Sylvia and Carrie shared a lot of time together last year. What's it to you she borrowed a good friends name for her daughter? You don't need to be snide."

"I didn't mean it that way, Susan. I really did mean that it was sweet, as you put it."

"It's okay guys," Sylvia interjected. "You two sound like an old married couple."

"Should we tell them?" Mike asked as he glanced into Susan's eyes.

"Tell what?" Sylvia's curiosity was stirred.

"Well," Susan began, "Mike and I . . ."

"Susan and I are engaged!" Mike finished.

"You two are engaged! Hallelujah! Who would've surmised that would happen? Hey everyone," Sylvia shouted out, "did you hear? Mike and Susan are engaged to be married!"

The crowd all clamored together in giving congratulations. Carrie remembered back to their first gathering at the Forsberg's when Susan set her sights on Ben. My, how things evolve, she thought.

Ben and Carrie had little contact with each other during their second year in school. Carrie took the clinical track, whereas Ben took the policy and administrative track. They had no classes in common and only passed each other on campus briefly a time or two. Carrie secretly was glad their paths rarely crossed. It helped to deaden the yearning she felt the first year for him. In fact, she knew she would see Ben this night and began to feel anxious apprehension about the encounter. She talked herself into the notion she was a mature adult, and she would be fine. After all, they were friends. If both of them respected the needed relationship boundaries, then the evening could be fun. She knew she wasn't going to cross the line. She sure hoped Ben wouldn't. Besides, Jane would be by his side, so no problem, she convinced herself.

The evening was a pleasant one. The group genuinely came to care for one another and they were glad to be in each other's company. They all knew this evening was likely the last evening they would have an opportunity to be together. The energy was bittersweet and inevitable. When Carrie was happy the night went well, it happened. She came out of the bathroom into the long hallway, when Ben approached her. They were alone. The others retired to the basement recreation room, where Carrie was heading. A nervous but pleasant twitch began to rise within her.

"Carrie, I'm glad we have a chance to talk alone," began Ben.

Oh no, thought Carrie, please Lord do not let this be happening. Things never went well when she and Ben were left alone.

"Carrie, I had plenty of time to think about us and the last time we really spoke. I've felt terrible this entire last year about the last conversation I know I forced upon you. I wanted to say you were right. You were right to send me home. You've always acted with honor and grace. I know if I didn't press you into that conversation, it never would've happened. You said one day I would be thankful for not acting on our feelings and, again, you were right. I love my daughter with all of my heart, and for me to leave Jane would've crushed her. And I know in my heart of hearts, relationships starting out by breaking up marriages would be no good. Jane and I do well together. We've come to respect each other and as a result I see Alexis thriving."

Carrie began to plea, "Ben, Ben no, you don't have to revisit that day with me. It's best left in the past." But Ben wasn't listening.

Ben continued, "I want you to know I think you're the most incredible human being I've ever known. I do love you more than you can possibly know. And I know I shouldn't have said it. But it's the truth, Carrie, and I wanted you to know I'm not some kind of wandering gigolo trying to capture hearts wherever I go. But you did capture my heart and I know it wasn't your intent. I'll always love you even if I never see you again. It pains me to say this, but I do hope you find a man who's free to love you as much as I do. And that's all I needed and wanted to say to you. " A tiny tear streamed from Ben's moistening eyes.

Carrie felt like a deer caught in the headlights of a car. A million different fleeting thoughts were freely flowing through her brain. She wanted to reach out and wipe away his tear and tell him everything would be alright. She knew if she even dared to touch him, she wouldn't be able to simply stop without embracing him. At the same time, a raging anger was building inside of her. How dare he return to this? How dare he stir up feelings she spent more than a year burying? She thought she accomplished the feat. It was now apparent she played a game of self delusion. She loved him desperately. He was again compelling her to face it, and the reality it could never be. Damn him to pieces.

Ben turned away from her without requiring her to respond. He simply left her standing in the hallway as he headed to join the crowd. She felt smothered and was in frantic need of some fresh air. Her emotions were bubbling inside begging to erupt. She ran outside through the sliding glass doors of the family room and onto the back patio. The rain turned to a sprinkle which was a blessing, as her tears which couldn't be stopped joined with the rain drops.

As she slowly gained command over her emotions, she heard quiet chattering coming from the far corner of the yard. She noticed a flash of light as if someone lit a match. As she peered into the darkness, she realized some people were gathered inside the screened in cabana. She hoped they didn't witness her outpouring. Curiosity replaced the painful emotions and she approached the group. To her surprise Tamara's husband Steve was entertaining Matt and Eloise and Eloise's current boyfriend Cliff, who happened to be thirteen years younger than Eloise.

"Are you alright?" Eloise asked in her gentle and compassionate voice.

Damn, they saw her. What do I say now? Then she realized what the small group was up to. They were smoking weed! She could smell its distinctive odor lurking in the air. That explained the momentary firelight.

She avoided answering the question by asking one of her own. "What are you guys up to out here?"

"Chilling out a bit with some ganja," Cliff said nonchalantly. "Want some?"

"You look like maybe you could use some," Eloise interjected.

Carrie didn't incorporate smoking marijuana into her life. She was exposed to it, having dabbled with it briefly in her undergraduate college days. And of course she saw it many times in her daily work with her clients. She really didn't have any strong feeling about it one way or the other. It was never important to her. But something deep within her suggested the universe may have offered her the perfect cup of medicine for her emotional pain. Why the hell not, she thought.

"Sure," she replied as she reached for the joint from Cliff.

"Well, I'll be," exclaimed Matt. "I would never have figured you as the sort who would liken up to weed. Carrie, I think I may have a new appreciation for you."

Carrie looked up at Matt and smiled.

Eloise announced, "I think Carrie may be far more complex than what we've given her credit for. I never have thought she was the goody-two-shoes you have, Matt. Now Carrie, don't you mind these men. Don't let them spoil your evening for you."

That was funny. Men spoiling her evening. If they only knew the real truth.

"And I guess you're more than a simple country boy, Matt," Carrie remarked.

"What do you mean? Us country boys were smoking weed long before the city folk caught on to it," Matt laughed out loud boisterously.

Carrie awkwardly put the joint to her mouth.

"Allow me," Steve stepped forward as he provided a flame to relight the joint.

Carrie inhaled slowly. She didn't want to push her luck, having not smoked in over eight years. Yet her body reacted quickly causing her to choke on the smoke and cough uncontrollably.

"Easy!" Steve calmly directed.

Carrie handed the joint back to him. Each took another hit. It came back around to her again. She didn't hesitate. She didn't want to appear wimpy. Another toke and she appreciated the unique pleasant lemon flavor of the bud. After the third hit, she needed to sit down and flopped into one of the cushioned chairs. It was apparent to all she was a novice, which caused them to laugh uncontrollably. It felt good to laugh. It was the perfect balm for her beleaguered soul.

She closed her eyes momentarily and didn't fight the weed's effect.

"Another hit?" Steve inquired.

"Maybe one more. You know I'm not used to this. It's been quite a long while."

"We did notice," Eloise whispered while holding her breath.

"And Eloise, haven't you been the sly fox all this while. I never would've pegged you as a smoker."

"Nor I you."

"Well I'm not," Carrie said defensively. Then she broke into a wide grin, which turned into another round of laughter.

Oh yes, it feels good to laugh thoroughly and completely, thought Carrie. She closed her eyes again. This time she drifted away from the group as her energy touched the unfolding universe only weed could take you to. It was a deeply personal journey. Carrie forgot about this effect, but she was glad to revel in it. She imagined her body assumed the posture of a stoner. Deadheads they called it. Sitting in the chair, head tilted back, and non-communicative. Dopers. There was no way for people to understand weed could transport a person's essence on a journey of enlightenment unless they also joined the throng of smokers. From the outside it does look like people are wasting time in a land of nothingness. But nothing could be further from the truth, she thought.

Then she heard the message weaving its way into her psyche. Do not despair. You'll be surrounded by love greater than you can imagine in your lifetime. This is your truth, your future. Love. Love. Love.

Carrie was curiously comforted by these words. She became aware she dropped out of the conversation and willed herself back into the group. She didn't want to open her eyes, but her nano journey was over. She slowly regained her focus and called out, "Hey Cliff, I think you sent me over the cliff!" They, again, burst into raucous laughter. "What kind of marijuana is this?"

When he could capture his words, Cliff replied, "We call it giggle weed!" Again the laughter erupted uncontrollably. Makes sense thought Carrie. I might have to get me some of this! But she never did.

---

chapter 26

Graduation came and went without incident. Carrie returned to Children Services and began her life without school once again. It was freeing in some ways, but she missed the camaraderie of her school friends. They all scattered about throughout the state and beyond. Ben and Jane moved across the state where he secured a job with the Public Children Services Policy Initiative, an organization working closely with communities and legislators to advance the profession of child welfare. It fit him perfectly. Carrie was relieved distance would separate them. She knew she needed to move on emotionally. The separation by miles would help her. She was now keenly aware accomplishing the needed emotional break from Ben was far more difficult than she originally imagined. Her encounter with Ben at Tamara's jolted her out of her delusions. She loved him, but he wasn't hers to have.

On a happier note, Sylvia received a teaching job at the local community college and wouldn't be leaving the area. Carrie was thankful, for she came to love Sylvia as a sister, and they remained fast friends. She delighted watching her namesake grow and thrive and experience the world through a child's eyes. This was one child who kept Carrie grounded in the realistic possibilities of how a child without trauma grew and thrived. To a great extent, she needed that perspective for her own well being and balance.

After dating a few men, she met Jeff. He seemed to be the most stable, sane and genuine of men she encountered. She hated the dating scene, and at age thirty she was ready to get serious about settling down and starting a family of her own. She remembered back to the night Jeff asked her to marry her.

He was quite clever setting up the "will you marry me?" scenario with the Scrabble board. Carrie appreciated the thought and work that went into the proposal. However, she was taken by surprise when he popped the question having dated only six months. It was apparent to her he was more resolved than she was. That's why she first spelled out the word 'maybe' as her response. As she was assembling those letters, thoughts of Ben ran through her mind. She couldn't help but compare him to Jeff. Of course, she knew possibilities with Ben weren't even on the table. Try as mightily as she did to dismiss Ben from her life, he continued to dwell in the inner recesses of her mind. He would simply pop up here and there, always cause her pause. Damn if he didn't insert himself into this situation as well.

She had to reconcile with herself she unexpectedly and thoroughly fell in love with Ben, like in a fairy tale, only without the happy ending. Now here was this wonderful man, Jeff, who adored her and was a good, caring and loving man asking her to marry him. She, too, fell in love with Jeff, only in a quieter manner. They had many wonderful times together. Jeff was patient with her. He gave into her wants too easily. It was only because he wanted to make her happy. She knew and understood this. She appreciated the security he provided her. He was well grounded, not a risk taker. Carrie knew many women would consider him to be the perfect catch. He often talked about wanting a family, a loving home and the perfect woman to wrap his arms around at night. Jeff would never be on the cover of a magazine for his looks, but he was gentle on the eyes and was always flashing a smile Carrie's way. It was hard not to love him. But what possessed her to initially respond with the word 'maybe' was her concern the high voltage electricity she felt with Ben wasn't present with Jeff.

She and Jeff shared many intimate moments together. He was tender, considerate and occasionally filled with great passion and energy. Spontaneity wasn't his strong suit. He was a planner. Carrie knew she was built differently than Jeff. She was the greater thrill seeker of the two. Jeff was easily contented with simple things. Carrie appreciated quiet times as well, but not all of the times should be quiet. Friends all believed them to be the perfect couple. Carrie reflected on their differences. Perhaps it was the difference between them keeping the energy of the relationship flowing along. After all, it would be boring if they were alike. Wouldn't it?

The final element influencing Carrie to change her 'maybe' to a 'yes' was she knew, with every part of her being, Jeff loved her, adored her, and would do absolutely anything for her. How could she reject him? And she did love him. She was sure. She listened to the sounds of fate in her head and acceded to the moment.

They had a small wedding the first weekend in January of 1981. Jeff wanted to marry her sooner. When Carrie discovered part of his reasoning for wanting a December wedding was it would create another tax deduction for him that year, she stubbornly refused. She knew he was only being practical. After all he was an accountant. She also knew it didn't mean he wanted to marry her only for the tax deduction. Jeff fully loved her. But it didn't seem right to pick a wedding date for that reason. She knew if she objected he would relent and abide by her wishes. She proposed the wedding should begin with the New Year, symbolic of their new life, rather than symbolic of a tax deduction. Jeff agreed as long as he could plan the honeymoon. He wanted it to be a surprise for her.

Carrie never relished the thought of a large wedding production. She cherished the commitment of the wedding vows and held them sacred. The wedding ceremony was sacrosanct and not to be staged as a Broadway play in her mind. It was to be a treasured moment between her and Jeff and their closest loved ones.

As a result they were married in the beautiful small chapel at Dane Forest cemetery on January 3, 1981. Carrie's parents passed away the previous year, and it gave her some solace the ceremony would be near their final resting place. She could feel their spirits around her in the beautiful setting. She knew that would probably be considered silliness by some. She didn't care. Jeff attended Good Shepherd Lutheran Church his entire life. The kind reverend agreed to marry them. Jeff's parents were present. His father was his best man. Sylvia stood next to Carrie. Howard and little Carrie, Carson and his wife, Colleen, rounded out the guests. When the reverend pronounced them husband and wife, Carrie felt like the moment couldn't have been more perfect. Looking into Jeff's soft brown doe-like eyes, she couldn't have loved him more.

The honeymoon was also full of splendorous surprises. Jeff even packed her luggage for her, not wanting her to get a hint about what he planned. They spent their wedding night at a cozy turn of the century bed and breakfast. It was filled with stylish antiques and decorations. The hosts were a married couple in their mid-fifties who were filled with down home charm themselves. Jeff and Carrie were the only occupants, allowing them all the privacy they needed. Carrie later discovered Jeff rented all four available rooms, so he could have her to himself. He was a true romantic at heart. There was an antique four poster canopied bed in their room along with a wood burning fireplace sporting an already lit fire upon their arrival. Carrie felt like she was a princess from days of yore. It was magical.

They made love not once, not twice, but three times on their wedding night. She never knew Jeff to be so ardent. It was as if the wedding provided him with a surge of energy unlike any she saw before with him. Her feelings changed for him, erasing any doubt she made the wrong decision. Awareness crept into her this was where she belonged. It snuggled up to her, warmed her, and comforted her like Jeff did that night.

"Good morning, Mrs. Cathers," Jeff greeted her early Sunday. Mrs. Cathers sounded strange to her. She thought about keeping her maiden name, as part of her embraced the burgeoning feminist movement. Why should women have to rearrange their life around a name? She knew, though, Jeff was more of a traditionalist and it meant a great deal to him for her to fully embrace his name's heritage, so she did. She rationalized she wasn't simply a name. She defined herself as spirit energy and it mattered not how one referred to her on the earthly plain. It didn't change her essence. So Mrs. Carrie Cathers it was.

"Good morning, husband," she responded as she caressed his hair.

"You know I'm the luckiest man on earth," Jeff continued as he began stroking her back. "You're the angel of my dreams." He covered her with kisses. The both giggled and kissed and hugged and then giggled, kissed and hugged some more. "If only I could, I would ravage you once again. But honestly you've sucked all of my mojo from me. I'm the most contented, spent man I know. Please forgive me. But I'll never run out of kisses for you!" Upon which he threw the sheets off of Carrie and immersed himself in her total beautiful nakedness again kissing her here, there and everywhere. Her nipples hardened and she knew they were offering Jeff some sexual teasing which gave her secret pleasure. Then her goose bumps began to appear, whereupon Jeff covered her again with the soft thick down blanket. After all, it was January and the fireplace fire died in the wee morning hours.

The winter sun streamed in through the Victorian lace covered window. "Oh, this is the perfect time for me to give you your wedding present! Jeff hopped out of bed and retrieved a box wrapped in white satin paper with a fire red satin bow tied around it. Carrie delighted in observing Jeff's nude body. He lost thirty pounds during their courtship, and he was trim and inviting. Although her mind wasn't spent, her body was, like Jeff's. It was an exhilarating and exhausting evening, but the morning air began to perk her up.

Jeff eagerly handed her the carefully wrapped eight inch cube. "The red bow reflects my love for you," he commented. Carrie carefully studied the package trying to guess what might be inside. She had no clue. "Open it!" Jeff encouraged her excitedly. Carrie untied the bow and carefully removed the paper not wanting to damage or tear it; it was of such beautiful quality. "I wrapped it myself," he said grinning proudly.

"It's beautiful!" she smiled back at him.

Inside the box the gift was heavily wrapped in layers of tissue paper. Removing the tissue, she found exquisite, delicately crafted, hand blown angel wings. "Wings for my angel, so you can fly high and free!"

"Oh, Jeff, they are absolutely stunning!"

"Did I do good?"

"Perfect, they are perfect." Carrie thought about the time and energy Jeff devoted finding this perfect gift. She felt another swelling of love pass over her. A tear of absolute joy trickled down her cheek.

"Now, you're not going to start crying on me, are you?" Jeff half chided. He placed his hand on her cheek and tenderly moved her face towards his and brushed his lips against her. "I love you with all of my heart and soul," he said as his body began to press against hers once again. And to the surprise of them both, they languished into another love making session neither could have imagined this morning. But it felt good and natural as if it was simply meant to be.

"We've a plane to catch in about four hours," Jeff announced.

"A plane! I had no idea we would be flying somewhere! Where are we going?"

"That's for me to know and for you to find out. But I think you're going to love it."

"I think I've already flown into outer space several times in the past twenty-four hours," Carrie mused happily.

"At least one more flight today, if not more," Jeff twinkled slyly.

As they were driving up the winding mountain road, Carrie couldn't believe Jeff planned a honeymoon trip to Sequoia National Park in California, especially in the middle of winter! But he knew she never had the opportunity to travel out west. He knew it was one of her life dreams to see Sequoia trees up close and personal. Jeff premeditated every single detail to the nth degree. A four wheel drive vehicle was reserved for them at the airport. He contacted a local grocery store in Sacramento a week prior and had them gather a list of food ready to pick up. It included a cooler for storage, some Dom Perignon champagne, filet mignons, salmon, bison burgers and many fresh vegetables. He didn't overlook incidentals either such as cheese, crackers, fruits and desserts! And of course he didn't forget to include some of their favorite wines and beers. He bought enough food to last them for a month, sparing no expense.

He rented a cabin near Mariposa Grove, the heart of the Sequoia trees, discovering only three total cabins were rented this late in the season. Privacy wouldn't be an issue. There was the lightest of snowfalls for the region, but it was bone chilling cold at the high altitude. He even prepared for the possibility of the coldest of weather having purchased complete down coveralls for them both. Jeff left nothing askew, which was in keeping with his accounting style. He created the perfect honeymoon experience. The landscape and sights were breathtaking, especially with the snow lightly covering the ground and branches. The snow highlighted the stellar jays and other birds against the white background. As they approached the park's welcome center, they unexpectedly encountered two small bears at the road's edge. They looked like yearlings. Every twist and turn of the road led to another new awesome sight.

Carrie remembered how she was young and full of wonder. She and Jeff walked to the top of Moro point, where to their surprise some rock climbers lifted themselves up onto the top ledge having grappled with the granite mountain's side. She was amazed by their stamina. The hike up the prepared visitors' path and stairway was quite a challenge for her at the high altitude. She couldn't imagine what it would take to master the side of the mountain by rope.

Jeff rented some cross-country skis for them to slide their way through some of the forest's paths. They also joined up with some other vacationers for the lantern led snowmobile trek through the mountain pass at dusk. If he tried harder, Jeff couldn't have planned a more perfect start to their marriage. They ate by candlelight in their cabin, having cooked their meals on top of the wood burning stove, which kept the cottage well heated. Occasionally it became so warm they opened the windows to cool it down. Jeff read poetry to her including Elizabeth Barrett Browning's poem 'How do I love thee, let me count the ways.' And of course they made love often. They made love tenderly. They made love passionately. They made love to the point of total exhaustion. They laughed uncontrollably when they both acknowledged their sexual encounters left their sexual parts quite raw and tender to the touch. But it didn't stop their longing for one another. The small details of this physical inconvenience were easily dismissed. The thrills of their climaxes were all encompassing. Carrie thought Jeff found the secret to heaven via Sequoia.

chapter 27

Carrie took two weeks off for her wedding. Returning to work she realized she should have taken yet another week for recovery, but her office wouldn't approve three weeks. She was still soaring high. Work would soon put an end to that.

She was transferred to a new experimental unit. The staff was responsible for conducting intake investigations as well as providing continuing services for the families, if the case needed to be opened for longer termed services. The rationale was families wouldn't have to endure relating to yet another assigned worker after the intake process. It was experimental because it went against traditional thinking. Intake workers generally have the difficult task of confronting the families with the original allegations of maltreatment. Often this wasn't a welcome intervention. On occasion, the intake worker would have to remove the children from their parents and place them into either relative care or foster care. Typically this didn't make for happy parents. They would often vent anger like a dragon spews fire. When the case was transferred to an on-going worker for continuing services, the on-going worker could easily play the role of savior. Implementing a case plan addressing the needs of the family, caseworkers were able to help the family reunify with their children. It was child welfare's version of good cop, bad cop.

There were downsides to the system, although children services employed it. Downsides included the client had to establish a new relationship with a new worker. Workers have different talents and skills and many times the intake workers actually were more adept at working with the clients, a result of putting the more experienced workers at intake. As a result the parents often would complain their new on-going worker was useless.

Additionally, intake workers rarely got to see any happy endings. They always gave their cases away to the on-going caseworkers. This could lead to some devastating emotional trauma and burn-out for the workers. Being on the front end of a family's situation in child welfare was the more difficult end, confronting the workers with the worst of the worst family dynamics. At the closing end of the case, families increased their parenting skills and improved their responses to difficult child behaviors, thus giving on-going workers the joy of success.

The new unit was called the full-cycle unit to distinguish it from a strictly intake or on-going unit. The fundamental goals of this unit would be to minimize clients having to relate to numerous workers, and to create a work environment that would reduce worker burn out. Turnover in the profession was problematic. The system realized it needed to keep talented and experienced workers. The average worker stayed for about two years. This was their innovative idea. Carrie was up for the challenge and was eager to see if such a system was feasible.

Once again she was assigned to a male supervisor, Brian Galloway. She didn't mind he was male as much as she minded his reputation for sexually hitting on his staff. Two previous workers filed sexual harassment suits against him. The outcome of those suits was the workers resigned. Brian remained. Brian was a personal friend of the executive director, John Mitchell. Carrie believed this caused him to have a conflict of interest, and therefore couldn't or wouldn't see the situation through clear and unfettered eyes. Additionally Carrie felt he was intimidated by Brian because he was an African-American, and the executive director didn't want to be tagged as a racist. As a result, staff didn't feel there was a clear path to effectively deal with Brian's behavior. Carrie hoped Brian would leave her alone and stay within his boundaries of his supervisory role. Unfortunately, such wouldn't be the case. It started slowly and burgeoned with time. Carrie reflected on the many statements she endured.

"Carrie, welcome to our unit. I understand you're coming back from your honeymoon. Boy, you have one lucky husband. I'm sure you made him feel real good."

"Carrie, with your eyes being of a different color, you can understand why I sometimes find myself looking elsewhere on your body. You sure are beautiful."

"Carrie, if your husband ends up working late at night during tax season, you know I could keep you company."

"Carrie, if you get lonely, call me."

"Carrie, I want you to understand I mean this as a compliment, but I sure would like to do you."

Brian also invaded her personal space routinely. He would stand too close. He would come up from behind her and reach around to touch her hand to get her attention, whispering something in her ear. It drove her nuts. He made her feel uncomfortable. Carrie convinced herself she could easily ignore his unwanted advances. She certainly was never going to act upon any of his suggestions. She didn't want to spend any extra energy dealing with this lothario.

Carrie knew she couldn't confide in Jeff about this circumstance. It would only lead to misery of a different sort. Jeff wouldn't understand. He would want to physically harm Brian. He would want to call out the executive director for some action. He would want to write a letter to the editor to call attention publicly to this guy. He wouldn't be content, as Carrie chose to be, to put up with the behavior.

What he wouldn't understand was the politics which played into a scenario such as this. He wouldn't care John Mitchell was fearful for his own personal reasons. Jeff loved her and would step immediately into the role of protector. She wanted to work with her families, and not deal with this nasty situation. She was gifted in her ability to ignore unwanted input. That's how she wanted to deal with this. Deep within, she knew Jeff was right. No one should have to put up with this behavior.

Did she have the energy to fight this fight too? Did she have to be the strongest of the strong all of the time? In this case she decided no. Was it right? No. But the fact of the matter, in Carrie's eyes, was life wasn't fair. And this was one of her unfair burdens. She knew you taught people how to treat you. She would find a way to teach Brian how to treat her. She needed more time to think on the matter.

One day she found the perfect answer to Brian. It was quite accidental on her part. Brian called her into his office, once again, for some trivial matter he insisted needed to be dealt with right away. This was usually a clue Brian's sexual inappropriateness was about to surface. She begrudgingly marched herself to his office.

"Close the door, please," he requested.

Carrie always left his door open when she met with him. She decided to ignore his request.

"Okay, I guess I'll close the door," Brian said irritated. Carrie had yet to sit down in the chair across from Brian's desk.

When he walked by her after closing the door, he intentionally brushed up against her breasts as he walked past her. Carrie responded without thinking. "Brian, I've had enough of your unprofessional behavior. I want it to stop right now."

"Really? What behavior are you speaking of?" Brian taunted.

Carrie was fast losing her interminable patience. It was time to call him out. "You know exactly what I'm talking about. If you don't stop your sexually harassing behavior, I'm going to. . . ."

"To what?" Brian interjected as he bore into her eyes. "What? The great and mighty Carrie Cathers is going to stop me? Don't you realize neither you nor anyone else can touch me? They've tried twice and it hasn't worked."

Carrie couldn't believe what she was hearing. How could this man be this arrogant and so sure of himself? How could he walk around with such impunity? Well he picked on the wrong woman this time.

"Or what, Carrie, please finish," Brian bullied. "What are you going to do if I accidentally touch your boobs like this?" whereupon Brian cupped one of her breasts in his hand. "Who's going to believe you? There will never be any witnesses. I'll make sure of that."

Nice sweet Carrie no longer existed, at least not in this moment. She slugged him in the face trying to push his nose into his brain. As he grabbed his nose, her knee bent straight up, back and then with the swiftest and strongest kick she could muster, she soundly and squarely delivered a full motion impact directly to his balls. At the same time she thanked the good Lord for all of those self-defense classes she took.

Brian fell to his knees, obviously in great pain. He held his manhood with one hand and his nose with the other hand. Blood trickled down toward his upper lip. Carrie turned around, swung the door open and started to leave. Directly on the other side of the door was the executive director. He stood there with his mouth wide opened, gaping at Brian, who was moaning gutturally. He turned and gave Carrie a bewildered look as if asking, "What's going on here?"

Carrie wasted no time in responding. A side of Carrie surfaced no one in the work place saw previously or imagined. "Do with me what you want, but I'll no longer tolerate this despicable man's sexual groping. If you don't do something to stop this man, I'll file a sexual harassment suit against you and him. I'm sure I can locate many more victims who'll stand by my side. In fact, if you insist I continue to work with this maggot, I'll personally contact the president of our board, Judge Keyes. I'll let her know exactly what has been going on. You may have been able to make the other complainants go away, but I'll not. I love my job and I've no desire to leave. I only wish to work in a non-invasive and non-combative office environment. What we deal with on the streets is bad enough. No one should have to deal with this within the office environment. He is," she pointed to Brian, "the lowest form of human life. If I didn't have a shred of dignity left in me, I would gladly spit on him." Carrie walked off. Two clerical staff noticed and heard the encounter. They clapped their hands as she walked by them. Brian stayed on his knees moaning.

John Mitchell quickly entered Brian's office and shut the door. That was Brian's last day at the agency. Carrie became the heroine in the office. News of her encounter traveled fast. People congratulated her the rest of the day to her dismay. She didn't want this attention. She wanted Brian to go away. Thankfully, they replaced him with Becky Harrell, a compassionate and skilled clinician. It wasn't until Brian was gone Carrie realized the magnitude of negativity he brought into her life. She was able to shed the feeling of dread which was her constant companion when she was in the office. She didn't understand how badly Brian's behavior affected her. She felt free. It felt marvelous.

***

She never told Jeff about the incident. There was no need to burden him with the negative energy it produced. She wanted home to be a loving refuge, not a place to rehash the vagaries of her work. Carrie was cautious about keeping her work at work. As a result she didn't invite coworkers into personal friendship roles after work hours. There would be precious few exceptions to this rule. She didn't need to commiserate with others. She stayed out of gossip. She knew some staff considered her to be anti-social or snippety or a bit odd. But all knew if they needed a helping hand with a case situation, Carrie would be one of the few who would volunteer to help, especially if the situation would require you to work after your traditional work hours. She was surprised when Becky advised her other staff were jealous of her skill and tenacity, her calm in the middle of a storm. Becky wrote on her annual evaluation Carrie was most effective as a silent leader. It struck Carrie as rather curious. She never gave any thought to her effect on her coworkers. She got up each day and tackled the challenges of the moment as best as she could. Some thought she was a perfectionist. Although Carrie knew she wasn't. She was her own harshest critic.

chapter 28

Carrie and Jeff reveled in each other during the beginning of their marriage. Carrie was always glad to walk through her front door after a hard day's work and into the loving embrace of Jeff. He fully doted on her. Yet, at the same time, Carrie became acutely aware she needed to separate her work life from her home life. She found this avoided bringing negativity into the home, and lessened potential disagreements between her and Jeff. When Carrie originally discussed her work situations with Jeff, it brought out his protective nature. At first this enchanted her, likening him to her knight in shining armor. She thought it was sweet. However, the more Jeff learned about Carrie's daily activities, the more he railed for her to quit her job. Carrie understood his point of view. It disagreed with her own personal calling to immerse herself in this field. As a result she spoke less and less of her work to him. She kept it to herself. Instead she concentrated on the joy of their relationship.

Jeff became Carrie's soft place to fall. Young and in good health, they stayed active. They joined the local gym and fell in love with playing racquetball. It served as a fantastic release for Carrie. Jeff could easily beat her in any game, but Carrie enjoyed the challenge. Then one day she suggested he give her a fairer advantage. "What do you want me to do? Give you a handicap of ten points?" he asked.

"No, you know better. It wouldn't suit me to not win fair and square. No. I'm not asking to be given points. What I want you to do is play with your opposite hand."

"You mean you want me to play with my left hand?"

"Yep, that sums it up."

"Okay. But I'm warning you, this won't afford you much of an advantage. I'll play with my left hand under one condition," he counter offered.

"What?" Carrie's curiosity was awakened.

"The winner of the game gets to be the recipient of a total one way love making session."

"What the hell is a one way love making session?" Carrie inquired as she adjusted her sports head band.

"Well," Jeff began shyly, "it's where only one person, the loser, has to initiate, touch, fondle, and make love to the other with no expectation or allowance of any reciprocal action." He grinned widely.

"Oh, you think you have the game in the bag already, don't you. Okay. I'll accept your condition. And I won't feel one speck of guilt when I luxuriate in my orgasm."

The game was on. Jeff floundered with his left hand more than Carrie anticipated. She realized playing with your opposite hand also required changing how you moved on the court. Jeff didn't adjust quickly enough. She won. She won big.

Now a wide grin adorned her face as Jeff meekly approached her that evening and gently, slowly and with great deliberation tantalized her body. He kissed each disc of her spine as he reached around and played with her nipples. He lifted her up and carried her to their bed, whereupon he ravaged her with kisses. He placed his hand between her legs and stroked her with a deliberate rhythm increasing her pulse rate.

Throughout the lovemaking he whispered into her ear the most endearing sentiments. He told her with detail exactly what he was going to do to her next. He breathed words of great love into her ear. He would place his fingers over her lips, beckoning her to not speak but to merely enjoy. Carrie didn't see this side of Jeff before, but she liked it. Typically he was the strong, silent type, but not this evening. It was as if his cloak of reticence was lifted. This evening was creating an indelible memory for Carrie. It was hard for her to not reciprocate. She wanted to touch and caress Jeff. When she would try, he would grab her wrists, and place them on the pillow. He would admonish her and remind her it was a one way street this time. It drove her crazy and admittedly caused her body to react with even more excitement. It was the best game of racquetball she ever won.

There were many wonderful moments such as these. They would fill their hours with numerous activities: biking, swimming, movies, dining out, walks in the park, picnics, bird watching. They even tried roller blading which led to unanticipated hilarity. The evening hours were quieter times. Books were important to them, often lending one to read to the other. Carrie joyfully reveled in Jeff's voice as words would roll off of his tongue. She snuggled against him as he kept his arm wrapped around her. They would sip on wines, compare their different tastes, and then compare the taste of the wine as it mingled upon the other's lips. This, of course, led to another session of lovemaking. Carrie knew she was blessed by Jeff, even if he wasn't a social butterfly. He loved her unabashedly. He would die for her. This was their absolute truth.

***

Carrie was in the Book Alcove. She was searching for the right book for Jeff. Unbeknownst to him, tonight was to be a gigantically special evening. Thinking about it sent rays of excitement through her. She wanted it to be a perfect evening. "Ah, here it is," she remarked as she was filled with great excitement.

She made reservations at the Windjammer, the place where it all started. The place Jeff told her time and again, where he fell in love with her. It fit into her plans precisely.

She wrapped the book in a dark purple shiny paper and adorned it with a deep bright blue ribbon, and slipped it into her oversized purse. She wrapped herself in a simple but elegant black dress and bejeweled herself with a strand of her mother's pearls with matching earrings. She glowed and she knew it.

"Hi sweetheart, I'm home," Jeff called out as he entered their home. "What's this big surprise you called me about?"

As Carrie rounded the corner from the kitchen and walked into the room to greet him, Jeff's eyes opened wide as he gazed upon her. "Oh God, you're absolutely stunningly beautiful!" he declared. "And to what do I owe this?" He stepped forward to grab her and cover her with nibbling kisses.

"I made reservations for us at Windjammer this evening. I hope you don't mind?"

"Mind, are you kidding me? Of course I don't mind. What's the occasion?"

"Oh, I don't know," Carrie said slyly. "I thought we would have an impromptu celebration of us. You know we haven't been back there since our first date."

"Since I first fell in love with you," Jeff reminded Carrie. "That's what I love about you. I never know what you might be up to."

"Well tonight, we are up to good food, good memories and creating new memories. I promise I'll try to not spill hot butter on *you* this time," Carrie sniggered.

They snuggled into the wooden booth next to each other. Jeff put his arm around Carrie as she lifted her lips to his neck and gave him some warm slightly lingering kisses. "To what do I owe those kisses?" Jeff whispered.

"For being you. For loving me."

"And I do. I'll always love you. You're the best thing ever to happen to me," Jeff reminded her, as he did frequently.

"Well, I may not be the only best thing to happen to you," Carrie began as the waitress approached.

"Welcome to the Windjammer," the waitress said as she beamed a broad smile. "May I get you something to drink as you review the menu?"

"Yes," Jeff interjected. "Could you bring us two glasses of your best Sauvignon Blanc please?"

"Make it one glass of wine and one sparkling water please," Carrie requested. Jeff looked at her curiously.

"What? You aren't going to drink wine with dinner? What's up? You're breaking our tradition?" Jeff asked with some disbelief.

Instead of responding to his question with words, Carrie slipped her hand into her purse and handed him the wrapped book. "Here, I brought you a little present."

Jeff held the present in his hand and began to guess its contents. Carrie was having a difficult time containing herself and blurted out, "Oh, I can't tell you, open it up!"

"Well I clearly know it's a book. I can tell by the feel of it. Is it poetry?"

Carrie realized she rarely felt as excited as she was. It was a challenge for her to remain calm. She failed the challenge. "Jeff, please open it. Here let me help you." She began to untie the ribbon.

"That's okay. I can open my own present," Jeff gently chastised her as he pulled the gift away from her fingers.

The ribbon pulled off and the paper unwrapped. Jeff dumbfoundedly stared at the cover. "A Child is Born" by Lennart Nilsson bore a picture of a fetus inutero. Jeff remained painstakingly quiet as he considered the book. Carrie thought she was going to burst with her excitement. Jeff gave her a long look with the softest of brown eyes. "Are you trying to tell me you're pregnant!" he managed to eke out.

Again, without words, Carrie answered his question by flipping to the inscription she placed inside the book. *To my love, you've given me the greatest gift in the whole world, our child. I'll love and cherish you forever.* Jeff pondered for a moment. "That's why there's no wine for my love!" he exclaimed. "Oh Carrie, I can't believe it. Is it really true? Are we going to have a baby?"

Carrie vehemently nodded her head up and down and could no longer be quiet. "Yes, yes, yes, oh yes!"

Jeff grabbed her into a bear hug and whispered, "I don't even want to eat dinner any more, I want to go home and make love to you. You've made me the happiest man on this Earth."

The waitress approached with their beverages. She eyed the wrapping paper on the table. "Somebody's birthday?" she asked.

"No," Jeff said in an almost whisper, then changed his tone to a near exuberant shout, "I found out I'm going to be a father!"

Then to Carrie's shock, Jeff scooted out of the booth, stood up and yelled to all in the restaurant, "Hey everybody, we're having a baby, we're having a baby!" He, then, tried to do some version of what looked like a drunken Irish jig. Carrie never saw Jeff express his emotions publically. She started to laugh and then the giggles usurped her. Before long the entire restaurant shared in their joy. Later, Jeff took her home and made love to her in the most gentle and loving of fashions.

Kate was born April 17, 1983. Carrie loved children but she was never able to imagine the breadth and depth of a mother's love until Kate. Kate filled a spot in Carrie's spirit unlike any other being. The love she felt was indescribable. Her life was inalterably changed for the better. And Jeff was the perfect father. He absolutely adored and loved Kate. Sometimes Carrie was a tad jealous of their relationship. She intellectually knew she was being ridiculous. She would stop and quietly admonish herself regarding this. She reminded herself to bask in the numerous blessings bestowed upon her in her life.

Six months later, Carrie's maternity leave was up and it was time for her to return to work. She was torn about her decision. Jeff, of course, was against it. He was against her working even before Kate. But no one understood how deeply she felt called to her profession. It fulfilled her in ways no other activity could. It was their biggest argument. Carrie should have seen it coming. Jeff was a traditionalist in many ways. He would've been happy for her to be barefoot and pregnant and home. Carrie understood it was his protective and loving nature blowing him in this direction. He would die for her. He didn't want her to die or suffer because of the call of duty. He knew she worked in dangerous areas and worked with many who would eventually be tagged criminals, because they were. He didn't want any harm to come to her, and couldn't understand why she couldn't sacrifice her career for her family.

On the other hand, Carrie knew in the six months of being home with Kate, motherhood alone wouldn't sustain her and allow her to keep her sanity. She loved every minute with Kate. Kate was her precious and perfect daughter. But she found herself going crazy being tied solely to her home. She didn't know how stay-at-home mothers did it all of the time. She rationalized to herself she would be a better mother, wife and role model if she fulfilled herself with her work as well as her motherhood. She believed she could possibly have it all, especially with the support of Jeff. In the end, Carrie knew she would win the argument. Jeff always gave into her. At times she wished he would stand and hold his own ground more than he did. Challenge her more. But that wasn't Jeff. He would give a small measure of fuss, and then cave in. However on this issue, Carrie knew for her own well being, she needed to return to work.

Jeff refinished the garage into an office and moved his accounting practice to their home. Jack and Betty Cathers, Jeff's parents, lived nearby. Betty was always eager to help care for Kate through the day. It felt like a perfect set up for all. Most importantly Kate grew into a happy, healthy, and generous spirit. Leaving Kate each morning was filled with bittersweet memories for Carrie. It was a profoundly confusing emotional roller coaster ride for her. In the end, she decided it was for the best that she went back to work. Kate was well cared for, and Carrie was filled with great excitement each evening getting back to her. Kate would always beam and run to her with hugs and kisses. Carrie was reminded with every reunion what a special place Kate held in her heart. Carrie and Kate were inseparable when they were together. Carrie went to bed each evening thanking the good Lord for all of her numerous blessings. Work, Kate and Jeff kept her grounded in gratitude for the bounties given her.

chapter 29

Becky Harrell and the rest of Carrie's unit members at work were thrilled to have her back. They decorated their entire office area with welcoming banners, balloons, and crepe paper. Carrie was overwhelmed with the warm greetings. She was surprised and acutely aware that not all returning workers from leave were fussed over. She didn't expect this upon returning to work. Her only anticipation was that she would be hitting the streets soon again, wrestling with her forlorn children and their families.

The unit members gathered around Carrie, all chattering away. They were bursting with stories to tell during Carrie's absence.

"You've got to listen to this case scenario," Jenny insisted. "You won't believe what these parents did! I had a mother who is intellectually limited, not severely, but functional. She was highly dependent upon her boyfriend, the father of her four daughters to lead her through her day. Well, he decided they should commit suicide together. For whatever reason, she went along with it. The only good part is they sent the children to their grandmother's home, when they attempted to end their lives. This guy, well he had mom go out and purchase some toilet bowl cleaner and bleach. They blended this with a bottle of aspirin, some alcohol and who knows what else. Then they drank it!" Jenny's eyes widened and her mouth gaped opened as if she still couldn't believe it.

"Well, I know this isn't funny, but it gets funnier. Well, you know, funny the way we understand funny. They both passed out cold. Mom came to first and called for the emergency squad. Dad was still passed out. Mom ended up having burned her esophagus and tongue a bit, but recovered. They pumped his stomach, which was the only thing that saved him. Dad, now this is where it gets funny," Jenny interjected, "dad passed out face down across his arm. His body vomited up the nasty mixture, and before he was revived the vomit dissolved his arm and the doctors had no choice but to amputate it! Now he has only one arm. He blamed this on the mother saying it was her fault because she didn't make the drink strong enough. He was also angry with her she didn't drink enough of the concoction. If she did, they both would've died. But now it's her fault they weren't dead. When he got out of the hospital, he beat her up for screwing up! Can you believe it!"

"Oh my God," Carrie responded as the other unit members were laughing hysterically, "those poor children."

"Oh, and for the children it ended up being a blessing in disguise," Jenny continued.

"How so?" Carrie questioned.

"Well, when we interviewed the children, they revealed their father was sexually abusing them. At least, that is no longer happening."

"But can you imagine what you would say as you went through life," offered up Julie, another unit member. "How did you lose your arm? Were you in an industrial accident, did you have a medical condition? No, it was a failed suicide, I was an idiot! Can you imagine how many times you would have to respond to that question? Serves him right, kind of a poetic justice! Doesn't happen very often."

"Well he is in jail now," Jenny offered up. "Wouldn't want to be him. You know pedophiles are on the bottom rung in prison. He'll get his just desserts. Even rapist and murderers are thought better of than pedophiles."

"Yeah, you're right," Donna inserted, "I surely wouldn't want to be him, especially in prison. He may get his wish yet to die, or he certainly will have greater reason to want to die!"

Carrie was never surprised any more about what humans were capable of doing. She lost all shock value. She was also struck about how caseworkers were able to laugh regarding the worst of circumstances. They had to or they would go crazy. Of course the general population would find their humor appalling. They laughed at tragedies. What they understood, however, was the situations they encountered were first and foremost tragic. Children suffered greatly. This was what they didn't have to explain when sharing their stories with each other. No one made light of the underlying consequences for the children. But if they didn't see the humor in the surrounding events of some of the scenarios, they would go insane themselves.

Carrie remembered back when she watched the Joseph Wambaugh movie, "The Choir Boys", a gritty story about police culture. It showcased how police officers belonged to their own special fraternity after hours, and how you needed to be a member of the group to understand their culture of humor. The same dynamic played out here with the caseworkers. Carrie knew she could never share some of these stories with her friends who didn't work within this framework. They couldn't understand.

"Carrie," Donna tapped her shoulder, "I've another list of names."

"Really?" Carrie proffered. The list of names referred to the first names parents gave their children with peculiarities built into them. "What are they?"

"Brandy, Tequila, Champagne and Amaretto!"

"And mother is an alcoholic?" Carrie said with a raised eyebrow.

"Yep!"

"Well, at least that's better than naming your children Crack, Smack and Pop like my mother did!" Julie added.

"Yeah, or Sir and Mister," Jenny added. "Or Cinderella, Rapunzel, Snow White and Prince Charming!" These were all names given to real children.

Carrie could have added these names to the growing list of names she encountered in her short career. There was Ginger, Rosemary, Saffron and Basil. There was Lily, Rose and Tulip. She remembered Georgia, Georgette, Georgejean, and Georgeann, all named after their father George. Such an ego trip, Carrie contemplated. Carrie thought he had a George Foreman complex. He named his kids George 1, George 2, George 3 and George 4. Then there was the mother who actually named her children First, Second and Third. The worst name list was Chlamydia, Syphilis, and Gonor, short for gonorrhea. Then, there was the sad name Female Black White. Carrie remembered asking her client what she named her newborn daughter. The mother said she didn't name her because someone else at the hospital already named her Female, as she pronounced it fem-all-lee. It was already on the birth certificate. This mother was intellectually challenged and didn't know how to read or write. As a result the child's name stayed as a description: female, black with her last name of White.

Life was filled with its own cruel ironies. And on the lighter side there was the family whose last name was Trees and of course they named their children after a type of tree such as Jack Pine, Douglas Fir, Virginia Pine and Merry Christmas. Jack, Doug, Ginny and Merry didn't sound strange until you said their full name. Carrie's favorite strange names came from the Sparrow family with their children all being adorned with bird names: Robin, Cardinal (known as Card), Downy and Hairy (twins named after woodpeckers) and often called the peckers.

"Speaking of names," Becky interrupted, "are you ready for your next case Carrie? I have a family here with the last name of Marvelous."

"Are you kidding me?" Carrie smiled.

"Nope, welcome back."

Well the Marvelous family didn't turn out to be marvelous, but they were interestingly creative. The report read the mother of four children, two boys and two girls took an Exacto knife and sliced up the leg of her second child Emily. Emily has scar marks all across her calf. The report came from a concerned unnamed neighbor.

Upon investigation Carrie was able to interview all four children and observe their well being. They were shy and quiet children, not forthcoming with a lot of information. None of them had scarred legs. All denied anything happened. Carrie asked the mom if she had any idea why someone would call in such a referral regarding her children. She admitted she was in a verbal argument with the neighbor the evening before. He told her he was going to call child welfare on them. She wasn't surprised when Carrie showed up. She said she didn't have anything to hide. Carrie thanked the mother for being cooperative and advised her she would be closing out the concern. Carrie chalked it up to another false referral. It surprised her when neighbors or relatives would get back at others by using the child welfare system making false claims. It boggled her mind. It did happen frequently. What a waste of time and taxpayers money. You could never know which reports were true and which weren't until you went and checked on them. This one was apparently not true and thankfully so.

The next day Carrie was greeted with an angry phone call. "Excuse me, but can you tell me, for the love of God, how you could close out the referral on the Marvelous family?" was shouted into her ear. "Did you even bother to look at the poor child's legs? You guys are some kind of lame excuse for caseworkers."

"I'm sorry, sir, but I'm not allowed to reveal to you the circumstances of our case findings. It's legally confidential."

"I figured you would say something like that. Well let me tell you, you missed the mark. I saw Emily this morning, and she looks worse for the wear today than she did the other day."

"Sir, could you please tell me what it is you saw this morning?"

"Well, if you did your job, I wouldn't have to do it for you now, would I? The girl is all marked up. She's wearing knee socks to cover it up.

I swear to you, her mother is crazy. If you don't do something about it, I'm going to the newspapers. You got it?" The caller slammed down the phone.

Carrie felt disconcerted. Generally with false referrals this response never came. She saw all four children. All of them. None of them had marks. She took it in to Becky for a consultation. After sharing the caller's emphatic vehemence, Carrie wanted to check on the children again. Becky agreed.

This time Mrs. Marvelous wasn't at all as cooperative. She was, in fact, disturbed greatly with the second visit by the caseworker and didn't want her to have access to the children again. It was a beautiful autumn day and the children were outside playing. She refused to call them into the house. As Carrie was trying to conjole the mother into cooperating, she watched the four children among others playing outside. Her eyes traveled to the girl wearing knee socks, as she remembered what the caller said. Then her brain woke up and Carrie realized she wasn't the girl she interviewed yesterday. One of the older kids came in for some water, and briefly acknowledged Carrie with a weak, "Hi."

Carrie asked the mother, "Who's the girl wearing knee socks?"

The older child responded without hesitation, "That's Emily!" and then he ran back outside.

Emily! Carrie's heart sank instantly. "Mrs. Marvelous what's going on here?"

"I don't know whatever you're talking about," she responded.

"What I'm talking about is, that isn't the same child who identified herself as Emily yesterday. She isn't the same child I talked to. The person who called us said Emily wore knee socks to cover up her scarring and this child has knee socks on. The child I talked to yesterday, who said she was Emily, didn't have knee socks on. And she wasn't the child I see wearing knee socks today on this hot day. Something is going on and I need you to be honest with me."

Mrs. Marvelous stammered and stuck to her story about not knowing what Carrie was talking about.

"Listen, Mrs. Marvelous. I'm not here to judge you. I'm here to help you. Now if the child out there is Emily, and if she does have cuts on her legs, you know as well as I we need to address the situation. Either you can tell me what happened here, or I can call the police department and have an officer come out here and assess the situation. If you don't cooperate with me, he likely will take custody of Emily and remove her from you."

"Are you threatening me?" Mrs. Marvelous asked in an agitated tone of voice.

"No, I'm not threatening you. I'm trying to tell you the reality of the situation. Now you know I can't walk out of here and do nothing if that child is Emily, especially if she has injuries to her legs. I don't know what happened yesterday. I don't know who the child was yesterday, who said she was Emily. But I've a sneaking suspicion I didn't get to talk to the real Emily. I suspect the real Emily is the one I see now wearing the knee socks."

Carrie wasn't going to give up. She wondered for a minute if Mrs. Marvelous might become a physical threat to her, but dismissed the idea as she saw the anger lift from this mother's face. Carrie continued.

"Look, Mrs. Marvelous, whatever has happened, we need to fix it. I know you're not okay with your situation. I believe you love and care about your children. We can find a way to remedy what's going on, but we can't do it without your help."

"How can you know this? You don't even know me?" Mrs. Marvelous asked.

"I can know this by seeing how your children are cared for overall. You've provided them with a nice home. They are doing well in school. They have friends. It looks good on the outside. You do have strengths. But I need to know what's going on inside of you. Please let us help you."

Then, Mrs. Marvelous broke into sobs. "I didn't mean to hurt her. She pushes all of my buttons. She's always questioning my authority. I say no, she says yes, I say up, she says down. She took the Exacto knife from the kitchen drawer and started carving her name into the woodwork baseboard. I told her to stop. Of course she didn't. She said you can't make me. That's when I lost it, I just lost it. I grabbed the knife from her hand and started to swipe at her calf with it. I wanted to get her attention. I didn't mean to hurt her. She didn't even cry or scream. She kept staring at me. I threw the knife down and ran out of the house."

"I see," said Carrie. "Then what happened?"

"I don't know. It's all such a blur. The other kids came inside and saw she was bleeding all over the floor. They began to scream and ran outside hysterical. The next thing I know the next door neighbor is yelling at me, saying I'm a crazy woman. I ran back inside and Emily was putting a paper towel around her leg to stop the bleeding. It didn't bleed long, the cuts were superficial. I apologized to her and we both started crying." Mrs. Marvelous began sobbing uncontrollably. Carrie approached her and gave her a hug and helped her to calm down.

"We can work this out. The hardest part is done. You've acknowledged what happened and it's always the hardest part. It can only get better from this time on."

"Really, do you think so? Even after I fooled you yesterday and Emily's cousin pretended she was Emily? I knew you would be coming, so I arranged for her to spend the night and pretend she was Emily. We pretended it was a game and it worked, or we thought it did."

"All of that doesn't matter now," Carrie reaffirmed. "We need to get you some help and make sure Emily is safe from here on in. Please understand my mission is to make sure the children are safe. No different from your own mission. And the only way we can keep Emily safe is to make sure her mother has all of the resources she needs to be a safe mother. It may take some time, but we can do this."

Carrie, once again, immersed herself in her work. After the first week, it felt like she never left. Going home at the end of the day was always sweet. Little Kate would instantly warm her heart, and Jeff greeted her with endearing comments. Life was good in this home. Love lived there.

chapter 30

Carrie woke up and began to get ready for work following her usual routine. First and foremost, check on Kate. If awake, spend wondrous moments holding her, feeding her and loving on her. This morning she was sound asleep in her crib. Carrie stood there in awe of her, sending her love energy as she gently brushed a wisp of hair from Kate's forehead. She could hear Jeff getting ready for the day, singing in the shower. She loved to hear him singing. He was not in tune, but it warmed her heart. Today he was singing "Jeremiah was a bullfrog". She then retreated to the kitchen for a cup of tea, some cereal and a look at the morning newspaper.

It was with mild trepidation she read the newspaper daily. Carrie never knew if one of her clients might be in one of the headlines. She hoped not. Today her wish wouldn't come true. On the third page, a story snuggled at the bottom corner announced: "Child dead, smothered in bed." The article went on to describe how a mother slept with her infant son. He apparently wiggled himself down to the bottom of the bed, got himself caught between the footboard and the mattress and suffocated. Immediately Carrie began to tear up. What a tragic event, she thought. She knew this mother, although she wasn't currently on her caseload. In fact, she delivered a crib to her, even though this mother didn't see the value of the item. Carrie talked with her about the danger of sleeping with infants. This mother insisted she knew she would never roll over on her child and accidentally smother him, as it happened with other children in the community.

The article went on to say a crib was also in the room, but it was filled with baby items and other stuff. It was used as a place for storage. Well, Carrie thought, this mother didn't roll over on her child. Nonetheless the child was no longer alive. She said a prayer for the little boy. She wondered how this mother was going to handle the death with his three older siblings. She felt for them as well. She made a mental note she needed to attend the funeral, for the children as well as the mother. She left for work with a heavy heart, but not before checking on her own precious child first.

She loved Kate fiercely. Having become a mother, Carrie carried a new perspective on the parenting role. Before becoming a parent, she was able to work with her clients and not be as angry with them for their shortcomings and misdeeds. After becoming a parent, her viewpoint shifted. It became more personal. Having her own child made it more difficult for her to understand how a parent couldn't put their child's well being above their own. Carrie would've died for Kate. She would've killed for Kate. Kate was the most precious spirit in her life. Nothing rose above her, not even Jeff. She struggled with managing her own feelings around her clients during these times. In the end, her intellect ruled and not her emotions.

She understood her clients didn't have the same wonderful opportunities in life she did. She imagined no one was there for them as children. Their needs weren't routinely met as they were growing and developing. Their brains likely didn't get the nutrition needed to be fully maximized into clear thinking logical beings. When they were young, no one soothed their fears and told them everything would be alright. In many cases they weren't safe. Good parental role models weren't in some of their lives. The adults once were the same vulnerable children she was now serving. Many of her clients were children of the system. She didn't know what it said about the system, except it wasn't perfect.

Longitudinal studies suggested the most intensely difficult cases have a recidivism rate of thirty percent. At least, seventy percent of the severe cases never re-entered the system. This alone was a remarkable number in Carrie's mind and kept her going.

This morning the agency called a meeting of all three hundred employees. They met at one of the local movie theaters early in the morning. It was one of the few places having room and seats enough for all of the staff. Popcorn typically wasn't on the agenda. All staff meetings were a rare event, occurring twice a year, maybe. Carrie was curious what was on the agenda.

Carrie settled comfortably in her seat. She loved to people watch and noticed who aligned themselves with whom, who were loners, who were social butterflies, how people carried themselves, who held his head high, who gazed at the floor, whose shoulders were slumped, whose back was tall and rigid, who were gabbers, who were gossipers, who was shy, who was aggressive, who was fearful, who was pathetic, who was loving, who beamed, who held darkness around them, who was energetic, who was tired, and many other characteristics. People fascinated her.

She imagined people probably grouped her into any number of categories: workaholic, socially distant, competent, and helpful. Some may have thought her arrogant, others as caring and approachable. Carrie learned a long time ago not to care about what others thought of her. She cared more of what she thought of herself. She was her own worst critic and judge. She held herself to a very high standard. Some may have called her prideful. She called herself responsible. Carrie tried to make the best of every moment. It was one of her life mantras. What sense did it make to make your moments anything but the best they could possibly be? Moments were the only time one actually lived their lives. She chose to walk on the brighter side, even in the thorniest of situations. She strove to keep her heart filled with love, compassion and hope.

Two staff members were busily chatting as they seated themselves directly in front of Carrie. "Did you hear what happened to Tim?" one said to the other. Carrie recognized the two workers from their foster care department: Bess and Joella. "No, what happened?" Joella responded.

"Well, Tim was fired last night," Bess said in animated whispers.

"Fired! What are you talking about?" Joella exclaimed.

"Yeah, he was apparently holding a mother's visitation with her child hostage for sex!"

"What?"

"Well, at least that's what I heard. And you don't see him here today do you?" Bess said as she waved her arm across the room.

"What do you mean he held a mother sexually hostage for visitation?" Joella persisted.

"Do you remember his client Debalyn?"

"Yeah, I've taken a few phone calls from her on his behalf," Joella offered. "She wasn't bright, but she seemed to genuinely care about her kids."

"Well, then you know one of her daughters was placed in a foster home about an hour away. She called juvenile court and complained she wasn't given any visitation with her. She told the court worker she did everything Tim told her to do to see her daughter. She was getting pretty angry she still didn't have any visits." Bess then added, "She apparently called Alan, you know Tim's supervisor, and he didn't do anything about it. He didn't believe her. He didn't even apprise the director when she told him she gave Tim oral sex the last three times he came to her home. She didn't want to, but he insisted, or he wouldn't let her see her daughter."

"I can't believe this!" Joella exclaimed.

"Believe it," Bess continued. "Ryan told me, you know my lawyer friend. He said Tim came into their office and hired his partner to represent him at the disciplinary hearing. You know when we thought he was taking a two week vacation, well; he was apparently on leave with pay."

"How do they know Debalyn was telling the truth? Maybe she was mad and making it up."

"Oh no, it happened. Debalyn said her last visit with her daughter was seven months ago. She told the court worker that during that visit Tim sat down next to her on the couch and unzipped his pants and pushed her head down onto his dick. She, Debalyn, started crying because she didn't want to do it. She said Erica, her daughter, was in the next room and she could see what was happening. Then Tim threatened Erica and Debalyn that if they ever told anyone about it, that he would make sure they never saw each other again!"

"I can't believe this. Not Tim. He was always nice. This makes me want to vomit," Joella declared.

"Ryan said that the police sent out Detective Allison Baldwin to interview Erica in her foster home. Apparently Erica confirmed the entire story. The foster mother also confirmed that there was no visitation or communication of any kind with Debalyn. There was no opportunity for mom and Erica to concoct this as a story." Bess shifted in her chair and shook her head up and down. "I think Alan may be in trouble, too. Debalyn told him all about it, and he didn't do one damn thing about it."

"Well then he is as guilty as Tim. That poor child and poor Debalyn. You know she was sexually victimized as a child too. Life isn't fair, especially for those who are easily taken advantage of like Debalyn. She has a good heart, but makes bad choices." The movie theater began to fill up with loud chattering. Bess and Joella stopped their conversation and began talking to others.

***

"Good morning ladies and gentlemen," John Mitchell began the morning's program. "I would like to welcome you all here today. We have three items on our agenda today. I want to talk to you about some goals that our county commissioners and board members have set up for us."

"The rising cost of paid placement is killing our budget. More and more children are entering placement and staying longer. Currently we've approximately one thousand children in out of home care; about three hundred are in relative placements. The rest are in foster care, group homes or residential treatment. The cost per diem for these children has risen by twenty percent. Currently paid placements eat up over half of our total annual budget. We simply can't sustain this and maintain any kind of fiscal solvency. What I'm asking each caseworker and supervisor to do is review each caseload with eagle eye scrutiny and determine if any child in paid care can be processed home sooner. Additionally see if there are any children who can be moved into relative care. I know when children first enter placement, we look for relatives. I'm asking we relook. Sometimes relatives may be more amenable to helping out with child care after the initial crisis has passed. Perhaps some children can return home sooner than we thought. Currently the average length of out of home care is fourteen months and we need to reduce it to nine months, if we can."

Carrie mulled this over. Perhaps this might happen in a few cases. She couldn't readily think of any child that she removed who was ready to return home and could be reasonably assured they would be safe from further maltreatment. This request bothered her. It suggested caseworkers were allowing children to linger in care. Was child well-being going to be sacrificed due to budget issues?

John Mitchell, the executive director continued. "For those of you who do not know, we have separate allotments of money from different sources which are legally earmarked for specific use. We can't borrow from Peter to pay Paul. As a result, we are working with all of our contract providers and reviewing our agreements. We are asking each of our providers to take a five percent decrease in their daily rates. Additionally we've established a panel from each agency to partner with members of our agency to see if any of the treatment plans can be altered, so children can step down from care into a less expensive alternative or possible earlier return home."

"Listen guys, these are tough times. The whole country is in a recession and we are feeling the pinch. We need your help. I'll expect each supervisor to give me in thirty days a list of children we can transition."

"The next item on our agenda concerns the Adderly group home. As some of you may know, Mrs. Adderly has suffered a stroke. As a result, she and her husband have no choice but to close their home. This unfortunate news saddens us all. We currently have eight children residing in the home. The caseworkers who have children placed there were notified a few days ago. Arrangements have been made for them to be moved elsewhere. Regrettably, we weren't able to keep these children together. They were placed into five different sites. As you know this home was one of our most coveted and therapeutic settings for our children. This is a sad and tragic loss for our kids. Not only have they lost their beloved "mother", they have lost the support and comfort of each other. We couldn't find a placement site able to embrace them all. It's an irreplaceable resource, as Mrs. Adderly was the heart and soul of the home. A newspaper article will be in tomorrow's paper regarding this event, and we wanted to update all staff, as community members may inquire of you about it as you work throughout your day. Our thoughts and prayers stay with the Adderly's, as Mrs. Adderly continues in her recovery efforts."

"Lastly, as you know, this year is an election year and the county commissioners have agreed with us to request a .2 mil increase in our tax levy. Our costs are continually increasing as everything else rises. Our local tax levy provides about sixty percent of our total revenues, followed by thirty-five percent of federal dollars and five percent of state monies. As you can see, this levy is extremely important for us to pass. We will need each and every one of you to help us get out the vote for this levy. We have two board members who have agreed to volunteer and organize our efforts – Agnes Whitmore and Dody Jones. This is going to require staff volunteer their free time to canvas neighborhoods, make some speeches at community gatherings and raise money towards financing our efforts. Unfortunately state law prohibits us from setting aside any of our work time towards this effort. I tell you now, if you want to be assured of maintaining your jobs, we need your help."

"If this levy fails, we will be forced to start downsizing our staff by at least ten percent. There's little else we can cut except for staff. As you know, our office space is anything but luxurious and we pay the lowest possible rent. Our overhead costs can't get any lower. The only place we do have any discretionary spending is in staff allotments. If this levy fails we've one of two choices – start staff layoffs or reduce staff pay to lessen the layoffs. Either way it isn't a pretty scenario. As a result we need you all to become community advocates and help with the passage of this levy."

A hand rose up in the front row. "What do you mean by becoming a community advocate?"

"That's a good question. There are several ways each of us can participate. We've identified key neighborhoods needing to be canvassed at a grassroots level. We will have flyers and information cards to pass out to each household. We will need volunteers to go door-to-door, promote the levy and answer any questions the public may have."

"Additionally we've a list of several different groups and citizen council meetings throughout the county. We will want to have a representative at each of those to deliver a 'levy advertisement' in the form of a short speech."

"Last, but not least by any means, it takes money. It takes money to print the materials and pay for needed radio and television advertising. All together we will need about fifty thousand dollars to launch this campaign and see it through to the end. Unfortunately media advertising isn't cheap. On the up side, we've already garnered half the amount from some concerned anonymous citizens in the community, so we only have to come up with twenty-five thousand dollars."

Another hand shot up. "What revenue resources can we access to get that money?"

"Again, another excellent question. Unfortunately, that rests solely upon our shoulders. At this time we can think of three ways to achieve the goal. First, staff can possibly create and plan some fund raising activities such as bake sales, car washes, or any activity we've the ability to run, to raise money from the community, except raffles. We are legally not allowed to hold raffles. Secondly, we can all ask for donations directly from individuals we may personally know who may be interested in helping us. And lastly, if each of us can find some way to donate fifty dollars, we'll bring in fifteen thousand dollars."

An elderly woman in the clerical staff stood up and asked, "As you know we are not well paid. Some of us even qualify for food stamps because our pay is so low. I mean, we don't even get one tenth of the salary you get paid as the executive director. What happens to us if we simply can't afford to personally contribute our own money? I know I struggle to feed my family and buy gas for my broken down car."

Carrie could hear some grumbling behind her. "We already work more than forty hours a week and don't get paid for those hours. Now they expect us to donate even more of our time for this effort, too."

"Yeah, we don't even get paid as much as teachers, only get two weeks of vacation a year, and work in dangerous areas. This sucks," boomed another voice from behind.

"They have our asses lassoed and they know it," responded the first voice. "We don't have any choice. Give them more of our time, for free, or maybe lose our jobs."

Carrie wanted to turn around and smack these workers. What they said was absolutely true, but she hated whiners. If they were unhappy, she wanted to tell them to quit and find another vocation. She hated negativity. Obviously this job wasn't the path to financial riches, but it provided benefits of a different nature. Yes, it could and would easily usurp your waking hours with little compensation or thanks, except for the thanks delivered through the eyes of the children. What price could you put on that?

Carrie refocused her attention to the stage. "I know this request may be very difficult for many of you. For those who have more funds, we would be glad to take a larger donation." The entire auditorium began to laugh. "We can't require this of you. If you can't give a dollar donation, hopefully you can help with some of the other fundraising activities. Again the stakes are high. If this levy doesn't pass, there will likely be layoffs, I'm sorry to say."

"Yeah, but you won't get laid off will you," an angry voice was heard from the back of the room.

"Listen, I know this is tough. These are tough times. I can only implore you to understand and help wherever you can. Passage of this levy is critical for us to maintain our staff and many of our services."

"I believe that concludes our agenda for today. Thank you all for coming."

The crowd gathered their belongings together and began exiting the theater. Chattering could be heard throughout the group as they shuffled about.

"Hey Carrie!" called out Jenny. "We're going to catch some lunch. Want to come along? We thought we would go to the Bohemian Grille."

"Oh, I'd love to except I have to stop by the Kane home."

"What? I thought you went there yesterday, or was it the day before?" Jenny remembered.

"Yes I did, the day before. I took her some food that should have lasted the family for a week. But her neighbor called and told me she threw most of it out, and put a lot of it down her garbage disposal because she thought it was poisoned."

"Are you kidding me? Really?"

"I wish I were kidding. I'm afraid I'm going to have to figure out if it's safe to leave her two children with her. Her thinking ability is deteriorating. She likely is off of her medication. I'm going to try to get her to go to the mental health center for another assessment. I know they won't declare her homicidal or suicidal, but she definitely needs another intervention. I'm worried about the children. They are only four and six years old. I checked with the school and she hasn't sent Bonnie to school the last four days either. I'm afraid I may have to place them," Carrie declared with a loud sigh.

"Gee, I'm sorry," Jenny responded. "If you need any help later in the day, let me know."

"Thanks, I will," Carrie smiled as she walked out the door.

***

That's how Carrie's days went. When she walked into work, she never knew what might be waiting for her. An internal agency concern to be addressed, a committee meeting, a fellow employee needing a comforting voice or helping hand, a hungry child, a beaten wife, a cluttered unsafe home, a sick child, an angry delinquent, a dying mother looking for someone to care for her children, an overwhelmed mother with a colicky baby, rat and roach infested dwellings, a burnt home from a fire due to condemned wiring, a suicidal parent, families struggling every way you could imagine. Big, forlorn, begging eyes of children filled with hope for someone to rescue them from their pain: physical pain, hunger pain, emotional pain, devastating pain, psychological pain, and the pain of torrential fear. She couldn't walk away even if she wanted to. Her internal spirit wouldn't let her turn her back on the children or person in need. There were days when she would come home tenaciously tired, sometimes more emotionally tired than physically tired, sometimes both. She felt enormously blessed to come home to Jeff and Kate. Her reward was to come home to love and great caring. Kate filled her with a delight only known to mothers. Kate provided her with the balance she needed in her life. It was rare for Carrie to see a happy and thriving child during work hours. She needed to know up close and personal there was hope for the world's children. Katy gave her that solace.

Jeff didn't understand her calling to minister to the needy. In rare moments he would rail against her for continuing her job. He came to realize this would always be a no win argument for him. He loved Carrie for the exact same reasons he loathed her vocation. The essence of her being was the most loving soul he ever knew.

chapter 31

Carrie remembered back clearly to the day of Kate's first birthday. Unknown to her and Jeff, they were about to take passage on an unexpected life journey, changing them in ways unforeseen. Jeff, himself an only child, was quite content with having one child. Carrie, on the other hand, didn't want Kate to grow up without the joy only siblings provided. She cherished her relationship with her brother Carson. When their parents died, Carson became her strength and she became his. She didn't want Kate to feel the loneliness of being an only child. Jeff wasn't opposed to more children. He was, though, quite satisfied with Kate alone.

After Kate was snuggled in bed, Carrie plopped herself down into Jeff's lap and approached him with her desire for more children. She was six weeks away from approaching the age of thirty-four and she didn't want to wait longer to try to have another child.

"Jeff, darling," Carrie began, "can you believe our little Kate is already one year old!"

"It's hard to believe. It seems like the year has flown by. I'm already regretting the day when she grows up and leaves our home. I never knew such a small child could capture my heart the way she has," Jeff smiled. "I love her so much! In fact, how did I get so lucky to get the two greatest females in the world to live with me?"

"And to love you, too," Carrie teased.

"Yes, and to love me, too. I do feel blessed. I love you both with every breath I take. I know I'm one of the luckiest men walking this earth." Jeff hugged Carrie and gave her a gentle lingering kiss.

"Well what would you say if we tried for another precious angel to add to our family?" Carrie offered.

Jeff looked Carrie straight in the eye, "Are you serious? Do you want another child?"

"Well, only if you do, too," Carrie countered. "Don't you think we should consider another child, at least for Kate's sake? I mean, wouldn't it be nice for her to have a brother or sister to share her life with? You know when we die I really don't want Kate to be alone in the world. There's something special about having another person with which to share your life history."

"Gee, Carrie, I don't know." Jeff had a serious look on his face. Carrie was afraid her dream of another child might be headed for the trash heap. She began to feel slightly panicked.

"What about another child would cause you to be unsure? Kate is terrific. Wouldn't you love to have another little Cathers to dote on?"

"Carrie, it's not that. I love Kate so much I can't imagine dividing my love, giving her less. It doesn't seem fair to her."

Carrie knew how to approach Jeff's dilemma. It eased her panic. "Jeff, do you remember how you loved me the day we got married?"

"What kind of question is that?" he retorted. "Of course I do. I've never loved anyone like I love you. You've filled my heart entirely. In fact, I've grown to love you more deeply each day." Jeff tenderly stroked her arm as he talked.

Carrie continued, "So when Kate was born, did she usurp some of your love away from me?"

"Of course not. What a silly notion."

"Is it any more silly than you thinking another child of ours would take away any of the love you have for Kate?" Carrie raised her eyebrow and cocked her head to the side. "You see, my darling accountant, in my world, love isn't divided, it is multiplied. Wouldn't you like to invite even more love into your life?"

Jeff sat silently, pondering for what seemed like an eternity to Carrie. "You got me again!" Jeff conceded. "Come closer and let me kiss those lips again." This time his kiss was less affectionate and more passionate. "Yes," he whispered in her ear. "Yes, let's get on that right away." He took her hand and led her to the bedroom, whereupon they reveled in each other's body as if they were making love for the first time all over again. The next day Jeff sent her a dozen roses. The enclosed note simply read: *We can have as many little Cathers as your heart desires. For what your heart wants, so does mine.* Carrie was ecstatic.

The desire for another child revived their sex life. After Kate's birth their sex life diminished. Carrie wasn't concerned about the change. She was often fatigued from work. When she would come home, she spent every hour with Kate until she tucked her in bed. But she missed the connection with Jeff. It was something about the knowledge of creating a new child which sparked their passion all over again. Jeff wasn't this amorous in months. Carrie didn't realize how greatly she missed their intimacy. She loved coming home to Kate. She acknowledged her own passion for Jeff took a back seat, until now. It was all glorious and wonderful. Home certainly became her sanctuary from her day life.

A year passed and it was now Kate's second birthday and the hope of a second pregnancy wasn't fulfilled. It wasn't for lack of trying. This past year was one of Jeff's and Carrie's most passionate. Yet they didn't achieved conception again. Carrie feared she waited too long and her eggs were too old. After six months of trying, she and Jeff were referred to an infertility expert, Dr. Schmidt. Thus they began their arduous journey of solving the problem.

Jeff was first tested for his sperm count. No problem there. They sent them home with instructions for Carrie to take her basal temperature each morning before she got out of bed. They wanted to discover her cycle of ovulation. The mornings her temperature was higher for two or three days from the other days in her cycle were likely the days she was ovulating. They became obsessed with temperature taking and graphing it. Clearly two or three days each month Carrie's temperature was higher by two degrees. On those days, they sent Kate to stay with her grandparents. She and Jeff stayed tangled together for as long as their libidos allowed. Six months later and they still had no positive results.

More tests followed. They injected Carrie with dye to determine if her tubes were blocked. She particularly remembered the test, a salpinogram, never wanting to repeat it again.

"First we are going to insert the speculum," Dr. Schmidt instructed. "Then we are going to attach the dye injector. You should feel a slight pinch or tweak." A slight pinch my ass, Carrie thought. It felt like someone grabbed all of her female organs and twisted them violently upside down. She let her male doctor know, in no uncertain terms, he didn't know what he was talking about regarding a slight pinch. She thought he should be informed, so he didn't misguide future patients.

"Okay, I hear you loud and clear," he acknowledged. "Next we are going to need you to lie as still as you can. Do not move a muscle. You can watch as we inject the dye into your vaginal canal on this monitor screen. When all the dye is injected we will be taking some x-rays which will require you to be absolutely still. Okay?"

"Roger," Carrie replied. She watched the monitor. She saw the dye fill up her uterus. Kind of cool, she thought. She was fascinated by the distinct shape of the organ. As she was enjoying the experience, all bets were off. As the dye entered her fallopian tubes the pain and pressure became excruciating. Even Kate's childbirth wasn't this painful! Her body wanted to jump up to the ceiling and back, off the table and out of the door. 'You need to lie absolutely still' rang through her mind. Was he kidding? Couldn't they have knocked me out first for this? But Carrie remembered she was a trooper, a non-complaining trooper and she took it like a man, no like a strong, determined, woman. No man could take this she thought and made herself laugh. And they complain about having to whack off to give a sperm donation!

"Another minute or so," the doctor spoke, "and we'll be done."

Another minute or so, Carrie thought frantically as she clenched her teeth. You've got to be kidding me. "Well that does it," Dr. Schmidt continued. "The good news is there are no blockages here. Everything looks normal."

Carrie took a big sigh of relief, not only for the normal pronouncement, but for the end of the simple procedure as they called it.

The doctor sent her home and told her to be patient and to keep trying. They did. Nothing happened. Three months later the medical team decided perhaps there was something wrong with her uterus's ability to maintain the vitality of a fertilized egg. They wanted to perform an endometrial biopsy. It would require a procedure scraping off some cells from the inner lining of her uterus, a procedure easily done in the doctor's office. They did the procedure once, twice and then a medical student announced to Carrie they would need to do it a third time after he checked her charts. Carrie loudly protested.

"I'm not submitting to the intervention again, especially not by a medical student. You're not even an intern. Besides they have already done it twice."

"But your charts indicate differently, ma'am."

"Are you suggesting I don't know how many times this has been performed on me? And don't you call me ma'am. I'm not that old." Carrie was a bit testy. This procedure, too, was no picnic. "Where is my doctor? I want to see him."

"He'll be along shortly."

"Well, you and I are not doing anything together, so you can boogie on out of here, okay?" The medical student exited and returned with Dr. Schmidt.

"Hello Carrie, how are we doing today?" Dr. Schmidt started the conversation.

"I don't know how we are doing today. I brought my brain with me. I don't think your medical student has one. The important question is how are you doing today?" Carrie knew she was acting like a brat but couldn't help herself. This process was wearing on her. Perhaps it was the straw breaking the proverbial camel's back.

"Well we've some test results I want to discuss with you and Jeff. Why don't you meet me in my office in five minutes?"

"I'm sorry, but Jeff couldn't come today. He has an important meeting with one of his larger accounts."

"No problem. I'll see you in a few."

Carrie seated herself in the large comfy armchair opposite the large walnut desk of Dr. Schmidt. She eyed all of the framed diplomas and credentials on his wall. "Carrie, my team has thoroughly examined all of your test results. All of our tests have shown you to be normal. However the last blood test we took indicates you've a slightly elevated level of testosterone in your blood. This may not be problematic as it's still within the high normal range, actually the very top of the high normal range. But we need to discover from where the testosterone is being produced, either the adrenal glands or the ovaries."

"I see. How do you discover that?"

"I promise you, this will be the least painful and easiest test you'll need to take. All you have to do is collect your total urine elimination into this receptacle for the next seventy-two hours." Dr. Schmidt held up a container resembling a large paper milk carton.

"That's it?" Carrie said.

"There is one caveat," Dr. Schmidt continued. "You'll need to keep it refrigerated between urinations and then bring it to us immediately following the seventy-two hours."

Carrie's mind raced. She was going to have to take this contraption to work and keep it in the refrigerator. Unbelievable! Her co-workers would die if they knew their lunches were sitting next to her urine. And the darn thing was so large, it wouldn't go unnoticed and there was already a fight to find refrigerator space for the sack lunches. "Can I wait until this Friday to collect it?" Carrie was thinking it would only need to be in the refrigerator at work for one day, and would only have begun to fill up. Less opportunity for odor her mind reasoned, always the rational thinker.

"Unfortunately I don't think that will work," Dr. Schmidt hesitated. "It would require for you to bring it to us on Sunday and we are not open then. Perhaps you could start on Saturday. You'll have two days at home. Perhaps you could take off Monday, if you're concerned about this at work. I can give you a medical note for sick leave if you need."

Carrie's heart sank. That wouldn't work either. She had to testify in court on Monday for a trial that was continued three times. The judge admonished all of the attorneys for the delays and said he would accept no excuses from anyone for another trial date. All were ordered in, even if they were on their deathbeds. She resigned herself to the inevitable. She would take the pee contraption to work on Monday, the third day of peeing into it, store it in the refrigerator at work and if she had nosy co-workers, so be it. It would serve them right. Then her thoughts became obtuse and she found the whole scenario funny. She started to giggle.

In a concerned voice Dr. Schmidt inquired, "Are you okay Carrie?"

"Oh, it's nothing," Carrie squeaked out and then began to laugh louder. "It's so. . ." her laughter increased, "it's just so, just so, just so . . ." She laughed so hard she began crying. Then the tears turned into a torrent of tears and she began sobbing. They were no longer tears of laughter, but tears of emotional pain.

Dr. Schmidt got up from his chair, grabbed the tissue box and sat next to Carrie. He was fond of his patient and admired her strength and tenacity. He could sense her pain. "Carrie, can you tell me what you're feeling?" he offered.

She blew her nose and tried to compose herself. "Why does it have to be so hard? Why can't I get pregnant like my clients do? They pop out babies as fast as popcorn pops. Why is this happening to me? All Jeff and I want is another child to hold and love. Why is that asking for too much?" She began to sob again.

"Carrie now isn't the time to give up hope. We still have things to check out. You'll get pregnant again. We need to tweak a few things. Your prognosis still is very promising."

When Dr. Schmidt spoke of tweaking things, she remembered the salpinogram test. It was going to be a slight tweak. It got her to laughing again. "Gosh, I'm sorry. I'm a mess today. I feel really embarrassed. I don't know what's wrong with me."

"The infertility process can be quite stressful. You hang in there. And don't be embarrassed. There's no need. Now, are you going to be alright? Do you want me to call Jeff or someone else to see you home?"

"No, no I'll be fine. It is what it is, isn't it?"

"Well, yes."

"I'm good now. Hit a little bump in the road. All's okay." Carrie stood up and began to leave his office.

"Oh Carrie," Dr. Schmidt called to her.

"Yes?"

He held up the urine receptacle with a slight grimace on his face. Carrie laughed again, retrieved the carton and left.

She dropped off the urine sample on Monday to Dr. Schmidt. They scheduled an appointment for her at noon on Wednesday, so she wouldn't have to miss work time. Wednesday came quickly.

Dr. Schmidt began, "We've received your test results back and have discovered it's your ovaries producing the testosterone. We can easily ameliorate this with a shot of progesterone. Are you alright with that?"

"Whatever you say, Doc."

"Okay, well the nurse will administer the shot into your upper hip. It's an oil based formula, so the best action would be for you to go home afterward and soak in a hot tub of water. The hot water helps the oil to thin out and enter your system."

"No can do," Carrie sighed. "My work schedule prohibits that. Will it be a problem?"

"There is an alternative action you can take. The goal is to keep the oil warmed, so if you can remember to rub the site of the injection vigorously every five minutes or so, you'll be okay. Do that for about three hours and it will work as well."

"You know Dr. Schmidt, you come up with the most potentially embarrassing of predicaments for me. So you want me to spend the day rubbing my ass?"

"Pretty much, sums it up."

All Carrie could do was laugh. How on earth was she going to explain this? She decided to get real with her co-workers. She vowed the private Carrie would have to share her infertility life with them. It would make life easier. She intellectualized there should be no embarrassment about infertility any more than there was with cancer, broken bones or warts. It was time to be honest. Honesty was the best policy, wasn't it?

It didn't take long for her co-worker, Donna, to notice Carrie rubbing her derriere. "What's up, Carrie. Do you have an itch that won't be scratched?"

"I wish," Carrie answered as she continued to massage her hip.

"What do you mean you wish?" Donna said taking greater interest.

Carrie knew it was now or never to spill the beans. "To tell the truth, I've been dealing with an infertility problem. Jeff and I decided to have another child about a year and a half ago, and to date we haven't had any success, obviously." Carrie sighed and slowly continued with her thought, "I was referred to Dr. Schmidt, an infertility expert, and have been undergoing a lot of different tests. Today I was given an oil based injection and instructed to frequently rub the injection site to help with the absorption of the medicine. It was either this or soak in a hot bath tub all day. And with my schedule there was no way I could do that."

Donna looked flabbergasted. She never imagined anything was difficult for Carrie. "Oh, no! You too! I'm so sorry. But I've heard Dr. Schmidt is one of the top physicians in the field."

"He's been great. We haven't discovered what the problem is. Still working on it. What do you mean you, too?"

"Haven't you heard? There are at least three other women working here who are struggling with the same issue. You know them – Katrina in clerical, Joella in foster care and Maggie in Pam's unit."

"I had no idea," Carrie said in surprise.

"You're so good with children. People like you were meant to be mothers. I bet it hasn't been easy for you either, I mean working here and seeing all of the mothers who get pregnant at the drop of a hat, and then won't or can't take care of them. That's got to be tough."

"Sometimes it gets me down. But if it's meant to be, it'll happen. At least I do have Kate," Carrie offered.

"Well, I wish you all the luck in the world," Donna continued.

"Thanks, Donna. I'll take all the luck I can get!"

Gossip was never lacking at the agency and before the day's end, Carrie was approached by at least five other people offering their words of encouragement and support. She even discovered two additional women at the agency struggling with the same issue. She had no idea infertility was so prevalent.

***

Carrie discovered infertility issues ushered in a host of other potential problems. First, one had to learn patience. Typically in a year's time there were only twelve opportunities to get pregnant. After each medical intervention, the patient was told to go home and try again. Dr. Schmidt usually waited at least two months or longer before he could rule things in or out, and then begin a new test if needed. And in Carrie's case, it seemed like another test was always needed.

Secondly, one had to constantly ward off the depression following the start of each monthly menstrual cycle, announcing no baby yet.

Thirdly, one had to awaken each morning and stick a damn thermometer in their mouth for three minutes before arising. Carrie fell back to sleep twice with the thermometer in her mouth and bit down on it breaking it in two pieces. Other times when she would fall asleep with it in her mouth, she would wake up slobbering all over herself as her saliva would drool down her chin. This didn't create any kind of early morning romance.

And lastly, it changed the whole meaning of the sexual relationship between her and Jeff. It no longer became a loving act, but a required chore. It could easily become the death of a relationship. It was especially frustrating when they needed to complete a post-coital test for the doctor. They were to successfully complete the sex act at home. Then Carrie needed to rush to the doctor's office within two hours for them to examine if her body fluids were killing Jeff's sperm. It sounded easier than it was. For Jeff, even as much as he loved Carrie, being able to perform this act at an exact appointed time became quite stressful. Three times they were unable to achieve any success. The entire process simply tested both partners to the point of exasperation.

Carrie felt Jeff withdrawing emotionally from her during these times. He no longer approached her for lovemaking unless the temperature chart suggested this was the right time for conception. Their days of carefree romance and lingering in each other's arms disappeared. When they did make love, Jeff fell back into his ultra conservative mode and demanded only the missionary position. There was no imagination, no creativity, simply a quick plain sex act – wham, bang, thank you ma'am, lucky to get a thank you. Carrie began to wonder if this was all worth the effort.

The last test they performed was the laparoscopy, a minor surgery requiring the doctor to cut a small incision in her naval and look into her body's cavity with a miniature camera to actually observe the condition of her sexual organs. They discovered she had some non-malignant fibroid tumors growing on her ovaries and fallopian tubes. They were able to remove them successfully. This outcome surprised the medical team involved as Carrie never reported any pain in this area, which was the most common complaint of those so afflicted. But Carrie had an unusually high tolerance to pain.

"Go home and relax," Dr. Schmidt told Carrie. "This should take care of your problem. In fact, I'm not even going to see you for six months, not until November. I know how stressful these procedures can be, and my advice to you is to forget about trying to get pregnant. Take some time for you and Jeff to get back to a normal routine. Get rid of the thermometer. You both can use a break. I'm sure of it."

"Well you're right about needing a break. You really think this was our problem all along?" Carrie persisted.

"We generally have great results with our patients after removing fibroid tumors. Don't worry. Really. Carrie, relax."

"So do you think the fact I'm thirty-six years old is another problem for us?"

"Carrie, relax, relax. Now go home and find yourselves again."

Carrie couldn't help herself. "What if I still don't get pregnant? Are there any other avenues left for us to explore?"

"Carrie," Dr. Schmidt began, "you're impossible. You need to think more positively."

"I know. I know you're right. I'll try. But are there? Are there any other paths to explore for us?"

"Yes, there is one more. But it's relatively new and the results are still pending on its effectiveness. It's call in-vitro fertilization. But we're not even going to consider it now. I want you to go home. Hopefully I won't even need to see you six months from now. Take care, Carrie, and . . . "

"I know," Carrie acceded, "and relax. I'll try. Thank you for everything Dr. Schmidt. I hope I'll have good news for you soon."

"Me, too," Dr. Schmidt smiled as he gave her a hug good-bye.

chapter 32

It was late June, 1986. Kate was three and her personality was taking shape. She was a bright and inquisitive child. She seemed to be quite empathic even at this young age. She knew how to make Carrie smile and could sense when her mother was troubled, even though Carrie could effectively hide her sadder emotions from others. Kate intuitively knew what her mother needed and was happy to provide it. She might sing her a silly song, smother her with kisses or make up a story to tell her. All of her stories had the same happy ending, "...and everyone would fall to sleep at night with smiles on their faces."

Carrie tried to implement Dr. Schmidt's advice and relax. She vowed to herself she wouldn't speak about having another child during this time. Jeff was good with that, too. Kate was enough for him. He hated to see Carrie so disappointed time and time again. Even though she relaxed, it didn't change the downturn in her and Jeff's intimate relationship. He immersed himself in his work and didn't seem to require any sexual contact. When they did make love, it was robotic and unfulfilling. Carrie thought about Scarlett O'Hara in "Gone with the Wind" and decided she would deal with that tomorrow. Perhaps they both needed a vacation from lovemaking, or should she say sex. The love component seemed to have taken a back seat.

At work there was always another crisis to address. Carrie channeled her energy back into her caseload during the day and spent her evening hours loving on Kate. In many ways her world became simpler. Jeff was content to sit on the sidelines and watch over his two women. Life was good.

This night was the agency's annual employees' banquet and reception. It was a time for staff to gather together and forget about the day's worries and enjoy one another. It was a time to reconnect with each other without the overlay of work. The agenda included the invocation, the food, some songs from the talented youth of the creative arts program in the area, a local keynote speaker, the presentation of the awards for years of service (given to each employee for every five years they served), and the announcement of the coveted "Employee of the Year" award.

Carrie sat with her unit members: Becky, Jenny, Donna, Jim and their newest employee, Andrea. Spouses were also invited but not children. Jeff attended along with many others. He seemed to be in high spirits and was quite jovial. Carrie was glad. It was quite relaxing.

"And now for the employee of the year," John Mitchell announced. "Let me read the winning nomination." Any employee could nominate another for this award. A selection committee was chosen to include at least one board member, the executive director, two supervisors and three staff members.

"This employee comes to work each day with boundless energy. A smile can usually be seen on this employee's face even during the most troubling of circumstances. This employee always exudes integrity and is a willing and accommodating spirit to any of us who may need a helping hand. She, aaah we know it's a female," he interjected, "sorry guys." He continued. "She keeps her nose to the grindstone, and is an exemplary example to all who serve in this field. She's mentored countless new employees as well as students. She's routinely seen working well beyond quitting time and has been known to complain only once. Only once?" John Mitchell repeated and arched his eyebrows in disbelief. "Really, only once? I wonder what it was about, don't you? Well, continuing on: this employee has been nominated yearly for the last ten years. She started the initiative to secure bus tickets for our clients so they would have transportation to needed appointments. She lobbied for a child friendly visitation center for parents with children in foster care. She's highly thought of among our many community partners including Juvenile Court, the police department and Children's Hospital. It's with great honor I present to you…." Jeff looked lovingly at Carrie and gave her a wink. ". . .Ms. Carrie Cathers! Come on up here Carrie."

Jeff leaned over and gave Carrie a hug and a kiss as all the other attendees immediately stood and gave her a resounding standing ovation. "You knew!" Carrie said to Jeff. He merely shrugged his shoulders.

As Carrie walked up to the podium, she couldn't believe what happened. She thought for sure the award would be given to Rachel Glowacki, a dedicated employee for the last twenty-six years. Carrie thought she didn't do anything special to deserve this award. She simply did her job.

John Mitchell shook her hand, and offered her an engraved plaque stating: Carrie Cathers, Employee of the Year, 1986, followed by a picture of the agency's logo. John Mitchell spoke again into the microphone, "So Carrie, do you want to share with us what your one complaint was?"

"Well Mr. Mitchell," Carrie paused for a moment to gather her thoughts, "I really don't think we want to infuse this room with negative energy, now do we?"

"Oh, come on Carrie, we can handle it!"

Carrie thought again for a response. How could she help him save his own face? "Mr. Mitchell, if you think hard enough you should remember, for it's to you I complained." The crowded room broke out with uproarious laughter. Mr. Mitchell's face carried a stymied look. Carrie motioned with her finger for him to lend her his ear upon which she whispered softly, "Brian Galloway."

"Oh," came out of his mouth. "Well once again, Carrie has demonstrated her iron integrity and professionalism. Shall we all give her another round of applause?" John Mitchell vigorously clapped his hands again. "Now before you leave the podium Ms. Cathers, we have one additional announcement. As our employee of the year, you've been selected to receive the honor of attending the Public Children's Policy Initiative's National Conference in September of this year as our representative." Carrie was flabbergasted and speechless. "That's not all folks," John continued, "It's being held in San Francisco, California!" Once again the crowd came to a frenzied roar of approval.

John handed the microphone to Carrie for some words. "Oh my, oh my Lord. Never in a million years would I have dreamed all of this would happen in my life. Thank you all so much. I gladly accept this award. San Francisco? Really?" Carrie was still stunned and searching for the right words. "I gladly accept this award as a symbol for all of the hard work each and every one of us do daily. I could never do what I do without the support of my co-workers and supervisor as well as my dear husband. All of you deserve this award, but I'm happy I got it. Thank you all, once again!"

She left the podium and was once again swept up into the loving embrace of Jeff, who was grinning at her from ear to ear. "If anyone deserves this award, you do sweetheart," he announced above the noise and kissed her again.

⁂

Summer came and went as fast as a hurricane blows through a town. Carrie could hardly believe September arrived as she was packing for her trip to San Francisco. She hadn't visited San Francisco before and was excited. The last and only time she was in California was when she and Jeff honeymooned in Sequoia National Park.

She was conflicted about leaving Kate for a whole week, but knew she would be in the loving and capable hands of Jeff and his parents. Grandma Betty was the best of grandmothers and Kate loved her dearly. Betty and Kate sat at the kitchen table yesterday and planned their itinerary. "We must go to the zoo and see all the animals," Kate proclaimed. "Mommy, do they have a zoo in San Francisco?"

"Yes they do sweetheart, the biggest zoo in the whole country!"

"Are you going to get to go there?"

"I don't know. I hope so. Sure wish you could come with me if I do go."

"Me, too, but don't worry mommy, Grandma Betty and I'll have fun at our zoo." Carrie was enveloped in a swelling love for this curious and bright little girl.

"Grandma Betty and I are going to make cookies. See all of these new cookie cutters she brought to me. There is a star, and a heart and a moon, and a sun! I'm going to make heart cookies for you because I love you so much!" she declared.

"You'll probably have way more fun than I will, sweetheart," Carrie smiled as she tousled the hair on top of her head.

"Prob'ly," Kate announced. "And don't worry about the birds at Dane Forest. We will go and feed them too!"

"We'll be fine, "Jeff announced as he entered the room. "Now don't worry your pretty little head about us."

Carrie continued packing as Kate was taking her afternoon nap. She quickly reviewed the conference's workshops and activities. The theme of the conference this year was "The Importance of Cultural Considerations." Additionally they offered side field trips to the San Francisco zoo, the Golden Gate Botanical Center, the famous Pier 39, a city tour to include Lombard St. and the legendary trolley car, and Fort Point, an old civil war fortress located under the infamous San Francisco Bay Bridge, coupled with a stop at Alcatraz. She hoped she would have time to take advantage of at least two of these offerings in addition to the daily workshops.

Jeff quietly ascended the steps to join Carrie in their bedroom. He didn't want to wake up Kate.

"What? Taking a break from the office?" Carrie said.

"Yep."

Jeff stood behind her and wrapped his arms around her and began kissing her neck.

"For what reason do I deserve this attention?" Carrie asked.

"Because," Jeff responded. He continued kissing her neck and turned her around to face him. He then nuzzled his lips directly on the spot of Carrie's neck he knew was extremely sexually sensitive. He began moving his lips down to the top of her breasts and laid protracted kisses upon them. "You know I'm going to miss you," he murmured. "This will be our first separation. I don't know if I can handle it. I need you Carrie. I could never live without you."

"Don't be silly, Jeff. I'll be coming right back."

"You better," he said. "I know I haven't been the ideal lover these past few months, but I do love you." He kept kissing her. "How about you get out of those clothes and let's hop into bed. I want to give you a going away gift you'll remember."

"Alright," Carrie said as she pulled off her top. "I'm up for it."

They cozied up against one another. Jeff stroked her breasts. Carrie could feel his swelling manhood. He separated her legs and entered her. Within five minutes he was spent. "Well I better get back to the office," he announced. "Besides you need to finish packing. I love you sweetheart." He threw her a kiss.

Carrie lay in bed not knowing what to think about what happened. She was glad it happened. She was glad Jeff came to her. She was glad he was fulfilled, but she couldn't say the same for herself. She loved his gesture. She understood his meaning. He did love her. She felt her breasts and noticed her nipples were hardened. Carrie placed her hand between her legs and began stroking herself. It was so long since she climaxed, and Jeff awakened her need for the release. She let her mind wander back to their earlier days of slow lovemaking as she stimulated herself to orgasm. Maybe when I get back, we can find ourselves again, she thought.

chapter 33

Bags packed and checked in at the airline's reservation counter; Carrie was ready to depart for California within the next hour. Jeff and Katy warmly hugged her, wished her well and said their good-byes. Katy warned her "not to let the lions eat her up" at the zoo. As she walked down the concourse to her gate, she turned around for one last look. She saw Jeff's back as he walked away, and Katy waving to her enthusiastically as Jeff carried her up near his shoulder. Carrie waved back as she threw her a kiss. She sure was going to miss her little girl. At the same time she was excited for the change of venue away from her daily work routine. Sunny California, it couldn't get better. The last month at home was rainy more than it was sunny. She felt a momentary sense of freedom from everything. She didn't know if she should feel guilty or blessed. She settled on a bit of both.

Six hours later the plane touched down in San Francisco. She grabbed a cab and went to the swanky International Wyeth Hotel. She was issued a room located on the twenty-first floor with a window view looking westward toward the ocean. She could see Coit Tower and Alcatraz floating in the far distance. There was no curtain in the window, as the hotel had glazed glass windows allowing the visitor to see out, but didn't allow people outside to see in. It felt strange to be able to undress in front of such a window and not worry about being exposed. She had a king-sized bed with luxurious linens, a television, a refrigerator and a microwave. Carrie was never before in such a lavish room. This was certainly a treat beyond her expectations. It was ten o'clock back home, but only seven o'clock in the evening here. She was hungry. She decided to stroll down to the restaurant and bar lounge to grab a bite to eat.

The menu was as daunting as the hotel. She decided on some fresh albacore tuna with char grilled vegetables and rice pilaf. A glass of Perrier water complemented her dinner. She shifted into her people watching mode as she waited for the entrée. The bar area was crowded. A roar of raucous laughter could be heard. There were people of all types. They did dress differently here than what she would typically see in the Midwest. The culture appeared to be more youth oriented in its fashion sense. Carrie threw on some black linen pants with a white knit top and a brightly colored silk scarf covered with cats sitting next to each other. She hoped she didn't look too obviously out of place. In the end, she really didn't care, but the thought crossed her mind.

Her gaze settled upon the outline of a black woman sitting at the bar with her back to Carrie. Something felt curiously familiar about this woman's stature. Oh, it's probably nothing, Carrie thought. But the curious thought wouldn't leave her. The woman turned her head to the side and Carrie caught her profile. Oh my God! It's Lydia, Carrie thought. She hadn't seen or heard from Lydia since the day of their graduation. Carrie couldn't believe it. Then, her food was served. It was delicious. The fish was obviously fresh, not frozen, and cooked to perfection with a lemon basil sauce. Carrie thought it far beat anything she ate at the Windjammer. And the char grilled vegetables were to die for, especially the white asparagus. She kept her eye out for Lydia, wanting to catch her should she get up and leave.

Lydia jumped off of her barstool and started heading towards the exit as she passed closely by Carrie's table. "Oh, Lydia," Carrie called out. Lydia swerved her head to the left looking right past Carrie and then to the right searching for the caller of her name. "Over here, Lydia," Carrie called a second time. Lydia turned her head to the left again, finally settled her eyes on Carrie, and then reacted as if a thunderbolt struck her.

"Carrie! Oh my God! Carrie! Is that you? I can't believe you're here!" Lydia took a chair at Carrie's table. "You look great! You must be here for the conference too! This is so awesome. It's so good to see you!"

"Look at you," Carrie said warmly, "you look stunning."

"I feel terrific!" Lydia offered with great enthusiasm.

"So what have you been up to? It's been how long now since I've seen you? Seven years I think."

"Gee, has it been that long? Well I guess it has. Oh, I've been busy fulfilling my dreams," Lydia said as she placed her elbows on the table and rested her head lightly on her hands. Carrie cocked her head, asking her for more. "After graduation I worked a year for the Regional Planning Center and then the following year I went to NYC University and got my PhD. Can you believe it? I'm Dr. Lydia Greenly. I can't believe it. But as my grandmother always said, 'you're the only thing standing in the way of your successes. I kept her voice in my head and trudged on. Now I'm on staff, you won't believe this because I don't believe it yet even myself, at UC Berkeley, right here."

"Awesome," Carrie responded. "I'm so happy for you."

"Do I see a wedding band on your finger?" Lydia inquired. "Did you get married?"

"Oh, yes, I did. His name is Jeff. He's a CPA, and we have a three year old daughter named Kate."

"He must be quite a guy to catch you. What does he look like?"

"Oh, he is a little taller than six feet, brown hair, and brown eyes."

"He's one lucky guy," Lydia continued.

"And you? Have you found someone?" Carrie wondered.

"Me? Well I did discover one thing. I hope I won't offend you Carrie, but I have come out of the closet. I'm gay. What do you think about that? A black, gay woman!" Lydia began heartily laughing at herself. She slapped her hand on the table. "You know it wasn't easy coming out, the whole African-American culture really doesn't want to acknowledge that we exist at all. That's why I'm here. I'm giving a workshop about the gay/lesbian population in the minority cultures. Oh, do come to it if you can. I value your input."

"I would love to come. Do you have a significant other?"

"This one is going to grab you, too. I do. She's a tall blond white woman about six inches taller than me. She's a knockout. You should see the look on the faces of men when they realize she's with me! It's such a hoot! In fact I'm meeting her at nine o'clock tonight. Want to come along? I would love for you to meet her."

Carrie declined, "Maybe another time. I'm really tired. Your nine o'clock is my midnight I'm afraid."

"Oh, right. Well, promise me we'll get together again before you head home. I want to hear all about Jeff and your little girl. By the way, you didn't change your last name when you got married, did you?"

"I did," Carrie smiled, "it's Cathers, now. Carrie Cathers."

"Well you'll always be Carrie Singer to me. I hate I have to get going. It was great seeing you! Now remember to save some time for me. Bye-bye."

"Good bye," Carrie waved back.

Carrie finished her meal and headed back to her room after she ambled through the lobby and caught some fresh air outside. She still couldn't believe she was in California. There were no signs of the city quieting down for the night, but she was tired. She put on the silk pajamas her mother-in-law gave her for her birthday and sprawled out in the bed. After a few body stretches and a couple of loud yawns, she repositioned herself to sit up in the bed and look at the conference schedule possibilities. She knew she would need to declare which workshops she would attend in the morning.

There were so many to choose from: Culture: What is It?, Minority Disproportionality in the Social Service Systems, Building Cultural Advocates from the Grassroots, Codes of Conduct as they Apply to Universal Mores, Gay/Lesbian Population in the Minority Cultures (Lydia's workshop), Understanding the Essence of the Cultural Phenomena, Where Culture Ends and Laws Begin: Ethical Considerations, Respecting Cultural Diversity in Practice, Melting Pot or Salad Bowl?, Culture-Does It Matter?, How Culture Impacts Non-Verbal Communication: What was Your Meaning? So many choices, which to choose? Thinking about it made her tired. She flipped to the page outlining the credentials of the various speakers. Like a bright neon sign, flashing bells and whistles at her, his name jumped out and she felt her body fill with adrenaline. Benjamin Randall. Ben is here! That's all her mind would allow her to think in the moment. Ben is here! Ben is here! Ben is here!

At first she felt elated, happy and ecstatic. She hadn't seen or heard from Ben since they graduated from school together. Her mind quickly reminisced to the year they spent together working the evening shift. Then she remembered their last parting where they both declared their love for one another, a life moment filled with an internal happiness, only to be followed by great emotional pain in the realization such love could never be realized.

Carrie thought she moved past that moment. She moved on with her life, gotten married and had a beautiful daughter and a steadfastly loyal husband. But seeing his name on the pamphlet resurrected emotions she thought she long ago vanquished. Ben is here! Carrie checked herself and couldn't believe the emotional turmoil to which her mind quickly reverted. Ben is here!

Now calm yourself down, Carrie reflected. So what if Ben is here? This changes nothing. Ben's presence doesn't change a single thing. She began to rationalize. Ben and I were good friends, and that's how it will stay, good friends. We probably won't even run into each other. Ben is here! If I signed up for his workshop, I could see him. Do I want to? No, it's best to let sleeping dogs lay. Carrie decided to take the high road and avoid any interaction with Ben. If she saw him at a distance, she vowed to turn and walk the other way. She hadn't seen or heard from him in seven years, and she was none worse for the wear. It's best she decided. Employ avoidance was her plan, though there was a gnawing ache in her to see him.

She turned out the light and curled up in bed begging for sleep to come. Ben is here! Sleep. Ben is here! Sleep, let me go to sleep, she begged. What she so longed for seemed to evade her. Sleep finally came and snuffed out her last waking thought: Ben, Ben, Ben.

chapter 34

The telephone rang providing Carrie with her morning wake-up call. She was still tired. With her travel and the time zone changes the day before, it was no wonder. She foggily transported herself into the shower hoping the water would refresh her. As she was scrubbing her shampooed hair, clearing her head, the thought resumed: Ben is here! Carrie was jolted once again. This time she quickly recovered and started singing, "I'm going to wash that man right out of my hair." She began to laugh at the absurdity. She had a plan. It would work: avoidance. There would be no potential for any type of complication whatsoever. I'm a married woman, he's a married man. He's probably long forgotten our youthful silliness.

Carrie threw on a pair of blue jeans and a light green sweater. She grabbed the conference scheduled and reviewed it once again. She looked to see when Ben's workshop was being offered: Wednesday at three. She felt a surge of relief. Why, he probably isn't even going to be here until Wednesday. Presenters typically didn't stay as conference participants. She grabbed her purse and scampered out of her room towards the elevator. She met Kylee, also waiting for the elevator. They chatted on their way down to the lobby. Kylee was also attending the conference, having hailed from South Dakota, near Mt. Rushmore and the Crazy Horse Memorial. They chatted about their homes, family and work as they stood in the registration line. Carrie was thankful to have someone to talk to and she gladly entered into the conversation. "Can you believe Dick Gregory is going to be our keynote speaker?"

"No, but I'm excited to hear what he has to say," Kylee continued. "And I heard Bill Cosby came with him!"

"You're kidding," Carrie chided, "*the* Bill Cosby?"

"Yep, I overheard some of the event planners at the bar last night. They were so excited. It was a surprise to them as well. They were lamenting it was too late to insert him onto the written agenda. But what a great surprise it would be for all of us! This is going to be the best conference."

The registration line slowly moved forward as the throng of attendees chattered among themselves. Carrie immersed herself into conversation with Kylee to the point she didn't pay particular notice to anything else. It was her turn to register. She turned around only to find herself looking at the top of Ben's head as he was processing registrations behind the table. She knew that head and that full, thick, beautiful light brown hair. Her immediate reflex was to run, run as fast as she could. But she stood frozen.

"Name please," Ben asked without looking up.

"Carrie Cathers," eked out of her mouth.

"Carrie Cathers, oh yes, here you are," Ben said as he looked up. A bolt of recognition lit up his face. "Carrie! Oh my God, Carrie. Is it really you?"

"Hello Ben," Carrie said warmly trying to hide the exuberance her whole being was experiencing, "Surprise!" So much for the avoidance theory, she thought.

"Oh my goodness, what a surprise this is." Ben stood up and bent forward to give Carrie a big hug. Carrie felt the electricity starting to hum with his first touch. There was no denying their connection. "I can't believe you're here!"

"Well, here I am," she mustered. "What are you doing here?" she asked as she pointed to the registration table.

"Oh, I'm on the board of the National Public Children Services Policy Initiative. I volunteered to help with the registrations since I needed to be here as a presenter as well. I can't tell you how good it's to see you!"

"Yes, it's good to see you too. You look great! Well here's my registration request packet." Carrie handed him the envelope. She thought Ben's hand lingered a second too long touching her fingers as he retrieved the packet from her. Then she thought herself silly. "How's Jane?" Carrie offered to deflect the conversation elsewhere.

"Jane, she's good. Listen, promise me you'll have dinner with me Wednesday night. I have to leave the conference after registration is done, but I'm free Wednesday night. Please, Carrie," Ben said beseechingly. "We've so much to get caught up on. I still can't believe you're here!"

Say no, just say no. Carrie's mind was racing. Make up some excuse. You've other plans. Say no, for God's sake. Say no. "Dinner? Wednesday? I'd love to!"

"Great!" Ben's eyes lit up. "I'll meet you in the lobby, let's say seven-ish."

"Sounds perfect. "

"Hey, I see you didn't sign up for my workshop. What's that about?"

"Oh, I was in such a rush. I didn't really study the venue. I think I overlooked it," Carrie lied through her teeth, an uncommon act for her. "I mean I'm really surprised to see you here. Please sign me up for it. I wouldn't miss it for the world."

"Okay, got you all set up. Here's your packet. See you Wednesday. I can't believe you're here!" Ben handed her packet to her. His eyes sparkled.

"See you then. It's good to see you, Ben." Carrie turned and walked away. She couldn't believe what she assented to, dinner with Ben. After all we're adults. I can handle this, she thought.

Carrie had some time before her first workshop. She found a pay phone and dialed home. "Hi sweetheart," she answered back to Jeff. It was good to hear Jeff's voice. It grounded her as Jeff always did. He assured her she need not worry about him and Katy. They were fine. Jack and Betty were happy to keep Katy during the day. He was busy with his own work. He missed her, etc., etc.

"Now don't worry your pretty head about us. Take this time and enjoy yourself, Carrie. You work long and hard and deserve this break from work. Come back to us refreshed. You know we love you with all of our hearts and we miss you. We'll be here safe and sound when you come back. Love you. Bye."

"Love you too. Bye," Carrie said and hung up. She missed Kate immensely but knew she and Betty would be having fun together. She thought of Jeff. She thought of him sitting at his desk, working his figures. She thought about how he was so devoted to her and how lucky she was to have him in her life. Yet, something felt different. She couldn't quite put her finger on it.

***

Monday, Tuesday, Wednesday, the conference was flying by at supersonic speed. Dick Gregory gave a wake-up call of a speech. He seemed to be an angry man. He spoke of institutional racism by the white culture and how the minority culture was affected. He suggested while the white population was moving toward zero population growth, minorities would increase their numbers. It was the only way they would get a political voice and effect change. He also suggested the culture needed to move toward inter-racial marriages to even out differences. Many who attended the conference were shocked and appalled at his statements. Others felt strangely uncomfortable. Still others applauded.

In only a fashion Bill Cosby could deliver, he humorously brought all back to the notion of our common humanity. It was a good balance to Dick Gregory. Both left participants invigorated. It also stirred up lively discussions as the workshops broke out. Carrie found herself immersed with great interest. She realized how sheltered she felt from these macro political problems. Her world of local child maltreatment seemed to be a smaller focus. But, then, that's why she was a caseworker and not a policy planner. She preferred the direct contact with families. Let the visionary minds tend to the larger picture, she thought.

Late Monday afternoon she took advantage of the field trip to the Golden Gate Park and Botanical Conservatory. She hadn't been to such a large garden facility before. She once visited the Franklin Park Conservatory in Columbus, Ohio but it wasn't nearly the same size and stature. The California version was breathtaking and exhilarating.

She also went to Alcatraz on Tuesday. Walking into Alcatraz gave her an eerie feeling. During the guided tour they were locked into a cell, and even though she knew it was only momentary, it created a fleeting moment of panic. She could only imagine how the real criminals felt as they festered in this facility. They were shown Al Capone's cell and many other notorious criminals' cells. Some prisoners could see San Francisco from their small windows. It was designed this way to be a constant reminder to them what their lifestyle didn't deserve.

Wednesday afternoon came fast. It was three o'clock and time to attend Ben's presentation. Carrie was curious what the content would be. She tried to stay focused on the task at hand and pushed to the back of her mind any personal thoughts of him. It was impossible. Try as hard as she could, such thoughts came poking through all of her defenses. She knew the energy she carried into his lecture was unlike the energy she felt with all of the other workshops. She was extraordinarily excited on many different levels. She found a seat in the back row nearest the exit door. She wanted to keep all of her options open for whatever she may need or decide to do. The room was filling up and Carrie counted more than one hundred people in attendance. She was glad, hoping she could remain anonymous and out of site. Why she didn't know, because she did agree to have dinner with Ben the same evening. Her stomach fluttered at the thought.

'Where Culture Ends and Laws Begin: Ethical Considerations'

"Good afternoon ladies and gentlemen," Ben began projecting his melodious voice.

"Good afternoon," roared the seated professionals. Ben already captured his audience with those five words. Carrie thought back to the first time she heard Ben speak publically for the mandated reporter meeting. His level of confidence had certainly risen and he was more compelling than before. It was in his body language, his tone, his posturing, and in his eyes. His eyes gave away the back story. She could see it in his face, even though she was seated one hundred feet away from him.

"Culture and laws are in a formidable struggle with one another. Yet as a civilized society we must consider cultural mores as we design our laws. We pay homage to overarching cultural values such as do not kill and do not steal. Many of our current laws are based in Judeo-Christian values, which at the time of our country's founding was the pervasive thought of the public. But as we've grown, our country has not been void of our own social growing pains. Let me try to bring this closer to home for you."

"Please close your eyes. Think of your family. You and your siblings were all raised by the same parents. You all experienced life together, had the same experiences, went on the same vacations, lived day to day with each other in your house. Your family members sat around the dinner table at night and ate the same food. You laughed at the same things, held similar political views as well as religious views. So, given you had the identical same influences in your life, it would only be fair and accurate to suggest you and your family members were identical, entirely interchangeable. Right?"

The whole room groaned and disagreed.

"But how can that be?" Ben continued. "Is it perhaps given those same influences, you were able and did come to different conclusions even though you were all exposed to the same information and taught similarly? Some of you became extroverts, some introverts, some curious, others content, some risk takers, others homebodies, some more challenging, others more compliant. Some of you may have chosen to try illegal drugs, like marijuana or LSD, others chose to rely on prescription drugs only, and still others lived in fear of all substances both legal and illegal. Some of you remain steadfastly monogamous, others have multiple partners with no problems, others have partners of the same sex, and others are non-sexual.

How do you account for the differences and whose point of view should take center stage when writing and enforcing our societal laws? There's our dilemma. Who gets to decide what ethical behavior is and isn't? Whose perspective is honored? This is our struggle and likely shall be until the end of time."

"When it comes to child welfare, what behavior towards our children, our most precious resource, can we tolerate and can we not tolerate? When does a spanking become a beating? When do we cross the line, when caring for our children becomes a criminal act? I'm sure I could individually poll this audience and the answers would lie on a long continuum from no physical hitting of any kind on one end to anything short of death is a parent's right on the other end, well maybe not quite, at least not in this audience." The group tittered with laughter. "But don't be surprised if all of these responses can be found in the general public. And if you expand the boundary to include the entire world, we have cultures which are fine with parent's having the right to even kill their child."

Ben had them mesmerized. Carrie looked around the room and saw no side chattering happening at all. Amazing! She also was mesmerized.

"So where do we draw the ethical line in creating our laws? How do we establish what good social policy should look like. Often we look to statistics for answers. You all are familiar with the Bell curve, right? Remember those dreaded research and statistic classes we took in college?" Again the room filled with laughter. "Even if we take the middle sixty percent of views on the Bell curve and disregard the extreme twenty percent on either end of the curve in formulating our laws, we are likely going to piss off about forty percent of the population, while we placate to the middle. But then again statistics are limited in their information and are only informed by the populations polled or studied. So how does all of this apply to fabricating social policy laws and your job as child welfare caseworkers?"

The crowed stirred with various responses. "Good question!" "You're telling it like it is." "I've wondered myself." "Yeah, I want to know."

Carrie was enthralled. She even felt a false sense of personal pride, although she knew she shouldn't. She watched Ben move about the room, not hiding behind a podium like many speakers. She watched him make eye contact with his attendees. His features were animated and he demonstrated his passion easily. He had them eating out of his hand. He knows it, she thought. He knows how to deliberately use his self to capture his audience. He wasn't arrogant or flashy about it, making it so persuasive. And his message was pertinent. She found herself looking forward to dinner with him and continuing to explore his ideas.

She thought of Jeff and realized he was unable to share these kinds of conversations with her. He didn't understand them in the same context and had no real interest in them. People are people he would say, and be done with it. She missed this kind of dialogue. Carrie momentarily forgot about her unrequited love with Ben, and happily eased back into his presentation.

"Ethical standards in a modern society can't remain stagnant. Current legal mores must be continually examined and challenged as our society grows, diversifies and changes, for culture is dynamic. The 'old guard' will fight to the death against such change. But without change we are sure to self implode."

***

Carrie was glad to retreat to her room. She closed the door and let out a long sigh. Images of Ben danced through her mind. He was a master at public speaking. She admired his skill. As the workshop ended, people didn't rush to exit, but clustered around Ben to continue the conversation. He was in his element. He was right not to take the clinical path. Social policy was his forte as well as his passion.

She felt exhausted. She knew she also was on an emotional treadmill the last couple of hours. And now she was about to face the moment of truth, so to speak, which she approached with dread and exhilaration, dinner with Ben. She yawned loudly. She didn't want to think about it. Maybe if I take a short nap, I'll feel better. She called the front desk and asked for a wake-up call for six o'clock, giving her a full hour to primp, as much as Carrie primped. She lay down on the bed and slumber quickly enveloped her.

Carrie bolted up in her bed as the phone rang to wake her up. As she reoriented herself to her surroundings, she began to doubt she should meet Ben for dinner. Leave well enough alone, she thought. Then she began to giggle as she realized she blew this entire Ben encounter out of proportion. They were old friends, old good friends. They experienced a year of life closely together at work. They learned from one another, laughed together, cried together, and even dodged potential real danger together. Why did she focus only on the last days of their meeting in her apartment and at Professor Forsberg's and not their entire shared experience? I'm such a silly goose, she thought. I'm sure Ben has easily gone on with his own life with Jane and Alexis, as I have mine with Jeff and Katy. It will be good to reconnect, she rationalized.

It was a warm September evening. She wore a simply fashioned black background flowered sundress with a matching black short jacket. She dabbed some rosemary oil behind her ear to provide the faintest of scents. She preened in front of the mirror. "Well, it's now or never," she murmured.

As she rode down the elevator, her stomach churned but it wasn't from the thrill of the ride as one would feel on a roller coaster. "Oh, stop," she told her stomach. It didn't work. It became more excited. She took in a deep breath as the doors opened. She clutched her small black purse in her hand as she strolled towards the lobby.

There he was. Standing there, gleaming, and waiting for her. He grinned hugely upon seeing her. He walked towards her with outstretched arms ready to give her a big man sized nearly crushing hug. "Carrie, it's so good to see you!" he pronounced as he wrapped her in his arms. Carrie almost began to cry for joy, but mustered the ability to stop short, allowing her eyes to glisten with wannabe tears. "You look absolutely stunning! You've only gotten more beautiful with time." Ben wasn't filling her ears with false sweet talk, but with genuine delight and charm.

"It's great to see you too, Ben. Time hasn't hurt you one bit either," she returned the compliment. In fact, time didn't harm him at all and only made him more endearing. He lost his youthful cockiness and replaced it with measured self-confidence. She noticed his demeanor in his workshop. "Your workshop was terrific!" she continued.

"Really, you think so? It means a lot to me coming from you."

"Absolutely," Carrie smiled sincerely.

"Thanks, I appreciate the compliment. How about some dinner? Are you hungry?"

"Believe it or not I feel starved."

"I've always appreciated you Carrie, and your unabashed love for food. You aren't like all of those other women, obsessing about food and weight. But, then again, you've always looked great. What kind of food are you up for?"

"Oh, I thought we were going to eat here in the hotel."

"Here? I imagine you had your fill of food here. I know a place down the street a few blocks. A quaint Chinese restaurant called "Geem Loong". Are you up for some Chinese food? I know you didn't have any here."

"Chinese would be great! Let's do it."

Ben placed his arm around Carrie's waist and guided her out of the hotel and towards the restaurant. It was a short walk, but she floated there instead. Carrie couldn't believe she and Ben were spending time together.

Her last encounter with him in her mind was her final encounter with him. Life sure did take some strange twists and turns.

They were seated in a small rounded corner booth. The lights were dim, illuminated with Chinese lanterns, dropping silk decorative cording. There was scenic Asian wall paper depicting Chinese pictographs. The menu was expansive. Carrie ordered Wor Dip Har and Ben ordered Holy Basil Chicken. Both had egg rolls as an appetizer along with some Sake. The Sake warmed Carrie's tummy and helped her relax. "To old times," Ben toasted.

"Old times," Carrie repeated as they toasted their glasses and sipped on the Sake.

The booth didn't allow them to sit across from each other due to its rounded nature. They sat not quite side by side allowing for a sense of greater intimacy. Ben began the conversation. "Carrie, you got married! Whoever he is, he is one lucky guy!"

"Yep, I got married. His name is Jeff and he's an accountant. Do you believe it! I married an accountant."

"It does strike me as kind of funny, but then maybe my picture of an accountant is skewed. I imagine accountants to be logical, pragmatic, and exacting. You're all of those things as well, in a different kind of way. I guess I don't give accountants credit for having a heart."

"Trust me," Carrie said, "Jeff has a heart. You wouldn't question it, if you could see him with our daughter, Katy."

"You have a daughter! That's great. Tell me about her. Is she a little Carrie clone?"

"No, she's brilliant. Even at age three she's so intuitive. Her verbal skills are impressive. Before I left she warned me not to let the lions at the zoo eat me up!" Carrie laughed.

"Oh, I would love to meet her some day. She sounds precious. And Jeff, what's he like?"

"Jeff, well, Jeff is tall and has brown hair and eyes. His stature is quite similar to your own. He has his own accounting business, a CPA. He's more reserved than I am," Carrie lightly snickered, "more conservative. He's content to stay at home, kind of a homebody, you know. He's a devoted family man, strong and stable. He takes great care of me. We spend time reading together, we take walks, have picnics, and he has a good sense of humor." Carrie thought for a minute she was trying to convince herself of these things.

"Sounds like a great guy. For sure he's a lucky guy to have you."

Carrie shrugged her shoulders. "I don't know, maybe."

"Of course he is," Ben persisted.

"What about you and Jane? How are you guys?"

"Jane and I, well Jane and I are not together any longer. We remain good friends. You know we got married so young and we grew apart. We don't harbor any bad feelings for one another. In fact I highly respect her. We've stayed friends. She lives in Texas and I actually am living in Washington D.C."

"My goodness," Carrie shifted in her seat, "and how did Alexis respond?"

"Alexis is fine with it. We waited until she graduated from high school to get our divorce. It's only been about a year or so. She's easily gone on with her own life. She's attending Northwestern University, majoring in journalism. I'm really proud of her."

"It's hard to believe she's grown! Where does the time go?" Carrie remarked. "And you, do you have any special woman in your life now?"

"You, right now." Ben gazed at her with those emerald green eyes. Carrie's body was begging to go into overdrive. She tried to ignore her overactive hormones coming alive.

"Seriously, Ben, certainly someone must have caught your eye."

"Me, no. I've been too busy with other stuff. I'm really excited about my career. I joined the Camden Institute, a social think tank in D.C. We do a lot of research and treatises on social issues."

"Sounds interesting, and do you lobby congress as well?"

"Not me, personally, but some of my colleagues do. It's a whole different culture there. I think you would thrive there as well."

"I don't know," Carrie fiddled with her fingers, "you know how I love my families. You were the one who wanted to create the big changes. I'm quite content at the agency. Hey, did you happen to run into Lydia? She's here at the conference."

"Lydia, she's here?" Ben said as he pointed his finger in the air towards the conference center.

"Yes, I ran into her the first night I was here. She's Dr. Lydia Greenly now, and she's a professor at Berkeley! Can you believe it!"

"Wow, what an accomplishment! Who would've believed 'I need to question everything Lydia' would be a professor at Berkeley? Kudos to her. Did she ever get married?"

Carrie began to chuckle. "She's a lesbian!"

"A lesbian! You're pulling my leg."

"No, I'm not. She told me. She says her partner is a tall, blond, white woman, a 'knock out' I think was the term she used."

"Oh, that's too funny," Ben said as he laughed. "I would love to see them together. But if it works for her, then hey, great. I can't picture it. Have you kept up with anyone else in our class?"

"Not really. You know how I get so involved at work. And now with Jeff and Kate in my life, I really haven't, except for Sylvia. She gave birth to a baby boy about four years ago. Otherwise, I know I've been bad about keeping up. I did hear Professor Forsberg died of breast cancer."

"Yeah, I read about it in the college alumni news. She sure was one tough old bird, but not tough enough for cancer. It was too bad. Mike calls me every once in a while. He is working in corrections at Baker State Prison. Says he's trying to upgrade their uniforms to be a bit more fashionable," Ben began laughing again. "Remember how meticulous he is! And he told me Vanessa married, has three kids and is a stay at home mom now. Things sure can change, can't they?"

"I guess so," Carrie said.

"So you're still at the agency, eh? Why am I not surprised? You were always so good with your clients. Those kids love you and so did their moms. You were incredible with them. They are lucky to have you! I wish I was that lucky."

"Oh, Ben, stop." Carrie squirmed uncomfortably.

"Why? Carrie, my feelings for you've never changed. You asked me about other women. Well, I certainly haven't lacked for opportunities with other women. But then I think to myself: Do they meet the Carrie standard? And inevitably none of them do. So here I am, an overachiever workaholic, alone and waiting."

"Waiting for what?" Carrie said earnestly.

"Waiting for you, or for your clone," Ben laughed to lighten the air.

This was the moment Carrie dreaded. Her body was reacting as her mind was trying to get the upper hand. Adrenaline was coursing through her body. "Ben, seriously, stop. There is no point. I'm married. Can't we be friends, please?"

"I'm sorry I shouldn't have said that. Friends it is. But you taught me to tell it like it is." Carrie gave Ben a furtive glance. "I promise, friends only, Scout's honor," Ben held up his fingers in the Boy Scout pledge. "Please don't be mad at me, please!"

Carrie could never stay mad at Ben. His impish boyish grin and dimples would get her every time. Deep down her true feelings for him were tightly sequestered. Now they were knocking on the door to emerge into the open air. She, once again, went into the jail keeper mode with them. Why, oh why, could they never both be free to love each other at the same time? First he was married. Now she was.

"So Carrie, tell me about how you met Jeff?"

"I fell into his wastebasket butt first, and got stuck!" she laughed remembering. "He had to pull me out!" The evening wore on with reminisces. Ben was true to his words and kept the evening light and fun. Carrie hadn't laughed as hard in months. Her sides hurt she laughed so much. She admitted she thoroughly enjoyed Ben. They had an easiness together she and Jeff didn't have.

"Hey Carrie," Ben began, both of them slightly tipsy on the Sake, "Why don't you play hooky tomorrow and skip out on the last day of the conference? Let me take you to some great site-seeing spots? What do you say? I know of some awesome not so famous spots. I come here often for work."

"Oh, I don't know Ben. I don't know if that's such a good idea."

"How many opportunities do you get to come to California? Do you want to spend all of your time here on the beautiful west coast cloistered inside of the hotel? Come on. Let's drive down Highway 1 to Big Sur. My nature loving friend couldn't refuse, could she?"

"Well, it's awfully tempting. I've longed to see California's coastline. I hear it's beautiful!"

"Breathtaking," Ben added.

Carrie was conflicted. Should she take the high road and stay at the conference or should she throw caution to the wind and indulge in a life dream? After some rumination she said, "What the hell!"

"Does that mean yes?" Ben queried with a hopeful look.

"Yes, that does mean yes. Let's go for it!" Carrie responded as she looked into Ben's eyes and saw her reflection mirrored in them.

"Great, wonderful, oh, this is going to be amazing."

They walked back to their hotel, Carrie holding onto Ben's upper arm. He helped to steady her as she was still feeling the effects of the Sake. They headed towards the elevator. As the doors opened Ben gave Carrie a quick kiss on the forehead and told her goodnight.

"Aren't you coming up the elevator, too?" Carrie questioned.

"My room is a little higher up, I need to board the other elevator," he said as he pointed to the elevators servicing floors 25-40.

"Oh, I see. Thanks for the evening Ben. See you tomorrow." She waved goodbye as the elevator doors closed.

Safely back in her room, she felt giddy. The evening was overwhelming. She attributed the feelings to the Sake, but she knew in the back of her mind it was Ben's presence. She curled up in her bed and fell fast asleep. She even forgot to call home.

chapter 35

Carrie woke up feeling happy. The sun was up. As she sat up in the bed a slight throbbing pulsed through her head. Probably from the Sake, she thought. Her awareness became fully focused and she remembered the prior evening. Suddenly a surge of guilt flooded her body. Guilty about what, she didn't know. She didn't do anything wrong. She simply and thoroughly enjoyed her evening with Ben.

She dragged herself into the shower and felt the refreshing lukewarm water cascade down her body. It helped to clear the birds' nests nestled in her brain. Then she suddenly remembered. She didn't call Jeff. She called him each evening to wish him goodnight and to check on Katy. He was probably worried about her. How could she be so forgetful, she wondered,

It was seven-thirty. He would be up and about. She dialed home. "Hi, sweetheart," she began, "I'm so sorry I didn't call last night."

"I guess I had a little too much to drink last night. We went out to a Chinese restaurant and I indulged in a little too much Sake." She never told Jeff about her relationship with Ben. Sylvia might have mentioned his name a few times. He maybe knew his name in passing as a former school mate of hers, but she never spoke of him or about him to Jeff. Jeff assumed she went out with a group from the conference.

"Don't worry about it, darling. I'm just glad that all is going well for you. We miss you and can't wait for you to come home. It's not the same without you here. Enjoy your time away and don't worry about us. We're fine. I love you, but I need to get going. Have fun."

She hung up the phone and felt genuinely guilty she didn't tell him the truth about her plans today. It wasn't in her nature to be secretive with

Jeff. There was no point of causing him some undue concern, she rationalized.

As she was getting ready to meet Ben in the lobby, she was excited for the day. Big Sur was a place she dreamed about seeing. And Ben was true to his promise to maintain appropriate personal boundaries with her. She couldn't deny she and Ben had the best time together the evening before. It reminded her of old times when they worked together.

She put on a pair of khaki shorts, and a red form fitting tee shirt, and a pair of sneakers. She bunched her hair into a ponytail, checked herself in the mirror and declared herself ready to go. She met Ben in the hotel's café for a light breakfast, some granola and juice, and off they went.

Ben rented a blue Chevy convertible. The day would prove to be warm and sun-filled. Carrie marveled at the scenic coastline. She was glad she could sit and enjoy the view while Ben adeptly managed the curving road. She was amazed at the steepness of some of the cliffs and the lack of any road berm, with only the guard rails to keep one from careening off the edge. The sea oats danced in the gentle winds, the tall grasses exhaled their distinctive aromas, and the birds, oh so many of them flying effortlessly through the sky. She imagined she entered a small piece of heaven. They would stop here and there at various pull-offs to soak in the scenic views.

They passed by one road pull-off with a few cars scattered about but no people in sight. "What's the view there?" Carrie asked.

"Oh, I'm sure you wouldn't be interested," Ben declared as he stole a glance at her with a mischievous look.

"What makes you say that?" Carrie chided.

"Well, it leads the way down to the nude beach," Ben smiled. "Want to go? Ready to bare all?" A quiet pause ensued. "I didn't thinks so," he smugly smiled.

"Don't be so sure of yourself," Carrie said.

"Oh, I see, my dreams may come true?" Ben teased. Ben pulled into the next available U-turn lane to return Carrie to the nude beach pull-off.

"What are you doing?" Carrie yelped.

"Giving you your wish. You said I shouldn't be so sure of myself. Kind of translates into a yes, I want to go there, to me."

"Ben you're impossible!"

"Me, impossible? I think the teapot is calling the kettle black here."

"Ben, stop," she pleaded. "No, I don't want to go there. You were right."

"Ah, music to my ears. Can you say that again, you know the part about me being right?"

"Well, you're kind of right. I mean I don't want to go there. But the thought of being naked in the outdoors seems like a natural thing we humans have denied ourselves. We must cover up even when the weather suggests not. It's the organization of society taking away our true nature."

"So what you're suggesting is our cultural mores may be in direct opposition to our natural instincts?"

"Perhaps. Look at the more primitive cultures found in the islands of New Guinea and the like. The tribal people do not adorn themselves with clothing. Yet, we persist and call it civilized. We make a big deal about public nudity and act shocked. The island people accept each other as they are, not for how they appear to be. I think they are freer than us in a nature/spirit kind of connection. They don't waste their time thinking vainly to the same degree we do in first world countries. Perhaps what we've lost is our true connection with our spirit energy. We've lost it to human ambitions and egos."

"Carrie, are you talking from personal experience about what being naked outside is like?" Ben asked teasingly and half seriously.

"No, but if the right opportunity came up I might. Imagine what it would be like to be in total honest communion with nature. No outside influences at all to accost you, not even clothing. Try to envision connecting only your authentic spirit energy with nature's life force, leaving behind all physical manifestation of care and concern. I think it would be awesome!"

"Carrie, you're a little crazy, but I love you anyway," he teasingly patted her thigh. After Ben drove southward a few miles he proposed an idea to Carrie. "Are you up for a challenge?"

Carrie looked at him curiously as if to say without words, what are you talking about? "That's not fair, Ben. You know I could never turn down a good challenge?"

"I don't know, you may want to consider what it is before you jump in this time." An impish smile returned to his face, accentuating his dimples.

"Okay, I'll bite. What are you thinking?"

"I challenge you, and me, to live this entire day as a free entity. We cast off our external selves and live and act only from our spirit energy. Approach the rest of the day without ego, without the demands and trappings of our over arching culture. To live and act from what we believe is our true spirit energy. Of course we will have to keep our clothes on, though." He flashed Carrie a grin as wide as the Cheshire cat in 'Alice in Wonderland'.

Carrie raised both eyebrows and studied Ben. "Let me think on this for a minute." This was enormously intriguing to Carrie. She tried to look at the purpose of the challenge: to live with total authenticity. Was there a downside? Was she fearful of what she might discover about herself? Could she even do it? She wasn't sure. Was she up for the challenge? Was she emotionally strong enough to maintain total honesty for one day with herself and share it with Ben? This felt big to her. She had some reservations. She couldn't deny she was titillated by the challenge to be free and true to her spirit driven energy.

"I accept your challenge with one caveat. In addition to this being a free day, as you suggested, we must also approach the day as a sacred one, one giving homage and respect to our spirits. It won't work for me unless we understand this opportunity for these few hours of total freedom for our authentic life energy to solely drive our thoughts will be held as sacrosanct by us. I can accept it as a rare and special gift from the universe, forever to be cherished and sacred for you and me."

Ben instantly gazed adoringly into her eyes. "I promise, free and sacred."

❋❋❋

Before she knew it, they reached Monterey Bay. "Oh, let's get out and explore a bit, if we could," she implored Ben.

"Certainly, anything you want today. Today is for you." He parked the car near the Monterey boardwalk. They strolled the wooden planked walkway and watched the surf roll in and out. Fishermen's boats were tethered to the dock along the way. Carrie never saw so many boats in one spot.

"Oh, look! They are adorable!" Carrie pointed to a group of sea otters swimming in the ocean. She was fascinated. Some were floating on their back and looked like they were drumming their bellies with their hands. "What are they doing?"

"Opening up shells for the food," Ben replied as he softly gazed upon her. He was delighted by her delight. "Speaking of food, are you hungry for lunch? I see there is a restaurant up there on the second floor of that building: 'Pelican Alley'. Want to try it? It looks like it has a good view."

"Sure, why not. My stomach is always ready for food," she laughed.

They ordered lobster rolls. "Want some wine or beer?" Ben asked.

"I think it's too early for alcohol. I'm still getting the Sake out of my system. How about some sparkling water instead?"

"Sparkling water it is."

As they waited for their food to arrive they watched the ocean from their window seats.

"Oh, check it out, Carrie," Ben pointed to a chubby fisherman sitting in the stern of his boat with their back to him. Carrie began to laugh as his pants were so low you could see the beginning of his butt crack. Each time he leaned forward his pants revealed a little more.

"What's he doing?" Carrie asked.

"I think he is getting his fishing lines ready."

A big old pelican landed on the rim of his boat and started to peck his beak into the back of his pants. The fisherman instantly got up and started to wrestle with the pelican, which began to flap his wings wildly about. For a minute Ben and Carrie didn't know who was going to win the battle. Suddenly the pelican grabbed a fish from the boat's deck and jumped onto a wooden sea post and lifted his head high as he gulped down his find. The fisherman stood there and raised his fist to the pelican, likely yelling some cuss words at him, as his other hand was trying to pull up his pants. It was all too funny. They both began to laugh hysterically.

Their lunch was delicious. "Ready to head on down the road?" Ben asked. "We only have about another hour to go.

"Ready," Carrie declared.

It wasn't long before Ben pulled into the Julia Pfeiffer Burns State Park parking lot. The park was located east across the highway from the Big Sur Coast line. "Want to hike up?" Ben suggested.

Hiking sounded marvelous. She sat far too much the past few days and her legs begged for the workout. "Absolutely," she grinned.

Hiking trails in the park led up the forested cliff sides filled with eucalyptus and juniper and lodge pole pine trees. Along the way a bountiful two hundred foot waterfall thundered alongside their path. At the top of the trail was a striking scenic view of the ocean and the rugged rocks which defined Big Sur. Robber jays flew about in their glistening coat of black feathers and Persian blue hooded heads. Carrie felt like she was transported to paradise. If she had any doubts about her decision to skip the last day of the conference, they were all erased from her mind. She thanked the good Lord for the bounty this day gave her.

As they began their descent down, Carrie noticed a brightly colored lizard on a log looking like he was doing Marine Corps push-ups. "What's that about?" she looked at Ben.

Ben did a quick scan of the area and found another lizard mimicking the same activity, and not far behind was a less brightly colored lizard. "It looks like we've some male competition going on here for this female," he said with a wry smile. "Look!" and he pointed to the other lizards. Carrie watched fascinated. Her spirit was dancing to nature's incredible song.

As they reached the path's end, Carrie was excited to cross the road to get down to the beach area and feel Big Sur up close and personal. "Not here," Ben said as she headed toward the road crossing.

"Why not? I thought we were going to explore the beach, too?"

"We will, trust me. There's a better spot a few miles down the road."

About fifteen miles south of Pfeiffer Burns State Park, Ben made a right hand turn onto an unmarked graveled pathway. "This used to be a service road at one time, now abandoned," he explained. "One of my D.C. colleagues told me about it some time ago." They traveled about a half mile reaching the magnificent coastline. The car pushed through some overgrown tall grasses and was hidden from sight. They exited the car and walked to the edge of the cliff. Below them was a small horseshoe beach outlined by a myriad of Big Sur's landmark protruding rocks, standing guard as the ocean's surf bathed them continuously with sprays of water. A once accessible rock peninsula jutted out from the land and still had a partial staircase. An earlier landslide wiped out the house and any access to the peninsula's most western point. The only accessible part was the deserted beach, once you descended a steep two hundred foot trail. Carrie was breathless. Tears of joy came to her eyes. She wasn't before so moved by nature's beauty as she was in this moment.

"Oh Ben, this is so beautiful. It's more than I could have imagined. My spirit is singing out with joy!" Then a golden eagle silently flew above them gliding effortlessly through the air, as if to greet them.

"Are you ready to go down there?" he said pointing to the faint overgrown pathway down.

"Really? We can go down there?"

"If you're game enough to conquer the trail. I think you can do it! Wait here a minute. I threw some beach towels from the hotel into the car. Let me grab them and we'll clamber down."

Ben led the way down the trail with Carrie following close behind. His strong hand steadied her on some of the steeper inclines down. Once again, Carrie became keenly aware of Ben's touch upon her and how it magically awakened every fiber in her body. When they reached the sandy beach, they kicked off their shoes. The feel of sand upon their feet and between their toes was soothing and warm. The smell of the ocean salt water filled her nose. Carrie felt strongly physically reconnected with earth's energy. She could feel the ocean's pulsing vibrations on her soles, as if she was experiencing Earth's heartbeat. She stood in wonder and thanked God for the blessing of the vision, the sight, the sound and the feel.

Ben placed the beach towels side by side in the center of the horseshoe. He grabbed Carrie's hand and they ran up to the shoreline and immersed their feet into the water. "Oh my! It's freezing cold!" Carrie remarked. "I never imagined the water to be so cold." She kept her feet steadfastly in one spot as the waves began to bury her feet with sand. She began to feel a slight numbing in her toes, but found it strangely satisfying. It reminded her, her body was merely a vessel, an earthly mortal vehicle housing her true essence which defined her, her spirit. She tried to move her feet into the warm sunshine and was surprised how great the force was burying them in the sand. She tugged with a burst of energy to free them. She thought it a metaphor for what it might take to truly live these moments with a free spirit. It would take resolve.

They sat on the towels drinking in the horizon and the surf. Juniper trees lined the cliff tops with their branches leaning far eastward as the west winds blew them mercilessly day in and out. The ocean was alive offering an occasional massive wave spray against the ancient jutting rocks. Ben and Carrie sat side by side silently, reverently.

"Oh, look," Carrie said excitedly as she spotted a distant spray of water coming from the blow holes of a humpback whale. "There's a pod of whales swimming by! You can see their long backs flowing in and out of the water. This is so awesome. I can't believe it!" Both remained mesmerized by the family of whales. It was another gift the universe delivered them far beyond anything Carrie could imagine. She felt as if this cove held them in the heart of God's loving energy. She was moved to silent tears. Ben noticed and tenderly wrapped his left arm around her shoulder and pulled her near to his side and held her silently.

Magpies shared their beach. Some were loudly chattering as they hopped among the rocks. Seeing them close up, they were larger birds than Carrie realized. They looked like giant distant cousins of the blue jays living in her backyard. Ben broke their silence. "Carrie, I hate to do this, but I must make a phone call back to D.C. I promised one of the senator's aides I would contact him this afternoon about one of our initiatives. I know I'm breaking our free spirit pledge and heading back to the external world for a minute, but I really don't have a choice. There's a phone booth at the little local grocery store we passed about three miles up the road. You're welcome to come with me, or you can stay here if you like. It'll take me about thirty minutes."

"If you think it's safe for me to be here, I think I would prefer to stay," Carrie answered.

"I don't blame you one bit. I, too, would prefer to stay here. But yes, you'll be safe, absolutely safe. I don't believe too many people even know about this beach. Did I tell you a friend of President Reagan's told me about this? "

"Really? A friend of Reagan's? You must walk in some pretty powerful circles."

"Well, I don't know about that! How about I bring back some bottled water to drink and something to snack on?"

"Sounds great."

"I hate to leave you, but I'm sure you'll be fine." Ben stood up and started walking toward the trail back up the cliff.

"Be careful," Carrie yelled back. "Come back to me. I don't want to be stranded here, although I can't think of a better place to be if I were."

Ben turned around and bowed to Carrie signaling his acknowledgement.

Carrie was enthralled with the opportunity to commune privately with nature in this glorious corner of the planet. She sat with her legs crossed in the lotus position, meditating. As she slowly inhaled the ocean air, noticing the unique odor of the salt water, she felt revived. Air in, air out, air in, air out. The sand, the breeze, the water, the sun touched her skin, her outer body. Only life giving breath touched her inwardly. Carrie felt herself slightly shift to a different metaphysical state. It was subtle. The surf resounded strongly as the tides moved out. The spray of the water droplets fell, plunking gently back into their mother ocean. The pulsating energy of the sun's rays fell upon her body in gentle, small, almost imperceptible beats. She felt the vibrations. Her own body began to resonate to the same frequency.

She also noticed the unpleasant tug of her hair band. She reached up and pulled her hair free of its ponytail. She slowly shook her head left to right until her hair flowed freely in the wind. She thought about her spirit energy. She was closing out the external world.

What about your clothing, her mind inquired? Are you ready to be a free authentic spirit? Carrie drew in another long breath. This small beach cove was hers and hers alone at this moment. Even Ben would be gone for another thirty minutes. If she was going to have the opportunity to meet nature exposed, this was it. The thought excited her. The thought of not taking advantage of the situation depressed her.

She grabbed the bottom of her shirt and lifted it up and over her head. She moved her hands to her back and unclasped her bra. She looked down at her chest and saw her breasts immediately respond to the air. Her nipples unfolded as if to greet the sun. She stood up and pulled her shorts and panties off. As she threw them down on the beach towel, a flourish of exhilaration surged through her being. She stood facing the horizon, hands and feet outstretched, naked as the day she entered this world. Nothing to hide. No judgments. No shame. The true spirit of Carrie existed in this moment. She inhaled deeply, eyes shut, letting the sun bathe her. She felt humbled in a good way. She never felt so one with God, one with the life force of the universe. The wind gently licked her body with warm kisses. She was immobilized, paralyzed in the moment, never wanting it to end.

Her mind drifted back to the material world. She thought of all of the sorrow she carried day to day with her. She thought of her clients, the beleaguered children and their pain. Then a voice in her head spoke to her: not today. Today is free spirit day. Commune with me. Commune with spirit.

In her mind's eye negative energy pulsed out of her body into the air. Small tiny flecks of negativity escaped every small crevice of her body and were replaced with pure loving energy. She was overwhelmed with a joy beyond anything she knew. She was free of the Earthly plane. Her feet began to dance. She ran alongside the water's edge with her arms fully extended outward. She was lost to the physical world. She was aware God dwelled within her, was an inseparable part of her. No other entity could produce this joy with this intensity. She resoundingly thanked Him a million times over for the revelation.

All of her blessings scrolled before her mind's eye. She understood their universal connection. She couldn't stop her feet from moving. She danced and twirled and ran. Her heart was bursting with a love she didn't previously know in this awakening context. Not only did she shed her clothes, she shed all of her worldly thoughts. She became utterly unaware of her nakedness. The thought simply didn't come to her mind. Instead all of her energy focused on this enlightening moment of her connection with the infinite. It was supreme freedom. She was living from her authentic spirit energy. No, she became a manifestation of her authentic spirit. She transcended into a perfect meld of her body and spirit.

Ben watched her in bewilderment upon his return. He simply couldn't believe she was running around naked, as if it were nothing. She was the most beautiful, loving, and curious creature he knew.

She saw Ben approaching her in the sand. "Oh my good Lord," Carrie exclaimed. Immediately her arms began covering her body as her awareness of him brought her back to the reality of the moment. She ran to the towels and whisked one up off of the sand and immediately wrapped it around herself. What was she thinking? In her exhilaration she forgot her situation. She couldn't believe she so disassociated from her body. It was freeing and wonderful for as long as it lasted. She would be forever thankful. She was no longer Carrie the person, who came with a body, but Carrie the spirit of the body. She wished Ben could have joined her spirit to spirit, not human to human.

Her happy feet flew to him. Carrie was simply radiant beyond compare. "Oh, Ben! It's wonderful! It's so great! I was free, I am free." She raised her arms straight up to the sky and spiraled around him. "The energy, the spirit energy inside of you, you must let it out. It's so awesome,"

Ben sauntered to his towel with his hands in his shorts pockets. They both stood there peering into each other's eyes. His were deeply effervescent green and searching. Hers were brilliant and imploring. "Ben, I'm so, so, so . . . .'

"It's okay, Carrie. I know I embarrassed you. I ruined your obvious joyful high. I'm so sorry."

"Ben, you didn't embarrass me. That wasn't what I was going to say." Then she started to laugh. "Usually you know what I'm thinking, but this time you got it wrong." Carrie grabbed Ben's hands and said, "Ben, relax. Sit here with me as she glided into a sitting position onto the sand in one easy motion. She patted the sand in front of her for Ben to sit facing her.

"Ben, I want you to understand what happened to me. After you left I sat in the sand, closed my eyes and meditated. This place is so utopian in its feel and energy. I asked the universe to help me tap into my true spirit energy. I asked my earthly way of being, well . . . would take a nap." Carrie giggled. "I asked if I could greet the essence of who my being is. Oh, I know I'm sounding crazy Ben, but it happened." Carrie continued highly animated. "I tried to march fearlessly within myself to see what my essence was really made of. You know it felt scary. I thought maybe I won't like what I find. Maybe I'll face me and I'll see the truth of me isn't as good as I think it is."

Then a voice suggested I needed to come to the life force in the same form it delivered me to this world. If I wanted true freedom of spirit, I had to shed my earthly ties, which included my clothing! Ben, please don't think me crazy."

"The next thing I knew I began thinking about all of the sorrow in the world. I began seeing the faces of all of my clients. A real heaviness settled in on me. Then the voice told me today wasn't about absorbing the pain of others. I was to cast off all the negativity. It was blocking my path."

"And then it evolved into thinking about love. The voice told me this was my true essence. Love was the path. Being on Earth was a way for our spirits to grow and learn about love so we can pass it on to all others. This world desperately needs love. All of us troubled humans have come for the greatest lesson of all – love. We need to learn to meet and greet each other not with our eyes, not with our body, but spirit to spirit. The body given us is a mere conveyance vehicle for our spirit." Carrie continued on with her excited chatter as Ben adoringly listened.

"The more we come to understand our spirit to be about love, the better our body will be. For it's important to love everything, including our body regardless of our look or shape. It's our spirit defining the essence of who we really are. Not our hurts, our pain, our anger, but our love and how we spend our love while we are here on Earth." Carrie was speaking rapidly and passionately. She was so excited Ben was falling more deeply for her. But he knew she was on a different plane right now. She didn't think about human love at all, but a higher form of pure love. He was a bit envious.

"I forgot about being naked Ben! I transcended my body! It was glorious! Oh, how I wish you could have shared this experience with me."

"Maybe I could try now," Ben said. "How could I not want what you described?" He let out a big grin. Carrie's heart heartened. He didn't think she was a nut case!

"Seriously Ben? I don't know. I mean I was alone. I don't know if I could have reached that place with other people around?"

"I hope you don't think of me as other people," Ben said in all earnestness.

"Of course I don't," Carrie countered. She became increasingly aware of how she wanted to connect with Ben in every possible way. Could she set aside her human desire she knew she harbored for him, but always neatly tucked away? Would she be tempting fate? Could he focus without succumbing to his desire for her?

"Carrie, if only you could have seen your own face when I saw you. You were completely oblivious to me for quite a while when I returned. I couldn't believe you were dancing and running so free of everything, including your clothes. I have to admit I was enthralled. But when you came running up to me so unabashedly unashamed, I knew there wasn't a sexual thought in your mind. I've never seen you so perfectly aglow. Carrie, my sweet Carrie, how could I not want to know that state of being? Please, take me with you. I promise I won't act on my human desires, and I've many for you. This I can't deny. And I understand the boundaries required in our relationship. But this is different, isn't it? At least that's what I gather. This isn't external. This is a journey of the internal, right?"

Carrie was touched by Ben's honesty. Should she trust him? Could she trust herself? Was she brought here to this place, with this man by accident, or was it a part of a grander plan?

"Carrie, I promise. I would never do anything to compromise you. If you feel too uncomfortable then we can leave, if you want. But I can't stay here with you and pretend something uniquely special isn't happening with us. Please, it was my challenge that started this. Let's not quit now." He reached out and held Carrie's hands as he sat cross-legged opposite her. Immersing completely into her eyes, with a voice genuine and loving he whispered, "Please, take me to the energy of spirit. Help me find mine."

"We'll try together," she said realizing she couldn't toss away the gift designed to be shared.

Without speaking he pulled off his white polo shirt exposing his sun bronzed well toned chest. The sun bathed them as if washing them from all desire and shame.

"First you must have an absolute intention to close out the world and find your inner spirit energy. Close your eyes," Carrie quietly instructed. "Feel the beat of the Earth's energy. Focus on the language of the water, the force of the gentle wind, the touch of the sun upon your body. Banish away any thoughts of the external world: no work, no people, no tasks. Go inward. Greet your innermost, deepest energy, the highest part of your being. Tell your ego to go away. Invite in your perfect authentic energy. Let go of all past judgments including your own self-judgments. Allow yourself to greet your spirit with no walls. Go deep within, quietly."

They remained silent for a long time. Carrie journeyed back to being one with her spirit. Happiness rippled throughout her body. She knew she was meant to be even more loving to all crossing her path. Only love would stamp out pain, and she was intimately familiar with the ramifications of pain and negativity in life. It could swallow you up, if you allowed it. Most people didn't know how to access their loving parts. Fear was the enemy. Love was the peacemaker.

Carrie could hear Ben's breathing slow down. His energy felt relaxed next to her, not as tense. They remained still and silent in synchronicity for what seemed like forever and was in fact about twenty minutes. She glanced at his face and knew he left her. She quietly stood, retrieved her clothes and dressed as Ben meditated. Quietly returning next to him, she noticed a tear streaming from his closed eyes. She reached over and gently squeezed his hand. He opened his eyes and gazed into hers, not moving to wipe away the pooled remaining tears. He greeted her with total honesty of self, no pretenses.

They stood up and embraced, hugging each other in perfect unity of spirit. He understood. He was changed.

"Wow! I felt the connection with a greater spirit energy. It's so awesome. There are no words, are there, to capture this?" his voice gently floated to Carrie.

"No, none."

They stood silhouetted against the horizon, two free, joyful, happy, and enlightened spirits.

***

Returning to the car, it was time to head back. Neither wanted to leave, but the external world weighed heavily upon them. They both were lost in their thoughts of the afternoon. Their departure from their cove was bittersweet. They each were given the gift of a life truth. They were given a glimpse of their true energy. It felt sacred to them. It was sacred. Now if they could only hold onto it as life marched on. Carrie realized it would be difficult to lead her life solely from her authentic energy, but it would be easier than it was yesterday. Awareness was the key.

Ben turned the car into the Big Sur Inn, a quaint looking cottage styled restaurant. It was wrapped with a checkerboard of windows and vines creeping up trellises and bearing red and pink flowers. The ocean surf provided its own song on the wind's breeze as they entered. The Victorian decorated interior was once someone's rambling house, with fireplaces in each room. The tables were covered with white tablecloths and accented with a second printed cloth of roses. Each table had a soft glowing candle, and floor lamps provided additional soft light. It reeked of romance. They were seated in a windowed corner in the third of four adjoining rooms.

Carrie noticed a tabby house cat lounging in a chair near the fireplace. She was delighted and surprised to see such an animal within the restaurant. It gave it a homey feel. The waitress came and took their orders and returned with two glasses of David Bruce Pinot Noir, a smooth and velvety red wine. They both were still overwhelmed with their earlier beach experience.

"Carrie," "Ben," They both began simultaneously, and then laughed. Ben reached across the table and held Carrie's hand. "I don't know what to say," Ben began. "I've never experienced such a powerful feeling as I did with you today. The connection I felt with my spirit was so . . ." Ben was lost for words.

"I know," Carrie replied placing her free hand on top of his. "You don't have to explain, I felt it too."

"I'll never be the same. There is no way to go back to your old self is there? I see I can be a better man than I've been."

"I don't know how. It's like a door was unlocked to my spirit. It spoke to me, told me about my ability to love universally. How do you ignore such a message?" Carrie rhetorically asked.

"Exactly!" Ben exclaimed. "The challenge will be to not let life snuff it out."

"Awareness is the key, I think," Carrie smiled. She thought of Jeff and acknowledged he likely wouldn't have been able to immerse himself in such a revelation. She felt a bit saddened. "At least we were given a glimpse. I'm still overwhelmed. It felt like I was in perfect communion with God's energy."

"Honestly, for me Carrie, I've never felt so intimately connected with everything," Ben momentarily paused, "but especially with you. It was like my spirit joined with yours and made love. And it wasn't one bit sexual, but so illuminating. It was like the ultimate level of emotional intimacy." He lightly squeezed her hand as he allowed himself to gaze into her bright eyes, as the reflection of the candle danced upon them.

A warm glow coursed through Carrie's body. She never felt such love before, but was scared by it as Ben was putting words to her own identical feelings. Their reverie was interrupted by the restaurant's busyness. Carrie was glad for the intrusion. The hostess ushered in a couple to a table nearby. He was an older gentleman with a full white beard. She was a tall brunette, who stood rigidly straight and moved more as if she was marching rather than walking. He immediately excused himself to go to the men's room. As the waitress delivered the house's watercress salads to Ben and Carrie,

Carrie noticed the woman scanning her environment. She saw her eyes land on the cat sitting far from her table. Her face grimaced.

Carrie quietly sniggered. "See that woman who entered the room?"

"Yes, what about her?" Ben replied.

"She isn't going to like the cat being in the room. She's going to make a scene. I can feel it in my bones."

When the gentleman returned to the table, the woman immediately began. "This is outrageous," she said in a loud irritating voice, "they have a cat in here! I can't be in this room. You're going to have to tell the hostess that either the cat leaves or we do. And if they don't remove the beast, I'm reporting them to the Health Department."

"Now calm down dear," the gentleman requested. "I'll speak to the hostess."

"And don't you tell me to calm down. This isn't right, it's an atrocity. Well, get moving and go talk to someone," she ordered.

Carrie and Ben both began to laugh. "How did you know?" he asked.

"I don't know. I felt her energy. She needs a day on the beach!" she laughed.

"I doubt it would do her any good." Ben raised his wine glass and Carrie followed suit. "To authentic energy," he toasted, "and to you!"

Carrie simply replied, "Ditto."

They ate voraciously, and every single bite was delicious. Seven o'clock approached and they still had a long drive back. They rode back in comfortable silence between them, but Carrie felt like they talked the entire way home without words. Occasional glances turned into broad smiles. He would randomly pat her leg. She massaged his neck a time or two. She never had a friend such as Ben. He was so gentle, bright, and perceptive. He treated her with respect and rarely crossed any boundaries with her. She knew he loved her, always had, as she had always loved him.

As they approached San Francisco, Carrie was aware of her incredible longing to freely love Ben as a human, not as a spirit. She couldn't deny her strong physical attraction to him. She tried to erase such thoughts from her mind, but they persisted. She tried accessing advice from her new found awareness, but it remained silent as if to acquiesce to her need. The mere thought of holding and kissing Ben, being entangled with him almost brought her to orgasm silently. She tried to avert her thoughts from this subject, but failed miserably as the thought seemed to permeate every cell of her body. She couldn't deny she was drawn to his muscled body which moved so joyfully with her on the beach. He exuded maleness. Ben remained quietly serene. She sensed his thoughts weren't so dissimilar.

She focused her thoughts on Jeff. She loved him. But it was different from the love she felt for Ben. Jeff was stable, predictable, and provided her with security. She knew he loved her desperately. He also blessed her life immeasurably. He gave her Katy, the joy of her life. How could she love him and Ben at the same time? She knew she did. It felt like a betrayal of Jeff, but she couldn't deny the reality of the situation. She loved them both. She didn't ask for this, but the energy field between her and Ben was there long before she knew Jeff. It was what it was. They each secured a place in her heart.

⁂⁂⁂

Carrie was saddened as they approached the hotel. She didn't want the evening to end, but knew there was no alternative. She was leaving for the airport at seven o'clock in the morning to catch her ten o'clock flight home. Six hours of flight time and she would land at seven o'clock due to the time differential and be home around eight. She was excited to see Jeff again, but leaving Ben was going to be difficult. She reminded herself to telephone Jeff as soon as she reached her room. It was shortly after nine when Ben left the car with the valet service.

He grabbed Carrie's hand as they walked into the hotel's lobby. She melted with his touch and was agonized the evening was over. "Do you want to stop by the bar and have a nightcap?" Ben asked hopefully.

"Ben, no, I can't." She could feel tears welling up inside and she fought hard to push them back. "I need to call Jeff, and I need to pack, and . . ." she buried her face in her hands. Her shoulders began to heave. The dam was cracking and her tears started flowing. She was quietly crying. Ben ushered her to a couch in a distant corner of the lobby.

He held her in his arms and gave her a corner of a beach towel to catch her tears. He lovingly whispered to her, "my sweet, dear Carrie. Everything will be fine. I remember the last time we said good-bye seven years ago. You were strong, stronger than me. I left when I so desperately wanted to stay. But you were right, it was for the best. Nothing can erase the sacred day you and I had today. We were blessed. You'll live in my heart, do you hear me, always. You always have. But you've a home and a husband and a daughter to return to, even though, I wish they'd all disappear. This day has provided us with the rarest of love I have known. It will forever be on the top of my list of the most precious moments in my life. I love you Carrie, and I know you love me. That alone, will be enough."

He placed his hand under her chin and lifted her face towards his. "But I can't and I won't go without a kiss this time. Please, one kiss." He pressed his lips against hers and the moment swept them both away. Carrie's entire body begged for more, but Ben gently released her mouth.

"Don't say a word. I'm going to leave, but you'll be with me in my heart." Ben left Carrie, knowing if he didn't leave now, he never would. She watched him step into his elevator and disappear. She gathered herself together and hurried to the sanctuary of her room. As soon as she closed the door behind her, the dam burst open and she sobbed like she never sobbed before. She knew she could never see Ben again.

She pulled herself together as she remembered to call Jeff. Sniffling all the way to the phone, she blew her nose before she dialed. "Hello sweetheart," she began.

chapter 36

Carrie busied herself with packing her luggage, sniffling the entire time. She changed into her silk cherry pink pajamas, called the front desk for a six o'clock wake up call, and crawled into bed.

Her mind raced reviewing the day's events. Each time she thought of Ben, her body yearned for his touch. She tossed and turned. Sleep simply wouldn't come. She tried counting sheep fruitlessly. She went into a logical mode and reviewed in her mind everything she packed to assure she wouldn't leave anything behind, except for Ben. The pearls! Her mother's pearls! She left them in the safe at the hotel's concierge desk. She didn't want to forget them as it was her most precious remembrance of her mother. Not finding sleep, she scampered out of bed and threw on the white cotton guest robe and went down to retrieve the necklace.

"May I help you miss?" the concierge politely inquired.

"Yes, I secured a pearl necklace in your safe." Carrie handed him the security ticket needed to garner the item. "I would like to take it up to my room please."

"Ah, yes. One moment please." The concierge left through the door behind the desk.

Carrie waited patiently. Arms slipped around her waist from behind. "I couldn't resist," the melodious voice whispered in her ear, and then he withdrew his arms as the concierge returned.

"Yes, miss, I believe this is the item you wanted." He placed the necklace in her hand.

"Yes, thank you." Carrie turned around to, once again, face the smiling Ben. "What are you doing here?" she said in astonishment.

"Oh, I came down for a nightcap at the bar. I couldn't sleep. And you?"

"I needed to pick up this necklace so I could pack it. I couldn't sleep either." Carrie's body began to percolate with hormones again.

Ben declared, "It's turned out to be kind of a rough night, hasn't it?"

"You could say that."

"Would you like to see one more awesome view before you leave?"

"Ben, I don't know. I should probably get back to my room. Besides I'm not dressed. I didn't plan to hang out anywhere in my robe and pj's"

"No problem. Come with me." He held her arm and they began walking. "I want to show you the stars from the rooftop. We both can't sleep, so why not? And the night skyline is something you won't regret seeing. I promise. Please?"

Carrie knew there was no sense in fighting him at this point. She couldn't deny without lying she would've given anything for a few more moments with Ben. And he said please so beseechingly.

"Alright, show me the way."

He pushed the button to summon the elevator. "Let me put those pearls around your neck. You don't want to lose those." He carefully handled the necklace and secured the clasp for her. They lay perfectly on her slim neck. Even the lightest touch of his fingers brushing against her sent her stomach into flip flops. "You look stunning!"

"I doubt that," Carrie retorted feeling frumpy in her robe.

"You can't see you like I see you," Ben admonished. Carrie felt their magnetism coming alive.

They stepped into the elevator. "I didn't know they had an observation deck at the hotel," Carrie said.

Ben pushed the button marked PH. "Well, they do and they don't," he said.

"Ben, we can't go into the penthouse. What are you thinking?"

"This is the way to the rooftop," he smiled mischievously.

Carrie braced herself against the elevator's wall rail as the car whirred up to the top floor. They entered the short hallway which had a door to the left and another to the right: PH1 and PH2.

"Ben, you must be mistaken. I don't see any door to the rooftop here."

Ben pulled a key from his pocket and dangled it for Carrie to see. It was marked PH1. "They ran out of regular rooms due to the conference, and because I'm on the board of the host provider, they, ah, gave me the penthouse."

"No way!" exclaimed Carrie.

"Way," Ben grinned as he adeptly inserted the key into the lock and swung the door open for her to enter. "After you."

Carrie stepped into the spacious room and was awestruck. The suite used one half of the entire floor. Plush leather couches sidelined the gas fireplace. A grand piano was positioned in one corner. A fully stocked bar offered any libation you could want. A teakwood table was adorned with a candelabra and a vase of fresh flowers. A small kitchenette nestled in another corner. And the windows, the windows lined the entire outer walls from floor to ceiling. The bright lights of San Francisco glittered as far as her eyes could see. It was magnificent. She was speechless.

"Oh, Ben, oh Ben, oh Ben," was all she could muster. She walked close to the windows and soaked in the sight. "I never could have imagined this!"

He handed her a glass of brandy. "Glad you came?" She sipped the brandy. Every fiber in her body wanted to merge with Ben. She longed to kiss him, touch him, and feel him. "Wait, it gets better." He walked to the wall and turned out all of the lights which caused the city to brighten even more against the dark night sky. "To you Carrie, to the most precious friend I'll ever have," Ben touched his brandy sniffer to hers. She took another sip and felt the liquid warm her.

"It can't get any better than this," Carrie whispered.

"Don't be so sure." He took the brandy sniffer from Carrie's hand and placed them both on the table. "It's awfully warm in here, why don't you take off your robe?" She didn't protest as it was warm and the brandy warmed her even more. He stood behind her and helped her remove her robe as she untied the belt. The full moon hung high in the sky and its light silhouetted Carrie in its beam. Her nipples were evident as they brushed against her silk top. Her breasts gently swayed under the garment. Ben stared longingly at her. He couldn't help but be stirred by her essence. He removed his shirt letting it drop to the floor near her feet. He folded her up in his arms and kissed her ardently, passionately, yet gently. She didn't fight. She longed for this. She welcomed his embrace. The electricity generated between the two of them was palpable. Her body began to sing unashamedly with growing fervor. She let out a light moan as her body throbbed and arched into his chest. She parted her lips inviting his tongue to explore.

Every cell of her body began to dance with excitement. She grew wet between her legs as she felt his hardening girth press against her. She was in heaven. Everything about Ben awakened her unlike anyone else. As she was ready to give in to anything Ben wanted, Ben stopped and stepped back. She stood there trembling with excitement.

Ben could sense Carrie wanted him as he wanted her. But he didn't want to complicate her life any more than he had. "Are you sure?" he implored her. "Absolutely sure?"

Carrie stepped forward and answered him with yet another passionate kiss. He stopped her again. "Come," he simply said and held her hand. He opened the door leading to the bedroom. Carrie couldn't believe what she was seeing. Three of the walls were windowed as in the living room, but so was the ceiling. The room felt like it was floating in the sky. She felt like she was back on the beach again, only this time she was riding on a cloud with all of the twinkling stars and the moon surrounding her everywhere she looked.

Ben dropped his pants exposing his fully engorged manhood. He unbuttoned Carrie's shirt, kissing each newly exposed skin area with each button. He lifted it off her shoulders and let it glide to the floor. He hungrily kissed her breasts and adeptly used his tongue to massage and suck her nipples until they felt like they were going to explode. Her breath was quickening and she longed for him to kiss her mouth again.

He placed his fingers inside her pant's waistband and knelt down as he pulled her pants to the floor exposing her beautiful muff. He kissed her naval and slowly traveled downward. His tongue explored every crevice of her womanhood. She began to tremble, moaning as she buried her fingers into his thick hair.

He stood up and lifted her onto the luxurious four postered bed. His hands guided her legs apart, and he entered her easily as her entire vaginal wall was coated with her thick warm wetness. As his body pressed against her clitoris with his swaying motion time and time again, she climaxed extraordinarily, as did he. He withdrew and lay next to her holding her tightly. No words needed to be spoken.

Moments later they were consumed with their desire for one another. They began to kiss again, deeply, passionately, lost in their ecstasy. Carrie straddled him, and gently glided her body down his long hard shaft. She began moving rhythmically, massaging him inside her. She could feel the mounting tension of yet another climax approaching. Her vaginal muscles began to throb against his penis with increasing speed. She came over and over again, spewing liquid from her body onto his.

She felt Ben come inside her, filling her with his primal essence. They were bound together physically, yet her mind drifted to another place. She could no longer feel her body, but felt as if her spirit left it and joined Ben's in another realm. Bright colors filled her mind as she was interwoven in rapture unlike anything she before experienced. Hers and Ben's energies entwined and she couldn't tell where she began and he ended. The magnetism between them was unbreakable. They were one entity floating in the cosmos. Her body was completely electrified. It felt like it dispersed into the universe and disappeared. She never wanted to return to it as they lingered mingling in mind, body and spirit. It was the closest thing to heaven she experienced. She felt like she might have died, but didn't care.

Consciousness slowly returned to her. She was aware she was snuggled next to Ben with his strong arms wrapped around her. Her entire body involuntarily convulsed every few seconds as if her body's entire electrical system was shorting out. It was as if her spirit was rejoining her body bit by bit. With each trembling twitch the intensity lessened. Yet the jolting continued long enough Ben broke the silence, "Are you okay?" he asked with grave concern in his voice.

"I'm not sure," she whispered and twitched yet again. Then she began to laugh as if to release even more of the sexual tension their bodies created together. "I'll never be the same."

Both she and Ben knew the gift they were given could never be repeated again. There was no way this evening preceded by the day's events could be duplicated. It was magical leading to the perfection of two loving spirits mingling, connecting, and merging their elemental energies.

"I love you doesn't capture how I feel for you, Carrie," Ben whispered in his low captivating voice. "There are no words. You invaded my spirit and are indelibly etched into my soul. You're a gift from heaven. God blessed me this day beyond measure. I'll be forever yours."

Carrie started to speak but Ben gently placed his fingers on her lips and simply exhaled, "Shhhhhhh." They both drifted off to sleep cradling together.

***

Carrie woke up as her bladder urgently commanded her to pee. She carefully lifted Ben's arm from her side and quietly left the bed, grabbed her pajamas from the floor and relieved herself. She reentered the room and watched Ben sleep as she remained in total awe of him and the evening's events. Her heart throbbed with hurt as she knew she must leave him – forever. He was the most beautiful being she knew. Her soul belonged to him.

The barest glimmer of sun peaked over the horizon. It was five-thirty in the morning when dawn began to think about approaching. Carrie silently left the bedroom, her heart heavy. She sat at the desk with paper and pen at hand. She wrote as she silently cried within:

To my most loving soul mate,

> There are no words for us that can capture our feelings adequately. Know I'll always cherish you with every fiber of my body. Leaving you is the most difficult action that I've been compelled to take in my entire life. If you truly love me, please do not follow me. What we have together is sacred and needs to be left unscathed. Not a day will pass by you won't be remembered in my heart, and it's with enormous sadness I must leave you. Take care, my sweet love. Peace to you always.

Carrie placed the note on the teakwood table, grabbed her robe and returned to her hotel room. As she showered, her tears blended with the water. She was spent physically and emotionally. She thought of home. She was anxious to see Katy and Jeff. Home grounded her.

As she left the hotel lobby, the doorman hailed a cab for Kylee who was also returning home this day. "You're welcome to join me on the way to the airport," she cheerily offered. Carrie gladly accepted, thankful for a distraction from her thoughts of Ben.

"Wasn't that the best conference?" she excitedly pronounced.

"Yes, it was," Carrie smiled.

"What was your favorite part?" Kylee continued.

"Oh, I don't know. There were many different things."

"Well I have two favorite parts. First I loved the site seeing tours they gave, especially Pier 39. But my favorite workshop was the one Ben Randall gave. Isn't he the dreamiest of guys and so sexy? Did you get a chance to go?"

"Yes, yes I did. It was rather interesting." Carrie could feel her body responding to the mere mention of his name.

"I'll tell you whatever woman gets hold of him is one lucky woman. I noticed he wasn't wearing a wedding band. But of course that doesn't necessarily mean anything now, does it?"

"No, no it doesn't. Not in this day and age," Carrie smiled again. She needed to change the subject. "Are you anxious to get back to South Dakota?"

They chatted easily all the way to the airport.

Seated on the plane, Carrie had six hours to think things over. She knew she should feel guilty about breaking her marriage vows. Somehow guilt seemed trivial to the awakening and fulfillment of her spirit and love she had with Ben. She decided to render a new vow unto herself - To keep their alliance forever sacred in her mind, and to never see or contact Ben again. She drifted off into a deep sleep the rest of the plane trip home.

chapter 36

The plane's wheels touched the runway. In Carrie's mind she said one last goodbye to Ben. Jeff and Katy would be waiting for her and she was anxious to see them both. As she walked toward the airport's main area she spotted Jeff robustly waving to her with an expansive smile on his face. He approached and gave her a big bear hug and an ardent kiss. "For you," he said as he offered her a bouquet of red roses. It reminded her of all of the times he sent her roses when they first met, and she was charmed.

"Oh, Jeff you shouldn't have. Thank you." She gave him a kiss on the cheek. "Where's Katy?"

"I left her with mom and dad for the night. It was getting late for her. I missed you and I wanted you all to myself. Mom is going to bring her by first thing in the morning. She's been asking for you all week."

As they drove home Jeff caught Carrie up with all of his activities since she left. Carrie told him about the conference and the botanical gardens at Golden Gate Park and Alcatraz. It felt easy and comfortable to be back in their every day conversation.

Jeff hoisted her luggage out of the trunk and they went inside the house. Another dozen roses were displayed in a vase on the table. "Oh, you shouldn't have," Carrie smiled and turned to gaze at Jeff. She added the roses he gave her at the airport to the vase.

"You know Carrie, I was thinking I was acting like a jerk the last time we were together, and I wanted to make it up to you," he smiled. She rounded the corner into the living room and noticed rose petals lining a pathway up the steps. "What? What are you up to?" she queried.

"I thought I needed to make it up to you big time," he broadly grinned. "Follow the petals". They led her directly to the bathroom. He set out candles all along the bathtub rim. He came in and started running some warm water in the tub as he lit the candles. "I figured you might be tired from the traveling and thought you might appreciate a good warm soaking." He added some soothing bath salts to the water. It looked tantalizingly inviting. "Come, get out of those clothes and step into your awaiting sanctuary," he beckoned.

For the first time, she felt a bit self conscious about undressing, but did and gently lowered herself into the water. Jeff grabbed a sponge and lightly stroked her back with it. "I'm so glad you're home, sweetheart. I missed you terribly. Promise me you'll take me with you the next time."

Carrie was touched by his sentiment. "Promise," she responded.

"Take all of the time you need. When you're done I'll be waiting for you in the bedroom," he smiled. "I love you, darling."

"I love you, too," Carrie said with all sincerity.

As she basked in the water, a myriad of feelings flooded her. She forced herself to push thoughts of Ben away and concentrated on all of the loving and tender moments she and Jeff shared. She felt herself incredibly lucky to have both men in her life. But Ben had to go from her mind, only the memory could belong there. The man she committed her life to was expecting her to join him. And she was happy to go to him.

Jeff was patiently waiting for her, lying in their bed. Carrie slipped under the covers and snuggled close to him. It was comforting to smell his muskiness and feel his strong hands touch her. He didn't hurry his lovemaking, causing her to hunger for him even more. They made long slow love together and fell asleep in each other's arms. Carrie was satiated and thankful for sleep.

She woke up the next morning. Jeff was already up. She could smell coffee brewing downstairs. She suddenly heard the familiar sound of little feet come running up the stairs. "Mommy! Mommy!" She heard Katy calling excitedly to her. She jumped up on the bed and they both eagerly hugged and kissed. "I love you, Mommy."

Carrie's heart melted. "I love you too, sweetheart."

"I've a surprise for you. Come on downstairs." Katy's face was filled with pure happiness.

"And I've a surprise for you!" Carrie responded. She grabbed a bag from the nightstand and gave it to Katy.

"Pooh bear! Oh, I love you, Pooh bear!" she squealed as she tightly squeezed him. "Come downstairs Mommy. Grandma and Grandpa are down there, too."

"I will darling, give me a minute to get dressed." Katy scampered off. Carrie threw on some jeans and a sweatshirt and met her daughter in the kitchen.

"Good morning, love," Jeff said with a knowing smile. "Coffee?"

"Please." She gave Jack and Betty a warm hug. "I hope Katy wasn't too much trouble?"

"Are you kidding me?" Betty lit up. "She's the joy of our life. When can you leave again?" she laughed.

"Not any time soon, if ever," Carrie answered as she sipped on her coffee. Katy tugged on her mother's shirt.

"Mommy, look what I made for you." Carrie picked her up and sat her on her lap at the kitchen table. She handed her mother a picture she drew in a style unique to a three year old. "That's you, and that's Daddy, and that's Grandma and Grandpa, and that's me right in the middle! It's our family!" She exclaimed. "Do you like it?"

"I love it," Carrie said as she kissed her daughter. "We'll have to hang it up on the refrigerator." She thought about how blessed she was to have her family.

Katy put her nose to her mother's nose and said, "And there is one more surprise for you," as she held up her little index finger. "Grandma, where is our bag?" Betty handed Katy a plastic bag tied with a ribbon. "I tied it myself," Katy proudly declared. "Grandma Betty taught me how to tie a bow. I can even tie my shoes now. I'm a big girl!"

"Really?" Carrie looked up at Betty, who was nodding her head affirmatively. "Well, then you're a grown up big girl!"

"Open it up," Katy excitedly instructed and started helping her mother undo the tied ribbon. "You need help, don't you Mommy?"

"Well, I guess I do." Carrie was overwhelmed with her feelings of love for her daughter. Jeff watched them adoringly.

"Katy opened the bag and said, "See, they're cookies. Heart cookies. I put pink icing on them. I gave the other cookies to Daddy, but I told him all of the heart cookies were for you because I love you so much."

"And I love you, too," Carrie kissed her daughter and tickled her all over. They both giggled. It was good to be home.

Saturday and Sunday were wonderful decompression days. She stayed close to home and reveled in her family. Monday came far too quickly, bringing work back into her life.

"Glad to have you back," Becky smiled as she greeted her. "It's not the same without you here. I was hoping to give you a break and a chance to catch up, but this weekend was horrendous. We've a bunch of new reports to investigate, and referrals from the school systems have started to ramp up after the long summer."

"So what's new? Isn't it always the case in late September? What's on the agenda?" Carrie asked.

"Thus far I'm managing to hand off only one case to you. It was called in by the fire department. Apparently the house caught fire due to some faulty wiring. However, when the firemen surveyed the situation after putting out the fire, the living conditions were horrendous. In fact, two of the firefighters ended up in the hospital due to the extremely noxious odors emanating from the home and not from the fire. Their pulmonary systems have been extremely compromised as a result of human feces!"

"Whatever are you talking about?" Carrie shifted in her seat.

"This home had no running water for months now. The upstairs bathtub was entirely filled with shit. Apparently they would use the toilet and then shovel their bowel movements into the bathtub and leave it there. Maggots and flies were crawling everywhere on it."

"Oh my God, are the kids alright?"

"It gets worse. Not only was the bathtub filled up, they hauled in two fifty gallon old metal oil drums which were also full. One in the bathroom upstairs and one in the kitchen right next to the stove for when they used the half-bath off the kitchen. These conditions have existed for a long, long time. It's an old brick Victorian type home located on the fringe of the Renaissance neighborhood, yet to be renovated. The linoleum floors throughout the house are filthy and cracked, and have shards of glass laying about everywhere from broken unrepaired windows. A couple of the children had some tiny glass particles embedded in the bottom of their feet. The two youngest had seeping diaper rash and one of them has impetigo. All four kids were filthy. We also suspect the mother wasn't at home when the fire erupted. A neighbor saw smoke coming from the home and called the fire department. It was lucky for the children she knocked on the door and saw the kids inside. She ran in and retrieved them. Mom was charged with endangering children. She's in jail. That's about it."

"Great," Carrie said wryly. "Where are the children now?"

"Right now they're in foster care. A maternal grandmother came forward and wanted to take the children but she reeked of alcohol. Besides she was aware of this situation for some time and did nothing to help fix it. She didn't call anyone for help. We've some serious concerns about her ability to care for them. The four of them are ages one, two, four and five."

"Any fathers around?"

"Mom hasn't given us that information. I don't know if she knows where they are or who they are. That's something else you'll need to follow up on. Carrie, I'm sorry to have to hit you with this. By the way, how was the conference?"

"It was good, Becky. It was an awesome opportunity. It's unfortunate more of the staff couldn't have attended," Carrie remarked.

"Oh, yeah, I forgot to tell you the staff development department wants a full written report within ten days about your experience." Becky shrugged her shoulders as her hands twisted into palms up position. "What can I say? Welcome back!" Becky ended as she handed the file to Carrie. Carrie stood up to return to her office.

"Oh, and one more thing."

"Yes?" Carrie turned and questioned.

"Could you please call Mrs. Kane? She's called at least a hundred times for you. She won't listen or talk to anyone else. You know how she loves you," Becky teased.

"Will do," Carrie retorted and headed back to her desk. As usual, life trudged on at Children Services.

chapter 37

Life settled back into its normal routine, countless crises, long hours, needy clients, forlorn faces, and a few successes here and there, widely celebrated. Home felt good. It was her refuge where Jeff continuously doted on her.

It was the second week in October and her monthly menstrual period plagued her as usual. Soon she would have to visit Dr. Schmidt again as her six months of respite from him would soon be over. She re-examined if she really wanted to continue trying for another child. It was another disappointment to add to all of the misery she encountered at work. In fact, the prior week was particularly troubling to her when an unruly fourteen year old called Becky and accused Carrie of kicking her in the belly during her seventh month of pregnancy. Of course she didn't do that, and no one believed the child. But it was hard to listen to the complaint. It felt like a fatal stab wound. It wasn't fair these kids could pop one kid out right after another, and she struggled to have a child. Others easily dismissed her pain because she had Katy. But it didn't take the hurt away.

Jeff, on the other hand, reassured Carrie he was fine having only Katy. She began to wonder if he even wanted another child. Was he placating her? Maybe he wanted to make it okay for her whatever the outcome.

Monday, November 3, 1986 came. Today was her appointment with Dr. Schmidt. She advised Jeff there was no need for him to come along. She knew not much would be happening this day. The nurse escorted her to an examining room and asked her to put on the clinical paper gown as she was due for her yearly pap test.

"Good morning, Carrie," Dr. Schmidt began as he was flipping through her medical chart. "How have you been?" he said without looking up.

"Okay," Carrie answered.

Dr. Schmidt looked over his half glasses sitting on the lower rim of his nose. "You're due for a pap test today, eh?" After he completed the test he asked Carrie to join him in his office after she got dressed. She figured he would want to talk to her about what they might do next.

Carrie plopped herself down in the brown leather chair across from his desk. "What's up doc?"

"Carrie," he began as he removed his glasses, "can you tell me when you had your last period?"

"About three weeks ago."

"Was it the same as usual?"

"It might have been a little lighter than usual. Why?"

"Now I don't want to get your hopes up, but from my exam your vaginal tissues and cervix suggest you may possibly be pregnant. Have you any increased tenderness of your breasts?"

"A little bit, but that usually comes before my period arrives. I guess thinking about it now; they may be a tad more sensitive than usual."

"Well, I think we should do a blood test before we embark on any more procedures, to be on the cautious side."

"Do you really think there's a possibility I may be pregnant?" Carrie said excitedly.

"I don't want to get your hopes up. I could be wrong. Why don't we wait and see. We should have an answer in three days. Take this down to the lab," he handed her a lab order. "Complete the blood draw, and we'll call you as soon as the results come in."

Those three days seemed interminable to Carrie. She became hyper sensitive to any sign of pregnancy, but was fearful of her hopes being dashed once again. She didn't share with Jeff what Dr. Schmidt told her. She didn't see any reason to bring him along on this ride if it was headed for a crash and burn. At least he could be spared the crushing disappointment.

Her work phone rang as she was compiling a report. She was behind on her paperwork. "Hello, Carrie Cathers speaking," she answered.

"Carrie, this is nurse Roxanne in Dr. Schmidt's office." Carrie's heart immediately began to flutter with anxiety. "I wanted to be the first to congratulate you on your pregnancy!"

"I'm pregnant!" Carrie said in disbelief.

"Yes, that's what your test results indicate."

"I'm pregnant! Oh, I'm so excited. I'm really pregnant!"

"Now, Dr. Schmidt will want to see you within the next week. Will next Wednesday, the twelfth work for you, around ten in the morning?"

"Absolutely, I'll be there."

"Alright, see you then. And congratulations one more time."

Carrie sat there in disbelief. She kept repeating to herself I'm pregnant, as if to convince her of the reality. She couldn't wait to get home and tell Jeff. First she had to spend the afternoon testifying in court.

The agency petitioned the court for permanent custody of an eighteen month old infant named Bart. Bart was born to a thirty-three-year old African-American woman, named Mary. Mary had a good soul, but she was easily taken advantage of by others. She was of lower average intelligence and a follower. She was another child of the 'hole'. She claimed to be a lesbian and became pregnant during an alleged voodoo ceremony held in an after-hours joint. It was likely she became drunk and passed out and was raped.

She really didn't have the wherewithal to take proper care of Bart without constant overseeing. When he was two months old, Mary asked Carrie to place him in foster care. She said where she lived was unsafe for him. In fact, she slept with a wicked hunting knife under her pillow to secure her own safety. Her partner, Francine, was dominant in their relationship, berated Mary constantly, and really didn't want Bart around. Carrie monitored this situation closely due to her concerns for the child, but didn't want to remove him from Mary as long as she could give him minimum appropriate care. She was saddened, but not surprised when Mary urgently called and asked her to take Bart. Carrie knew, once he was in foster care, Mary had little chance of getting him back due to her chaotic lifestyle, especially with Francine. It was bittersweet. Good for Bart, terribly bad for Mary.

Carrie would never forget the tenderness with which Mary said goodbye to Bart. It was clear this was an emotionally wrenching moment for her. She stroked his hair softly, and kissed him gently. Her eyes glistened with tears. It was a courageous act of motherly love for her child. She handed Bart to Carrie. "I know you'll take good care of him Ms. Carrie. Won't you?" She said that more as a statement than a question. "I trust you."

And now today, she was to testify in court and demonstrate what the agency did to try to effect a reunification with Bart and his mother, and why that wasn't possible, even if given more time. She didn't know if Mary would be attending the court session or not.

Carrie thought about life's continuum of pleasurable and painful events. Today was one of her happiest days, but likely one of Mary's saddest days.

Carrie was on the witness stand for over three hours. It was grueling. In the end the judge declared the child in the permanent custody of the agency and now available for adoption. Mary attended, sitting next to her court appointed attorney, whom she met with for thirty minutes before the hearing. Her head hung low the entire trial. Carrie could see her sadness turn to melancholy as the trial wore on. Carrie felt her pain.

After the trial Mary approached Carrie. "Don't blame yourself, Ms. Carrie," she said. "It wasn't your fault. You did everything you could. Make sure he gets some real good parents, okay?" Mary gave Carrie a huge hug and left. She walked slowly down the hall's corridor. Carrie could see her shoulders shaking as she lifted her hand to wipe away tears from her face. Carrie's heart broke for her. She knew Bart got the best deal of all.

***

Carrie constructed an idea of how to tell Jeff she was pregnant. She took the basal thermometer she stuck in her mouth every morning for four years to determine her ovulation dates, broke it in two and wrapped it in a tie box. She wanted him to solve the mystery of the gift. This was part of their lifestyle, solving puzzles.

Carrie tucked Katy into her bed for the night and came down carrying the gift box. She walked over to Jeff, bent down and gave him a kiss and handed him the box. "What's this for?" he wondered aloud.

"Oh, nothing. A little gift I picked up for you."

"What is it?"

"Open it up and see for yourself," she encouraged him.

He opened the box and stared long and hard at the broken thermometer. He looked up at her and then back down at the thermometer again. Suddenly, Carrie could see the meaning of the gift register with him. "You're pregnant?"

"No," she teased and paused a long while. Jeff's face grimaced in disappointment. "No, we're pregnant!" Carrie announced gleefully.

"We are? Really?" he said looking into her eyes questioningly.

"Really, my dear heart. We finally did it! We're going to have a baby this spring!" Words couldn't express the happiness they both felt. Jeff pulled Carrie onto his lap and kissed her tenderly over and over. Then the telephone rang.

"I wonder who's calling at this late hour," Carrie remarked. She picked up the phone. "Hello. Yes, this is Carrie Cathers. Oh my God, yes of course, I'll come down right away. I'll be there in about a half hour." Carrie turned pale.

"Who was that?" Jeff said curiously, "and where are you going at this hour of the night?"

"That was Detective Holbrook. They want me to come down to the morgue right away."

"The morgue! Carrie what's happened?"

"A woman was found dead. She apparently jumped off of a bridge over the freeway. A car dragged her for a long while. They want me to identify her?"

"Why you?" Jeff asked. "Why don't they call her family?"

"They have no idea who she is. All they found in her pants pocket was my work calling card. They couldn't give me her description as she was extremely mutilated by the impact. All I know is she's a black female." Carrie's stomach was churning. She was afraid she knew who it was. She began to feel partly responsible for this death.

"I'm so sorry," Jeff said. "I'll go with you."

"No, you can't. You need to stay here with Katy. I'll be alright."

Detective Holbrook greeted Carrie in the morgue's lobby area. "I'm sorry to have to disturb you this evening. But we really had no choice. You were the only identification she had on her." Carrie nodded her head. She didn't want to do this. She hoped her intuition was wrong about who it was. "I need to warn you, the body is a pretty gruesome sight. Most of her face has been torn off."

"I understand," Carrie stated. "Well, let's get this over with."

Detective Holbrook took her into the body holding room. The temperature was quite cold. There was a body lying on a steel table covered with a white cloth. Shivers coursed through Carrie. It all seemed sterile, impersonal and smelled antiseptic. The coroner's assistant lifted the sheet. Carrie gasped as she quickly looked away. Her stomach wanted to retch. She recognized the tatters left of what was once a shirt. It was the one Mary wore to the trial that day. She began to sob. Mary's face was grotesquely disfigured with her skin hanging as if a potato peeler worked on her. Detective Holbrook placed his arm around Carrie's shoulder and asked her if she was going to be okay. Carrie shook her head affirmatively.

"Her name is Mary Ferris. The court granted us permanent custody of her child earlier this afternoon," Carrie robotically stated.

"Do you think this was a suicide?" Detective Holbrook asked.

"I don't know. It could have been. She was an alcoholic. Maybe it was an accident and she stumbled somehow onto the freeway. Anyway, it really doesn't matter now, does it?" she looked up at Detective Holbrook.

"Do you know if she has any family members we can contact?" Detective Holbrook continued.

"She lived in the 'hole' with her partner, Francine Becker. She was gay. I don't know any other relatives. I can give you Francine's contact information if you like."

"Yes, that would be helpful. I want to thank you for your cooperation. I know this wasn't easy for you. Do you need someone to escort you home?" Detective Holbrook asked. "I could have a cruiser come and pick you up."

"No. Thank you for your concern. I'll be alright. My car is parked right outside." Carrie slipped into her car, turned it on, and then cried for a long while before she engaged it into drive. She never would've believed her job would require this of her. Poor, poor Mary, she lamented. She's in your good hands now, Lord. Take good care of her.

She kept reliving in her head her interactions with Mary. Was there anything else she could have done to prevent this outcome? Was it her fault? Maybe she should have tried harder. Doubt wouldn't leave her, even though it was unfounded.

Jeff anxiously greeted her at the door. Carrie explained what happened. "Don't you think now is the time for you to stop working?" he suggested. "With this, you've another heart ache to pile on top of your heap of heart aches. You know Katy and I would love to have you home. And think of our new baby. You know I don't like you traipsing around, I worry about you."

Carrie wasn't ready for this conversation at this moment. She wanted Jeff to put his arms around her and hold her and tell her everything was going to be alright. She didn't want him suggesting what she should or shouldn't do with her life. She didn't tell him how to run his. She vowed, once again, she needed to share as little as possible with him about her work life. He didn't understand. Well this planned joyous evening of celebration turned into a fiasco. Carrie put her hands up to Jeff as if to say stop. "I'm going to bed," she announced, "I'm exhausted."

She lay in bed and thought of the evening's events. What was supposed to be one of their happiest evenings, ended in this debacle. She was elated with her pregnancy. However, the tragic ending of Mary's life haunted her. Additionally Jeff's overprotective nature was more than she wanted to deal with.

Her mind couldn't help but wander to thoughts of Ben. He would've understood. He would've soothed her. But he wasn't her husband. She knew Jeff loved her deeply and was only worried about her, but sometimes his protective nature felt smothering.

chapter 38

Carrie was in her fourth month of pregnancy and due for her first ultra sound. She and Jeff anxiously awaited Dr. Schmidt's arrival. She drank the requisite amount of water to assure her bladder was full so the best picture could be captured. She was ready to burst.

"Good morning, Carrie, Jeff," the doctor nodded his head. "Are you ready for the big moment?"

"Good morning," they replied in unison. "I sure am," Carrie replied. "I think I may burst before you're done," she giggled.

"Well, then, let's get started. This cream is going to feel a bit cold on your belly, but it helps to transmit the image to us." Carrie could feel the chill of the salve and squeezed Jeff's hand.

The doctor began to move the wand across her body and a black and white image was emerging onto the screen's monitor. "My, oh my, it sure looks crowded in there," Dr. Schmidt remarked. "Well, the good news is all is developing as it should. The other news is you're carrying twins! See here. Here is one heart beat," Dr. Schmidt tapped the monitor of the screen with his pen, "and here is the other one. Well we can tell by what we see here one of them is a boy. We won't be able to tell the sex of the other child as this one is blocking the view."

"Twins! Are you serious?" Carrie couldn't believe what she was hearing.

"Oh, my good Lord," was all Jeff could muster.

"I wouldn't kid about something like that. If all progresses as it should, they'll arrive sometime in early June. Congratulations!" the doctor smiled and shook Jeff's hand. "Everything looks fine. At this time, keep up what you're doing. No special restrictions are needed. Carrie, you're as healthy as an ox."

Carrie looked at Jeff still bewildered by the news. "I never thought of this even as a possibility!"

"Come to think of it, twins do run in my family. You know my mom's sisters are twins. Well, I'll be! We're having twins and at least one boy! Carrie, you always make me happy."

"Well, you had something to do with this as well," she winked at him. "Does this mean I get to have special treatment?"

"What? Nose to the grindstone, dedicated, tough Carrie is asking for special treatment. Do my ears deceive me?" Jeff asked as he gave her a kiss on the forehead.

"Well?" Carrie allowed her question to linger still.

"Absolutely, not," Jeff chided. "Come on, you've time to catch something to eat before you head back to work. Let's celebrate with lunch at the Windjammer." So off they went on their merry way. Jeff treated her like a fragile princess whenever he could, and when Carrie would let him. He didn't like she continued to work, but he learned the subject was a closed one.

***

Back at work Carrie decided to keep the news of twins to herself. Staff members commented on how quickly her belly was swelling. She attributed it to her second pregnancy and her muscles weren't as toned as she would like them to have been. Most nodded their head in understanding.

"Carrie, can you take a case this afternoon? You'll likely have to run out to Emerson Elementary and talk to this boy," Becky asked as she handed the file to Carrie.

"No problem," Carrie answered, "Emerson Elementary is on my way home." She read the referral a teacher called in. Eight-years-old, Hunter Crenshaw presented with a black eye. The teacher suspected foul play at home, as the boy could provide no explanation for his injury.

"Hello, Hunter. My name is Carrie Cathers and I work for Children Services. Do you know what that is?"

Hunter hung his head down staring at the floor and barely audibly said, "No," as he shook his head.

"Well it's my job to check up on kids who might have gotten hurt. And someone is worried about you and called me. They were concerned about how you got that big old shiner I see on your left eye. Can you tell me how you hurt your eye?"

Hunter simply shook his head to indicate 'no'. Carrie was drawn to this pale fair haired young boy. His demeanor was quiet, making Carrie suspect he was too frightened to talk. She noticed his slightly trembling hands. "Sometimes I know it's hard to talk about when we get hurt. Does your eye cause you any pain?"

"A little," he quietly muttered.

"Are you sure you can't remember how it happened?" Carrie said in a soothing voice as she gently patted his hand. Again, he shook his head no. His breath quickened a bit and Carrie knew she needed to not push the subject with him right at this moment. "I want you to know you haven't done anything wrong, Hunter. I needed to do a quick check with you, and I can see you're doing fine. I was glad to have a chance to meet you. Do you have any questions for me?"

Again, a quiet 'no' came with another head shake. "Well, I think I'll go now, and I'll let you get back to class. I wouldn't want to keep you here and have you miss your bus ride home. Everything's okay, okay?"

"Okay," he said quietly. He turned and left the small office they were in. His shoulders slumped as he slowly moved onward. Carrie knew she would be working well past quitting time today. She had enough time to stop by Hunter's house and speak to his mother before Hunter came home on the bus.

Carrie pulled into the apartment complex where the Crenshaw's lived. It was a townhouse. She took a deep breath of air before knocking on the door. Everything about Hunter's demeanor suggested to her his injury was anything but accidental. After all these years of seeing maltreated children, she developed an instinct about which kids were imminently at risk. In her mind, Hunter was one of them.

The door was opened by an extremely thin woman, a bit taller than Carrie. She had two black eyes! "Hello, Mrs. Crenshaw, Alice Crenshaw?"

"Yes," she simply answered.

"My name is Carrie Cathers and I'm a caseworker with Children Services. Are you familiar with our agency?"

"I've heard of you folks," Mrs. Crenshaw responded.

"Well then you know we are the legal agency required to look into all concerns of child maltreatment. We receive many referrals each day, and today we received one concerning Hunter. Now, I've no way of knowing which referrals we receive are accurate or not. It's my job to check out the information we receive to figure that out. May I come in and talk with you?"

Mrs. Crenshaw opened the storm door and invited Carrie in. They stood in the nicely furnished living room. "Here, I want to give you this pamphlet explaining your rights when we work with families. Now you don't have to talk to me if you don't want to."

"No, it's okay. I've nothing to hide."

"I want you to know I did get a chance to visit with Hunter at school and noticed he has a black eye. But he could give me no explanation for how he got it. Can you help me understand?" Carrie inquired as she studied Mrs. Crenshaw's two black eyes. Carrie knew sadness dwelled in this house. The energy in the air hung with it.

"Oh, yeah, he got into a fight with some of the neighborhood kids here. You know there are some rough kids living down the way, and they pick on him a lot. He came running home Friday night crying after they punched him."

"I see," Carrie offered. "Why do you think he wouldn't share with me?"

"I don't know. He's a pretty shy kid. I've taught him not to talk to strangers."

"Good. It's a good thing for kids to be wary of strangers. You did well to teach him. Most kids don't listen to that kind of stuff, you know. Mrs. Crenshaw, can you tell me how you got your . . . . "

"Oh, you think I have two black eyes, don't you." She nervously laughed. "Well, these aren't black eyes. I get these real dark circles under my eyes due to an extreme iron deficiency I have. My doctor has even given me a prescription of these huge iron pills to take." She quickly walked into the kitchen and returned. "See, here they are." Mrs. Crenshaw showed Carrie her prescription bottle filled with large brown looking pills. "I forget to take them. Well you can see that. The jar is still pretty full."

"I see. Mrs. Crenshaw, I'm required to speak to all of the children in the household. I understand you have a four year old son, Dallas."

"Yes, he's upstairs taking a nap. He should be waking up any minute now."

"Do you think you could rouse him for me so I could talk to him for a second? I really hate to disturb you all, but it'll take a quick moment."

"Sure. No problem. In fact why don't you come upstairs with me?"

"I'll wait down here if you don't mind. Maybe it will be better if you let him know I'm down here and want to talk to him for a minute. That way he won't think I'm a stranger, if you give him permission."

"Okay, whatever," Mrs. Crenshaw said. She left Carrie and went upstairs. Soon she brought down a sleepy-eyed looking Dallas. He had brown curly hair and bright blue eyes. He was adorable. He was rubbing his eyes with his little fists as his mother introduced Carrie to him. "Why don't you talk to Mrs. Cathers while I go and get you something to drink?" she said to Dallas, as he sat in the corner of the couch holding onto a teddy bear.

Carrie smiled at him and made small talk with him before she asked about people hurting him or his brother. In the end, Dallas gave her no information to cause concern. His mother returned with a glass of Kool-Aid which he greedily gulped down. "I have to pee, Mommy."

"Okay, why don't you go on upstairs and use the bathroom. If you want, you can go back to your room and play with your toys."

"Okay," he said sleepily as he yawned."

"Your children are adorable," Carrie complimented. "You must be very proud of them."

"Yes, I am. They're good kids. I would be lost without them."

"Do you have anyone to help you with them?"

"You mean like family?"

"Yes, family or friends."

"Well, my sister lives across town. She has three kids of her own. We see each other about once a week. We're pretty close."

"Well, that's good. It's always nice to have family support." The front door swung open and Hunter walked in.

"Hi, honey," Alice Crenshaw greeted her son.

"Hi," he whispered.

"Hello, Hunter. It's good to see you again. I came here to talk to your mom. She and I have been talking about how you got your black eye."

Hunter glanced up at his mom.

Mrs. Crenshaw nodded her head affirmatively. "Yes, we have."

Carrie inserted herself into the conversation again. "Your mother wants you to tell me how it happened, don't you Mrs. Crenshaw?"

Alice hesitated, sighed and then said, "Well, of course."

Hunter looked up at his mother again. He remained silent.

Carrie began again, "Hunter, do you think you could share with me how you got hurt?"

He looked at his mother a third time and then blurted out, "Mick punched me in the face because I wouldn't eat my broccoli."

"Can you tell me who Mick is?" Carrie persisted.

"He's my mom's boyfriend."

"I see," Carrie said as she caught Mrs. Crenshaw biting her lip.

"And how often do you see Mick?"

"Everyday. He lives here."

"Are you afraid of him?"

"Kind of."

"Has he hurt you before this time?"

"Sometimes he hits me with his belt, but he hasn't done that for a while. Mom, can I go to my room now?" Hunter asked.

Alice looked at Carrie who nodded her head she was fine with that. She didn't want to overwhelm Hunter. She knew she would have to make a plan with Alice about keeping her child safe from Mick, and it was best Hunter not be present right then.

She also knew Alice didn't tell her the truth about how Hunter got his black eye. And she likely lied to her about her own two black eyes. Carrie didn't buy her iron deficiency story. She hoped this mother would be cooperative. If not, she would have to invite the police into this scenario immediately. She didn't want to, if it could be avoided. It would only traumatize the children more. She sent up a silent prayer for help.

Mother agreed Hunter could stay with her sister across town; however, she wouldn't consent to Dallas leaving the home as well. She said Mick could get a bit heavy handed with Hunter sometimes, but he never took his anger out on Dallas. She also continued to deny he was physically abusive with her. Carrie knew she was lying.

The appropriate criminal and record checks were made to assure Hunter's aunt was a safe place for him to be. Carrie followed Alice as she took the children over to her sister's house, so she could care for Hunter. Carrie carefully went over the conditions of Hunter's placement with his aunt, to assure all the adults understood he wasn't allowed to return home until the agency was able to fully investigate the situation and assure Hunter would be safe from harm before he returned home.

She attempted once again to get Mrs. Crenshaw to agree to leave Dallas there as well, but to no avail. Because Dallas had no injuries and gave no information about being hurt by Mick, she couldn't force the issue this evening.

Seven o'clock was approaching and Carrie was now heading home. The Crenshaw family weighed heavily on her mind. Hunter was safe for now, but she wasn't sure Alice would stick by the safety plan once Mick realized what happened. She also worried about Alice's safety, suspecting

Mick Norris likely abused her as well. And her heart broke for little Dallas, as he had no ability to keep himself out of harms' way.

When she arrived home, Katy ran up to her excitedly and jumped into her arms giving her many hugs and kisses. Jeff walked in and also gave her a loving embrace. "Rough night?"

Carrie didn't respond to his question. She didn't want to talk about it. "I'm starved," she said. "We have to get these children fed," as she rubbed her belly and smiled up at Jeff. "Twins!"

"What's twins, mommy?" perceptive little Katy asked. Jeff and Carrie looked at each other. They didn't tell Katy about the babies yet, but it looked like now was going to be as good a time as any. Jeff prepared some meatloaf, mashed potatoes and green beans. They ate happily as they shared the news of their pregnancy with little Katy.

"When can I play with them?" Katy asked.

"It will be a long time from now. Your birthday will come first, then Mommy's birthday, and then the babies will be born and have their birthday.

"Me first?" Katy asked. "My birthday is the first one?"

"Yep, you got it right," Jeff answered as he rubbed the hair on her head lovingly.

"Oh, goodie!" Katy clapped her hands. "I like birthdays. I'll be four years old." She lifted her hand up and demonstrated four fingers and counted, one...two...three...four!"

The next morning Carrie reviewed the Crenshaw case thoroughly with Becky. They decided, at the very least, they should approach the court for some court orders to compel mother to follow the safety plan. They wanted to ask the court to give them orders to keep Dallas safe as well.

The court decided to give the agency temporary custody of Hunter. They didn't receive any orders at all for Dallas, citing he needed some evidence of maltreatment. Otherwise they would be overreaching their authority. Carrie felt sick. She didn't feel that Alice was capable of keeping him safe, as evidenced by her own inability to keep herself safe. She couldn't prove it, but knew Mick likely gave Alice those black eyes as well. At least the agency would keep this case open and try to work with this family towards better outcomes.

chapter 39

The months flew by. As Carrie progressed in her pregnancy, her co-workers became quite accommodating to her condition. This second pregnancy became far more taxing on her than her first pregnancy. Perhaps it was because she was carrying twins, perhaps it was because she was an active mother as well as a wife and caseworker, or perhaps it was because her body placed extraordinary demands upon it for greater than usual nutrition and energy requirements. Carrie knew she was tired all of the time, a condition previously foreign to her. Her back began to continuously ache and it was getting harder to move around.

Sylvia remained a steadfast friend for her throughout. Her daughter Carrie doted on Katy, and Sylvia kept Katy with her two days a week. Sylvia also had a son, Eli. Katy was delighted to be in their company. It turned out to be a wonderful arrangement for all. Often times Sylvia would prepare enough dinner to send some home for Carrie, Jeff and Katy. Carrie thought of her as a godsend. Sylvia became a second place of refuge for Carrie. She could share her work day with Sylvia, as she couldn't with Jeff. Sylvia understood. Sylvia also kept up with all of their old school mates, keeping Carrie informed about what was happening with them all. The recent news was Eloise married Cliff, and Matt left social work to farm full time. It was in his roots and blood to do so. Carrie didn't blame him. Growing food was also doing God's work, she thought, except the food didn't talk back.

Carrie received a recommendation from Dr. Schmidt to get off of her feet. She was beginning to experience some edema, and she needed to put her feet up more these last two months. Carrie didn't want to stop working at this juncture, knowing after the delivery she would be out of commission for six months with her maternity leave. She didn't want to use up any leave before the birth of the twins.

It ended up being a blessing in disguise. She was able to transfer back into the evening hours screening position during this time. She could keep her feet propped up, stay in and answer the phone, and have all day to spend with Katy. Jeff, too, was happy for the change. He worried about her constantly whenever she was out on the street.

Tanner was more than happy to have Carrie back once again. He admired her integrity and skill. She seemed to bring calm to chaos, and right now his staff could use some calming influences. Most of them were young, inexperienced, and easily freaked out by many of the unpredictable evening events. He also appreciated having an old colleague around he could banter with easily. He appreciated Carrie was able to challenge his thinking.

Jeff was a sweetheart throughout, being extra attentive to her. Carrie never complained, but Jeff could see it in her eyes and her movements she was wearing down. Her delivery date was drawing near. They recently completed the Lamaze refresher course.

It was her birthday, May 30. They celebrated earlier in the day. Sylvia came to her home and prepared a grand lunch for them. Sylvia supervised Katy in the preparation of a birthday cake. It was a good day.

Katy propped herself next to Carrie as they snuggled in a chair, as she no longer could fit on her mother's lap. This was their special time together reading books. Katy learned to read some of the small words, or she memorized the books from the numerous readings of them. Carrie adored these times and hoped they would never stop. Katy would often fall asleep listening to the sound of the twins moving around in Carrie's belly. She was sent into fits of giggling when one of them would give her a slight kick with a foot. "Calm down Chloe, Scott or Todd," Katy would say to them as she put her lips against Carrie's stomach.

"Now you had your birthday, Mommy, will the babies be here tomorrow?" Katy asked.

"I don't know, sweetheart. They get to decide what day they want to come, but it will be soon."

"I can't wait to play with them," Katy smiled.

"Me, too," Carrie laughed.

***

Carrie struggled to get herself ready for work and wondered how much longer before the birth. She had to admit even she was losing her enthusiasm for trudging into work daily. It was Monday, June 1, 1987, a day about to rock her world.

"Children Services, this is Carrie Cathers. How may I help you?" Carrie said robotically after taking the twentieth call of the night. It was late, and she was tired and ready to go home.

"Hello. This is Officer Ellen Lewis of the police department." Officer Lewis sounded extremely stressed. "I've never called your agency before. I need to report a child's death." Officer Lewis started crying. "I'm sorry for being emotional, but I'm new at this."

Carrie became immediately alert. A child died. "It's understandable," Carrie responded to Officer Lewis. "There is no need to apologize. Let me help you by asking a few questions, when you're ready."

Ellen blew her nose and though sniffling proceeded.

"What's the child's name, please?" Carrie began.

"Dallas, Dallas Crenshaw, age four."

Carrie was speechless. Her steel trap armor protecting her emotions began to crack. "Did you say Dallas Crenshaw?" Carrie said unable to hide her own emotions.

"Yes, that's his, I mean was his name," Ellen Lewis continued.

"Oh my God, I know this boy!" Carrie said in disbelief. "What happened? Did he get killed in a car accident?"

"I wish it happened that way. It would've been a kinder death. I'm afraid he died at the hands of his parents. We are still investigating the exact cause of death. Both of his parents were present at the time of his passing. He died at home." Ellen began to sob. "It was horrible."

Carrie began to cry while trying to maintain her professional composure. For the first time in her career she thought, perhaps, someone else should take this call. At the moment no one else was available. Pull yourself together, she challenged herself. You've a job to do. But this time it felt personal. She knew this darling boy. This time it was different. Something deep inside of her warned her to brace herself.

With her own voice beginning to crack a bit, Carrie continued on. "Can you tell me what happened exactly?" She could hear Officer Lewis trying to catch her own composure. "Take all the time you need," Carrie said sympathetically.

She could hear Ellen draw in a deep long breath. "He was tortured," she briefly paused and then added, "slowly." She began to cry again. "I can't believe parents could become such monsters," she said in agonized disbelief.

Carrie's hand began to shake. She didn't want to know the details. Yet she had to know them, both professionally and personally. She needed to give homage to this boy in some fashion and the least she could do was hear his story.

Ellen continued. "I wrote down some notes. Maybe it will be easier if I read them to you. But they're cryptic."

"Okay, take your time."

"Dallas has the following injuries: large contusions and bruises on his face, patches of hair pulled from his head, hot sauce and tobacco stuffed down his throat . . . ."

Carrie heard enough. She desperately wanted to remove the phone from her ear. Her hands would no longer write down what she was hearing. She, too, was falling apart. Ellen continued mechanically. ". . . . a broken right arm, skin removed from his extremities due to apparent rug burns or had his skin rubbed off with an abrasive substance, and numerous cigarette burns about his body. He also appears to have been thrown up against a wall numerous times due to the nature of the holes in the dry wall." Silence ensued, a long hard silence. Both women were speechless, lost in a well of unfathomable sorrow.

Ellen began again. "Both parents have been arrested and likely won't be released from jail anytime soon. We understand there is an older brother, a Hunter Crenshaw, in the care of his maternal aunt, and your agency still holds temporary custody of him."

Carrie's suit of armor cracked and shattered. Her ability to absorb the emotional pain of her clients and stay sane was teetering on the edge. "Yes," was all she could muster.

Ellen continued. "One of our patrol officers will bring our police report to your office tomorrow. And for the record, I'm sorry for your loss. I can tell this has hit you hard. If there is anything else, please call me."

"Thank you. I will. You take care of yourself," Carrie responded before hanging up the phone. Carrie sat in her chair, staring out into space. She left the material world, lost in her own sea of emotions. She didn't even see Tanner as he stood in front of her. He was waving his hand in front of her face.

"Carrie, Carrie, Carrie," he said to capture her attention. She looked up at him, all color gone from her face. "Carrie, are you okay?" She simply shook her head to say no. Her demeanor scared Tanner. He never saw her like this before. "What happened?" he quietly inquired as he half sat on her desk keeping one foot on the floor. He came to genuinely care for Carrie and was alarmed with her appearance. "Is something happening with your pregnancy?" Again Carrie simply shook her head no. "Carrie, you're scaring me, please tell me what's wrong," he pleaded.

She slowly turned her eyes toward him. They were reddened. Tears streaked down her cheeks. "It's Dallas Crenshaw, he was tortured to death. I knew him. I opened his case before I came here. He was only four years old." A sharp pain stabbed Carrie in her belly, then another, and another. She cried out as if in agony. She recognized the pain, labor pains, but they never hurt like this before with Katy. She knew Dallas was crying out through her.

Tanner was frantic. Carrie didn't look good at all. He immediately assessed she needed to get to the hospital immediately. Tanner instructed the receptionist to call for Jeff and alert him Carrie was in labor and he was rushing her to the hospital.

The resident on-call checked Carrie. "These babies are not going to wait for anyone. They'll be here within the hour," he proclaimed. Jeff rushed to her side and barely made it to her before the birth.

"Hey darling, how are you doing?" he greeted her and tenderly kissed her. She answered him by squeezing his hand as another excruciating pain swept her body. She could feel a child emerging.

"It's a boy!" exclaimed the doctor.

"Scott," Carrie proclaimed, before her body ramped up for more labor pains. Three minutes later and another miracle was born. "Todd," she happily noted. "We have a set of boys," she looked lovingly at Jeff. "Life gets better for us, doesn't it?"

"My life became eternally better the day I met you," Jeff replied grinning. The boys were making quite a ruckus. Both peed the minute their pink little bodies felt the cool air outside of their mother's womb. "That's my boys," Jeff remarked proudly.

The children were wrapped in warm blankets and placed in Carrie's arms with their full heads of hair poking out. She kissed each gently and knew her family was, once again, blessed.

The next day Jeff brought Katy to the hospital to see her brothers. They went to the special viewing room for siblings. Katy stepped up on a small stool to peer through the glass window. Carrie stooped next to Katy and Jeff brought Scott up to the window. "That's your brother Scott," Carrie said.

"He's so little!," Katy replied. "I love him, Mommy."

Jeff kissed Scott and returned with Todd. "And that's Todd," Carrie smiled.

"He looks like Scott!" Katy observed.

"Yes, he does," Carrie affirmed.

"But Mommy, where's Chloe? I don't see her."

Carrie laughed. Chloe was the name they picked out if the other twin was a girl. "Oh, sweetheart, we didn't know if one of the babies would be a boy or a girl. But he turned out to be a boy. Chloe would've been the baby's name if it was a girl. Remember, we were only having two babies?"

"Oh, that's right. I love the babies, Mommy. I love you too, Mommy."

Carrie's heart was breaking with love. "And I love you too, sweetheart. You'll always be my very special little girl." She squeezed Katy with another hug. "Tomorrow Mommy and the babies will come home. Grandma Betty and Grandpa Jack will come and visit too. Will you help me take care of everyone?"

"I promise," Katy said in her little grown-up voice.

Carrie's in-laws picked her up from the hospital to take her home as Jeff waited with Katy. Jack held Scott and Betty carried Todd. Carrie purchased a gift earlier to give to Katy for this moment. "Hi sweetheart," she smiled at Katy. "I brought you a present."

Katy was overflowing with excitement. She ripped opened the large gift and lifted out a life sized doll which could pass for one of the twins. "Oh, Mommy," she exclaimed, "Here's Chloe!" And with that, the doll was forever christened as Chloe. "I have a baby, too!" Katy excitedly exclaimed. And she did. As Carrie took loving care of Scott and Todd, Katy was alongside her taking care of Chloe.

❊❊❊

Carrie reveled all summer long in her family. She didn't have to return to work until December, although her mind didn't abide by the timeline. She couldn't remove thoughts of Dallas from her mind. She continuously rechecked herself to make sure there was nothing more she could have done to prevent his death. She tried to gain court orders to keep him safe and was denied.

Images of this sweet little boy being tortured haunted her. Mick Norris and Alice Crenshaw were both charged with Dallas's death. Mick pled guilty to manslaughter charges and received the maximum penalty the law allowed. However, he would be eligible for parole within five years with good behavior. Five years wasn't nearly enough of a price to pay for what happened to Dallas, thought Carrie. People spent far greater time in jail for less serious offenses. She secretly hoped his time served would be hard. She hoped his fellow inmates would see to that.

Only one of them could be charged with the murder for having delivered the final death blow. Alice was charged with aiding and abetting. She pled guilty by reason of insanity and "got off," as much as one could "get off," having to live with the consequences of her actions. Carrie knew she was also a victim of domestic violence. But her mind couldn't wrap itself around the notion a mother wouldn't have given up her own life to prevent her child's torture and death. It was likely Alice may have been murdered by this animal if she didn't follow his commands. She reminded herself it wasn't her place to judge such events unless she walked in similar shoes, and she hadn't.

Carrie received some small solace she helped to keep Hunter safe. Yet, still, she remained troubled by these circumstances. She realized the law was the ultimate problem. Children Services had no recourse to intervene on behalf of a sibling of an abused child unless the child also showed evidence of having been maltreated. The law simply didn't allow for it.

It didn't help the newspaper lambasted the agency with shocking headlines: "Children Services fails to act, a child dies." They needed to find a scapegoat for this child and the agency was it. Articles noted the family's case was opened for services at the time of Dallas's death. They suggested the agency was negligent by mere virtue of Dallas's death. Nothing was noted about attempts to get court orders so they could legally intervene on behalf of Dallas, and were denied such orders. Nothing was said about the flaws in the legal system. And the agency wasn't allowed to publicly or privately respond due to laws of confidentiality. They had to sit there and take it. It was a rough time for the caseworkers in the community following the tragedy, even though they held no responsibility for what happened to Dallas.

Carrie's mind wouldn't let her rest. She decided on a course of action and did what little she could. She wrote letters regarding the law's loopholes about being able to intervene on behalf of siblings to try to spur some legislative changes. She sent them weekly to her state representative and the Public Children Services Policy Initiative organization. She received back kindly form letters thanking her for her concern as a response.

chapter 40

Carrie returned to work. She realized she had to shift her mental energies around. Having a family of three children was more demanding. She tried to leave work at work, which wasn't easy for her. She loved coming home. It was her sanctuary. She and Jeff had a comfortable giving relationship with one another. Both of them calmed their careers down and focused on their family. Jack and Betty continued to be a dream of support for them. She and Sylvia remained close friends, and as the years wore on she and Ellen Lewis also became fast friends. Their relationship started with Dallas Crenshaw and evolved as their paths frequently crossed.

Katy, Scott and Todd were her heart and soul. She and Katy shared an unbreakable bond. Katy was her rock and anchor. When all hope would leave Carrie, she would return home to Katy and be revived with renewed awareness of possibilities. Katy represented all that was good. People, who saw them together, remarked about the undeniable connection between the two of them. Katy knew inherently how to lift up her mother's spirits from the day she was born. She was a gift from God. Katy resembled Jeff in her appearance and the twins favored Carrie.

Every now and then, when the sun glimmered off of the eyes of Scott and Todd, Carrie thought she detected the most brilliant green emanating from deep within. Each time this happened, she was flooded with thoughts of Ben. Secretly she felt Ben's energy was captured in their souls. When Todd developed that same unique jaunt in his step which Ben had, she knew. She knew even though she couldn't have Ben, the good Lord gave her a piece of him. This filled her heart in a deep and meaningful way, and she was thrilled to have this small part of Ben. This was her truth alone and she would carry it with her to the grave. It filled her with an uncommon peace.

Jeff never suspected. He was a loving and caring father. The twins adored their father. All was good.

When the twins were ten years old, Sylvia shared with Carrie, during one of their alumni updates; Ben was remarried, some Washington, D.C. socialite. Carrie was filled with a mixture of emotions upon hearing the news. First she was jealous, and then she was happy for him. She could never deny to herself her connection with Ben was soul deep, even deeper than hers with Jeff. That's why she removed herself from any potential possibility of including him again in her life. It was best. She was happy. She was content. She was loved.

May 29, 2014

It was a long evening of remembering. Carrie was amazed at how her life could be reviewed in a mere evening. Tomorrow was *the* big day and she was ready for it. She changed into some comfy pajamas and crawled into her bed. She grabbed some of her journals she kept in her nightstand. She faithfully recorded her thoughts nightly throughout her years. It was her therapy, a way to let go of all she experienced. In fact, her nightstand was filled with years of journaling. Jeff respected this ritual. He understood this need. He also honored her privacy and never read her world of thoughts. It was her safe haven.

During the past year, she didn't write. Even she realized writing the words wouldn't heal her heart. She flipped through some of the journals catching glimpses of her life here and there. A small piece of a singular fiber of a rope was taped to one page. Beside it she wrote the words, "never forget". No other entry was made regarding the rope strand. She realized she didn't need the rope fiber to remember Paula. Like Dallas, Paula haunted her memories, except she knew Paula was saved. She fortunately never had to look down upon Dallas and see him after his torturous abuse, but she did see Paula. In fact it was Dallas who was the persistent voice in her head to find Paula.

1995

Carrie was searching for Paula. Two weeks passed and she hadn't found her. The referral came from an anonymous source. It was filled with multiple concerns. Carrie suspected one of their neighbors called it in, thankfully. The Thompson home was located in a working class neighborhood of white families only. The culture in this small section of town was known for its white racist bent. Living in this area was hard. Motorcycle gangs, theft rings, chop shops, and drug trafficking were all known to exist here. Tattoos and alcoholism and domestic violence were common family traits. Most were undereducated. Men ruled this part of the world.

The report indicated the Thompson family was composed of three children: Paula, age six and bi-racial, Davy, age four and Barry age three, both white boys. Ed Thompson was linked to a white supremacist gang. Darlene often had black and blue bruises about her arms, legs and face. The caller was concerned because she hadn't seen the little girl for two weeks. The boys were out and about in the neighborhood, but there were no signs of Paula. When the caller would ask the mother about Paula, she would simply say she was inside.

What prompted the caller to make the report was she could hear some blood curdling screams come from the home, sounding like they came from a young female child. This happened several times. She admitted she had no real evidence of harm to Paula, but then again, she hadn't seen Paula. But the screams she heard "sent blood curdling shivers through me to match the screams."

She also mentioned Ed came across as a ferocious bully. She was frightened of him. The last additional alarming detail the referral source mentioned was she knew Paula was born as a result of her mother having been raped by a black man. Ed hated black people and anyone with some black blood in them.

As Carrie reviewed the report she knew this child was possibly in severe danger from the likes of Ed. She approached the home and noticed it was a bit run down, paint peeling on the outside, no window screens, but it appeared to be clean and tidy. She could hear the boys scrambling about within the home. The mother answered the door and allowed Carrie inside. It was four-thirty in the afternoon. School aged children should be home by now.

Darlene's face looked sallow, her eyes deeply set and sad. She continuously ran her fingers through her thick dark hair as she talked, perhaps in a nervous gesture. She was a bit plump and wore baggy sweats. She was missing a couple of teeth and had cigarette stained fingers. The smell of bleach permeated the house.

The boys looked fine. They were watching television and irritating each other as only boys can do. Carrie shared with her the concern called in.

"Oh, those boys get after her terribly," she said as she pointed to her sons. "It ain't unusual for a lot of screaming to happen 'round here." Carrie noticed a slight tremble in her finger as she pointed to her boys.

"Do you think I could talk to Paula?" Carrie asked.

"Well, you could, 'cept she's not here right now. She's at her Brownie meeting. You know the Girl Scout stuff they have after school."

"I see. What time do you think she might be home?"

"Not anytime soon. They ain't nothin' wrong goin' on 'round here," Darlene persisted. "Well, you can see that for y'urself."

"Okay," Carrie said. "I'll need to see Paula before I can close out our investigation. Can we set up a time when I could come out and talk to her?"

"Sure. Anytime."

"How about tomorrow, about this same time? Will that be good for you?"

"I don't see why it wouldn't be," Darlene answered as she began to pull her upper lip nervously.

"Okay, I'll see you then."

The next day came and Carrie returned to the Thompson home. This time no one answered. She returned to the home each successive day for three days. No one answered. On an off chance, Carrie stopped by the Thompson home one morning around ten. She hoped to catch Darlene at a different time.

As she knocked on the door, Carrie could hear the boys running through the house. Davy, the oldest yelled to his mother, "That lady's here again." Still no one answered. Carrie persisted. Her radar alert was high. She knew without a doubt Darlene was inside. She wasn't going to give up.

She walked around to the back door and could see Darlene in the kitchen smoking a cigarette and tapping her fingers on the kitchen counter. She knocked loudly. This time Darlene couldn't hide from her.

"She ain't here," she told Carrie through the door. "She's at school." Carrie knew better as she checked with the school regarding Paula's attendance. She hadn't attended school for the past four weeks. This alarmed Carrie even more intensely. The school assumed they moved out of the area.

"Now, Mrs. Thompson, I know that isn't true. Please, let me in so we can talk." Begrudgingly Darlene allowed her in as she admonished her to talk quietly. She didn't want to wake up Ed, who was sleeping upstairs.

"Mrs. Thompson," Carrie began, "I want to be able to close out this investigation as much as you do. But first, I must see all of your children. That's our legal mandate and it includes Paula. Is she here?"

Davy and Barry came running through the kitchen and Carrie thought she heard Davy say, "She's in the basement," as he quickly ran past her and into the dining room.

Darlene responded, "No she ain't here. She's at my mother's house. She was getting on Ed's nerves and I thought it best she stay away for a while."

"Okay, can you tell me where your mother lives? I can go see her over there."

"She lives way on the other side of town. I don't rightly recollect her address." Darlene began running her fingers through her hair again.

"How about a phone number? I can give her a call and set up a time to see her." Carrie was trying to remain hopeful but, she saw this avoidance dance before with others.

"She ain't got no phone. She's on SSI, can't afford one."

Carrie decided to take another tactic. "Mrs. Thompson, I can't deny I'm concerned for Paula's well being, but I'm concerned about you too. Does Ed treat you right?"

"Ed, oh he's a lot of bluster, but we do okay. Sometimes he can get pretty angry. He can get a bit rough. I know it scares the kids, but we're okay."

"What does he do when he gets angry?" Carrie questioned.

"He does what all red blooded American men do. Listen, I don't want to be rude or nuthin' but I think it's best if you leave, I can hear Ed stirrin' upstairs. He don't take kindly to strangers in his business. It's best if you got going."

"Okay, but I'll need to come back. Please help me, Mrs. Thompson." Carrie decided to take a giant leap of faith, "Please, help Paula."

"Who's that you're talkin' to?" Ed bellowed as he started coming down the stairs.

"It's the welfare lady," Darlene said extremely nervously. "You'd better git going," she whispered to Carrie. "He's going to be real mad."

Ed appeared in the kitchen doorway. "What the hell are you doin' in my house?" he said intimidatingly. "Get the hell out of here."

Carrie knew when to exit, and did out the back door. As she walked around to the front she could here Ed working himself up into a rage with Darlene. Her heart sank for Darlene. She was even more determined to find Paula. The neighbor heard blood curdling screams probably for a good reason. She sent up a prayer to God she would find Paula safe and sound.

Carrie reviewed the case with her current supervisor, Judy. "I want to ask the prosecutor for a search warrant. There is no other way we are going to get access to her. I'm positive she's in that house."

"What evidence do you have?" Judy questioned.

"Very little. Just the boy suggesting she was in the basement as he ran through the room. I wouldn't put it past Ed to lock her up down there. I noticed the door has a deadbolt lock on it. How many people do you know have a deadbolt lock on their basement door?"

"Anything else?" Judy asked.

"Nothing more, other than mom's demeanor. She's awfully nervous and she's clearly afraid of Ed. I don't think she can help her daughter even if she wanted to. Plus, Paula isn't attending school. She's disappeared off of their attendance charts. Listen, I know it's not much. Let me try. Let me talk to the prosecutor. What can it hurt? Maybe we can use an educational neglect angle."

"Educational neglect won't get you a search warrant. It will only get you a court hearing scheduled sometime in the next month."

"I know," Carrie sighed. "But this child is in severe danger. I know it. Ed's a racist bigot and this child is half black. He wouldn't need any provocation from her to take out his anger on her."

"Alright," Judy relented. "You have a point. It can't hurt to talk to the prosecutor and see if there is anything we can do. Go ahead."

Carrie was a caseworker for twenty-seven years now. As a result she was afforded some deferential treatment by other professionals due to her stellar reputation of being honest and dedicated to her clients. She hoped to use her reputation in persuading the prosecutor to get a search warrant, even on the minimal evidence she had. Thoughts of Dallas Crenshaw began to invade her thinking and she would do anything to prevent another death like Dallas's. This situation with Paula had a similar ring. It was the look in Darlene's eyes. It reminded her of Alice Crenshaw, even after so many years passed.

Bernie Willoughby's assistant listened intently to Carrie. As assistant prosecutor he had the authority to secure the search warrant with a judge by the end of the day, if the judge agreed. "I'll give it a try. That's the least I can do for you Carrie. I'll give you a call and let you know what happens."

"You got it!" the assistant prosecutor told Carrie excitedly over the phone. "Come on over and get it."

Carrie elatedly called Detective Ellen Lewis, who was still with the juvenile bureau of the police department. She would need police assistance in activating the search warrant. Ellen was immediately on board with Carrie as she earlier learned of Carrie's concerns. They agreed to meet a block from the Thompson's residence.

Ellen brought police reinforcements with her. They ran a criminal check on Ed Thompson and he had a long list of petty crimes: assaults, menacing threats, receiving stolen goods, robbery, and one incident of domestic violence. Most of those charges were thrown out or plead down. He was known to be a member of the local white supremacist group. He was on probation. His rap sheet certainly suggested he could be a dangerous threat and likely armed. The police backup included six additional street officers all dressed in bullet proof vests.

Ellen instructed, "The officers will secure the home, and then we can do our search. We don't want to go in until we know it's safe for everyone."

The officers knocked on the door and Darlene answered. "Police department, we have a search warrant to search your premises for Paula Thompson," the uniformed man announced as he flashed his badge and the warrant. They pushed their way into the home. Two officers covered the back door entry and caught Ed as he was heading out of the door to escape through the back alley. Darlene and the boys sat on the couch in obvious fear as an officer stood over them. They motioned for Ellen and Carrie to enter.

Carrie looked at Darlene who turned ghost white. "Where is she?" Carrie asked.

Darlene pointed to the basement door. "She's in the basement," Ellen called to the officers. The door was locked.

Carrie said to Ellen, "Let me handle this please." Ellen nodded.

"Darlene, I promise we will try to keep you safe from Ed. But we have to think of Paula. Do you have the key?" Darlene reached inside her shirt and produced the key she had on a string hanging around her neck, as if it was a locket. She handed it to Carrie as tears formed in her eyes.

Carrie quickly took the key and unlocked the door. She headed down the steps with Ellen at her heels. She wasn't prepared for what she saw. There lay Paula, with ropes around her wrists and ankles lying on the damp wet floor. Her arms were in an upward position as they hung from the ropes wrapped around her tiny wrists and the water pipes on the basement ceiling. Her ankles were tethered to the supportive posts of the basement. She felt like she entered a medieval dungeon of torture. And there was the mere wisp of a little girl, barely alive. Carrie ran to her side and knelt down next to her. Paula was barely breathing.

"Cut down those ropes," Ellen ordered one of the officers.

Carrie ran a soothing hand through Paula's matted hair. The stench in the air reeked of urine. "You're safe now," Carrie said repeatedly to Paula. She was barely conscious. Her deeply sunken eyes gave Carrie a long searching look directly into her eyes. As soon as she was free of the ropes Carrie lifted her small body. She was as light as a feather. She was as thin and emaciated as a holocaust survivor. Her tiny hands barely had any strength to hold onto Carrie's neck as she carried her upstairs. Carrie kept telling her over and over, "You're safe now, you're safe now, you're safe now."

She heard Paula say only one word, "angel", and then she went unconscious. They rushed her to Children's Hospital. Emergency room doctors swarmed her and began to assess her condition. They immediately started IV drips as she was severely dehydrated. They told Carrie they didn't know if she was going to make it. Her vital signs were weak. Carrie immediately began sending up silent prayers for her. She calculated Paula was in the basement for more than a month.

Ellen gave Carrie a hug. "Are you going to be alright?" Carrie nodded affirmatively. "I didn't know people like this existed," Ellen said. "I'll do everything in my power to throw the book at that animal. He deserves to rot in hell!"

Ellen left and processed Ed's booking. They arrested Darlene as an accessory, even though they all knew she was also his victim. Davy and Barry were transported to Children Services for safekeeping. Carrie called Judy and let her know what happened. They would make arrangements for the boys. Carrie stayed at the hospital until she could get the full details of Paula's condition. It would be a couple of hours before the medical report was completed.

Carrie went to the small chapel inside the hospital as she waited. It was a small quiet room with two pews facing a stained glass window depicting Jesus Christ as an infant, held by His mother Mary with an angel wrapping her wings around them. How many desperate parents came to this room to pray for their children, she wondered. Today was her turn, to pray for Paula. She knelt down on the padded kneeling board, folded her hands together and spoke to the image of Christ in the window.

"Dear Lord, I've done all I can. She's in your hands now. Please spare this child and free her of her misery. I promise I'll watch over her to the best of my ability. She's so frail, but she has to have a giant spirit to have survived her ordeal thus far. Surely she was brought to this Earth for a greater purpose. Please send her some angels to wrap their loving wings around her and help her heal from all of her wounds, both physical and mental. And dear Lord, while you're at it, I could use a bit of your strength too, if it isn't asking too much"

Carrie bowed her head and began to sob from the depths of her own soul. No child touched her as Paula did. She felt bound to her. A smiling image of Dallas Crenshaw filled her head, as if he was sent to tell her, her prayer would be answered.

The attending resident approached Carrie as she re-entered the waiting room. "I'm happy to tell you your little girl is going to make it. It was precariously touch and go when you brought her in, but I think she's passed through the crisis. Her vitals are coming back and her breathing is more regular. If she came to us even a day later, I can't say she would've survived. Of course we will be admitting her. We've given her a mild sedative to help her sleep. It's what she needs now."

Carrie breathed a huge sigh of relief while offering up a big 'thank you' to God. "Can you tell me anything else about her condition? Is there evidence of other traumas?"

The attending physician knew what Carrie was asking. "In addition to being emaciated and nearly starved, she does show multiple contusions and bruises all over her body. Her wrists will likely have scarring ligature marks and she may need some skin grafts. We've wrapped them to prevent infection as they were so deeply cut into by the rope. She's missing patches of hair. It appears as if she's been repeatedly sexually traumatized, but she should be able to physically recover from those wounds. Additionally she has numerous cigarette burns on her lower extremities and the bottom of her feet. Only time will tell how all of this has affected her brain. Whoever did this to her was a monster of the worst kind. He should be tortured in the same way he did to this precious little girl. Surely there is a spot in hell waiting for him."

"Can I see her?"

"She's currently being taken to her room, but if you like you can visit with her once she's settled in. She'll be sleeping, but I'm sure she wouldn't mind if you looked in on her."

Carrie crept quietly into Paula's room. She gazed adoringly upon this child as she stroked her little face. "I promise I'll watch over you as long as the good Lord lets me," she whispered. She gave her a kiss on the forehead. A nurse entered the room and put her arm around Carrie's shoulder.

"You must be Carrie Cathers," she smiled.

"Why, yes. How did you know?"

"Oh, you're fast becoming the talk of the hospital. Everyone says if it wasn't for you and all of your efforts this little girl wouldn't have made it. I think you were her God sent angel this evening."

"I don't know about all of that," Carrie responded.

"We will take good care of her. She'll sleep through the night. Why don't you go home and get some rest. You look like you could use some."

Carrie caught the elevator down to the lobby. Ellen surprised her by greeting her in the lobby. "I realized you left your car at the Thompson's home. How about I give you a ride?"

"What a night!" Ellen tried to make small conversation, except there was no small conversation to be made this evening.

"Are you okay?" Carrie asked Ellen, realizing she was as involved in the rescue as was she.

"Me, I'm good. As long as you're good, I'll be good." She flashed a smile at Carrie. "It was all you, Carrie, all you."

***

No, Carrie didn't need the small thread of rope that bound Paula's hands to remind her of the precious child. She was indelibly etched into her mind. She watched over her as long as the system would allow, mostly from a distance. The case was transferred to the foster care department. She was placed in a wonderfully loving home. It took her a long time to trust anyone, especially men, if she could ever trust them again.

Two years later, the agency received permanent custody of Paula and she was available for adoption. Her foster mother's sister, Rena Cameron adopted her. She was single and longed for a child. She fell in love with Paula while she stayed at her sister's home in foster care. It worked out for the best. Paula didn't lose the love of her foster parents either, as they remained a part of her family upon her adoption.

As for Ed and Darlene Thompson, they were incarcerated for a long time. In fact they remained there to this day. Davy and Barry were sent to Ed's sister who lived in Florida. She also denounced and disowned her brother and all of his actions.

Carrie was comforted by this memory. It was one of the few times she knew she saved a life. It made working at Children Services all those years worth every minute of it.

She placed the journal back into her drawer among all of the others. She knew Katy read some of her journals during the past year. She didn't blame her for invading her privacy. She knew Katy was terribly worried about her. Perhaps it was her way of trying to understand her mother even better than she already did.

Carrie was aware this past year she was distant, sleeping most days trying to get through. Losing Jeff was one thing. You expect life will cause one of the spouses to have to deal with the death of the other. It was in the natural order of things. His loss served to sharpen Carrie's focus about how incredibly loving he was, and how she became emotionally dependent upon him more than she realized. He always gave her space. He respected her privacy. And he loved her through thick and thin.

She realized this past year how strong Jeff was. How well he provided for her in every single aspect and was always loving and tender. She knew deep down he was a far better husband to her than she was a wife to him. Even though everyone who knew them would be able to present a damn good argument to Carrie her assessment was wrong, she knew the truth.

But losing the twins was a deal breaker. Children are not supposed to precede their parents in death. She remembered the night Ellen told her. It hit her hard to hear about Jeff. She knew immediately she had to stay strong for Kate. Kate adored her father. She was his precious little girl. Carrie had the reserves to weather his loss and be a comfort for Kate. But when she heard the twins had also . . . . She still couldn't bear to think of it, even say the words in her mind. She railed at God this past year. What more did He want from her? Didn't she do enough good works? She rationalized He might as well have all of her. It was better than living with the tattered pieces of her life He left her with on the Earth. She was a burden long enough on Kate. Kate has Luke to take comfort from and love her now. Luke was a good man and was devoted to Kate. It was a good time to leave.

Carrie pulled the bed covers up and snuggled into her bed. She said a heartfelt silent prayer. Dear Lord, you know my heart. You know I've tried to live honorably and lovingly to all things. I haven't been perfect by any means and yet you've shown me great joy. You've blessed me and surrounded me with great love all of my days here on Earth. I've tried to return love to all you've created. But good Lord, I'm so tired.

I thought I would always be a pillar of strength. I thought I could handle all of the emotional pain sent my way, and I did pretty well, I think. But the holes in my heart continue to grow wider each day rather than smaller. I'm barely hanging on. Please forgive me for what I'm planning to do. I pray I may enter heaven. Please, if there is another path, please show me, but I see none. I only hear the call of Jeff, Scott and Todd, and I want to return to them. Please watch over Kate and Luke. Until tomorrow.

Exhausted Carrie fell off into a deep sleep.

chapter 41

May 30, 2014

She became aware she was dreaming. She was back in the arms of Ben, enveloped lovingly in his essence. Their souls danced together in perfect and exquisite lovemaking once again. He promised he would never leave her. He needed her. He thirsted for her as she did him. She swam in the pool of his deep green eyes and was refreshed. She reached out to touch his lips but her fingers couldn't quite meet them as he began to fade away. She screamed in agony. Noooooooooooo, you promised you wouldn't leave me.

Suddenly the sound of not one, but two pileated woodpeckers woke her. She jumped out of the bed frantically and looked out her window in a frenzy to make sure she could see them before they left. Two of them! Each pecked on the dead white oak trees that fell exactly one year before on that dreadful day. She imagined, as she did in the past, they were messengers of their distant cousin, the phoenix. She saw them as embodiments of Scott and Todd as if to say, "We are here. We will travel with you and take you with us. Our spirits will wait for you later this day." Carrie was filled with an uncommon peace and joy.

She looked at the hanging angel wings Jeff gave her on the day of their wedding. The sun's rays reflected perfectly off of them. Filling the glass wings up, the rays turned the wings into a blinding brilliant bright white light which was difficult to look upon, a sight never before seen by Carrie. Suddenly they burst and shattered onto the floor. Carrie was aghast and dumbfounded. Jeff's spirit was here, too, along with Scott and Todd. They knew of her plan and came for her. He, too, would wait and be her steady guide to the next world. This was her birthday. And it would be her birth day into the next realm as well. It was a good day. She felt strangely calm and gloriously happy.

She looked at the clock and was amazed she slept in until ten! Carson was picking her up in ninety minutes. It was going to be a great day. Anybody and everybody she cared about would be at the luncheon for Carson. It was her perfect opportunity to tell each and every one of them how much she loved them, and relieve them of all of their concerns and worries about her. She was moving on and leaving behind the all consuming depression. It was her birthday gift to herself. She was filled with an odd excitement. It's time for me to get my butt in gear, Carrie thought.

She went to the kitchen and put on some water to boil for her last cup of Chai tea. Meanwhile she took the shower liner out of its package and carefully unfolded it and covered the passenger seat of Zippy with it. She didn't want to leave any unnecessary mess. She threw the unopened prescription bottles of Xanax onto the driver's seat along with the bottle of Bailey's Irish Crème. She ripped off a piece of duct tape and wrapped it around the old hose. Next she grabbed the two hoses and placed one end of each hose into the tailpipe and the other ends into the top of the car's side window. That should do it, she thought. Overdose on some Xanax, drinking Baileys, as I drift off inhaling the fumes, and I should float to the next world. Lord, please understand. Soon her all encompassing permeating pain would be gone.

The teapot screamed for her attention. She dipped the teabag into the cup of water and let it steep while she took a shower. She took particular notice this morning of the refreshing quality of water as it spewed from the shower head. She opened her mouth to let some of its life giving properties fill her up. She dried off with a towel and slipped into her soft plush bathrobe. She retrieved the cup of tea, sat down on her back porch and took in the glory of the morning. The woodpeckers left, but she knew Scott and Todd didn't leave her. She could feel their spirits soothing her.

She set her empty teacup on the counter top and proceeded to get dressed. She looked in the mirror and was pleased. She actually loved the green tunic pants suit and noticed her cheeks were flushed with more color since her day out in the sun yesterday. She was ready to greet her world and secretly say good bye to all.

The door bell rang and Carrie opened the door to greet Carson and his wife Colleen with a big hello and a hug.

"You look stunning!" Colleen proclaimed. "I love your outfit."

"Thanks, a little something I picked up yesterday," Carrie replied.

"Well, it's beautiful on you. Oh yes, Carson, don't you have something for Carrie?" Colleen poked him in the ribs.

"I do!" He handed Carrie the box carrying the calla lily corsage. "Happy birthday, sis!"

"Now whatever have you gone and done?" Carrie said as she opened the box to find the beautiful white fragile flower contained within. "Oh my goodness, it's beautiful."

"I thought I'd get you a little something special for your birthday. It's your favorite flower isn't it?" Carson asked as he helped her to put it on.

"I can't believe you would remember that!"

"Well, I had a little prompting from Katydid, I must admit. There, that should do it. What do you think?" he asked Colleen.

"It looks perfect!"

"Is everybody ready to go?" Carson questioned.

"Ready."

"Yep, ready."

"Okay, off we go."

⁂

As Carrie, Carson and Colleen entered the hotel, Kate and Luke greeted them in the lobby. "You look beautiful, Mom!" Kate remarked as she gave her mother a big hug. "Happy Birthday."

The hotel's agenda was in prominent view on their easel board:

The Annual Benjamin Franklin Award

Ballroom – Noon

"Shall we head to the ballroom?" Carson suggested as he escorted the group in that direction.

"Hello, Welcome to our luncheon!" Barbara Douglas of the YWCA greeted them at the door. The room began to fill up with guests sitting here and there. "It's good to see you again, Carson. We've a table reserved for you up front and in the center, directly in front of the podium, if you don't mind."

"Not at all," Carson replied and gave Barbara a knowing wink.

"My, isn't this beautiful," Carrie remarked. "Look at all of the lilacs in the flower arrangements. They smell heavenly." She leaned down and inhaled deeply. By design there were no program bulletins placed on their reserved table.

"Allow me," Carson said as he pulled out a chair for his sister to sit on.

"Why thank you, Carson," she patted him on the cheek before sitting. "I wonder who else will be joining us for your celebration. I see we still have three chairs available at our table."

Ellen scurried over to their table and seated herself. "Hello everyone. I'm glad you invited me. It's good to see you, Carson and Colleen. It's been a while."

"Save a spot for us!"

Carrie couldn't believe her ears. Was that Sylvia?

"Hey Carrie," Sylvia said as she bent down and gave her a kiss. "Surprise! I bet you didn't expect me and Howard, now did you? I'm so excited." In her natural exuberance Sylvia kept talking while they sat down, greeting Kate, Luke, Carson, Colleen and Ellen.

Carrie began to get suspicious. "Carson, what are my good friends doing sitting at this table? Why are you not surrounded by your good friends?"

"You'll have to ask Katydid about that," he replied as he nodded his head toward Katy.

"Kate, what's going on?"

"Mom, now don't get mad at me. But we've gotten you here under false pretenses."

"Go on," Carrie instructed.

"You see, I entered your name as a nomination for the Ben Franklin award. I wanted something special and good to happen for you. I hoped you would be the selected recipient for the award, and you are! Mom, everyone is gathering here today to honor you. If you look behind you I think you'll see some familiar faces."

Carrie was absolutely speechless. She turned around and saw many of her former supervisors sitting at one table: Thomas White, Becky Harrell, Tanner Hill and Judy Graham, even Lysbeth. She couldn't believe it. Then there were other professionals she worked with from Children's Hospital, Juvenile Court, the Mental Health Center, and the Public Health Department to name a few. As she scouted the room many noticed her and waved cheerily to her. "Why I don't know what to say?"

"That's the good part," Carson interjected, "you don't have to say anything. Sit back and enjoy the ride Sis. If anyone deserves this honor, you do."

Carrie was in a state of mild shock. She never would've dreamed in a million years she deserved such attention.

"I've never seen you lost for words before in my life," Sylvia giggled. "Oh, I'm so happy for you."

"Me, too," Ellen said as she patted Carrie's hand.

"I can't believe you all knew and didn't tell me. When were you ever able to keep a secret Sylvia?"

"Trust me, it was hard, Lordy, Lordy, it was hard. You've no idea. I almost slipped and gave it away a couple of times, but I held it in. Yesiree, I kept the secret. And I'm mighty proud of myself, I must say." The entire table laughed.

Barbara Douglas stepped up to the podium and turned on the microphone. She tapped it with her finger to see if it was working. It was. "Good afternoon ladies and gentlemen. Welcome to our twenty-fifth annual Benjamin Franklin service award luncheon. Today I have the great honor of presenting to you our recipient, Ms. Carrie Cathers. Would you mind standing for a minute, Carrie?" As she humbly stood, the entire room began to clap. "Thank you. You may be seated."

"The servers will be bringing us our lunch momentarily, so at this time, I would like to present to you Chaplain Isabell Kennedy for our invocation. Please feel free to eat and enjoy your lunch, after which we will begin our program. Chaplain Kennedy, if you will."

"Good afternoon ladies and gentlemen, and Ms. Carrie. Please may we all bow our heads? Dear Lord, Thank you for all of the blessings of this day as we gather together to honor one of the most giving members of our community. May we all strive to serve one another with the same passionate strength and fortitude of spirit Carrie Cathers has delivered unto us. We are richer for her presence and grateful for her servitude. And thank you for the blessing of the food we are about to receive. May it nourish our bodies as Carrie has nurtured our souls. Amen"

"Amen," resounded through the room.

Carrie sat quietly through the meal. She was still astonished with what was unfolding before her. She loved listening to her dearest loved ones talk among themselves, capturing their joy and laughter. It convinced her even more thoroughly life would go on fine without her.

"Are you okay, sis?" Carson leaned over and gave her a shoulder hug. "You're being quite quiet. It's not like you."

"I'm flabbergasted," she smiled. "It's all too much to take in. There are so many people here!"

Barbara stepped back up to the podium. "Now we are all filled up with our lunch, it's time to begin our program. I would like to start our afternoon by introducing our city's mayor, Russell Stonebridge. Mayor Stonebridge, if you would be so kind as to start our program."

"Good afternoon everyone, and Ms. Carrie," the mayor began. "Carson, you never told me your sister was so stunning. Shame on you." The audience laughed. "I've known Carson Singer quite well for some years now, but I haven't had the pleasure of meeting his sister, Carrie Cathers. I've heard of this Carrie Cathers for several years. You may not know this," he was directing his comment directly to Carrie, "but you've been the talk of our community for some time now." He returned addressing the group. "Every time her name pops up in a conversation, it has been with the utmost respect and admiration. Typically Ms. Cathers has unintentionally impressed someone by being herself. Words like forthright, committed, bright, integrity, professional, and even a bit crazy," again the room laughed, "have all been used to describe her. But the word coming to my attention most often is honest. It's said you can't tell a lie. Is that really true?" Carrie shook her head no, as the rest of her table all nodded their head yes.

"Even Bernie Willoughby, our trusted prosecutor speaks highly of her, and trust me, he doesn't give out many compliments. Isn't that right Bernie?" the mayor called out to him. Bernie saluted back. Again the room was delighted by the comments. "It's with great pride and admiration I stand here in this beautiful ballroom to give my humble homage to Carrie along with the rest of you. And may I say from the bottom of my heart, and I believe I speak for all of us, thank you. Thank you for making our community a better place. Thank you for all you've done. We are lucky to have you in our city. May we all aspire to be as noble! Thank you." The audience followed suit with unanimous applause.

"I couldn't have said it better myself," Ellen told Carrie.

"Thank you, Mayor Stonebridge." Barbara returned to the microphone. "Next I have the pleasure of introducing one of two people who nominated Carrie for this award, her daughter Kate Cathers-York. Won't you please come forward Kate?"

Katy stood up and gave her mother a hug and kiss before she headed to the podium. "You deserve every bit of this mom," she whispered in her ear. "I love you."

"Good afternoon. I don't know how I was bestowed the good fortune to get the best mother of all. I can't begin to elaborate on all she's taught me as a mother, and through her example as a social worker. If you don't mind I think I would simply like to read my nomination."

"I would like to take this moment to nominate the most incredible woman I've ever known or will know, my mother. First and foremost my mother has taught me how to accept people without critical judgments. She would say: until you've walked in their shoes, you can't know their challenges, their pain, and their love. It isn't our place to judge, but to understand and give of ourselves where and when we can."

"These weren't mere words from her. She put them into action, and at times, dragged me along with her so I could understand. We volunteered years of Sundays in the shelter system, cooking and serving food to the needy. She wanted me to learn to appreciate what we did have by showing me up close and personal what it meant not to have."

"Each year she would make me sort through my closet and part with clothes to give to the needy. Of course, I never minded giving up old clothes I was no longer interested in, but she would always come in behind me and make me add my favorite outfit to the pile. It doesn't mean anything unless you give something that's precious to you, she would say."

"My mother worked in the child welfare system for forty years and she never left the front lines. She said she didn't want to get ivory tower forgetfulness." The audience laughed. "When I was young I often resented her work as her many long hours kept her away from me. But as I grew older and understood the nature of her work, my resentment turned into pride. I never did without. Every moment she was home, she dedicated herself to me and my brothers and our father. Those were the happiest times."

"As a family, we also volunteered at Dane Forest cemetery, maintaining the birding station and butterfly gardens. We often picnicked there, and many of my happiest moments were there. It was in this beautiful place she taught me about nature and the cycles of life. She taught me to appreciate the small things in life as the big things in life come rarely."

"My mother possesses a phenomenal strength of courage and wisdom. She was willing to take the toughest assignments. She came home often after having to overcome challenges the average person would've run from in a heartbeat. To give you an idea about what I speak of, my mother has been shot at, with four bullets flying past her head. That happened while she was trying to help a client get away from an angry husband."

"Another time she was greeted at a front door with a sawed off shotgun. He told her she had thirty seconds to exit his porch. When she turned around to abide by his request, her leg fell through the rotting porch plank and she got stuck and broke her ankle. Lucky for her, he gave her a few extra seconds."

"She once was nearly raped, as a client trapped her in his house, grabbed her and was about to assault her, until one of his drunken friends emerged from a back bedroom and talked him out of it. She said the drunken friend was an angel in disguise."

She read my journals, Carrie thought.

"She also brought home cockroaches and lice who hitchhiked on her clothing. Those weren't such happy times. But she never complained."

"She gave hope to the hopeless when they had none for themselves. I don't think I can even understand how many children she helped to save along the way, not only from physical harm, or sexual harm, or neglect, but from the emotional abyss of no hope".

"She stood up for the disadvantaged and tried to make wrong things right. She was a fierce fighter, and a strong advocate, and yet she spoke quietly. She would say a whisper resonates further than a shout."

"When she saw problems within the system, she didn't turn her head and walk away. She would carefully assess how she might promote needed changes and then went about it. This she did in her 'spare time'. She helped to get a program started providing bus tickets for those with no transportation. She designed several training courses, so new caseworkers didn't have to learn through trial and error as she did. She fought for better working conditions, so staff didn't have to work in unsafe buildings that were cheaper, but barely met the safety code. And where laws were lacking to keep children safe, she lobbied long and hard to change those laws."

"I would ask my mother," Kate's voice started to quiver. "I would ask my mother why she didn't leave her job. I would see her come home exhausted, only to get up and get moving again. I could see on her face she saw tragedies none of us will ever know, yet she spared us any knowledge of them. She told me, 'Somebody has to do it. They are our children. If we don't care for the most helpless, then I don't want to live in this society.' I would tell her she did more than enough time, she deserved a break. She would argue with me someone had to stay with experience. Someone had to stay behind and teach others through example. The real learning is done on the front lines."

"You must face reality, my dear Katy, she would say. The only way we can get through this life and maintain any sanity is by facing truth, seeing things for what they really are. You know she would say, "tell it like it is," is the only way you can free your own spirit and live a full life, otherwise, you'll remain trapped in delusions of your own self-imposed prison." Kate wiped her eyes.

"As many of you may know, my mother was delivered a crushing blow when my father and my brothers were tragically killed in a car accident one year ago. It took an event that enormous to take the wind out of her sails. She's faced the truth of this, and I can see she's still trying to get the wind back in her sails. I know she'll come through. I hope giving her this honor will move her one step closer to reclaiming her life and her joy."

"I know I'll never be able to fill the shoes my mother walked in. I'm instead glad I was blessed to have occasionally walked by her side. And as you taught me to "say it as it is," Mom, I've got to say – you're one impossible act to follow!" The crowd cheered.

"In addition to honoring you with this prestigious award, which you fully deserve, I want to tell you Mom, how much I love you, and how much your grandchild will love you." Kate broke out into a full faced grin as she placed her hands over her heart, and then extended them toward her mother.

"I'm going to be a grandmother?" Carrie said as she watched Katy leave the podium. "I'm going to be a grandmother!" Katy bent down and lovingly kissed her mother.

"Yes, Mom, you're going to be a grandmother this Christmas."

"Oh, I can't believe it!"

The entire room exploded in thunderous applause following Kate's presentation. Carrie's eyes leaked out tears of joy. She was happy for Katy and Luke. They would make excellent parents. She made the right decision this morning. Katy would have more time with her child and not have to look after her as she did for the past year. She would watch over her grandchild from above, she thought.

"Wow!" Barbara returned to the podium. "You sure do set a high standard, Carrie Cathers. I'm sure it will make all of us think about how we live our own lives. But folks, that isn't all. We have more to come. I would like to introduce our next speaker, who also nominated Carrie for this award."

Carrie looked surprised. She couldn't believe someone else nominated her.

"May I present to you Mr. Martin Barnett." Barbara moved away from the podium to allow Mr. Barnett to speak.

"Good afternoon everyone, and Ms. Carrie," Martin winked at Carrie. "Bet you didn't expect to see me again, did you?"

Carrie put her hands over her heart and shook her head, no.

"Well I can tell you right off what I might say is miniscule in comparison to Kate's tribute. Carrie may be an impossible act to follow, but your daughter is also one hard act to follow!" The audience tittered. "But what Ms. Carrie did for me was enormous. It literally changed my life beyond anything I could've imagined. I'm happy to take this time to honor her. I worked as a janitor for Children Services in the building Ms. Carrie worked in. Ms. Carrie was different from the other caseworkers. She noticed us, and acknowledged us. Even at Christmas she would remember us janitors and give us a small gift. I can honestly report no other staff member did that, except Ms. Carrie. She didn't singularly have a heart, she's the living essence of heart."

"Many of you may not know this, but the county hires illiterate janitorial help. You see, they didn't want anybody to read any of their written records due to reasons of confidentiality. As a result, having a staff of illiterate janitors fit the bill. There was no risk we would see information not meant for others' eyes."

"My working hours were from three until eight at night. We were given a thirty minute break sometime around five. Ms. Carrie was always nice to spend a few moments and chat with us. She would ask about our day and our families. One day she asked me about my dreams. What did I dream of most in my life? I told her I always dreamed of learning to read. It would mean the world to me. I didn't really understand how true that statement was until I learned to read. Reading opens up the entire world to you, but that's hard to fully comprehend unless you can't read."

"After she heard my dream, she took it upon herself to teach me how to read right then and there! "I'll teach you during your breaks. It may take us a while, but if you really want to learn I'll teach you a little bit each and every day I'm here." She looked at me straight in the eye and asked me if I was up for the challenge? I was speechless. I thought she was pulling my leg. I think I told her she didn't have to, but she wouldn't take no for an answer. I've got to tell you, she's one stubbornly determined lady."

"It took me a while, quite a while to catch on, well, actually, it took more than a year, but she wasn't about to give up on me. Do you know how many different rules the English language has? She started out by getting me to recognize the letters of the alphabet. Then I learned what sounds each letter stood for. And I'll tell you, when you're a grown man, your brain doesn't learn it easily, but she persisted. Then I learned some letters made different sounds depending on what situation they were in. For example the letter C sometimes sounded like a K, sometimes like an S. The letter G sometimes sounded like a G but other times when an E followed a G it sounds like a J. Then there's I before E except after C, or E before I as in neighbor and weigh. But it didn't stop there, or no. We have the double "oo" which sounds different in the word 'soon' than it does in the word 'wood'. Go figure. And then if you have a vowel followed by a consonant followed by an E, the E is silent and the vowel has the long sound. Oh, yes Ms. Carrie, I remember all of them rules. And there are more I won't bore you all with. My point is, it wasn't an easy process, but Ms. Carrie was never going to give up. Oh, and did I mention she did this after her working hours would end at five. She delayed going home to help me read."

"I can tell you God doesn't make many people like her. Ms. Carrie, I want you to know I now own my own Janitorial Service Company, and without you it would never have happened in a million years. I try and pay it forward and teach others to read, but it only happened because of your selfless heart. I owe my life to this wonderful lady. In my book you're an angel on this earth. Thank you."

Another thunderous round of applause rippled through the audience. Carrie stood up and embraced Martin in a big bear hug.

Barbara again returned to address the gathering. "If there are any more stories like these two, I'm going to have to go home and rethink my own priorities." Again the crowd clapped in approval.

"Who's next on the agenda? Is it Cindy or Elliot? Cindy. Okay. I now have the honor and privilege of introducing to you one of our state's legislators, Representative Cindy Prehm."

"It is my genuine honor to have the opportunity to pay tribute to Carrie Cathers this afternoon. I had the privilege of chairing a committee to explore changes in our laws regarding circumstances under which the state could assume custody of children. This hearing wouldn't have occurred except for the grassroots campaign Carrie Cathers launched with endless energy and wouldn't give up pursuing even in the face of defeat. I think she personally sent my office over fifty letters. And that was before e-mail became all the rage."

"The afternoon came when she was given the opportunity to testify before our legislative changes panel. She gave us one of the most gripping heart wrenching testimonies I've heard. I do not believe there was a dry eye left in our chamber. Every legislator will tell you it was her words that moved them to make the changes, even in the face of some strong opposition from parents' rights organizations. She presented two cases to us I would like to briefly share with you. First there was the case of Dallas Crenshaw. Dallas . . . . ."

***

Carrie came to accept Dallas as one of her guiding angels. It was his death first stirring her to try to effect some changes. The entire summer and fall of her maternity leave in 1987, she began her letter writing campaign. She did what she could. She believed no one was listening as she rarely got anything back except a standard pre-written response: Thank you for your concern, blah, blah, blah. When she returned to work, the daily duties of her job and home usurped her efforts and she kind of gave up, meaning she put it on the back burner to simmer for a while.

But then there was the case of the Mallory family who attached themselves to Carrie's very soul as well. They wouldn't let her rest until her mission was accomplished. It started in 1993.

A child, Steffani Mallory, was brought into the emergency room with a serious head injury. In fact her skull cracked opened. When Carrie saw her in intensive care, she could see her brain through the one-inch crack. She never saw anything like that before. Steffani was only sixteen months old and fighting for her life. Her head was encased in a metal halo to keep the skull from splitting even more. It was a heart wrenching sight. Carrie was informed the parents were in a small waiting area, and she could use the small viewing room area if she wished to interview them.

She found the parents in the waiting area, and many of the extended family members were present as well - aunts and uncles. Before she could even introduce herself, many of them began to openly grumble and admonish the parents they would be fools to talk to her. Apparently child welfare workers all have a tattoo on their forehead, remaining invisible only to them, but not the general public. The tattoo says CHILD WELFARE WORKER.

"Hello, are you Maxine Mallory?" Carrie asked the mother.

"Yes," the tearful woman answered.

"May I please speak with you and the father for a moment? There's a private room we can use down the hall, if you would." Carrie wanted to handle this with great sensitivity, understanding their daughter might not survive her ordeal.

After they were situated in the small private room, Carrie professionally introduced herself and stated the purpose of her visit. "Before I move forward, I want to express to both of you how sorry I am for your daughter's condition. I can't even begin to imagine how horrible this must be for you." She noted Maxine was unable to keep a dry eye; however, Carrie was disturbed by the father's reaction. Kenneth Gibson had no tears, but wore a half-smile on his face. Odd, thought Carrie. "Do I understand correctly you and Kenneth are not married but live together?"

"Yes," Maxine answered.

"And Kenneth, you're the father of both children?" Steffani had a younger four month old sister, Lizzie.

"Yeah," he responded.

"And for the record, am I correct to understand you work for the Langley Insurance Company, Maxine?"

"Yes."

"And I'm sorry Mr. Gibson, but could you please tell me where you work?"

"I stay home. I'm kind of between jobs right now."

"Oh, I see. So are you currently caring for your daughters while Maxine works during the day?"

"Yeah, you could say that," Kenneth answered as he stroked his moustache.

"Okay. If you could take your time and tell me in your own words how Steffani got injured, I would appreciate that."

"Well, we already explained this once to the doctor," Maxine explained.

"I know how hard this must be for you, but the doctor's not available and I really need to hear about the events from you personally." Carrie handed Maxine a tissue.

"Hey, I got this babe. Let me handle it, that's, if it's okay with you?" Kenneth said glibly as he pointed to Carrie.

"That's fine."

"Well you see, it went down like this. You know Steffani's learning to walk. She's still kind of wobbly on her legs, know what I mean? I decided to take the kids to the park and play. You know the park in front of the hospital. We only live three blocks away. Well, we were outside on the top step of the porch. I was carrying Lizzie. And Steffani, she was walking on her own. There are about ten concrete steps down to the side walk. Steffani must have tripped over her feet, and she came toppling down those steps and hit her head on the corner part of the last step down. Kind of went airborne, and then crack, split her head open. Yeah, that's how it happened." Mr. Gibson slouched back in his chair and nodded his head, still wearing that smirk. "It was a terrible accident."

"I see," Carrie said. She didn't believe a word of his story. His demeanor was all wrong, so was his energy. "Mr. Gibson, can you tell me what happened next?"

"I put her in the back of the car, along with Lizzie. I knew I had to get her mother, since I drove her to work that morning 'cause we only have one car to share. I'm the kids' dad. But I didn't have no papers to prove it. I figured I was going to have to go and get Maxine so she could get medical treatment."

"Wasn't her head bleeding badly?"

"Oh, yeah, real bad. That's why I wrapped a towel around it after I put her in the car. Well, I went and got Maxine and after I told her what happened we came to the hospital."

"What time of day did this accident happen, Mr. Gibson?" Carrie asked wanting to pin down a time frame.

"About noon. Yeah, we ate some lunch. The kids were getting restless, so I thought I'd take them to the park to tire them out some."

"And how long does it take you to drive up to where Maxine works?"

"It takes about a half-hour, don't it babe?" Maxine shook her head.

"Let me make sure I understand what you're saying. Steffani was hurt around noon, you drove to pick up Mom here," Carrie touched Maxine's knee, "and that took about thirty minutes. And then you drove to the hospital. Is that right?"

"Yeah, that's right," Kenneth acknowledge as he cracked his knuckles.

"Well Mr. Gibson, can you explain to me why the hospital recorded Steffani arrived here at four. Because according to your story, you went to pick up Maxine at noon. If you got there by twelve-thirty because it takes a half hour to drive to her work, you should have gotten back to the hospital by one o'clock or a little after. Steffani didn't get here until four. Can you explain that to me?"

"Well you know I wasn't exactly watching the clock. My kid's head was bleeding real bad and I was worried. And me and Maxine, we did have to talk a little about what happened. I mean she wanted me to explain it all to her and everything. And who says the hospital got the time right?"

"Okay, I understand. It was a stressful time. If Steffani recovers, will you be keeping the same arrangement for the children's care?"

"What do you mean?" Maxine queried while dabbing her nose.

"I mean, do you plan to continue to work? And is Kenneth going to continue to stay home and watch the kids?"

"Well of course. Why wouldn't we?"

"Sometimes when circumstances like this happen, families do things differently. Sometimes mothers decide to stay home, if they can. Or they find another relative, like a grandmother, to come and help out. You know, to relieve their partner once in a while from the stress of caring for young children. I wondered if you thought of that."

"No, no, not at all. I trust Kenneth. He's a good father."

"Why, thank you babe. I appreciate the vote of confidence," Kenneth said cockily. "Besides Ms. Whatever your name is, I don't appreciate what I think you might be insinuating here. Even the doctors told me her injury could have happened like I told you. Go ask them."

"Oh, I'll be talking to the medical staff. I'm curious why, if her head injury is as bad as it is, why didn't you rush her to the hospital that's three blocks away and call mom to come down right away?"

"I don't know. I was panicked. I wasn't thinking straight. Her head was cracked wide opened. I was scared and I knew I had to get Maxine."

"I can appreciate how scared you must have been. Well I'm sorry I had to have this conversation with you, but I appreciate your time. I do sincerely hope Steffani recovers. She looks like a precious little girl."

Carrie left the scene knowing with every ounce of her intuition Kenneth Gibson wasn't telling the truth. He hurt Steffani and her mother was blind to that possibility. She walked over to the nurse's station and pulled out Steffani's medical chart to read. INJURY: Skull fracture, one inch crack opening to brain. HISTORY: Fall from step one to step nine hitting head on concrete corner. ASSESSMENT: Such a fall that distance onto a hard service may cause above noted injury. It can't be ruled out. Carrie couldn't believe what she read: It couldn't be ruled out. It might have happened that way. That was utter nonsense and she was going to have to talk to the attending resident about his diagnosis.

"Dr. Loeber, are you telling me you actually believe the child received her injury from a tumble down concrete stairs?"

"I know how you feel Ms. Cathers, but I can't rule out the possibility. If she hit her head right, it could have happened that way."

"Does it concern you at all she had at least a three hour delay in her arrival to the hospital from the time of the injury, considering they only live three blocks away? And if you buy Mr. Gibson's story about picking up the mother, they were still here at least two and a half hours later than they should have been?"

"It isn't my responsibility to consider those factors. My role requires me to simply determine if the injury could have happened as explained to me, and I believe it may have. Now could there be other viable explanations? Possibly, but it isn't my job to figure it out. I'll leave that up to the police and your agency."

"I see," Carrie said.

"Look, I know why you feel the way you do. I don't like this scenario any better than you do. But I can't help you out any further. I'm sorry. I have to go. I'm behind on my rounds."

Carrie was beside herself. She knew these girls were in danger. She didn't sleep trying to think of ways to get Maxine to open her eyes to the possibility Kenneth hurt Steffani. When she walked into her office the next day the worst news awaited her. Steffani passed away during the night. She succumbed to her injury. Carrie's heart sank. She thought of how Kenneth was smiling and giggling inappropriately as his daughter lay on the other side of the viewing window, fighting for her life. She was more determined than ever to help intervene on behalf of Lizzie. Thoughts of Dallas spurred her on.

Everywhere she went, she was denied help. Her supervisor, the executive director, the court worker, the court supervisor, even Bernie Willoughby, the prosecutor, all turned her down for court orders to intervene on behalf of Lizzie. They were all good at commiserating, but none of them would take any action. It came down to the same issue that kept her from keeping Dallas safe. The law didn't allow for the state to intervene on behalf of a sibling of an abused child unless that sibling also exhibited evidence of maltreatment. Lizzie didn't. In fact, Steffani couldn't even be identified as a maltreated child, since the system bought into Kenneth's story. There was absolutely no way to help Lizzie.

It didn't help the police department didn't examined the scene of the fall, because they didn't think a crime was committed. She even called Ellen Lewis to enlist her help in getting some departmental investigation in the juvenile bureau. However, by the time they could act, the scene lost any evidence of blood or hair because it rained many times since the accident. She had to accept she came to a dead end. She carefully recorded absolutely everything she did in the record.

Almost exactly a year later, Judy asked her to come into her office for a moment. "Carrie, I need you to brace yourself. I have some tragic news."

Carrie's mind raced wondering what could be so grave from the look on Judy's face. "What, what is it?"

"Carrie, we received news of a child who arrived to the hospital 'dead on arrival'. It was Lizzie Mallory. She was sixteen months old, the same age her sister was when she died."

"No, oh no, tell me this is some sick joke." Carrie clasped her hands over her mouth. Tears began to spill immediately.

"I wish I could. Additionally the police found Kenneth Gibson in a corner of his apartment, in a fetal position. Carrie, he's admitted to killing both of the children, Steffani and Lizzie. He forcefully threw them up against the wall. Lizzie died from a brain hemorrhage."

"I don't give a damn what position he was lying in. Jail is too good for him. That poor mother, she couldn't see it. Didn't want to see it. I wouldn't want to be her."

"Carrie, there's more."

"What, what more?"

"It's the press. They are spitting mad. They want someone hanged for this. They are looking to blame the agency. They know we did the previous investigation on this family. They are suggesting we failed to do our job. They want someone fired." Judy hung her head down.

"Oh, I see. They want me gone? Is that what you're saying? What, they've formed a lynch mob?" Carrie felt like she was about to spin out of control herself. She was ready for the press. Bring them on. She'd give them a mouthful or two.

"Carrie, I know you don't deserve this. I know you did everything you could, and then some. Thank God, you were the caseworker on this case. No one else would've covered every base on this case as you did. We know what the problem was here. It's where our laws are lacking. Listen, the press will eventually figure that out. The director thought maybe it would be best if you took a couple of days off. Until things cool down."

"Are you kidding me? Tell me you're kidding me," Carrie said in disbelief.

"It will be paid leave, until the entire hullabaloo calms down. Why don't you and the kids take a mini-vacation together? It'll do you all some good. And don't worry. We all know you're not the problem here." Judy was half embarrassed to have to deliver this news to Carrie.

"And what about my cases in the meantime? I'm not prepared to leave. I have stuff on my schedule, client's to see."

"Give me your schedule and I'll cover for you. Only two or three days. I promise."

"I don't have any say in this, do I?"

"I'm afraid it's been decided. The Board voted on it. I'm sorry."

When the press realized what really happened, they immediately backed off. They didn't pursue the back story of why it happened. They didn't talk about the constraints of the law. That didn't sell newspapers. That wasn't sensational enough. That might indicate their politicians fell down on their job, especially when they learned that Carrie wrote letters to state legislators about this same gap in the law back in 1987. Nope, it quietly disappeared.

But Carrie didn't disappear. Her administrative leave increased her determination to get the law changed. She spent those three days of leave organizing a full-fledged effort to gain the attention of the legislators to change the law to allow caseworkers to intervene on behalf of the children with no voice. She became a tsunami-like force speaking to every group she could schedule. In the end her persistence paid off. The law was changed.

***

". . . . . and because of her unrelenting persistence we now have the Crenshaw/Mallory law which allows all caseworkers to intervene on behalf of the siblings of abused minors. Since its implementation we haven't had a similar death occur in the entire state. It was all due to the heart and soul of Carrie Cathers!" Representative Prehm closed her notes and clapped along with the audience, once again.

Carrie thought it was all due to the heart and soul of Dallas, Steffani and Lizzie. It hurt her to have to remember so much pain. She was tired of remembering. Each memory wounded her soul by taking out another piece of it. She didn't want to remember any more. Once again, she thought of the relief awaiting her in Zippy, and was comforted.

chapter 42

A quite tall, gangly, good looking, reserved man came to the podium. "Hello. My name is Elliot Marquette. I'm currently the director of the state office of the Public Children Services Policy Initiative. We often work closely with our state legislators and they have asked me to say a few words today about Carrie Cathers. But you know, I think I can take a cue when I get one. Given the magnitude of all of these prior speeches, what I would have to offer seems, well ridiculous. How can you improve on the acts they have asked me to follow?" He shrugged his shoulders and held his hands palms up. Again the audience laughed.

"You know what? I'm not even going to try because I know the person about to follow me has an even more phenomenal message to deliver, if you can believe that. It gives me great honor and pleasure to introduce to you a child, now grown, Carrie once helped. And trust me 'helped' isn't a big enough word. May I present to you Ms. Paula Cameron." Elliot stepped back a few steps and guided Paula to the podium.

Ellen began to gently rub Carrie's back, as she knew what effect seeing Paula might have on Carrie, for it was also Ellen who accompanied her that day to the Thompson home. Carrie gasped loudly. She couldn't believe Paula was standing before her. She matured into an absolutely beautiful and stunning young woman.

***

The last time she actually saw Paula was when she was six-years-old. But Paula was with her every day of her life since their initial meeting. She was woven into the very fabric of Carrie's being. Following her rescue from the dungeon-like basement, Carrie spent every day and night at Paula's hospital bedside for four days, until she was released and placed into foster care. No one could get her to leave her side.

Paula was in a precarious condition, nearly starved to death. There was concern she may have some internal organ damage due to her severe dehydration, not to mention the physical abuse and ravaging sexual abuse her body endured. She was sure Paula would never remember her. She was in and out of consciousness most of the time. But Carrie was compelled to sit by her bedside, not wanting her to have to spend another moment without the loving support of a caring adult by her side.

She would talk to her quietly as she lay there. Sometimes her eyes would gaze at Carrie, but mostly she stared off into space, as if she was trying to find her way back. Sometimes Paula would talk randomly as if she was speaking to someone no one else could see. She relived some of her nightmares. The doctors assured Carrie the sedatives they gave her would help her to forget in the short term.

Carrie couldn't help but cry silent tears as she realized what happened to this child. Ed was lower than a ferocious animal. What he did to this child was as close to demonic as Carrie ever saw. Carrie learned as she sat by Paula's bedside, Ed raped her nightly for several weeks. He and his white supremacist racist thugs violated this child over and over. Their hatred of black people transcended the charts. The fact they could take out their anger on this adorable bi-racial six-year-old helpless girl was unthinkable.

She was sexually assaulted orally, vaginally and rectally. The men routinely urinated on her. They would tie her up in different positions. They put their cigarettes out on the soles of her feet. And that's what Carrie could gather. She was well aware she was likely exposed to some other unfathomable acts of terror never to be known or understood. Her heart literally broke for this child. She would've liked to have taken her home to care for her, but agency policy wouldn't allow it. She couldn't stop her own personal judgments from wanting the transgressors to be tortured as well.

Carrie inserted herself into the search and final decision to decide Paula's foster home placement, even though it wasn't agency protocol. No one was about to tell Carrie she was overstepping her boundaries. They knew better. They could see the pain she was carrying for Paula radiate off of her. She took full responsibility for this child on her shoulders and no one was going to interfere, and no one dared to try.

Once the case was transferred to a foster care worker, Carrie knew she had to distance herself. She couldn't fully break her ties with this child. It wasn't within the realm of her abilities. She was able to contact her a few times through written letters which were incorporated into Paula's lifebook and given to her at the appropriate times. She knew Albert and Lena Hobbs, her foster parents, were top notch foster caregivers, extremely loving, giving, and patient. They had a lot of experience, and had won the foster care of the year award in years past.

Albert was the perfect male role model. He knew not to push himself onto Paula, understanding why she would be fearful of men. Men had done nothing but hurt her, and her mother all of her little life. They were scary beings. Albert possessed a soft and kind manner. He brought cheerfulness into the room. He would eventually win Paula's trust.

And Lena was the rock ruling the house. She was a loving Mother Earth incarnate. Carrie often thought if anything happened to her and Jeff, the Hobbs would be perfect parental surrogates for her own children, if she didn't have Carson. Carrie worked with the Hobbs before and was impressed by their empathetic nature as well as how they ran their well organized household. She knew if anyone could help Paula back to normalcy, it would be them.

It was hard for Carrie to let go of Paula. In fact, she never did let her leave her heart. When Carrie learned Lena's sister, Rena, adopted Carrie, she knew the good Lord knew what he was doing, and she was thankful.

Now she couldn't believe her eyes that little waif of a child was standing before her as a tall, composed young adult. Her eyes gave off a shimmering sparkle, and her voice exuded an assured self-confidence. Carrie's heart was melting.

***

"Hello, ladies and gentlemen. My name is Paula Cameron. I would like to share my life story with you this day, for I'm only here due to the heroic efforts of my angel, Carrie Cathers. And when I say I'm here, I mean I didn't actually die because Carrie Cathers literally saved me from the jaws of death consuming me slowly."

"I do not wish to shock you with the details of my early life. But I can tell you I was horribly abused in many ways when I was six-years-old: physically, sexually, emotionally, and neglectfully, not only by my birth mother and step-father, but additionally by many of my step-father's cohorts. And please, do not feel sad for me, for the good Lord delivered me into the loving hands of my adoptive family, who I cherish beyond compare."

"When you become a foster care child, the tradition of creating a Lifebook for the foster child is practiced. I was fortunate I only had one foster care placement before my adoption. Many children are moved about several times in foster care for a multitude of reasons. Lifebooks are the vehicle the agency uses to help them remember their pasts. They can be filled up with pictures, or school work papers, photographs, letters or anything that will help the child remember their past and move them towards having their spirits healed from their trauma. I take the time to explain this to you, so you'll better understand the impact Carrie Cathers had on my life."

My memories of my life with my birth parents still remain somewhat vague to me to this day. I must admit recently I had the opportunity to view the photo of Carrie Cathers as you see on your program bulletin. My wonderful mother, who works with the YWCA, formatted the bulletins for this occasion and it was by mere chance I saw her picture on the computer. I say mere chance, but I believe it was a divine intervention. When I saw her photograph, my memory was jolted and I began to remember some details of events in my life my mind long ago buried. I always had some rough memories of being abused and isolated, but Carrie's picture brought back many details into sharp focus."

"I was only six-years-old. I was relegated to be tied up to ceiling pipes and left in our basement for what seemed like an eternity to me. Many days and nights passed. I was given only scant amounts of food. My step-father would repeatedly come into the basement and rape me along with many of his friends. I could never figure out what I did wrong to deserve the punishment, but I tried hour after hour to figure it out. I thought if I found the answer I would be released from my confinement."

"When Kate talked about her mother giving hope to those on the abyss of hopelessness, she was talking about children like me. I do clearly remember having to struggle to want to keep living. As only a little girl could, I prayed over and over to God to send me an angel to take me away. Then one day, the angel came." Paula began to weep. "I'm sorry. Please give me a minute."

Carrie was beside herself, weeping openly along with Paula. Ellen also joined in the weep fest as did many of the other attendees. People were gently blowing their noses throughout the room.

"I remember some gentle being kneeling beside me and stroking my head. I opened my eyes and turned and looked at this beautiful angel cradling me in her arms. She kept saying "you're safe now, you're safe now." I thought she was the most beautiful angel, even if she did have one blue eye and one brown eye. I remember trying to talk to her, but no words would come out except one, angel. After my rescue, I have very few memories until I came to the loving home of Albert and Lena Hobbs, who are now my adopted maternal aunt and uncle, as I was adopted by Lena's wonderful sister Rena."

"I was told I nearly died. When my angel found me, I was emaciated, and in and out of consciousness. I was told Carrie sat with me day and night in the hospital, not wanting me to be alone and scared ever again. I never saw Carrie then, I never saw a human. I only saw a loving beautiful angel next to me while I was in that hospital bed. I would close my eyes and then open them again, sure the angel would disappear, but she never did. That's all I remember from those days. When I saw the picture of Carrie Cathers, I, once again, found my angel, the one who stayed with me and kept me alive." Paula wiped her tears from her cheeks.

"There is a little bit more to say," Paula continued holding up her finger and thumb, the sign for a little bit. "I discovered two days ago who sent me messages to add in my lifebook along the way. They were signed C.C. and I figured C.C. must have meant county caseworker, but I realized it wasn't the caseworker who sent them; it was my angel, Carrie Cathers. It all came into clear focus for me, as these were very special messages. They could have only come from someone who knew my past, someone who understood and deeply felt my pain and fear. These weren't accidental messages. They came infrequently, but were always poignant. Ultimately, even with years of therapeutic interventions, it was the words of my angel that helped me recover myself and be healthy. I would like to share some of her messages, if I may."

"When I was six, the first message read: Dear Paula, You did nothing wrong. It was never your fault. You're a good girl. They were bad men." Love, C.C."

"A few years later I received this: Dear Paula, You're a loving and gentle spirit, contained inside a body. What those men did to your body was wrong. No one can destroy your true beautiful self, your spirit, unless you let them. Be strong and let your loving spirit rule your choices. Love, C.C."

"And the last one, I wish to share, came to me when I most needed it." There wasn't a dry eye in the room. Everyone was listening as if on tenterhooks.

"Dear Paula, Life is full of good things and life can be full of bad things, but life is also full of choices. You'll come to a crossroads in your life when you'll have to make a choice between being a victim or being a survivor. The choice is yours and yours alone."

"If you choose to be a victim no one could ever blame you. It's easy to be a victim. All you'll need to do is revel in all of the bad things. If you do, the bad things will ultimately eat you up and win. It will take all joy of life from you. Nothing will be required of you except to live each day in negativity, to relive the horrors and nightmares of your past life. It will keep you down. It will slowly suck the very life you have left out of you."

"Or you can choose to be a survivor. You can choose to empower yourself and rise above your circumstances. You can let your true spirit fly away from the chains that have bound you, and soar to the highest heights filled with love, joy and peace. You can sing gloriously the song meant to be your most divine self."

"In deciding, know this: you're worthy. You deserve the joy filled path. You're a child of God. Please pick wisely. All my love, C.C." Paula looked at Carrie with tear soaked eyes.

"You're absolutely one of God's angels on this earth and He picked the best and wisest of all of the angels to come save me. You need to know you saved me more than once. The love I feel in my heart has always been the gift you've given me."

chapter 43

Carrie couldn't contain herself and her emotions as the crowd stood on their feet and created a deafening roar of approval. She stood and walked up to the podium and embraced this dear child in her arms. Their hug was so full of emotion, it emitted joy throughout the room.

"My angel!" Paula shouted.

Elliot approached the women with fresh tissues. "May I say a few words, please?" Carrie appealed to Elliot.

"Who am I to deny you? Please do."

Carrie approached the microphone. She looked back and smiled at Paula. The crowd quieted and retook their seats in excited anticipation.

"I'm not sure where to begin. I'm overwhelmed with so many emotions. But I've one thing I need to share. As my daughter earlier said, "tell it like it is." Today has been a life- altering day in my life. As willingly as Paula would like to tag me as her angel, you all need to know, today, she has been my angel from God. For you see, I had a plan this day."

"I was led to believe today's award was going to be given to my brother, Carson Singer, for all of his many good works to the community. This was the ruse he and my daughter used to get me here." Carrie looked down at the two of them and raised her eyebrows.

"As Kate mentioned, this past year has been a particularly difficult and troubling one for me. After the death of my husband and my two sons, I really didn't see any reason to keep living. All I loved dearly had been ripped away from me, with the exception of my Katy and her husband Luke, Carson and his wife Colleen. I had no energy. I've laid around for nearly a year basking fully in my misery. I had time to think, too much time. I let my mind wander to all of the numerous incidents of hurt, and violence, and hatred and pain which have become the textiles of my life. I didn't want to know about that any more. I allowed myself to dwell on everything I've loved and lost in my life. I became a constant worry and burden to my wonderful daughter."

The room reached a level of complete silence.

"My plan was to come here today, sit and enjoy my family for one last time. Then when everyone went home, I fully intended to kill myself." The audience loudly gasped in surprise. "I conjured up an elaborate plan to make sure I wouldn't botch my endeavor. I had many conversations with God about my plan, and I asked him to show me another path, but none was given to me until today."

"He sent me one of his angels, Paula Cameron. The courage she's shown sharing her story with you all today is overwhelming. I realized I was acting from a very selfish place. If this gentle spirit could overcome her tragic life circumstances, what the hell was wrong with me? And then my answer came. I chose the path of the victim, when I needed to be on the path of a survivor."

"Why that has not been clear to me all of these many past months, I do not know. But I do know Paula is an angel walking among us. I'll be eternally indebted to her." Paula and Carrie embraced again. The crowd roared.

Elliot Marquette approached the podium once again. "Wow! Talk about tough acts to follow! Ladies and gentlemen, we still have one more item on the agenda before we end our luncheon." Carrie began to walk back to her seat. Elliot caught her by her elbow. "No, no. Please stay up here. We want to present you with your award. Barbara, can you bring the plaque for us please?"

Barbara signaled one moment with her finger and exited out of the room. "You would think we would have our ducks in a row and have the engraved plaque up here near the podium. But your stories were so gripping we were unable to get everything in its right place at the right time," Elliot interjected as he waited for Barbara to bring in the plaque.

Barbara returned sans the award. She whispered into Elliot's ear. He nodded his head as if to indicate he understood what she said.

"Ladies and gentlemen, I'm pleased to announce we have a very special guest here today that has asked to present Carrie with her award. May I present to you the under secretary to the federal department of Health and Human Services, Mr. Benjamin Randall!"

Ben walked up from the back of the room and strode confidently through the crowd up to the podium. Age only made him more attractive. Carrie's heart felt like it literally stopped and she thought she might faint. He grabbed her and wrapped her up in his arms as he whispered in her ear in his low captivating voice, "I'm never letting you out of my sight again ever, never, ever." He forced himself to release her from the hug, but wouldn't let go of her hand. Magnetism hung strong between them.

"Ladies and gents, it's with my greatest of pleasure to bestow this award upon Carrie Cathers. I do not know of a more deserving and loving individual. Carrie and I became acquainted years ago in graduate school, where I first fell in love with her. She was my fellow student, my mentor and my teacher, and she became a close friend and advocate. I was blessed by her spirit and was always sad when life caused us to take different paths. But today my heart will only know joy, for once again our paths have met and I plan to never let her go. May we all leave in peace, and may our spirits shine a little brighter for the love of Carrie." Ben turned and embraced Carrie once again as the crowd magnanimously roared their approval with another standing ovation.

chapter 44

Ben and Carrie stayed in a long embrace as if they were the only two in the room. The love between them couldn't be denied. The low hum of electricity between them was continuous.

Katy, Luke, Carson, Colleen, Ellen, Sylvia, and Howard all approached them. Katy touched her mother's shoulder and managed to wriggle her free from Ben, and embraced her mother with a hug. "Oh, Mom, I love you so much. It would've killed me if you left." Then she turned to Ben, "I can't thank you enough. I'm overwhelmed you came!"

The wheels in Carrie's brain started to churn. How did anyone know about Ben? She never told a soul. "Ladies," Carrie began, "I don't know about the rest of you, but I'm dying to use the restroom. Anyone else?" She eyed Katy as if to say, you best come along too.

"You've a good point. I could use the restroom, too," Sylvia piped up.

"Why don't we make it a gal fest," chimed in Ellen.

Cindy Prehm approached. "If you all don't mind, I really would like to have a moment with Ben. I need to talk to him about a new initiative the state would like the Camden Institute to explore, if I could borrow him for a few seconds?"

As the women walked to the restroom, Carrie felt like she was transported to heaven on earth, a good kind of dying. Ben was here! Her sweet, darling, authentic spirit, soul mate, Ben, was here in the flesh. But how did he get here?

As they approached the powder room entrance, Paula was leaving. Carrie stopped her and gave her yet another hug. "I'm not going to lose you again," she said. "You literally saved my life today. Us angels have to stick together," she laughed.

Paula couldn't have agreed more with Carrie.

As the women huddled in the restroom Katy began, "Now Mom, don't be mad at us." She knew what her mother wanted to know. "I read your journals. I know I shouldn't have. But I was desperately scared with what was happening to you, and I was looking for any clue to help bring you back. I couldn't lose you, Mom."

Carrie nodded her head in acknowledgment. "And?"

"And I read about your trip to San Francisco. At first I didn't want to believe it. Not my mom. But then I saw the truth of it for you. I realized you chose Dad and me, and you loved us too, with all of your heart. But I came to understand what Ben meant to you as well. After I learned you were going to be the recipient of the Franklin award, I hoped that would get you out of the doldrums. But then I thought, if Ben could come too, surely that would work. I didn't know anything about him, so I asked Uncle Carson to help me find him. Then I thought of Sylvia and asked her to help me. I knew she knew him because you all went to school together."

Carrie simply said, "Go on."

"Well, Uncle Carson has a lot of contacts in government and Sylvia said she thought Ben was in Washington, D.C. Uncle Carson asked Cindy Prehm to help find him. She knew he once worked with the Camden Institute. But in the end it was Sylvia who located him." Katy pointed to Sylvia.

"Sylviaaaaa," Carrie said warmly. She could never be mad at Sylvia.

"What did you expect me to do?" Sylvia began in her own excited voice. "I was losing my best friend and I couldn't have that. When Katy told me about San Francisco, oops I'm sorry Katy," Sylvia put her fingers to her lips, "it all made sense. Everyone in our class knew how you and Ben felt about each other, even though neither of you spoke of it. We could see it in your eyes whenever you were in the same room. And you know me. I've tried to keep track of everyone. I knew he was in D.C. Well, I told you about that. Remember? I told you he married a Washington, D.C. socialite. Oh, by the way, it didn't last."

"Well, I want to know what the hell happened in San Francisco!" Ellen interjected. "I can only imagine. Carrie, he's a hunk. And those eyes! Did you all see those beautiful green eyes!" They all began to laugh.

"Mom, tell me you aren't mad at me," Katy implored.

Carrie embraced her in a hug. "I could never stay mad at you, even if I were, but no, I'm not. I love you so much. Hey, and I'm going to be a grandmother!"

The gaggle of women rejoined Howard, Luke, Carson and Ben who were engaged in men talk. Ben handed Carrie her award plaque saying, "By the way, I forgot to give this to you!" He put his arm around her shoulder and squeezed her into him. "I wasn't kidding when I said I'm not going to let you go."

"Carson, if you don't mind, I would like the pleasure of escorting Carrie home. That's if she doesn't mind. And I'm not taking no for an answer." They all laughed.

"Of course, Ben, I was counting on it. Happy Birthday, Sis. Love you." The group left leaving Carrie and Ben to themselves. This time with no holds barred. Ben stared lovingly into Carrie's eyes and placed his lips upon hers. First it was a gentle kiss, which quickly evolved into a passionate all consuming lip lock. Neither one of them wanted to break the moment.

"Oh, I'm sorry, I didn't mean to interrupt," the cleaning lady said.

Carrie and Ben both broke into hearty laughter. "Come on, let's get out of here," Ben said as he grabbed her hand.

***

Back in her home both Carrie and Ben couldn't believe they were together once again. It was long ago when they were last together, twenty-seven years, yet it seemed as if time stopped and nothing changed between the two of them.

"Is it true?" Ben asked, "Were you really going to kill yourself?"

"Oh, Ben, I was lost. I couldn't find my way back. I lost Jeff and the twins, and I lost you long ago. I had no hope. I wanted all of the pain to go away."

"I'm so sorry Carrie. If I knew I would've come running to you as fast as I could. I didn't know until Sylvia filled me in the other day. They made me wait until today to see you. It was killing me knowing you were there, right there."

Ben pulled out his wallet and opened it. "Do you remember this?" he asked as he showed her the note she left him long ago.

> To my most loving soul mate,
>
> There are no words for us that can capture
> our feelings adequately.
> Know I'll always cherish you with every
> fiber of my body.

> Leaving you is the most difficult action I've been compelled to take in my entire life. If you truly love me, please do not follow me. What we have together is sacred and needs to be left unscathed
> Not a day will pass by you won't be remembered in my heart, and it's with enormous sadness I must leave you.
> Take care, my sweet love. Peace to you always.

"I've always kept it with me. In fact it's this worn because I've read it so many times, to stop me from finding you again. It was the part about 'if you truly love me,' that kept me from kidnapping you, for I've always truly loved you."

"Oh, Ben," she reached up and cradled his face and kissed him once again. "I'm thankful you found me again."

"Carrie, can I ask one question?"

"Why of course, you can ask me anything?"

"How were you going to do it? How were you going to kill yourself?"

Carrie took his hand and walked him to the garage. She opened the door. He saw her plan, hoses in the tail pipe, prescription bottles and Bailey's on the seat. "You weren't kidding, were you? You were serious."

"I was, but not anymore."

"Do me a favor, please. Let me put this stuff away. Let me bury your sadness for you, please? Go on inside. Get into something comfy." He gave her another quick kiss.

"Alright, I won't fight you. I promise only to love you."

Carrie retreated to her bedroom. She realized the broken angel wings were still scattered about on the floor. "Oh, Jeff," she lamented. "You didn't come to take me away, did you? You left me so I could be free. I'll always hold a sacred place in my heart for you, my darling husband. I love you." She cleaned up the glass and took it outside to the garbage can. She could hear the call of the two pileated woodpeckers in the distance. "I love you too; she called out to her sons. Go with Dad, and peace be with you all until we can meet again."

Ben found her in the bedroom. He lovingly gazed upon her. He noticed a picture of Jeff on her dresser top. "He was the luckiest man on earth to have you," Ben said. "He must have been one hell of a guy to hold onto you."

"Yes, yes he was."

"Carrie, I haven't told you yet, but I'm so sorry for your loss. I can't imagine what you've gone through. To lose your spouse is one thing, but to have lost your sons. . . I can't fathom the depth of what your pain must have been."

Carrie knew she had to face the moment of truth. She wasn't sure how Ben was going to take the information, but she knew she had no right to keep the truth from him, even after all of these years. Tell it like it is, she reminded herself.

"Ben," Carrie began. She walked over to the night stand and picked up the picture of Katy, Scott and Todd. "Ben, here is a picture of Katy and our sons, not mine, but yours and mine."

Ben held the picture and studied it for a long time. He looked at Carrie with water glistened eyes. "Our boys?"

"Yes, Ben, yours and mine. I know I had no right to keep them from you all of these years. They were the one precious piece of you I had left. I didn't know until they were three. But Todd developed the same walk as you, and they both had your square chin and dimples. By the time I understood they were your children, it would've killed Jeff. He never knew. They were his boys, and he loved them completely. I couldn't break his heart." Carrie began crying. "Please don't hate me."

Ben began to understand her pain, as he began to feel his own loss. He was lost in the picture of his sons. He couldn't stay angry at her. "Carrie, I know your heart. I know you did what you had to do. I don't blame you. Carrie, you're my soul mate. I could never hate you." He sat down on the bed and held her next to him as they both shed tears.

"Hey, I've an idea. Let's get out of here. Let me take you somewhere else this evening. Okay?"

"Alright. Where do you want to go?"

"Leave that to me. Why don't you freshen up a bit, and let me make a couple of phone calls. I think it's time we celebrate your birthday!"

***

They were flying high in Ben's Lear jet. He earned his pilot's license along the way finding it helpful getting around for his work. They landed at San Francisco's terminal, caught a taxi and were soon riding on the cloud that was PH1 at the International Wyeth Hotel.

Ben lovingly looked at Carrie and said, "Now you're not going to start shorting out on me again, are you?"

"You never know," Carrie smiled. "But I'm willing to risk it, if you are." They made exquisite love. Their souls melted together as they traveled, once again, through the cosmos. Carrie nestled into Ben's arms and fell asleep never to leave his arms again, ever, never, ever.

Acknowledgements

This book couldn't have been written without the help and support of many.

I want to thank all of the members of my writers group who provided me continued support and encouragement during the writing of this book: Barbara Whittington, Justine Wittich, Sherry Hartzler, Pam Gary, Mary Ellen Donovan, and Luke Moore.

Additionally I want to thank the following persons for dedicating their time to help edit this work: Barbara Whittington, Sherry Hartzler, Pam Gary, Cindy Hartitz, Spirit Williams, Kathleen Dalton, and Charlotte Snead.

Thank you, also, to my dear husband, Randy Sanders, for his continued support and love throughout.

About the Author

Jill Sanders, M.S.W. worked full time in the field of child welfare for thirty-two years before retiring. After "retirement", she's continued to serve as a trainer in the field, teaching courses for Continuing Education Units (CEU's) for the licensure process of social workers.

She received the Pearl S. Buck Award for Writing for Social Change in 2013.

She also conducts workshops on how to reduce stress in one's life.

She and her husband, Randy, reside in the beautiful Hocking Hills area of southeastern Ohio. It's here, among the lush beauty of nature, that she finds inspiration for her writing.

You may contact her at: authorjillasanders@gmail.com

Other Books by the Author

Love Yourself More: Stress Less

(A non-fiction self-help book)

Made in the USA
Columbia, SC
18 July 2017